MW01137855

I DOn't

LEDDY HARPER

"A successful marriage

requires falling in love many times,

and always with the same person."

-Mignon McLaughlin

PROLOGUE

A thunderous knock jolted me awake. I sat straight up and slapped my hand over my mouth to keep from losing the contents of my stomach all over the... Through squinted eyes, I tried to assess where I was, the entire room unfamiliar and cold. And messy. Tiny liquor bottles littered the carpet, along with clothes. The bra dangling off the dresser left me cognizant of the fact that the only thing covering me was a thin sheet.

I had not a stitch of clothing on.

The knock sounded again and reverberated through the room. It echoed in my head, causing everything to spin and tilt. I quickly closed my eyes and wrapped my arms around my midsection, praying everything would stay put.

"Jelly, sweetheart...open up," my mother called from the other side, her saccharine voice already grating on my fried nerves. "We check out in an hour, which means you need to get up and pack."

I whined inwardly, realizing exactly where I was...and why.

"I got it, Mom. I'm getting up." I prayed she couldn't hear the hoarseness of my voice and know the reason for it. She'd be so disappointed in me, which was worse than almost anything else. I was the baby, the youngest of five children. If she found out I'd been up most of the night getting drunk—

at the tender age of eighteen—she'd lose her mind. "I'll be downstairs in forty-five minutes."

I flung the covers off my bare body, the chill in the air cooling my overheated and damp skin. The instant I slid off the mattress and stood on both feet, the floor seemed to give out beneath me. My thighs ached, the kind of soreness you'd expect to experience after running a marathon. Only, I wasn't a runner. Never had been and, more than likely, never would be. I'd walked a lot over the last few days, which could've explained the aches, but intuitively, I was certain that hadn't been the cause, either. The deep red marks forming bruises on my thighs and hips were enough to explain my soreness.

Hello, Vegas.

Goodbye, hymen.

I closed my eyes and groaned. Fear, embarrassment, and regret shook my body, and I struggled to stand upright. But my brain hurt too much to even think about it, about who I'd given my virginity to. About why, how, when. Or *if* I'd given it willingly. I took a shaky breath and combed a hand through my tangled hair. I needed a distraction—anything. A very large glass of ice-cold Pepsi. And definitely a shower.

I didn't quite make it to the bathroom when I heard the familiar clicks of a card sliding into the reader attached to the door. My stomach clenched when the lock disengaged. Panicked over my mother finding me buck-naked and severely hung over, I ran into the bathroom—which proved to be a horrible idea. The room instantly tilted, the floor curved beneath me, and a flood of sticky heat washed over my clammy body just as I made it to the sink and gripped the ledge of the vanity to hold myself upright.

Like a tidal wave, there was no stopping it. My stomach flipped, then flopped, and I threw myself to the tiled floor, not caring about the new set of bruises that would form on my knees from the harsh impact. Thankfully, the toilet lid was up;

2

I DO

otherwise, I wouldn't have made it in time. I hugged the porcelain and gave in to the rush of bile hurdling its way up my esophagus and into the bowl in front of me. Out of nowhere, someone knelt behind me and pulled my hair out of my face. Unfortunately, my stomach wouldn't relent long enough for me to turn to see who it was, but based on the large, rough palms rubbing my bare back, I knew enough to assume it wasn't my mother.

If I could've screamed, I would have.

But...*this man had a key to my room.*

By the time my gut finished wrenching itself like an overused washing machine, I was too drained and weak to turn around. I closed my eyes, rested my cheek in the crook of my arm, and said a silent prayer that this was just a horrible nightmare I'd soon wake up from. But I quickly learned that the likelihood of that wish coming true was about the same as willing my hymen to grow back.

While I sat as naked as a jailbird, on my knees, hugging a hotel toilet rim, my unknown hero dampened a washcloth and used it to cool me off. He wiped it along my brow, down the side of my overheated face, along the unnatural curve of my neck, and across my shoulder blades. Even though I currently resided in only my birthday suit, his gentleness was so soothing it almost put me to sleep. At least, it would have had he not opened his mouth and spoken.

"We need to get you cleaned up and downstairs before your mom comes back up here looking for you." Even though he used hushed tones, attempting to keep his words soft and quiet, I knew exactly who it was. Nothing could disguise the voice I'd heard almost my entire life. The same voice I used to dream about.

The one belonging to my brother's best friend.

The realization made me bolt upright, where I was met with his familiar bright stare. Then I remembered my lack of clothing and yelped. My arms instinctively crossed over my chest and my thighs clenched together in a vain attempt to hide my goods. Unfortunately, I got a very different reaction from him. One side of his mouth curled up, a light shade of red tinted his cheeks, and his eyelids grew heavy as his gaze lowered to my lap.

"Janelle, it's not like I didn't see it all last night." Holden's voice softened, and a light humor lilted his hushed words. With his bottom lip tucked between his teeth, as if he had to bite back his words, his eyes found mine again. "It's a little late to be shy now, don't you think?"

I was speechless. Utterly speechless. My mouth opened and closed, repeatedly, yet nothing came out. This situation wasn't something I could easily comprehend. Him…me…together…last night… It didn't take a genius to fill in the events that had occurred between us—a fantasy come true, except I had no memory of the dream. I eventually closed it for good, worried something other than words would make an appearance, and I wasn't about to chance that happening in front of him…again. Although, it's not like it would've made this situation any worse. Things were about as bad as they could get.

Crawling into a hole sounded amazing at the moment.

Suddenly, in my lack of response, his eyes snapped up, and his expression changed drastically. The curl in the corner of his mouth fell away, leaving his lips in a flat line while his jaw flexed with a tic. No longer did the illusion of humor dance in his greenish-grey irises. Now, they appeared darker, narrowed, locked on me. The creases across his forehead deepened, lowering his brows and casting a shadow across his eyes. I couldn't tell if the change had been caused by worry, fear, or anger.

I DO

At least, not until he slowly asked, "How drunk were you last night?"

I swallowed thickly and prepared myself to answer. "On a scale of tipsy to shitfaced, where exactly would completely wasted fall?"

"I'd say completely wasted would be about neck and neck with shitfaced."

I nodded and closed my eyes while a sigh slipped through my barely parted lips. "Okay...then I was about thirteen notches past that."

"Shit, Janelle." He couldn't hide the frustration in his deep, gruff tone. "What all *do* you remember? And *please* tell me you remember *something*."

Oh, how I wanted to give Holden a tiny sliver of peace. I wished more than anything I could recall one iota of the night in question—for his benefit *and* mine—but unfortunately, I couldn't. At all. For some reason, when I tried to think back on the day as a whole, everything seemed fuzzy, including my brother's entire wedding, even though I hadn't started drinking until much later. Knowing I needed to say something, I took a chance and said the only thing I could bet was a sure thing.

"We had sex. I remember that." Such a lie, but I didn't care. The pained look on his face made me want to give him reassurance. I would've spun the most elaborate tale just to ease his worry if I knew he wouldn't have had a clue how false it was. "Well, I don't remember *all* of it, but I do remember you taking my virginity." I tried to make my voice sound clear and confident, when in reality, I wanted to be deleted from this scene as swiftly as possible. My brother would kill me if he found out. After he killed Holden, of course. I was young...I still had so much life left to live.

"Oh, thank God," he breathed out and hung his head. "Your reaction just now had me worried you didn't remember that part. I would've hated myself if that were true. I mean, someone forgetting they had sex with me is bad enough…because I'm *not* forgettable." His sexy yet cocky grin made my head spin—worse than it already was. "But if you couldn't remember losing your virginity, I would be the biggest piece of shit on Earth. I'd never forgive myself for that."

That settled it—there was no way I could ever confess to him that I'd lied.

"Come on, we have to get you up and showered before your mom comes back to the room. If she sees this place, she'll never let you leave for college." He stood up and grabbed a few towels from the rack above the toilet. After he set them on the vanity, he started the water and then headed out of the bathroom.

I took the opportunity to pull my body off the floor and quickly jump behind the curtain. The water raining from the showerhead hadn't quite warmed up, and I screamed at the stabbing sensation of freezing needles hitting my body. As if hopping into a frigid shower while severely hung over wasn't bad enough, I almost died of a heart attack when a pair of arms wound around my waist from behind, and a snicker escaped the perfect set of lips closing in on my shoulder. Had I not been so thankful for his body heat, I would've shoved him away and wrapped my body in the curtain to hide myself from him.

"What are you doing, Holden?" My voice came out high and off key, a perfect representation of the confusion and shock twisting in my gut. An inner battle raged between my yearnings and the dire reality of this situation. "Matthew will *kill* you. You do know that, right? He's your best friend—and my *brother*. If he finds you in here—*in my shower*—he'll chop

6

I DO

you up into tiny pieces, and no one will ever find your body. I highly suggest you leave now before someone catches you in my room."

To my surprise, he took a half-step back. "I was here all night, Janelle. If someone was going to catch us, they would've done it by now. Matt and Christine probably won't get out of bed the entire day. And I was in the hall when your mom knocked on the door. She headed downstairs to have breakfast with the rest of your family. No one's up here to catch us. So come on. We need to wash up, because if we aren't downstairs when everyone else is ready to check out, someone *will* come up here, and that's when the shit will hit the fan."

"Fine. I'll wash up, but you need to leave. Now. Go take a shower in your own room." It wasn't that I wanted him gone, because I didn't. Nothing made me feel safer, more taken care of than having him near. But I needed to think, I needed to clear the fog weighing down every sluggish thought, and I couldn't do that with him here.

With a smirk, he shook his head and cast his eyes in a sweeping motion toward my feet—I did *not* miss the way his attention grazed my backside on the way down, though. Then he pulled me back into him again, flush against his firm, hot, intoxicating chest. If I concentrated enough, I probably could've felt his heartbeat. But I couldn't, because my focus was broken by the very hard, very large body part pressed against my lower back.

Holden apparently thought *something* was humorous, because his deep, airy chuckle fanned against my neck, covering me from head to toe with his heat. "I've already checked out. I did that while you were sleeping. And while I was at it, I grabbed us coffee, which we can drink when we get out of the shower."

The thought of bitter coffee hitting my stomach made me shudder. "That doesn't sound appealing. Like…at all. In fact, I think my gut may revolt again very soon at the mere thought of it."

"Way to kill a man's ego."

My heart sank, and with it, I let my head fall back onto his chest below his shoulder, not even thinking about the position we were in. "That's not what I meant. I just loathe coffee. You've known me for how long, yet you bought me a coffee instead of a Pepsi?"

His chuckle shook my entire body, which normally would've filled me with mirth, except the headache from hell prevented me from enjoying the soothing vibrations. "Well, considering I've never woken up with you before, I guess I didn't assume you'd drink it first thing in the morning."

He settled his hands on my bare hips and held me against him. In that instant, I froze, completely stunned and at a loss for what to do. I may have dreamt that he'd touch me this exact way, prayed that we'd somehow found ourselves in a position parallel to this, but that didn't mean I knew what to do when—*if*—it ever happened.

"I've been thinking of this ever since waking up this morning." His husky words licked the spot below my ear as his lips grazed the sensitive flesh.

His touch was so warm, so comforting, everything I'd ever wanted, but I couldn't bring myself to break free from the nervous disposition that kept me in a perpetual state of frozen fear. Once I was finally able to force myself to move, it wasn't the way either of us had wanted. My shoulders curled in and my head fell forward, my back hunching in what seemed to be an attempt to move away from him—even though that was the last thing I wanted.

I DO

"You okay?" His voice was different than the last time he spoke—not harsher in an angry way, but more of fear or concern. "Janelle?"

His hands fell away from my hips, and even though I could still feel him behind me, I knew by the sudden drift of cool air along my spine that he had shifted away from me.

Part of me wanted to grab his arms and put them back around me. Another part of me longed to explore what had poked me in the back. But the saner part of me knew there was only one way to deal with the situation at hand.

Holden took a step back and blinked several times, as if he'd gotten water in his eyes, even though his face remained completely dry. I couldn't help but feel as though I were missing something. As if this had been part of a conversation I was involved in, yet I couldn't remember any of it. I wasn't sure how to continue, realizing either way would more than likely cause some sort of damage to one of us.

Understanding relaxed his features, and he closed his eyes with a slow, inconspicuous nod.

"Holden—"

"You don't remember anything from last night, do you?"

My chest tightened, and my heart skipped a beat. "I already told you—"

"Just be honest with me. You don't need to lie to spare my feelings." Gone was the smug, carefree, sexy guy I'd known since I was a kid, and in his place stood a man on the verge of an intense emotion I was too scared to name. Either anger, hinted at by his fisted hands and taut mouth, or immense regret, given away by his soft, dark, almost pleading eyes.

But I couldn't lie anymore—no matter how much I wanted to.

He was right. I didn't remember a damn thing.

He must've read the truth on my face, because rather than giving me a chance to answer, he nodded, sucked air through his teeth, and then shoved the shower curtain aside. As he stepped out, he mumbled something beneath his breath, but I couldn't hear. I couldn't move, unable to do anything other than stare at the swaying curtain with a sense of loss settling into my chest. The weight of regret hung heavily over my shoulders until my body caved, falling to the shower floor on my already sore knees.

Holden York had been the man of my dreams since I was six years old. For the last twelve years, he was my brother's best friend and a constant around the house. Everyone used to joke that he was the sixth Brewer kid and that my parents ought to just adopt him with as often as he was there. Needless to say, I'd been in love with him since kindergarten, despite him being four years older than me. By the seventh grade, I could sign *Janelle York* better than *Janelle Brewer*. And when I blew out the candles on my thirteenth birthday cake, my wish was to one day marry Holden, because I'd believed the number thirteen held some sort of magical powers.

Yet here I sat, hung over in a shower in Vegas after an eventful night with Holden. I'd kicked him out of the bathroom, dripping wet, completely bare—and impressively hard. I couldn't explain why I'd turned him away, because it didn't make much sense to me. Up until about a year and a half ago, I had no interest in anyone other than Holden. He was the only guy I'd ever had eyes for. But that had all changed when Justin Moose waltzed into my third-period class junior year with his faded jeans and unkempt hair. Suddenly, I'd forgotten all about Holden and my obsession-slash-love for him. My whole world revolved around Justin.

A few months before senior prom, I'd decided it was time to give Justin, who I'd been dating for a year, my virginity. And there was no more cliché time than prom night. I'd

10

I DO

planned the entire thing and kept it as a surprise. He'd hinted a couple of times about getting a hotel room, and each time, I told him no—not because I didn't want one, but because I didn't want to ruin the surprise. Then, two weeks before prom, before the most important night of my life, Justin did something I never expected. He broke up with me. I was devastated, and even more so when my friends had started to tell me it was because I wouldn't put out. Apparently, the entire time I'd spent planning our first time together—my first time, *period*—he'd tried to do the same thing, and when he assumed it wouldn't happen, he lost interest. He lost interest in sleeping with me, taking me to prom, *and* dating me.

I was heartbroken.

And the one person who was there for me was Holden.

Even though I had four siblings, three of which were sisters, I was closest to Matthew, with only a few years separating us in age. The girls were much older than us. So, after Justin had finished slaughtering my heart and spitting on it, I found myself at my brother's apartment, the same apartment he shared with Holden. As it turned out, Matthew wasn't home—he was actually on a date with Christine, the woman he just married yesterday. I ended up spending the evening on the couch, crying to Holden while watching all the Marvel Comics movies in order of production. But certain words he said to me that night came back to haunt me, words meant to comfort me…

"Janelle, you're worth waiting for, and any man trying to rush it is a fool."

"You almost done?" His voice came from the other side of the curtain. His gruff tone startled me out of my daydream and reminded me of where I was. It made me question what really took place last night, and why.

"Holden?" I called out, hoping he hadn't left the room. When I saw his shadow pause, and then hover by the door, I asked, "How much did you have to drink last night?"

Static filled the air while I waited for his answer. Then, in his gravelly baritone, he said, "Quite a bit. Why?"

"Just wondering." I turned off the water, not at all caring that I'd done nothing but sit beneath the spray instead of washing any part of me. Suddenly, a towel appeared through the opening of the curtain, which I took and wrapped around my shivering body. When I stepped out of the shower, I found Holden leaning against the sink, staring at me as if I'd been in the middle of a sentence and he waited for me to finish. With a shrug, I asked, "How much do you remember?"

"Every single fucking thing." His response was immediate, and he didn't break eye contact, not even to blink. "Had I been sober, I may not have made the same choices, but there isn't a single moment of the entire night I don't remember…in *vivid* detail."

"Holden…"

"I know." He straightened his posture and moved toward the door. With his back to me, his hand on the frame, he peered over his shoulder and locked his gaze on mine. "We talked about this last night, before anything happened. You're leaving for college, and I just started my job. What happened between us doesn't change any of that." The way he said it made it sound like he expected me to give him excuses why we'd never work, but that couldn't have been further from the truth. I'd rather make something up as a reason why we *would* work instead of saying we couldn't.

I had the hardest time reading between the lines. I heard the words, listened to his dismissive tone, and witnessed his expression, but something seemed off. However, I had no idea what it was. My head was too foggy and my stomach too weak to allow me to put more thought into it. Rather than argue or question him, I nodded, suddenly desperate to finish getting ready so I could head down to check out.

When I returned to the room, I was surprised to find it all cleaned up. Not a single liquor bottle remained on the floor, and all my clothes were folded neatly inside my suitcase. Holden had even set out an outfit for me to wear on the plane back home. Holding the towel against my chest, I glanced around, almost hoping he hadn't left. But he had. I was all alone, just as I'd asked for. Yet for some reason, it created an ache in my chest, and the more the silence grew, the more I realized he wasn't coming back.

Later at the airport, the ache expanded when I found out he'd switched flights and wouldn't be heading back with us.

It nearly swallowed me whole when he didn't show at Matthew and Christine's housewarming party a few weeks later.

And when he came up with yet another excuse as to why he couldn't attend my going-away party, the ache had turned into a massive black hole, right in the center of my chest where my heart used to beat. I'd missed the opportunity to decipher his reaction that day in Vegas, seconds before he walked out of my life forever. And over the years, it meant less and less to me. Eventually, I became a careless, heartless, walking train wreck.

I had no one but myself to blame.

Although every chance I could, I totally blamed Holden.

ONE

(Janelle)

Five years later

"Are you sure he's your soul mate?"

I glanced across the room and found Connor talking to one of the other guys in the house. Appearance-wise, he was the furthest thing from my type I could get, but then again, I figured that was the whole point of this. I clearly had horrible taste in men, so it would make sense that my soul mate wouldn't be anything like the guys I typically fell for.

Tilting my head and squinting my eyes at him, I thought back on the last eight weeks since we'd met and tried to analyze it from a different point of view. I knew I needed a man who would protect me, but not be an ass. One who wouldn't argue with me, but at the same time, someone who wouldn't be a doormat or put up with my crap. I needed a strong man—both physically and mentally. Thinking about these things while looking at Connor, I knew without a doubt that he was, in fact, my soul mate.

"Yes. Definitely." I turned back to Carrie, who picked at her blueberry muffin across from me at the kitchen table, and then I asked her the same question. "How confident are you that Mike is your soul mate?"

I DO

A slow-forming grin overtook her face. "Very confident."

I rolled my eyes, unable to hide my reaction.

Carrie and Mike had spent almost the entire eight weeks locked in a bedroom, getting to know each other between the sheets. I didn't really blame them. After all, the island did have a sexy ambiance to it, and the people who'd put this completely absurd dating show together wanted as much spice, love, and drama as they could get to boost ratings.

But I had no desire to find a man who'd extend past a free vacation. Still, half the people in the house did come here to find true love — I was *not* one of them.

"How many couples do you think got it wrong?" I asked while looking around the room, taking note of everyone. I'd become friends with a few of the girls, gotten along great with most of the guys, but overall, no one here meant anything to me. I'd been burned enough times that I'd eventually learned to numb myself when it came to a relationship of *any* kind.

"Out of the ten couples, I think at least six of us got it right. I know at least two have it wrong."

"Which ones?"

"Donna and Eric are so not soul mates," Carrie answered with a flip of her hand. "Eric is the same kind of guy she normally dates. We even had a whole conversation about it in like week two. So I know they have it wrong, which means there's at least one other couple incorrectly paired, as well. But none of that means anything to me, because I have Mike. And we're gonna get paid."

I'd previously told her I didn't think Mike was there for her, but she'd made it clear she wasn't open to listening, so I knew nothing I said now would change her outcome. We were less than an hour away from the big reveal. All our questions would be answered. It was a little late to change minds at this point in the game. We'd been given eight weeks to learn about the other people in the house and find our "soul mates," or at least the ones deemed to be soul mates by the producers through some scientific method used to pair us up based on our likes and dislikes. Cue the eye roll. I wouldn't be surprised if their super-scientific technique was nothing but an eeny-meeny-miny-mo, point-and-pick process. But I didn't care, because I wasn't here for love.

The entire process began six months ago when I received a letter in the mail, asking if I would be willing to audition for a reality dating show, of sorts. Normally, I would have tossed it straight into the trash, but the premise was entirely different—and the ten-thousand-dollar prize at the end *really* grabbed my attention.

The letter detailed a dating game, but unlike anything that had already been done. There would be no roses, no elimination ceremonies that dragged on and on. Instead, twenty people—ten guys and ten girls—would live in a lavish beach house on a privately owned tropical island together for eight weeks. No neighbors and no civilians around other than the production crew.

We had random dating opportunities, and we were all trapped in the house and forced to get to know one another, either by talking or hooking up. At the end of the experiment, we were to pair up with our "soul mates," and if we chose correctly, we'd win the ten thousand dollars. If we chose wrong, we'd walk away with nothing.

I wanted that money more than anything, so I had made sure I played the game right—which meant no getting acquainted between the sheets for me. Now Connor, my "soul mate," had his fair share of hookups, which probably should've bothered me, but it didn't. I didn't care to see him after this production anyway, so his recklessness was irrelevant to my finish line.

I DO

After Carrie and I had finished breakfast, we went to gather our suitcases. Everything had been kept super secretive up until this point. We'd been instructed to set our luggage by the front door for the crew to load them into the cars, which told us we were leaving our tropical getaway after the "exit interview," but other than that, we were left without further directives.

We all sat together quietly on the couch while they called us away, two at a time. About every ten minutes or so, the production staff would send for another pair to find out their fate. By the time Connor and I were summoned, my heart was lodged in my throat. Only three couples remained. I quickly hugged the two girls left behind, waved to the guys, and took Connor's hand. We followed the staff outside to the idling black SUV with heavily tinted windows, and then rode in complete silence until we stopped at a private airport.

More staff led us into a secluded meeting room off to the side of the entrance. I laced my fingers with Connor's, the anticipation of our fate slaying my insides. Just because I didn't have feelings for Connor had nothing to do with the contest. My competitive nature had taken over long ago, and I aspired nothing short of a win. Cameras were set up inside the room with several suits sitting behind a staged desk. Many more crew members with mic booms and headsets watched the monitors as if we were nothing but puppets on strings awaiting their instructions.

"Janelle, Connor..." Larry, the host, gestured toward two chairs, indicating we take the empty seats in front of him. "How are you two feeling today? Confident about your choice?" His line of questions seemed as phony as his smile, but I guess it came with being on camera.

"Yes, we feel very good about it," Connor answered for me, and that was why I knew I'd picked right. It was no secret that Connor hated everything about this show, yet he sat here with his shoulder leaning into mine and gazing lovingly at me, like someone who'd just spent the last eight weeks in paradise with the love of his life. I'd thought numerous times since meeting him that he'd make an amazing actor.

"Ready to find out the results?" Larry's eyebrow quirked, indicating he knew some big secret we didn't. It didn't fool me. His reactions were meant for the viewers, for those long, drawn-out moments where the music gets intense and then they cut to a commercial break, essentially taking a five-second moment and dragging it out for ten minutes. All for the drama.

Connor and I nodded before Larry opened the sealed envelope—as if it being sealed made it official or something. The entire production was a joke. But I couldn't complain, because I was about to be handed a check for ten thousand dollars.

"The results show…" He paused dramatically and took a long breath. Impatience urged me to snatch the papers from him, but before I could make a move, he glanced up and looked back and forth between Connor and me. "You two *are* soul mates. Congratulations!"

I smiled and squeezed Connor's fingers, but honestly, that was for the cameras. I knew it wasn't a done deal until that cash was in my bank account, so I made sure to keep up the façade until the bitter end.

"Now, here's the fun part," Larry added with a mischievous grin that made my stomach knot. "For guessing correctly, you two will receive ten grand—which for you math wizards, is five thousand each."

"Wait," I interjected with enough obvious bewilderment I wouldn't have been surprised if all the blood drained from my face. It seemed I'd been played, and that thought made me physically sick to my stomach. "I was told I would win *ten* thousand dollars. Not five. *Ten.*"

"Yes, that's correct. The couples who guess correctly win ten…as a couple."

"That wasn't stated in the contract."

"I can have someone go over that with you, Janelle, once we finish here if you'd like, but I can assure you, it's clearly stated what the prize money would be. I apologize if you assumed that was for each of you versus each couple, but that unfortunately isn't the case."

I knew my reaction spoke volumes for how I truly felt, but I decided to shove down my frustration and keep it to myself. There was no point in arguing with the show's host, especially while on camera where anything could be edited to make me look like a moron or loose cannon. Not to mention, Larry always kept his composure, so no matter how the footage would get trimmed, I'd still come across as the villain, and Larry would be viewed the victim.

"So you can take the money, or you can both use it to buy a bigger pot."

"Excuse me?" Connor and I both leaned forward and asked for clarification at the same time.

"If you both choose the money, you each walk away with a five-thousand-dollar check. However, you also have the option to use that money to buy rings—specifically, the kind worn on your left ring fingers."

"Hold up." Connor lifted his hand. "Why would I give up my money to buy a ring?"

"Good question. Glad you asked." Larry's tone and expression sickened me. It was obvious he had something up his sleeve, and it didn't feel right. "If you choose the option of spending your prize money on wedding rings, and actually following through with it, you will receive fifty thousand dollars." He paused for a moment and looked both of us in the eyes before following it up with, "*Each*."

My jaw dropped. This was certainly unexpected, and not in the bad way. "Fifty grand? Each?"

"That's correct."

There was so much I could do with that kind of money, and the first thought on my mind was being able to put my freshly printed degree to good use and start my own business. "What's the stipulation?"

"Only stipulation is you have to get married."

"And stay married for how long?" This was too good to be true. I could feel it.

"As long as you'd like. There's no requirement. As soon as the marriage license is signed, you get your money."

I turned to Connor and recognized the dollar signs flashing in his brown eyes.

"But make sure whatever you choose is what you want, because once you give me your answer, you can't take it back," Larry continued, his voice droning on like background static on the radio.

"I'm totally down for this if you are." Connor's wide eyes implored me to agree.

I'd be a fool not to…and my momma didn't raise a fool. "Let's do it."

"Are you sure?" Larry paused dramatically while waiting for confirmation, which we both ruined by giving him very eager nods. I'm sure the footage would be edited later to dramatically draw out our answers. "Marriage shouldn't be entered into lightly; you're both aware of this…correct?" Again, we nodded. "Okay then. Your choices have been locked in and you will be spending your money on wedding rings." The song "Chapel of Love" blared from the surrounding speakers. I tried not to laugh as Larry theatrically announced, "You may head next door to pick them out."

We all stood and moved toward the door while the obnoxious lyrics continued to play. The entire walk, my chest tightened and my blood pressure spiked. My hands shook with adrenaline—the thought of receiving fifty grand was like an EpiPen straight to the heart. I had zero desire to get married, at least anytime soon.

I'd just graduated from college with a degree I'd never planned to use in real life, but had received my diploma because my parents promised to pay for school and all living expenses as long as I attended and made good grades. They never once said I had to pick a practical major. So at twenty-three, I was the proud owner of a business degree. I'd gotten the looks from my dad, and they hadn't gone unnoticed. They'd paid for five years of education for me to *learn* how to own my own business. Basically, the same things as spending five years taking lectures on how to ride a bike. But I didn't care, because I went to college and earned a degree, and that was all that mattered.

And here I was, about to pick out a wedding ring to get married to a guy I barely knew just to make money. I'd say my degree paid off.

When we walked into the other room, we found a man in a tuxedo standing behind a jewelry counter. As I approached, the light reflecting off the brilliant diamonds nearly blinded me, and all I could think about was how at the end of this, I could hock the ring for even more money. It'd come in handy for the actual business I wanted to start.

"Which one do you like?" Connor whispered in my ear.

"Honestly, I don't care." And I didn't, because this wasn't real to me. And I knew it wasn't real to him, either. Not for the first time since this whole thing started, I found myself grateful Connor was deemed my soul mate. I would've felt awful had they paired me with someone who sincerely wanted a relationship out of this.

Not wasting any time, Connor pointed to the largest princess-cut solitaire with a matching band. Then it was my turn to pick his. Knowing I would benefit from the rings more than he would, I tried to locate the one with the most value, and chose the platinum band with five diamonds decorating the top. The man behind the counter—who hadn't spoken a single word since we walked in—put the jewelry boxes in a fancy bag and handed it to Connor.

"So...what now?" he asked Larry. "We get married? Is that how this works?"

"You most certainly can if you want. But there's no rush. You have one year to obtain a marriage license and complete the ceremony to claim the money. If you aren't married—to each other—in three hundred sixty-five calendar days, then you both forfeit the prize."

"We don't need a year." I tried to swallow down the attitude, but it was difficult. It annoyed me how he spoke to us, as if we needed to hear every single minute detail. We were ready to hop on a plane and tie the knot. Then get home and file for an annulment. Then count the Benjamins. "Just tell us what we need to do, and we'll do it."

"Well, first...you have to get a divorce." His shit-eating grin made me want to throat punch him.

Connor and I both glanced at each other before turning back to Larry. "Divorce? Don't we have to get married first?"

Larry chuckled and clucked his tongue like we were imbeciles. "I don't mean a divorce from each other. I mean you, Janelle Brewer, must obtain a legal divorce from your husband."

I balked and looked around the room, searching for the prankster about to jump out of a corner or something. This

I DO

had to have been some sort of practical joke. I scoffed and said, "I'm not married."

"That's not what your marriage license says."

The laughter died from my tone, and all I could do was stand and blink rapidly at Larry. I knew it was a bonus to capture the element of surprise on camera, but this was borderline ridiculous. "That has to be a mistake—maybe it's someone else named Janelle Brewer. I'm sure I can't be the only one with that name. I think I would know if I was married."

"Well, when we spoke to your husband, he verified the validity of it."

"My *husband*?" My voice didn't even sound like mine. It came out too high pitched and squeaky.

"Yes, your husband." He then pointed a small remote over my shoulder, all the while grinning obnoxiously. Out of nowhere, a recording played throughout the room. At the first sound of his voice, I grew lost in it, adrift in the deep waves I used to drown in. The same voice that used to comfort me.

The same voice I'd grown to loathe over the years, aware of the heartbreak it could cause.

"This is Holden York."

"Mr. York, we just need to verify a few details. We have it that you married Janelle Brewer in July of twenty-twelve in Las Vegas, Nevada. Is that correct?"

A rush of air hit the recording seconds before he said, *"Yes, that's correct."*

"And since then, has the marriage been annulled or dissolved in any way?"

"No. We're still married."

More of the recording played around me, but I couldn't listen to it. Emotions I couldn't comprehend slammed into

23

me. Anger shook within my chest, while pain and fear knotted in my belly. I knew what he was capable of. And I knew I couldn't go through it again.

My heart fell to the pit of my stomach, and then the floor opened beneath me. I dropped to my knees in some dramatic, slow-motion stumble, perfect for TV had this not contained the crushing blow of real life. I just sat there, staring off into the distance, desperately trying to absorb the information Larry had just dumped in my lap.

Five years ago…

Vegas…

Holden York…

I didn't even remember giving him my virginity, but apparently, I'd given him more than that.

And this whole time, he knew.

He knew, and he never told me.

There was only one thing left for me to do…get divorced.

TWO

(Janelle)

I shook my arms and took a few deep breaths while I fought to compose myself. I couldn't believe after all these years I'd find myself standing in front of Holden's house, the same one he'd bought after graduating from college.

As I stood there, I could almost remember it all like it was yesterday. How we'd gone from being close friends and familiar with one another to ultimate strangers. At the time, I had no idea how to fix it, and now, five years later, I didn't even know how to talk to him.

I'd rung the bell when I first stepped up to the door, but he hadn't answered yet, and I started to wonder if he was even home since I'd been waiting for so long. Then again, with all the adrenaline running through me, it could've only been five seconds, even though it felt more like five years. Rather than ring the bell again, I knocked—probably a little too impatiently based on the way Holden yanked the door open.

Whatever word he'd readied himself to say fell to the wayside, replaced by widened eyes and a gaping mouth. The same shock he wore on his expression, I felt in my chest, and we both stood there, staring at the other, no words spoken between us.

Even though he'd continued to be Matt's best friend through the years, I hadn't seen him much. In fact, it'd been at least three years since we'd been in the same room together—could've easily been four. Once upon a time, we used to see each other often, and our conversations were effortless. All that vanished after one senseless night in Vegas—the same night I not only had sex for the first time, but also got married, all without a single recollection of either instance. As if we'd never met before, the man standing in front of me was a stranger. Not only did he *feel* different, but he looked different as well.

Holden had forever been good looking. Tall and in shape with abs I could trace with my fingertips, longish dark hair that always seemed mussed no matter what style he wore it in, and the most unusual shade of green eyes I'd ever seen— upon close inspection, they appeared to be more of a mixture between slate and hazel, but from a distance, they were a rare, forest green. His skin tone fluctuated depending on the time of year—tan during the summer, and the color of coffee with a lot of milk in the winter, creamy almost.

However, the matured version of him caught me completely off guard. I guess I'd expected the same guy from years ago to answer the door, expected the guy I'd left to be the same one I found. But that's not at all what I got. Still just as tall, he wasn't quite as lanky as before, his chest had filled out, and his shoulders seemed broader. In front of me stood a man—a *grown* man—with short, dark-brown hair that curled close to the scalp on the sides, golden skin, and the same hard, chiseled jaw I used to dream about kissing.

"Holden…" It was nothing but a whisper.

He pinched his brows together and squinted at me before glancing over my shoulder and then off to the side, as if checking the street for something or someone. A slight twitch of insecurity immediately struck me, leaving me to wonder if maybe he'd been expecting someone. Another woman perhaps.

Although, that insecurity lasted all of five seconds. It disappeared when he looked me up and down, practically appraising me, and asked, "What are you doing here?" His voice came out deep, heavy with disgust, the repulsion dripping from each word. It erased the desire coursing through me, acting like a bucket of cold water being splashed in my face.

It reminded me of why I was here in the first place.

I didn't come to reconcile with my husband—no matter what my unconscious thoughts tried to tell me during sleeping hours. They were nothing more than fantasies, lies told to me by the romantic voices driven by Disney fairy tales. The more realistic thoughts kept me in check, reminding me that had Holden truly spent the last five years in love with me, he wouldn't have kept this marriage a secret.

Suddenly, my hands molded back into fists, and an ache in my jaw ignited. "Mind if I come in?"

He glanced over my shoulder once more before taking a step back and begrudgingly inviting me in. Immediately to the right was the living room with a couch, loveseat, and recliner. Not waiting for him to offer me a seat, I took the middle cushion on the long couch and waited for him to join me.

"It's been, what…three, four years, Jelly? What brings you here now?"

I hated hearing my family nickname roll effortlessly off his tongue. It used to be a comfort, a reminder of how close we were, of how close I'd wanted to be with him, but that was no longer the case. Not after he caused the hole in my chest by his blatant avoidance of me following our trip to Vegas. And especially not now after finding out we'd gotten married and he never bothered to tell me. Not once. Instead, he'd let me carry on as if I were the single woman in my early twenties I'd believed I was.

"I think you know why I'm here, Holden."

"No, I honestly don't. I haven't seen you in years, and I'm pretty sure you've never stepped foot inside this house. You rarely come home, and when you do, it's for a major holiday. You stay for a day, maybe two, and then leave just as fast as you came. You've made it extremely obvious how much you hate this town and everyone in it. So no…I don't have a clue why you're here."

I huffed out a breath of frustration, having debated this same argument more times than I could count with my own family. "I don't hate this town. My lack of presence has nothing to do with my feelings for this city or the people who live in it." Although, it did have something to do with a specific resident, particularly the one sitting across from me. "I went away to college and spent the time enjoying myself. Being young and having fun. Isn't that what most college-age people do? And now that I'm finished with school, I plan on moving back."

"Yeah, heard you graduated a few months ago. Where have you been? Because you didn't come back here. So you can't say college has kept you away, because that ended, and yet you've still been absent."

I wanted to know what world he lived in where a twenty-three-year-old moves back home with her parents the second she graduates from college. It seemed everyone I knew lived in this world—except me. I'd spent my whole life living in someone else's shadow, come second—or fifth—to one sibling or another. The last five years away, on my own, being my own person was probably the best five years of my life, yet these people expected me to just walk away from it as if what waited for me here was better. I was the life of the party in college—literally, everyone used me to help plan their soirées. Here, I was nothing more than the youngest Brewer.

"I've spent the last couple of months on vacation...which brings me to why I'm here. Why don't you tell me what happened in Vegas all those years ago? I'd love to finally hear the story of how I so readily gave you my virginity."

"You still don't remember, do you?" he asked with a scoff and slight headshake.

The fact I couldn't recall what was meant to be the most important night of my life did nothing but frustrate me. Over the years, that frustration had burned into ire. It wasn't directed at anyone, just at life in general, but hearing him accost me for not remembering—as if it were a slap in his face, not mine—made me turn my anger on him.

"Did you expect it to come back to me in the form of a dream? I was drunk. *Very* drunk. The only reason I knew I'd had sex was because I woke up the next morning naked, bare as the day I was born, and sore in places no virgin should ever be sore."

Holden's lips tightened and the muscles in his jaw flexed. His gaze narrowed while his nostrils flared wickedly. I'd never seen him this...pissed off. Upset. I couldn't tell what emotion he felt because every part of him was a contradiction. Finally, he stood up and turned his back to me, his hands settling on his hips while his shoulders drooped, almost in defeat.

"An explanation would be nice," I prodded.

"Fine. You want to know what happened? I'll tell you." He dropped his arms and turned to face me again, this time, his cheeks red and his gaze filled with a painful amount of regret. "You had left your sweater thing that went to your dress downstairs. I went to bring it up to you and found you drinking alone in your room. You invited me in, and we drank some more together. I had no idea how much you'd consumed before I got up there. I also had no idea the reason you were drinking, which you later revealed was because you were upset over that douchebag you were dating before prom."

I'd forgotten all about being sad, or why I'd gotten inebriated to begin with. But now that he mentioned it, I recalled going back to my room to sulk in the depressing thoughts of forever being alone, being a virgin until the day I died, and no one ever wanting to marry me. Pathetic, but at the time, my adolescent, melodramatic fears were completely valid. I was eighteen, had just gotten my heart broken for the first time, and had watched my brother get married to the love of his life. Which meant I was officially the only Brewer child who wasn't married, and it all kind of hit me at once. Rather than take a step back and look in the mirror, if nothing more than to remind myself that I was only eighteen years old and on the verge of taking my first step into personal freedom by going off to college, I threw myself an over-the-top pity party and indulged a little too heavily in the small bottles I'd swiped from Matt's reception.

"And then what happened? Did we go anywhere?"

He sucked his teeth for a second, as if either trying to remember the night or figuring out how to tell me. If only he knew it wasn't a secret, then maybe he wouldn't feel the need to tiptoe around it. "I talked you into getting out of the hotel room to get some fresh air, so we took a walk along the strip."

"Where did we go?"

"We watched the fountains in front of Bellagio, made out in front of a mime, held hands while walking the streets of Italy inside the Venetian, and then hung out with Elvis before heading back to the hotel. We went to your room, where you started to strip before we even made it through the door. You refused to take it slow and promised me you were ready."

30

I DO

Anger ignited every word, but I could tell he wasn't pissed off over the actual events. No. What made him mad was his bruised ego over the fact I couldn't remember. It was obvious in the way he *reminded* me of that forgettable night.

But what he didn't know was how it angered me to listen to him. To hear about that night. Because that was the last night I'd had with him, and ever since then, a shattered heart resided in my chest. All because of Holden York. Giving in and listening to how I promised him I was ready did nothing but upset me. Even though I couldn't remember it, I knew it was true. He was the only guy I had ever wanted, and being here, listening to this, was nothing more than a reminder that he had never felt the same.

"You held my face, looked me square in the eyes, and told me it was what you wanted, and you'd never regret it. I asked you how drunk you were, which you said you were tipsy but knew exactly what you were doing." He shook his head and released a huffed, humorless chuckle. "I believed you. Only to wake up the next morning and feel like a fucking jackass."

There were so many things to tackle, but I had to take it one thing at a time. If I tried to get answers for everything at once, I'd only get sidetracked and end up with nothing—it was a horrible habit of mine. "If you knew I was upset about Justin, why were you so willing to sleep with me? Were you just *that* desperate to get in my pants?"

I thought I had him. I really thought this would get him right where I wanted him. The perfect setup for when I let him know I was aware of this secret marriage. Unfortunately, that's not what happened. He sank back into the cushion and leaned forward with his head in his hands.

"Believe what you want, Janelle, but I wasn't desperate to get into your pants. In fact, it very much seemed like the other way around." He dropped his hands and locked his stormy gaze on me, effectively trapping me in my seat, in my head, unable to do anything until he finished speaking. "*You* are the one who attacked me in the elevator when we got back. And again in the hallway on the way up to your room. My plan was to get you back into your room safe and sound. *You* were the one with a different agenda."

"You make it sound like I begged you. Like I threw myself at you." I tossed my head back and squawked out a humorless laugh, but my insides didn't react with the same indifference. My lower belly quickened and a flush of heat rippled through my body. I tried not to imagine doing those things with him—*to* him—but the sexy visions flashed through my mind, anyway. Me attacking him, hungry for him, kissing him, making love with him… Oh, God. "Not to mention, *if* I did, it would've only been because I was so upset. Which brings me back to my question. Why would you sleep with someone who's crying over their ex? Seems rather pathetic. I mean, you could have anyone you wanted…"

I gritted my teeth, furious at myself for saying that last part. I should've left it at "pathetic." Now *I* was the pathetic one. But to my surprise, he didn't even acknowledge the blunder.

"I didn't know you were upset about him until we were in bed. *After* the last time. I have no idea what time it was, but it had to've been around four or five in the morning. We were naked, sated, and about to drift off when you opened up about the reason you were upset in the first place, about thinking you weren't good enough."

The urge to run and hide was strong, but so was my determination to get answers and a divorce, so I could cash my fifty-thousand-dollar check and be on my merry way. "Let me get this straight…you come up to my room, see that I'd been drinking, partake in *more* drinking with me, then we go for a walk, come back, to which I throw myself at you and practically beg you to deflower me. We do our thing, and just before we drift off, I confess to feeling unwanted, and then what? We cuddle and fall asleep?"

"Basically. But it wasn't like you just blurted it out. We were talking about the future. You had mentioned that it wouldn't be long before your mom started in on you getting married. And to be honest, my first thought—actually, more like worry—was that *you* had jumped into bed with *me* out of desperation. The only reason I didn't believe that was because you curled into me and said I made you feel worthy." His eyes locked with mine, and it took everything in me to not choke up at his words, wishing I could remember any part of it. "You told me I made you feel like you weren't disposable."

I blinked a few times, if nothing more than to regain my composure before stating my purpose for coming. To remind myself why I was here in the first place. I refused to fall victim to Holden York again. Apparently, the last time it happened, I became his wife. If I did it again, I could end up bearing his child. "Whatever. I don't recall that conversation."

"Of course you don't, Janelle." He dejectedly fell back into the recliner, leaning his weight toward one side like a young, arrogant king sitting on his throne. He cocked his head and placed his thumb beneath his chin, his forefinger practically digging into his naturally hollow cheek, and the others resting beneath his sexy, plump bottom lip. "You've made that *very* clear. I get it. I took advantage of you that night without ever knowing it. I thought we shared something, only to find out I basically stole it from you. But thanks so much for pointing it out...yet again."

His anger bit into me, and it took a minute to regain my bearings.

"You're the one who ran off and ignored me for the last five years." I leaned forward in my seat, as if needing to get closer to him, showcasing my own frustrations that I'd kept buried since that morning in Vegas. I hadn't realized how much of an impact that had on my outlook on relationships until right now, encountering it for the first time. "It was like you wanted nothing to do with me once you left my hotel room that morning. I had whiplash. We were friends, then we fuck and you want nothing to do with me."

"Don't…" He held out his hand in a gesture to physically stop me, his expression hard and full of ire, maybe even disgust. His breathing turned ragged and he held me hostage with his piercing, hateful stare. Even though his body went rigid, he remained in the same position in the chair. "*You* kicked me out of your room. And within a month of us coming home, *you* ran off to college. *You* are the one who has barely shown your face here during the last five years. So if *you* have whiplash…it's all your fault, baby." With each "you" he spewed, he jabbed his finger in my direction.

And I swear I felt each one of them stab my chest.

Justin had ditched me only four months before Matt's wedding. That means four months separated the time I'd gotten tossed to the side by one guy after *not* sleeping with him, and being forgotten about by another—*after* sleeping with him. I wasn't often an unhappy person. I didn't typically feel bad for myself or suffer from low self-esteem. However, after those two life-changing blows, both by guys I thought were important to me, I'd emotionally boarded up my heart. That was the point in time when I threw my hands in the air and decided to live for me and not care about how men viewed me. I'd been in one more relationship since then, which only lasted five months before I caught my roommate licking him like a lollipop. That was pretty much the reassurance I needed to know relationships weren't for me.

"You pulled away from me, Janelle. You pushed *me* away. You told me to leave. Or do you not remember that, either?"

I DO

He now sat forward, both of us leaning toward each other with a coffee table between us. "What did you want me to do? I'd slept with my best friend's little sister. I took her virginity, and she didn't remember a damn second of it. I felt like a creep. Like I'd somehow conned you into bed. Like I'd gotten you drunk just to sleep with you. When the truth was…it was all *your* idea!" He scrubbed his hand down his face before continuing in a much softer, more remorseful tone. "I knew you'd been drinking, but I swear to you that I didn't have the slightest clue you were as lit as you were. You walked, talked, and acted perfectly fine. You don't remember your first time, and it's all my fault. I was angry with myself and didn't care to be around you, because all it did was remind me of the worst night of my life."

His words were like a dull knife ripping through every layer of skin on its quest to shred my heart into unrecognizable pieces. "The w-worst night of your life?" Appalled, confused, and incredibly hurt, I spewed my question, the words burning my tongue like acid. "If it was so horrible, why haven't you done anything to annul the marriage?"

Holden froze, only his chest heaving while the rest of his body turned to stone. It was clear he hadn't expected to hear that accusation, to bring up the union I had no recollection of. "So, that's why you're here. Makes sense, but how'd you find out about it? I know you didn't suddenly remember that and nothing else."

I couldn't help but blow out a huff of disbelief and shake my head. "Really, Holden? That's your response? As it turns out, we've been legally married for five years, yet we've barely spoken or seen each other since, and you're questioning how I found out? Were you ever going to tell me we're husband and wife?"

35

He covered his face with his hands and sighed before dropping his arms. "You can believe me or not, but I actually planned on telling you when you came back. *If* you came back. If you didn't, then I would've found some other way to let you know, but considering part of the deal we made when we got married was that you'd go off to college and then come home and live with me, I guess I kinda figured I'd wait until then."

"That was the deal? I don't get it. What benefit do you get out of being married?"

"Tax breaks."

I couldn't believe my ears. "You never told me we are legally married because you didn't want to give up your tax status? Is this some kind of joke?" My voice got higher and higher with each question. "I feel like I'm in the middle of a horrible prank, and everyone's in on it but me."

He resumed his relaxed, arrogant-king position in the recliner, coming across as the sexy kind of confident. "Now really...how'd you find out? You clearly didn't remember, so what was it?"

"I was informed when I tried to get married—to someone else."

Had I not been staring right at him, I would've missed it. I wouldn't have witnessed the slight drop in his shoulders, the split-second break in eye contact, or the falter in his breathing. If I didn't know better, I would've thought he'd been emotionally sucker punched. But I knew that couldn't be right. Maybe at one point in my life, many years ago, I could've romanticized the situation and convinced myself that Holden and I had a chance. There was even a brief moment after Vegas that I'd grown lost in the idea of being with him, falling for him like I'd dreamed of most of my life. But his intentional avoidance cured that possibility real quick.

I DO

Holden York didn't want me the way I'd once pined for him.

No matter how much thought I'd put into his reaction to me the morning after, I had never been able to come up with answers. It was something I probably wouldn't ever understand, and I'd given up on figuring it out long ago. If it'd meant anything to him, he would've done something about it.

The only explanation I could think of—and the one I'd convinced myself of over the years—was that he felt responsible for taking my virginity. I was his best friend's sister. He'd known me since I was six. There were times he'd acted protective over me, both when I was younger and again during high school. There was also the awkward stage of life we all suffered through when I apparently annoyed him and Matt to no end. Then again, they were busy with the popular crowd at school and had just started driving on their own, so they wanted nothing to do with me. I couldn't fault either of them for avoiding me.

But the one thing that hurt more than anything was the end of my relationship—friendship—with Holden.

In April, I'd sat on his couch and cried to him. I told him things I couldn't even tell my own brother, things about my relationship with Justin. Things no guy wanted to hear about his little sister. But Holden had listened. And not once did he make any move to leave me in the pursuit of kicking my ex's ass. Later, he'd admitted to finding Justin and having a rather intense conversation with him, but when I needed him, he was there. Wholeheartedly. Both physically and mentally.

Then, two weeks later, on the night of my prom, Holden was the one who'd taken me to binge on ice cream. Afterward, he took me to an empty softball field. The lights were on and lit up everything around us. However, instead of the fluorescent bulbs highlighting our every move, we basked in the silver light of the moon hanging above. And right there, in the grass, he blared horrible music from his speakers and gave me the most memorable prom of my life. The best part being the respect he'd shown at the end of the night.

Over the few months between then and Vegas, we'd grown even closer. It wasn't like we suddenly hung out all the time, but he'd occasionally check in with me to see how I was doing, knowing how much the breakup had affected me, and how I tended to stuff everything deep down and keep it hidden. Holden was the only one capable of pulling it all to the surface and making me feel okay again.

That was what I'd missed the most over these last five years.

There had been plenty of times I could've used his support.

But I didn't have it. Or him.

I didn't really care that I'd lost my virginity and couldn't remember it. And I certainly wasn't bothered by the fact I'd lost it to Holden, especially since I'd spent the better part of my teenage years daydreaming of the night I would offer it up to him on a silver platter, on our wedding night, with candles and rose petals decorating a lavish hotel room and music playing softly to set the mood.

Ironically, the reality wasn't that far off.

As it turned out, it *was* on our wedding night, and we *were* in a hotel room. From the sounds of it, I'd more than offered it up on a silver platter, practically begging him to take it, if his recounting of events were accurate. And even if it wasn't, I didn't have a leg to stand on to refute his claims. There could've been candles and rose petals—hell, we could've even had Adam Levine himself serenading us from a corner for all I knew.

I DO

None of that bothered me, other than my inability to remember being with *him*.

My God, I'd spent eleven years infatuated with the guy. I even had a binder filled with our wedding plans, all the way down to the napkins with our initials embroidered in gold thread. Spending the night with him wasn't the issue. My already broken heart had taken yet another beating when he'd vanished. When I had to fly back home next to his empty seat with the mental snapshot of his sorrowful eyes after he learned I had no memory of the night before, it haunted every second of that flight.

Then my bruised and battered heart shattered weeks later when we all gathered at Matt's new house. I'd prepared myself to crush the tension we'd had between us since Vegas, eager and ready to move forward—even if that meant we had to pretend he didn't know what I looked like naked.

Only he never showed up.

Feeling a little beaten down, my ego slightly bruised, I'd made a few more attempts to talk to him so we could clear the air. But either the timing was wrong, too many people were around, or he played Houdini at whatever event it was. By the end of summer, on my way out of town for college, I'd officially given up.

That was what had hurt me the most.

He hadn't cared enough to make things right.

"You're...you're getting married?" His question sounded forced, pained, like he'd swallowed shards of glass before asking. "Since when? To who? Do your parents know? Matt never said anything."

I wanted to believe he was hurt. I wanted nothing more than to hear the pain and shock in his tone and convince myself it was caused by the thought of my being with someone else. Even though I knew that wasn't remotely true.

Couldn't have been. He had to have known I wasn't celibate over the last five years, and not once did he make any effort to claim me. To tell me his wants and desires for me.

They say a picture speaks a thousand words.

Well, so does silence.

And his silence was heard loud and clear.

"It's really none of your business, now is it, Holden?" It was my turn to give him as much attitude as I could muster. "Until five days ago, I wasn't even aware we were married. You—for whatever reason—kept that from me. And now you want to question the status of my relationship? What right do you have?"

I knew I needed to cool it before he started to get suspicious. Truth be told, I didn't want him knowing anything about Connor, or about the prize money. If he knew, then my brother would know, then my entire family would find out, and they'd never let me hear the end of it.

"It's just surprising, is all. I mean, you haven't been in a real relationship in years."

"How would you know that?"

He tilted his head and gave me a dumbfounded expression complete with bored eyes and a disbelieving smirk. "Really? Your love life is your mom's topic of conversation any chance she gets—or should I say, your *lack* of love life is all she ever complains about. It's like she can't live her own life until all her babies are married off and stable. So trust me, I get an earful on a weekly basis when I'm at your parents' house for Sunday dinner."

I had to replay his words to myself a few times to make sure I hadn't misunderstood him. "You go to my parents' house every Sunday for dinner?"

His eyes grew wide when he said, "Yeah," as if my question was the most absurd thing he'd ever been asked. "Ever since Stacey moved home with her husband and kids,

I DO

your mom has been hosting weekly Sunday gatherings. Everyone attends."

Stacey was my second-oldest sister, and she'd moved back home a little over two years ago when her husband had been laid off. Dad had offered him a job to help them get back on their feet, but they never left. I was the last child to come home, and even though I had my reasons for staying away, I couldn't help but feel slightly rejected after hearing how they were all so tight and close in my absence.

"How cozy of you to welcome yourself into my family."

"Oh, Janelle." He shook his head and tsked. "I've always been a part of your family. I was included a very long time ago. Don't take your anger out on me—I'm not the one who kept you away. If you want to be mad at someone for being left out of the family circle, I have a mirror hanging in the bathroom, and you're more than welcome to look in it."

"What reason would I have to be mad?" I prayed I was able to mask the hurt I felt, because I really didn't want him privy to my inner emotions. "Clearly, it doesn't bother me that you and everyone else gets together every weekend behind my back, and this is the first I've heard about it." I jutted my chin out as if I'd proven a point. Then I replayed my words—and noticed the smug look on his gorgeous face—and realized I hadn't effectively hidden anything.

"What's going on, Janelle?" Once again, he sat with his elbow on the armrest, his thumb beneath his chin, his forefinger along his cheekbone, and the others draped beneath his mouth...like the arrogant ass he seemed to have become. "Are you really getting married? And if so, where did this guy come from? Why does no one in your family know about him?"

I almost turned away. *Almost.* But a split second before I did that, I happened to see the shade of his greenish-grey eyes shift the slightest bit. It was a small shadow, so easy to miss. And for reasons my heart refused to explain, the emotion I caught filled me with excitement. Concern was what I'd seen. And not just any concern, but deep, passionate trepidation. It was unexpected, but so worth seeing.

"No one knows because I haven't said anything. It's all happened so fast, and I didn't want to chance anyone scaring him away."

"How fast? Wait—" He held out his hand and narrowed his gaze. "How long have you known him?"

"Almost two months."

As if he hadn't already shown signs of worry, my confession seemed to shock him into a state of panic, bordering on complete outrage. "Are you kidding me right now?" He shot out of the recliner and leaned over the coffee table between us, hovering over me. "You just met this kid two months ago, and you're already getting married?"

"Yes. The sooner the better. So I need you to sign these divorce papers, please." I turned to my purse on the couch next to me and pulled out an envelope. With a smug grin, I stood up and held it out to him.

He stared at it, then at me, then back at the offending manila envelope. "No."

"Excuse me?"

"No. I'm not signing those. I'm not giving you a divorce."

THREE

(Holden)

I stared at her, attempting to take everything in, because I couldn't believe she was here. In my house. Even more disbelieving was that she'd come to ask me for a divorce…so she could *marry someone else*.

The thought made me sick. My stomach did flip-flops while I regarded her, taking note of her honey-colored hair, so much longer than it used to be. I could still remember how it smelled when she'd leaned against my shoulder while watching a movie together. The more I observed her, the more lost I became in her presence. Even though the sight of her made my stomach ache less, it made my chest ache even more.

She wore her hair styled in loose curls, pinned away from her face. I always loved her hair pulled back because her eyes seemed so much bigger when they weren't hidden. The dark kohl lining the edges brought attention to the subtle explosions of caramel in the vibrant blue. The golden webs stretching toward the dark rims of the irises nearly hypnotized me. It was hard to take my attention off the eyes I'd spent so many years looking into, but the splatter of freckles along the bridge of her nose and across her cheeks brought my focus to her fiery complexion, which reminded me that the woman in front of me was fuming.

"You can't deny me a divorce." Her cheeks flamed with the same anger lighting her wide eyes and causing her pink bottom lip to tremble. Janelle had always been so transparent—well, most of the time. Turned out that wasn't the case when she had too much to drink. "You can't force me to stay married to you—especially when I didn't even know we were married in the first place."

I struggled against the grin threatening to split my lips. I had no idea where this need to fight came from, but it was a powerful one. It wasn't like I had some sort of vendetta against her for anything, or a desire to piss her off, but for some reason, I couldn't seem to stop. Probably because she came here and demanded I give her what she wanted. And had it been anything other than a divorce...I probably would've done it.

"I may not be able to force you to stay with me, but I can certainly drag this process out for years and exhaust a good portion of your twenties, as well as your bank account."

"You wouldn't do that," she argued, though her voice sounded more like begging.

And that's when I knew I had her. I confidently reclaimed my seat across from her and stated smugly, "Watch me."

With a renewed sense of defiance, she crossed her arms over her chest, bringing my attention to her perfect breasts, the same ones I found myself still dreaming of years later. "Oh, yeah? And how do you plan on explaining this to Matthew? Huh? I'm sure he and the rest of my family won't be too pleased to find out you married me five years ago, *after* getting me drunk, and now you're refusing to grant me a divorce despite the strained relationship we've had since the night in question."

Giving in, I laughed. I tilted my head back and released a hearty chuckle, deep, from the pit of my stomach. Janelle had always been the baby. She always seemed to get whatever she wanted from anyone, which was why when Matt and I wanted something from his parents, we'd always send in Janelle to ask. And as much as it pained me to admit it, she always got what she wanted from me, as well. This may have been the first time she didn't bat her long, dark eyelashes and walk away the victor.

I refused to give in on this one.

"I see you're already practicing your legal jargon, *Jelly*?" That was meant to be condescending. Her entire family called her "Jelly," which she'd always hated, and I knew that. Anytime I had ever used it, it had been meant as more of an insult than an endearment. And I could tell by the way she squinted her eyes at me that she knew it, too. "Listen, if you can't afford a lawyer, then maybe you shouldn't push this. I don't suggest representing yourself. There's a reason officers of the court go through so much schooling. Not to mention...are you really prepared to tell your family all about the drunken night you *don't* remember? I can't imagine you'd be eager to let them know specific details, but hey...if you want them to know, I'd be more than happy to fill them in on the parts you don't remember—oh, wait...that's everything."

"I don't get it, Holden. Why? Why would you fight this? It's not like we've been together this whole time or have some fairytale romance. We've never dated. We had sex once—"

"Four times," I corrected, making sure she had the right information.

"Four times?" She rolled her eyes and waved me off before plopping down onto the couch across from me. "Regardless, it was *one* night. But if saying it was four times makes you feel better, then okay, you win. We had sex four times, and I can't remember a single one of them. What does that say about your performance?" Her claws were out. And it'd be a lie if I said those grazes didn't hurt. "I don't understand why you're so opposed to signing these papers so we can put an end to this."

"I'm not signing them because I refuse to allow you to marry a guy you met two months ago."

"So you're saying if he were someone I've been dating for the last however many years, you'd have no problem granting me a divorce? You just want to be stubborn and act like some overprotective big brother? Well, guess what? I already have one of those, and you're not him."

I swallowed harshly and licked my lips, needing the extra time to rein in my thoughts and feelings regarding this whole situation. When I first opened the door and saw her standing there, I couldn't deny the way my heart had slammed against my ribcage at the mere sight of her. For a second—a *milli*second—I thought she had come back. To me. Then I'd noticed the rigidness of her posture, the way she'd clenched her hands into fists, and the tightness of her lips. That's when it dawned on me that there was no way she had remembered anything, and even less of a chance that she had returned to me.

Then I'd reminded myself I didn't want her.

"This is pathetic, Holden." She dropped the envelope onto the coffee table. "You don't know him. You know nothing about my relationship with him, so you don't get to have an opinion. You don't get to have a say-so regarding my life—the one you've been estranged from for the last five years. You've shown no interest in me over the entirety of our *marriage*, so you've lost every right you've ever had to have input in what I do."

I absolutely hated how she had placed all the blame in my lap for what had happened all those years ago. As if she had nothing to do with any of it. Aside from briefly seeing her a few times while she was in town after she left for college, no, I hadn't seen or spoken to her. But that wasn't all my fault.

46

I DO

She was the one who took off. She tucked her tail and ran. Granted, I didn't chase after her, but then again, that had been the deal. Standing on the strip in Las Vegas, that's what we had agreed upon. So really, I stuck to the plan. It wasn't my fault she couldn't remember it—or the existence of one.

"What's his name?" I asked through clenched teeth.

"Connor."

"Last name."

She blinked a few times, and I knew immediately that she had no idea what the douchebag's last name was. Once again, she couldn't hide anything from me, and I began to doubt the reality of this guy. For all I knew, this was nothing but a ploy to make me sign the papers.

"Don't lie to me, Janelle." No matter how righteous I felt right now, knowing I had the upper hand, I couldn't seem to hide the doubt and festering anger from taking over. They riddled everything from my stern words and raspy voice to the sudden rigidness in my spine, giving away how I truly felt. "Is there even a guy, and if so, who is he really? And are you seriously marrying him?"

"I told you…his name is Connor, and yes, we're *trying* to get married, but there's this tiny little problem preventing us from doing so." Using two fingers, she slid the envelope across the table, closer to me. "If you'll just sign these, I'll get out of your way, and you won't ever have to deal with me again. This little mishap will be behind us, and we can both move on with our lives as if that night in Vegas never happened."

I tried to swallow, but it was as if my esophagus refused to work. My breathing hiccupped in my lungs, and I had to force myself to not rub the center of my chest, where it felt as though I had been hit with a professional curve ball. And I wouldn't have been surprised if my heart skipped a few beats—or a hundred.

Rather than speak right away, I stared at the envelope in hopes of hiding my reaction from her. I abhorred the notion of Janelle marrying this guy—or any other guy—yet I couldn't figure out why. She hadn't been in my life, and it wasn't like I'd lived the last five years in limbo, waiting for her, so I couldn't decipher why this bothered me so much.

Once I felt confident that I had my reaction under control, I lifted my gaze and held her stare. "I'm not about to give you what you want just so you can run off and marry some loser you don't even know. Why are you marrying him, anyway? Are you pregnant? Did the fucker knock you up? Is that what's going on?" The second the idea of her being pregnant with that asshole's bastard child came up, I about lost it. My face flamed with unimaginable heat, and my forehead felt so tight it ached.

"Again...you know nothing about it."

"So tell me about it. Make me understand."

"I don't have to." She tilted her head defiantly to the side, and after a moment of us both doing nothing but staring at the other, she started to laugh. "We aren't five, Holden. This is ridiculous. We somehow managed to get married while both under the influence, and for reasons I still don't comprehend, you've kept that a secret from me. We haven't once, since our drunken vows, lived as husband and wife. We haven't shared a single thing...not even a conversation. So what's there to fight for? Tax breaks for technically being married? Find someone else. It doesn't have to be me."

"Do you love him?" Raw pain hung in my voice, but I couldn't waste the energy to care. If it worked in my favor, I'd take it. "Just tell me the truth. That's all I ask."

"No." She dropped her chin and took a deep breath. "I've spent the last two months on a beach in Jamaica."

I DO

"He's Jamaican?" I flew out of my chair, shock heightening my voice.

Without hesitation, she laughed. It was real and honest and flowed so effortlessly from her. The kind of laughter I used to crave when she was around. The kind that embedded itself inside until your lips curled and humor bubbled out, even when you had no idea what was so funny.

And that's exactly what happened now.

When she glanced up at me, realizing I now laughed with her, she shook her head. Humor lightened her tone when she said, "No, he's not, so you can stop worrying about it being some ploy for him to get his green card. The truth is, we were both there for a reality dating show."

The shock of her confession forced me back a step. I didn't want to believe it, because the Janelle I knew wasn't desperate enough to stoop that low. Not to mention, she was too smart to be one of those contestants who quickly tied the knot, thinking what they had could survive in the real world. "You met him on a dating show, and now you're ready to rush down the aisle? You are aware of the success rate for those kinds of couples, aren't you?"

"It's not what you're thinking." She bit her lip and shrugged. "It's more of a game show than anything. Basically, we each won five thousand dollars, but before they gave us the money, we were given the chance to exchange what we won for ten times the amount."

"This sounds like a fucked-up version of *Let's Make a Deal*." I groaned and rolled my neck, desperate for some of this tension in my shoulders to be relieved. "Fifty thousand dollars, huh? What's the catch?"

"Well, to get that, we have to get married. They needed our answer immediately, and once we gave it, we couldn't take it back. So of course, we traded the small check for the set of rings, all so we could walk away with more money. Only problem is…as I'm sure you've guessed by now, I can't get married to him because I'm legally married to you."

"And that's why you want a divorce." It wasn't voiced as a question, but I still sought an answer anyhow. More like a confirmation. Something to go on.

"Yes. We have one year to follow through—otherwise, we both lose it all. And, Holden, I really need this money. I just graduated college, and I'm getting ready to start my life, make something of myself. This money will go so far in helping me reach my goal."

With a deep breath, I fell into the recliner again and waited for it to stop rocking before locking my gaze on hers. I knew what she was doing, playing up the sympathy card. Normally, this would've worked, but now that I knew the real reason she wanted this, I couldn't find it in me to give it to her. "So you get fifty grand, and I lose my tax status. Doesn't seem like a very fair tradeoff, Jelly."

Her instant show of irritation proved me right. "Fine…I'll give you five grand of it. But I can't go more than that. I need every penny of this money. I want to start my own business, and this would allow me a solid head start without so much debt."

"Five thousand dollars?" I pinned her with my stare, letting her know without so many words how ridiculous that offer was—I'd never accept it. Then again, she probably could've offered me the entire amount, and I still would've turned it down. This wasn't about the money. Never was, never would be. "You're gonna have to sweeten the pot a lot more than that if you want me to sign those papers. You said you have a year? How about this…you give me six months."

"For what?" She balked. "You just want me to wait six months? Why? *Oh*…" Her mouth opened into the shape of a perfect, pink *O*, and she raised her brows, as if suddenly

50

realizing something. "You need to wait until next year so you can keep the tax status for this year. Okay, fine. Deal."

She accepted entirely way too fast, which only made me hungry to sweeten the pot. I never would've let her go for simply waiting a few months. But her naiveté made me laugh. "No. I want a wife. Legally, you already are. All I'm asking is for it to be real for the next six months. You do that, and I'll sign. I won't contest a thing. It'll be a clean break—you go your way and I go mine. No fight, no court, just two adults dissolving a marriage."

Her perfectly arched top lip quirked in disgust. "You want me to be your whore for six months? You've got to be kidding me." She hurriedly grabbed her purse and attempted to make a swift exit, but I was faster. I slid off the recliner for what felt like the millionth time since she'd arrived, and stood in front of her, preventing her from reaching the front door. She shoved at my chest and argued, "I'm not agreeing to that. And you're an asshole for even suggesting it."

"Stop." I wrapped my fingers around her wrists and held her still, forcing her to crane her neck and meet my gaze. "I never said that. You're putting words in my mouth."

"You said you wanted a *real* wife for six months."

"Yes. I want you here. Under my roof. Living together."

"Why?" Her question was barely a whisper, floating across my face and doing things to my insides I wasn't sure I was comfortable with.

"Because, Janelle," I whispered back, lowering my face close to hers. "I'm in love with you. And if I have to give you up, then I at least want something I can hold onto after you're gone." With my nose grazing hers, I felt her long, slow exhale billow across my face. That was the breaking point, the point I couldn't hold it in any longer.

My lips parted and I laughed. Hard.

Janelle stepped away, ripping her arms from my grasp, and stared at me with a scorching gaze and quivering lip. Guilt immediately assuaged me, but rather than apologize for the cruel joke, I decided to offer a bit of honesty.

"Truth?" I waited for her to nod, and then continued. "You've missed a lot here. I get that you've been at school and doing your thing, but while you've partied it up, your family has been here battling real life."

She rolled her eyes and huffed with a wave of the hand. "Like what? They haven't said anything."

"And you think I'm going to tell you? They kept certain things from you for a reason. Whether I agree with it or not doesn't matter. None of it is truly my business, anyhow. But I can put my hand on a stack of Bibles and swear I'm not making this up. They have been dealing with one thing after another, and we've all been here as one unit to offer support…to *any*one who's needed it. You're the only one who hasn't been here, and you've made it very obvious you have no desire to be."

"I'm pretty sure I would know if anything worth mentioning was going on in my family while I was away."

I shrugged, growing rather irritated over her stubbornness. "What reason would I have to lie, Janelle?"

"Oh, gee…I don't know, Holden. Maybe to get me to agree to your stupid deal?"

I set my hands on my hips and cocked my head, fighting back the argument I so desperately wanted to have with her. "You seriously think I would make up shit about your family to get you to live with me? You think I'm that hard up, Janelle? If I were that lonely, I could choose from a long line of women, most of whom would gladly move in."

"And here I thought you've spent the last five years pining for me." Her mock puppy-dog eyes grated on my last nerve, but she didn't stop there. "I figured you'd be waiting for me to graduate from college and come back to you. I mean, that's what you said earlier, right?"

"Yes, that's what I said because that's what the deal was. I knew it didn't matter, though. You were drunk when we planned it and you don't remember anything, so clearly, I wasn't sitting around pining for you, *Janelle*. That was never part of the deal. I guess it was more of an unspoken understanding that our lives would go on while you went to school, but that night, we decided to go ahead and get married anyway."

"That makes no sense. Why the hell would we get married and both be okay with each other fucking other people for five years? Not to mention, what would've happened if I got pregnant or you knocked someone up? Or one of us actually fell in love with someone else? Did either of us think of the possibility of any of *that* happening?" She practically screamed her questions, each one getting louder than the last.

I hung my head and dug my thumbs into my temples, hoping to ease the ache started by her voice, and immediately doubted my decision to have her stay here. "First of all, let's take into account that we were both drinking that night. I think it's a safe bet to assume neither of our logic was sound. We decided to get married for fuck's sake. Which is pretty much the most illogical thing I've ever done. So, let's go ahead and give up on wondering why we would say 'I do' and then turn a blind eye to either of us having sex with other people while you were gone. Maybe we thought we'd be able to carry on a long-distance relationship. Who the hell knows. But taking all that into account, I think you can see why the other questions were never brought up."

"I'm so confused." She threaded her fingers into her hair and then fisted her hands, gripping the strands by the roots in pure frustration. "We planned on being together? That's what we discussed? *Both* of us?"

I took a moment before answering, knowing my response would give so much away, but I no longer cared. All these feelings were buried so long ago, and after her prolonged absence, I knew they'd never be uncovered. Nothing could dig them up.

"Yes. I told you that night, but since you don't remember, I might as well explain it now. After that asshat broke up with you before prom, and we started spending more time together, I began to fall for you in ways I never expected. Ways I'm infinitely sure would have had your brother kicking my ass. But you needed me, and I very much enjoyed the feeling of being needed. We kinda grew a bond over those months, and as we stood along the strip, watching the fountain dance in front of the Bellagio, we realized it was a mutual attraction. One we thought would last forever. So, we decided to make it official, and at that time, the only obstacle in our way was college. Which is why we made the deal to begin with."

Her posture softened, and I wondered what part had gotten to her. "Did we like...say the *L* word?"

"No." I smiled and shook my head, hoping to ease her fears.

Only problem was, that had been a lie. We did use that word—several times in fact. She'd even screamed it one of the four times in bed. But that wasn't something I wanted to throw in her face, no matter how much I wanted to get back at her. Truth be told, I didn't even know why I was so angry with her in the first place other than her refusal to visit her family.

"If you choose to take me up on my offer and stay, you'll have your own room, your own space. My agreement doesn't include sex—I have no problems getting that when I need it.

I DO

I just ask that you participate in things. That you spend time with your parents and siblings. Hang out with your nieces and nephew. Don't worry about this." I waved my hand between us. "I work all the time, so it's not like you'll even see me often. The six months will go by, and before you know it, you'll be a single woman, free to marry whoever you want for any reason you'd like. And *hopefully*, you'll have a stronger relationship with your family."

"And I have your word on that?"

"Absolutely. A thousand percent."

"And no sex?"

"None." I cleared my throat and amended my answer. "With *each other*."

She nodded and licked her lips, her gaze falling from mine. I knew I had her, but I needed to hear her say it. She had to tell me she would live with me, as my pseudo-wife, for the full amount of time I requested. "Okay, but we'll need rules before I agree to anything."

"Of course." I held my hand out in a gesture for her to take a seat on the couch while I once again reclaimed my spot in the recliner. After pulling out my laptop from beneath the coffee table, I opened the lid and began to type. "All right... Over the course of the next six months, you—Janelle Brewer—will live in my house as my wife. During this time, there will be no expectations for sexual favors between either of us. What else?"

"Maybe you should add in there that you won't bring your 'dates' home with you. You have to see how awkward it would be to sit in my room while you have a woman in your bed. Or how odd it'd be to introduce your piece of ass to your wife after you get done screwing." She held my gaze the entire time she taunted me, all while a grin remained on her face.

"Well, I obviously wouldn't want to make anything uncomfortable for you. I'll include that I won't bring anyone here, and the same goes for you." I nodded at her before adding her request to the Word document I'd opened, aptly titled *The Marriage Agreement*. I glanced back up at her and winked. "You'll also be pleased to know I've put in here that I will not flaunt or brag about my escapades, such as shooting you a text telling you I'm about to get my dick sucked."

"Oh, how nice of you." She may have said it with a smile, but I hadn't seen anything faker since my last date's set of tits. She crossed her arms and gave me a pointed stare. "Okay then. Next rule. Bills. I don't currently have a job, and you're stifling my ability to make money. So unfortunately, I won't be able to contribute financially."

My fingers tapped away at the keys, the sound filling the silence in the room. When I finished adding her requested rule, I repeated it back to her. "Okay, no paying bills. I've also included that items, such as food or things for the house, are also not your responsibility. You're more than welcome to pick up anything you want from the grocery store—for you or the house in general, like milk or bread—and I'll cover the cost."

"And by 'things for the house,' you mean…"

"If you need a pillow or blanket for your bed. Or towels for the bathroom. Laundry detergent. Light bulbs. I don't know, Janelle…anything you'd need while living here." I was almost sure I'd regret this idea, but she'd come too far to turn back now. One thing was for sure though, the more she pushed, the harder I'd shove.

This was a war she didn't want to get into with me.

I'd fucking win.

"Sounds good to me. Moving along now. You're a grown man. I will not clean up after you. That means you wash your own clothes, you clean your own toilet, and make your own bed."

"I had no intention of you being my maid, but sure, I'll include it anyway." Keeping my thoughts to myself, I added that to the list. Word for word. "Now, I have some rules. You are here temporarily. That means no permanent alterations to my house. I don't care to repaint walls or patch holes left behind by some ugly-as-sin decoration you felt the need to put up. At the end of the day, this is *my* house. You are more than welcome to make yourself at home while you're here. You can add pillows to the couch, move the furniture around in your room, add a DVD player to the TV, or decorate the patio with potted plants. I don't care. Go crazy. But please, all I ask is that you don't use my property to get back at me."

She may have nodded, but I could tell by her meek voice that I had hurt her feelings when she asked, "Anything else?"

"That's it. That's all I ask of you, Janelle. I don't want this to be like I'm holding you hostage or making you my prisoner."

"Well, you kinda are."

"If that's the way you're going to look at it, then it's going to be a long six months. But if you treat it like a free place to stay, an extended vacation—*free* vacation, might I add—with a clean divorce at the end, then the time will fly by. It's all in how you perceive it."

"I just don't understand your motive for this, but whatever."

"Listen, I have my reasons for wanting you here, for not wanting to sign those papers, just like you have yours for marrying some stranger for money. There's no point in us debating the issue further because neither of us will get it. I only hope that in six months, you'll see for yourself why I asked for this—because if you don't, then that means I've failed you and your family."

"And when does this start?"

I closed the lid to the laptop and set it aside. "The day you move in," I answered, sitting forward with my elbows propped on my knees, my hands hanging between my legs.

"I have a question…how are we going to explain this to my family? What's our story?"

"Let's come up with one. I'm sure you don't want them knowing about Vegas, and I assume you don't want them to find out about this dating show…right?"

"That's correct." She couldn't even look me in the eye, which told me so much about the shame she felt over the fact she'd be twice divorced before she turned twenty-five. "We can just tell them you offered me a spare room for a few months while I get on my feet after college. I can just tell my mom I didn't want to inconvenience her by moving back in."

"Your ability to form lies is worrisome," I mumbled with my sights locked on her.

She glanced up and caught me staring, more than likely heard my grumble, but at least she ignored it with a swift flitter of her exotic eyes. "And when's this going to happen? When am I moving in?"

"Whenever you want. Just keep in mind I'm not signing those papers until you've lived here for six months. The timer doesn't start until your things are here and you're sleeping under this roof. But the when is completely up to you."

"Okay. I have to sort some things out. I might have to find somewhere to store the rest of my belongings until I need them again." She glanced around my small starter home. "I'm not sure everything will fit in here."

I ran my hand over my face, hoping to hide the anxiety rushing through my body. Ever since Matt got married and moved out, I had lived alone, hadn't shared my space with a single soul. Not even a dog. Especially not a girl. More importantly, a girl who would more than likely try to one up me. I needed to figure out a way to make her back down long enough to see the bigger picture.

So…I decided to kill her with kindness.

"That's your call. If I have room here for it, you're more than welcome to bring everything with you. I have a guestroom with a bed and dresser that has been used maybe twice when my mom came to visit. But if you'd rather have your own furniture, I can move my desk and computer out of my office. Just let me know ahead of time so I can get things rearranged, if need be."

There didn't seem to be anything else to say. After we swapped phone numbers, she shoved the envelope containing the divorce papers back into her purse and left. I stood by the front door and watched her drive away, unsure of what had transpired.

I figured this idea would blow up in my face, but for the small chance things would go right, I knew I had to see it through. Her family needed her, and they meant enough to me to sacrifice my own feelings to make sure they got what they deserved.

I only hoped I would survive.

FOUR

(Janelle)

It was move-in day. The day I started my jail sentence. And yes, it was a sentence—six months without parole. I was being forced to live with a man who could melt the panties off a nun. As if that weren't bad enough, he also happened to be the only guy I'd ever truly loved. Ever since the last time I allowed myself to fall for his charm, I'd practically sworn off men. If he hurt me again, there was a good chance I'd join a convent. So…I basically needed to remind myself of the third-degree burn his rejection caused in the past in order to get through my stay with him.

Lucky for me, I already had everything packed and in storage. There hadn't been much time between the last of my classes and my departure for the dating show. So it only took about a week to get everything in place and ready to move into Holden's house. The one thing I knew from the very beginning was I had no intention of making this easy for him. After leaving Holden's house, I'd called Connor to inform him of the change in plans. He didn't like it any more than I did, but for a very different reason. My issues with the arrangement surrounded the fear of falling for Holden all over again, but Connor disliked the idea of it because that meant he'd have to wait that much longer to get his money. Where I'd resigned to my fate, he brainstormed a plethora of ways to make Holden's life hell in the hopes he'd sign the papers sooner.

If this was what he wanted, this was what he'd get.

First order of attack was to bring everything with me and expect him to accommodate it all.

Which, to my surprise, he did.

Following Connor's orders, I'd sold my full-sized bed and purchased a queen, along with the matching dresser, chest of drawers, and two nightstands, knowing he wouldn't have the space in his office for a complete bedroom set. I'd also included a very worn and extremely outdated loveseat and patio table with only three chairs that I "couldn't bear to part with." As if that wasn't bad enough, I loaded everything up in a moving truck, along with the bags upon bags of clothes that had outfitted a walk-in closet, and had Connor drive it all to Holden's house while I followed behind in my car.

Unfortunately, I had taken a little longer than Connor and arrived the next day. I had to admit I hated to miss the look on Holden's face when Connor introduced himself, but at least I got a play by play after all was said and done. Apparently, Holden didn't seem too happy, though he didn't do or say anything.

As I arrived at my new — albeit temporary — address, I was practically giddy, eager to see what he'd done with all my belongings. The first thing I noticed after walking through the front door was the absence of my loveseat in the living room. I was about to make a comment about it when he led me through the house on our way to my bedroom, and low and behold, he had the hideous loveseat set up in the formal room. It was off from the main part of the house just outside the second and third bedrooms. Then, he showed me what would be my room for the next six months. Only I discovered he'd moved the smaller set from the guest bedroom into his office and given me the bigger room that would hold the larger furniture.

The smug grin toying with the corners of his mouth gave him away. He'd figured me out, and this was his way of showing me he was one step ahead. That was fine, it just meant I had to up my game. There was no way he'd last longer than a month before signing the papers and begging me to get out.

"Your patio table actually fit inside my gazebo in the back yard perfectly. Although, there wasn't room for the chairs since it has built-in seating, so I stored the three of yours in the garage. And speaking of the garage, would you like to park in there or are you okay with the driveway?"

I hated how accommodating he was being. It made me feel like a bitch. Even though I'd basically gone out of my way to make him regret his decision, I wasn't normally this conniving or vindictive. This just proved how far Holden had pushed me. I didn't like being blackmailed or forced to do things I wasn't interested in, but if he wanted a wife, then I'd give him one.

He more than likely expected someone like Christine, a woman who absolutely adored her man. She took care of my brother better than anyone could, and made sure he knew how much she loved him. But if Holden thought I'd dote on him the way Christine doted on Matt, he had another thing coming. I had no desire to pamper anyone, let alone the one basically holding me against my will.

"The driveway is fine." While I did prefer the garage, I knew if I said that, he'd make it happen, and then once again, he'd be the good guy and I'd be the needy houseguest. I realized within the first five minutes that I had to rapidly change my approach if I wanted to speed this along.

He showed me the second bathroom tucked away between the bedrooms that would be for my use during my

I DO

stay, and then he led me back to the kitchen. He stood on one side of the breakfast bar, and I leaned against the other while he gave me my own set of keys and garage door opener. Then he went over the rules he'd typed up the last time I was here, all printed out with his signature along the bottom like a professional contract outlining the terms of our agreement. Lastly, he went over the little details, such as where he kept everything. Again, very hospitable.

"I stocked the fridge with Pepsi for you, because I know you hate coffee. If there's anything else you like to have on hand that I don't have, either shoot me a text with the list to pick up when I get time, or I can leave you with money for grocery shopping."

No matter how much it pissed me off that he looked like the hero and I was left to be portrayed as the nasty, estranged wife, I couldn't seem to draw my attention away from him. Clearly dressed for work in a pressed, button-down shirt and tie, paired with form-fitting black, pinstriped pants, he looked like sex on legs. Sex on legs that ended in a very expensive pair of shiny black shoes. Sex in a suit. Sex with oh-so-sexy bedhead.

"Janelle…" It was enough to catch my attention and make me aware of the fact I'd zoned out. He leaned over the counter, his face dangerously close to mine, which only made the need to touch him worse. Add in the palpable scent of peppermint wafting off him, and I was a goner. "You'll be okay?"

"Yeah. Yup. I sure will. Perfectly fine. Why? Where ya going?"

He picked at the corner of a piece of paper with his short fingernail and chuckled beneath his breath. With a quick shake of his head, he slapped the countertop and said, "Good. See ya later." And as if someone lit a fire under his ass, he pulled a set of keys from his pocket and made a beeline toward the front door.

"Wait! You never answered me. Where are you going?"

He stilled by the door and peered over his shoulder with the kind of smile any woman would gladly part their legs for. "I did tell you. You weren't listening. I have to get back to the office to catch up on some work. I'll probably be there late since I had to take off yesterday and this morning."

"What's considered late?" Suddenly, the idea of being in his home alone terrified me.

"After dinner. If you're in bed by the time I get home, I'll see you after work tomorrow."

"Hold on." I took a few steps in his direction as if I needed him for protection. "What do you mean you'll see me tomorrow? Will you really get home that late? What time do you think you'll get done with work tomorrow?"

"I've missed an entire day. On top of that, I've had to leave early on a couple occasions because I had to move around all the furniture so all we had to do was move yours in. I have quite a bit to catch up on, and there's a chance I won't get it all done until nine or ten o'clock tonight. I'm trying to finish today so I won't have to stay late any other day and leave you here alone. If everything goes as planned, I should be able to pull a really long day today—which wouldn't have been as long if I didn't have to go in late—and be home tomorrow by six." He paused, probably to make sure I heard him point out the sacrifices he'd made on my behalf. "You have my number if you need anything, and the address to my office is on the piece of paper along with the number to my direct line."

Even if I did have something else to say, it wouldn't have mattered because he didn't offer me the chance to respond. In fact, he didn't even say goodbye. He opened the door, stepped outside, and then swiftly closed it behind him. Had I

I DO

not heard the deadbolt engage, I would've assumed he didn't even stop in his hasty retreat.

There was something about the silence in his absence that felt cold and unwelcoming. Maybe it was the fact he acted like he couldn't get out of here fast enough, like he couldn't wait to make his escape from me. It made no sense, considering my being here was his choice in the first place. No...not a choice, a demand. One I had no voice in.

Finding my inner strength, I headed back to my bedroom to unpack, and I didn't stop until I had everything put away in its new place. I tried every trick in the book to keep myself from watching the time, but that didn't stop me from noting the fading sunlight through the windows, or the streetlights turning on.

I'd taken a bath and stayed in until the water cooled, yet when I got out, Holden still wasn't home. I poured a glass of wine and sipped it while flipping through the channels in the living room. I figured this way, when he walked through the front door, it wouldn't look as though I had waited up for him. Except when I'd finished the wine—sipping the entire bottle—he still wasn't home. The clock above the cable box read a quarter after eleven, and I couldn't imagine the kind of desk job that would keep someone there that late.

Then I began to wonder if he was still at work or had gone out to avoid coming home, to avoid seeing me. Maybe he was with a woman. Well, it didn't take long to realize I despised that thought. I absolutely hated the images it produced. I wanted nothing more than to call his direct line, eager to catch him in a lie—then again, I knew that would do no good. I didn't have room to be jealous; not to mention, there wasn't anything I could've done about it. He was a grown man, capable of doing whatever he pleased.

I did know one thing for sure, though.

65

If he was out sleeping with someone, I certainly didn't want to be waiting up for him when he got home.

I had no idea what time Holden finally arrived home last night, because it was after I'd gone to bed. And by the time I got up this morning, he'd already left for work. Then I started to wonder if he'd come home at all. I wasn't sure how I felt about the whole situation, but things didn't seem as bad after a good night's sleep. If this was how our lives would be for the next six months, I would have no problem getting through it. Honestly, I had no idea what I had been so upset about last night. The less I had to deal with Holden, the better off things would be.

Initially, I'd planned on being with Holden when I broke the news to my parents that I was back in town, though I had made other living arrangements, but considering I hadn't seen him in the past twenty-four hours and he'd been evasive regarding his schedule, I decided not to wait on him.

"Holden? You're living with Holden York?" My mother's voice rose higher each time she said his name, as if he were some Hollywood billionaire and the news of us living together temporarily was so farfetched she had a hard time believing it. "How did that come about?"

Luckily, I'd anticipated these questions and had come up with a very plausible story. "We were talking one day, catching up and whatnot, and I just happened to mention my plans to move back home now that I've graduated. I told him I wasn't thrilled about the idea of moving back in with you and Dad—no offense, Mom, but no twenty-three-year-old college graduate wants to move back in with her parents. I said something about possibly asking Christine and Matt if I could rent a room until I was on my feet with a job and had enough money for my own place, and that's when Holden

I DO🖊

said he had extra space. It made more sense than living with my brother and his wife. At least with Holden, there's only two of us there, not three."

"I've always wished you two would date. He's such a good guy. So handsome and polite, and he seems like the genuine type who'd treat a girl the way she deserves to be treated. I've never seen him with anyone before, but I can just tell. In fact, back when the boys were in high school, I wondered a few times if maybe they were a little more than friends."

"Mom!" It didn't matter what her suspicions were or why she had them, I didn't want to hear about it. "You have the worst habit of seeing a palm tree in the middle of a glacier."

"Oh, Jelly. That doesn't even make sense."

I blinked dramatically, wondering to myself for the umpteenth time what the chances were that I'd been adopted or found in a basket on their front porch. "It makes tons of sense. You see things that aren't there, yet you run with it. Matt and Holden—especially Holden—entertained quite a few members of the female population. Here. In your house. While you were asleep."

"What?" She covered her chest with her hand and gaped at me with unadulterated shock painting her features. "How do you know this?"

"I was thirteen, not three. How did you *not* know about it? You knew they went out back because you constantly had to get on them for not locking the door when they came inside."

"Yeah...I thought they were trying to find some privacy. Had I known they were entertaining girls, I never would've allowed that to happen."

I held up my hand to keep her from interjecting before I could finish. "So when you assumed they were...together for all intents and purposes, you had no qualms about them sneaking off to do whatever in the back yard after dark. Yet if you would've known they were sneaking off to get freaky with the opposite sex, you would've put an end to it?"

"When you say it like that, you make it sound wrong. Although, at the time, I assumed he might've been having a hard time coming out of the closet, and I didn't want to make it harder for him. So I figured I was giving them space to be who they were really meant to be."

"You did acid in the sixties, didn't you? That's the only explanation. Lots and lots of acid."

Mom waved me off and shook her head. "You're getting off track, Jelly. Let's get back to you living with Holden. I wasn't aware you two still spoke to each other. I know you guys used to be close before you left for college, although I guess I assumed that stopped after you moved away."

Holden had made me swear on the unknown name of my potential firstborn child that I wouldn't pry into whatever my family had kept from me. I figured it was because he'd made the whole thing up. Regardless, I kept my promise—as odd of a promise as that was.

"Well, I mean, yeah…we didn't exactly stay in touch or remain as close as we once were, but that kind of thing happens all the time. He's four years older than I am, so our lives were in completely different places—he'd just graduated from college, and I was getting ready to attend one. He was getting settled in, ready to start his career, bought a house. What was I doing? Packing up my childhood belongings and moving away…not to start a career or buy a house, but to go to school. So I guess we just didn't really have anything to talk about or have enough in common." I knew I had to stop talking before my emotions bubbled to the surface. Apparently, discussing that time in my life, especially regarding Holden, was too difficult and left my voice quivering and the backs of my eyes burning with unshed tears.

"Well, I'm just happy you two have found common ground again. You should really spend a lot of time with him while you're there. He used to look at you like you could spin straw into gold."

"Ma…that's Rumpelstiltskin. No one looks at *any*one like they're Rumpelstiltskin, especially if they like them—that's just worrisome. It's even more concerning that you would connect that with something romantic," I added beneath my breath.

"You know what I mean."

"If you mean he looked at me like I hung the moon, then yeah, I do know what you mean, although I disagree. I don't ever recall him looking at me that way."

"Jelly, it's a physical impossibility to hang the moon."

"Yet, it's somehow totally plausible to spin straw into gold? As entertaining as this visit has been, I think it's about time I head out. But plan on an extra setting for dinner on Sunday. I've heard all about your weekly meals and how everyone attends."

"Oh, absolutely! I'm so happy to have my baby back. Now I will finally have all my children around the same table again." Her eyes glistened with happy tears seconds before she wrapped me up in one of her emotional hugs. To be honest, I'd missed this—the raw form of unconditional love. When it came to my mom, there was no way to misinterpret it. She wore her heart on her sleeve with pride, and there wasn't a single person who didn't know beyond the shadow of a doubt how much she loved her kids. All of us, including the late additions and strays.

"I love you, Mom."

"I love you, too, baby."

Holden stood in the kitchen with the refrigerator door open, his head stuck inside. "Did you not make anything to eat for dinner?" he called out without even bothering to turn his head to the side.

Luckily for him, I was in the hallway behind him. "No. I ate leftovers from lunch. I wasn't sure what time you were going to get home." Granted, even if I had known what time he'd be home, I still wouldn't have made dinner.

I finished putting in my gold hoop earrings just as he straightened and found me next to him. "What are you all dressed up for?"

"I ran into some friends from high school, and they invited me out tonight. It sounded like fun so I figured…why not?"

Something flashed in his eyes and it immediately set loose a flurry of uneasiness in my stomach. "Great, give me a few minutes to change my clothes and we can go."

My stomach flipped with excitement—and that's when I knew I'd never survive it if he came along with me. I had to remain strong. Even though it seemed innocent enough, I knew it never would be. Spending time with Holden would only give him another chance to break my heart, and I couldn't afford that. I'd loved him once before, and he never returned the sentiment. Doing it a second time would be foolish.

"Uh, Holden…I don't mean to sound like a bitch, but they invited *me*. Not us. Not to mention, we're not a couple. This definitely wasn't part of the agreement." It'd been three days since I'd officially moved in. I didn't see him the entire first day, saw him briefly after he came home from work on the second day, and assumed today would've been the same routine. Although Holden wouldn't be Holden if he didn't throw a monkey wrench into my plans.

For a split second, he looked almost pissed off, but it disappeared just as fast as it came on. "You may have told your family and friends that we're just roommates and I'm this good guy who's helping you get on your feet after college, except that's not the deal we made. You're my wife."

"Yeah, yeah...I remember that part. You don't have to remind me all the time. But there's nothing on our printed agreement that mentions tagging along with me and my friends. And stop calling me your wife—it's a technicality."

"It's a *legality*. Regardless of that, what makes you think I'd be okay sitting at home by myself on a Friday night while you go out with a group of people? How does that make any sense?"

Rather than argue, I kicked off my shoes and carried them back to my room, Holden following close behind. He stood in the hall, gripping the frame and leaning his chest forward as if the doorway was responsible for holding him back.

"I don't want a roommate, Janelle."

"Well, I don't want a husband, *Holden*." I spat his name like it tasted foul and bitter. "You never said I couldn't go out with friends. It's not a date, if that's what you're worried about."

His posture melted before my eyes, and instead of the lion stalking his prey, the man before me resembled more of a beaten-down housecat. His eyes, dark and almost all slate-grey with hardly any noticeable green to them, lost the spark of fight they held a moment ago. And his normally adorable chiseled cheeks just looked pathetic. "I don't know what I was thinking when I brought this up. I guess I hoped we could rebuild our friendship, but it seems you put more effort into marrying a total stranger for money than you do dealing with the husband you've already got."

He almost had me. Had he not completed his thought, I might've been putty in his hands. However, he just had to throw the fact he was my husband in my face like I had anything to do with it—well, more so than the obvious. "You're such a jackass. You know that? I've already told you I have no interest in this marriage. Rebuilding a relationship with you? Sure. You got it. You want us to be friends again like we used to be? Then maybe you should start treating me like you used to—you know, like a friend, not a prisoner, not someone you're forcing to be your wife. This is going to be one *long* half a year if this is how you plan on treating me."

"No one's making you a prisoner. You can go out. I just want to go, too."

"With you as my babysitter? No thank you. I'd rather stay in."

A shadow deepened at the corners of his smile, just enough to bring attention to the humor he found in this situation. "Then that means you're the prison guard. Not me. But now that we're staying in, let me get changed out of these clothes, and I'll meet you on the couch."

"For what?" I stared at him unblinkingly.

"To watch TV. Your pick. Movie, binge on a show, or just flip through the channels like you used to do. I don't care. I've got some cold drinks in the fridge, and I can order pizza or whatever you like." No longer did he show any signs of the controlling "husband" or the downtrodden friend. He seemed almost giddy at the prospect of sitting on the couch all night watching whatever and stuffing our faces with shit. We'd only ever done that a few times in the past, all of which were during the weeks following my breakup with Justin.

The entire situation confused me. It was so difficult to understand how sincere he really was, and when he looked at

I DO

me like he just did, it made it harder to remember that I didn't want to be here. Not in his house, not as his wife, and sometimes, not even as his friend. I had to close my eyes and remember the way it felt to sit on a plane, next to an empty seat, and fly home alone...*after* having sex. I had to remind myself how degraded he made me feel that entire summer, when he treated me like some random hookup he tried to avoid.

I remained still while he walked away from the bedroom, and then I waited to hear the familiar sound of his bedroom door closing across the house. Feeling smug, I carried my shoes to the front door, slipped them on, and then quietly snuck out. If he wanted to watch TV and gorge on pizza, then he'd have to do it by himself.

Holden was about to learn that I wasn't interested in his games.

FIVE

(Holden)

I hated playing these games, but Janelle didn't leave me much of a choice. I knew her motive was to get under my skin so I'd kick her out sooner. Little did she know, I could tolerate a lot. More than she could fathom. And no matter how I felt about her, or what feelings I'd had for her long ago, I didn't ask her to stay here for me. This had nothing to do with me and everything to do with the family she'd turned her back on. The same people who had taken me in when I was a kid and held onto me. I'd do almost anything for them, and I knew how much it would mean to every single member of the Brewer family if they had her back.

Killing her with kindness didn't work.

So now I had to try something else.

When she finally came out of her bedroom the next morning, I was at the kitchen table, finishing up my breakfast and cup of coffee. She hesitated as she entered the room, her eye contact intermittent and full of doubt. I knew right away she either felt bad for her actions, or she was still half asleep. Either way, she lacked the haughty attitude I expected her to have. Rather than rub last night in my face, she awkwardly hung around, almost waiting for me to make the first move.

"Morning. I didn't hear you come in last night." Such a lie, but I wasn't about to let her know I'd laid in bed and

74

stared at the ceiling fan spinning 'round and 'round until I knew she was safely inside. "Did you have fun? I hope you didn't drink and drive."

"I had a blast. Hadn't seen them in a while, so it was nice to catch up. And no. I didn't have much to drink. I was good to drive home. What did you end up doing?" She grabbed a can of soda from the fridge and leaned against the counter, making it impossible to notice anything other than her long legs peeking out from beneath her cotton sleep shorts. So creamy and soft…and long.

It seemed this woman could torture me without even realizing it.

Doing my best to ignore her and all her first-thing-in-the-morning glory, I carried my empty fruit bowl to the sink. But as it turned out, washing a dish didn't stop me from thinking of the way her hard nipples showed through her thin T-shirt. Before I could chance speaking, I had to clear my throat; otherwise, I would've sounded like I was twelve all over again. "I watched a movie and made a few calls."

"Let me guess…work calls?"

I dried my hands and turned to face her, reminding myself to keep my eyes above her neck. Except, doing that only made me take notice of her hair, which she wore in some sexy, sloppy bun on top of her head with pieces falling out to frame her clean, fresh face. Damn…she really did just get out of bed. And that thought only made me think of what she looked like when she slept—which I had firsthand knowledge of.

"Actually, no. It wasn't work related, unless you count talking to your brother as work related." Considering I'd spent so much time at the office since she arrived, she more than likely assumed that was all I did. And to be fair, I did spend a lot of time there, but I wouldn't have considered myself a workaholic. What she didn't seem to understand was that between Matt and me, we'd both taken quite a bit of time off lately, and in order to keep our accounting firm from falling apart, we now had to pick up the slack. Which was why I ended up staying at the office until almost midnight her first day in town, and then well past dinner the next night. But this was the weekend, and unless something urgent came up, neither of us would go into the office.

"Oh, yeah? And what did Matthew want?" It was almost as if she called my bluff.

"We're taking the boat out on the lake today. Weather is supposed to be amazing, so we're going to pack up a cooler with some beer and sandwiches and spend the day on the water. It's going to be great." I gave her the smile I knew she couldn't resist—because she'd told me so many years ago while she was drunk, and I chose to believe that was the truth.

"Oh!" She perked right up, excitement lilting her tone. Her intoxicating blue eyes brightened and widened, adding to the broad, infectious grin on her perfect lips. As it turned out, I wasn't the only one with an irresistible smile. "That sounds like so much fun. Is Christine going, too?"

"Yeah. And I think Rachel and Steve might, as well, but only if your parents can watch Kennedy," I said, adding in that her youngest sister would be joining us. "Your other sisters already have plans, so they won't be able to go. But they'll be at dinner tomorrow, so it's not that big of a deal."

"When will everyone be ready?"

I knew I had her right where I wanted her. "Soon. I still have to stop by the store and grab some drinks and ice. Matt and Christine said they should be down at the dock in about an hour."

"Okay, then I'll make it fast. I already shaved my legs, so I won't need to do that." She just had to go and point out how her legs were soft and smooth, making me yearn to touch them just to see if she was right. And once again, I had her legs on my brain—so creamy and soft…and long.

She made it halfway down the hall before I managed to snap out of it and say, "Wait. You're not going. I have a package being delivered today, so I need you to stay here to sign for it."

She turned on her heel and met my stare with confusion. "I thought you said *we* are going out on the boat?"

"Oh, I'm sorry. I didn't mean you and me. I meant me and Matt, as well as a few other people."

"Yeah…my family."

This was where I had to hone in on my acting skills. I could match her defiance with more defiance. I could meet her moves with alternative ones, and silently call her bluff with bold actions. The one thing I couldn't handle was seeing her hurt or upset. It was never something I could deal with very well. Which was probably why she always got what she wanted from me. But if I had any desire to get through this, I had to remain strong and ignore the way she yanked on my heartstrings.

"Who also happen to be like family to me, too."

"But they're not. They're *not* your family, Holden. They're mine." She jabbed her finger at her chest and took a step toward me. "And you're the one who said I need to get closer with them. Isn't that why you made me move in here? To reconnect with *my* family? How do you expect me to do that when you won't include me in things they're involved in?"

I steeled my expression and took a deep breath. "Jelly," I said with a sneer, knowing it'd get under her skin. It's not like I sought to piss her off, but I needed something to replace the feelings of remorse I had toward her, and I couldn't turn back now. Not after the shit she pulled last night. "The Brewer family is rather large. Aside from your parents, you have your oldest sister, Nikki. She and her husband have three kids, all girls, who I'm sure would *love* to have some quality time with their cool, young aunt. Then there's Stacey and Tony with their two kids. Even if Rachel and Steve decide to go out on the boat today, you still have plenty of other family members to bond with. You don't have to be with me to do that."

"If I have to stay here to sign for a package, then how do you expect me to see anyone?"

I shrugged as if I hadn't already thought this out. Unfortunately for her, she left me with *lots* of thinking time last night to contemplate all kinds of scenarios to run with. "Who knows…maybe UPS will get here early enough for you to spend the rest of the day with one of your sisters or your mom. Or you can always call them. There's this neat invention called a phone, and it comes in handy when you want to talk to someone without being with them."

"I know what a phone is, jackass."

"You sure? Because no one around here heard much from you while you were away, so I just figured you didn't know you could call and keep in touch." With my hands on my hips, I hung my head and shook it in mock shame. "I really wish you hadn't told me the truth. Because now…" I glanced up at her and caught her smoldering attention. "Now I can't help but think you didn't reach out to any of us because you didn't want to. And the only reasons I can come up with are hurtful."

She closed her eyes and huffed, clearly irritated with my taunting. "Either that or I was busy with classes. You stayed here for college, which made it easier to stay connected to everyone. I was hours away. Don't judge. And don't act like you know what was going on—with me *or* my family."

"Whatever, Janelle." I had so much I could've come back at her with, but I didn't want to argue. I wanted her to accept

I DO

that I had the upper hand so she'd stop fighting and give in. But she seemed determined to block my every move, making it that much harder to stay on top. One thing was for sure, though—I had to stop letting her get to me. "If you want to spend time with your family, do it. This is your house now too, Janelle, so if you want to invite them over, by all means, invite them over. You don't need my permission to have one of your sisters come here." I pinned her with a stare, hoping she noticed my genuine disappointment, and then turned to walk away, leaving her with my words to chew on.

"Is this your way of getting back at me for last night?" Her question stalled my retreat and made me glance at her over my shoulder. From the quiver in her voice, I expected to catch her bottom lip trembling, but it wasn't. Instead, an angered woman stood behind me with her arms crossed over her chest and a fire in her eyes I hadn't seen in years.

I turned all the way around to face her, to look her square in the eyes and make sure she heard every word I had to say. "Get back at you for what, Janelle? There's nothing to get back at you for. You went out with your friends. Big deal," I added with a nonchalant shrug. "If you purposely snuck out to teach me a lesson...I hate to say it, but I didn't learn anything. Whatever it was you were trying to show me, I didn't see it."

"It didn't make you mad?" And there was her first card, reflected in the shades she thought cleverly shielded the truth in her eyes, but little did she know, it gave far more away than she anticipated.

"Why would it make me mad?"

"Because you said you wanted to go with me, and when I said no, you planned on us staying in."

"To be honest, I expected you to leave." And I did. Once I realized she had left while I was in my room changing out of my work clothes, I wasn't all that surprised. Let down, sure, but not surprised. "I guess I had hoped you wouldn't, but you did exactly as I anticipated...so again, why would I be mad?"

"Okay, fine. Maybe mad isn't the right word. Disappointed? Upset? Hurt?"

I licked my lips, and then celebrated in the way her eyes fell to my mouth and followed my tongue. The sight of her breath hitching pumped me full of adrenaline. But I refused to let that deter me from my plight. "Had I not already accepted the fact that you aren't the same person I once knew, then yeah. I probably would've been disappointed and upset. But you see, you're not the same. At all. Not even close to being the same Janelle who used to spend her afternoons with me on my couch in front of the TV. You don't at all resemble the girl who used to give me a run for my money in pop culture trivia. You're the person I expected to sneak out while I was in my room last night."

Her chest heaved with labored breathing and her gaze bounced around from one thing to the next. It was obvious her thoughts wouldn't slow down, and the longer she stood in silence, the more emotional she became. If I didn't walk away soon, there was a good chance I would cave and offer her comfort against the harsh sting of my words.

And I couldn't afford to do that.

Janelle would get her divorce just as she'd asked for. I had no problems granting her that. It wasn't like I wanted her to stay and fall in love with me because I'd spent the last five years plotting out our future or pining for her. I wanted her here for one reason and one reason only, and that was to be a part of her family the way they all needed her to be. But that would never happen if she spent all her time and energy battling me. My hope was that she'd exhaust her efforts soon and begin to focus on the real matter at hand. And that would never happen if I gave in first. She had to be the one to fold. I only had to keep upping the ante long enough to make her do so.

"If you're not doing this to get back at me…why are you making me stay here on a Saturday while you go out on the boat with my brother and sister?"

"I already told you. A package is being delivered today, and I need someone here to sign for it. As for me going on the boat with *your* siblings…I guess I don't see it that way. I'm going out to spend the day on the lake with my best friend, his wife, and possibly his sister and brother-in-law."

"If it's your package, don't you think you should be the one to stay home and wait for it?"

"Not really. I assumed you'd be hung over after going out last night. I didn't expect you to be awake before I left. Not to mention, you don't really have any friends around here since you've been away for so long."

"What if I leave? Huh? What will you do if I'm not here to sign for it?"

I shrugged and turned around to walk away, speaking over my shoulder when I said, "Do whatever you want, Janelle. We both know you're going to anyway."

"What's that supposed to mean?"

I stopped at my bedroom door and looked right at her, standing exactly where she'd been when I walked away. "If you don't want to stay here, then by all means, leave. Go hang out with whoever you were with last night, or go run into more people you used to know. I. Don't. Care. If you're not here when the delivery truck comes, they'll just come back another time. The world won't end. You won't stick it to me, it won't piss me off, and it won't keep me up at night. I'll still be out on the boat with my friends, having a good time. But there's one thing I *won't* be doing, and that's thinking about what *you're* doing."

Without waiting for her to respond, I walked into my room and closed the door behind me. Aside from my shoes, I was already dressed and ready to go, but I knew I needed to hang back for a few extra minutes. So I sat on the edge of my bed and ran my hands through my hair, wasting time before I could leave my own house.

I hated these games—usually avoided *all* games—and wished I didn't have to participate in this. Granted, I didn't *have* to. I could've given up and put an end to it all. I could've given Janelle what she wanted, signed the papers, and let her go off and marry that moron for money. But no matter how easy that would've been, something stopped me. Probably my need to fix things. And by this point, I needed to see it through. I refused to lose this, and the only way I'd be able to accept a loss, was if we'd made it all the way to the end of our arrangement and she still refused to reconnect with her family.

At that point, it wouldn't be my loss.

It'd be hers.

And there was nothing I could've done about it then.

It was eight by the time I made it back home. The sun was about to set, the streetlights about to come on, but there was still enough light to see the woman standing on my front porch. Without wasting a second, I parked the car and jumped out, hurrying around the corner to greet my guest. I only prayed she'd just gotten there, and Janelle hadn't already had a chance to answer the door.

I swept my gaze along the road in front of us, noticing her car in front of my neighbor's house, and I shook my head, unable to figure out why she always parked there. "What are you doing here?" I asked, almost out of breath—not from the

I DO

light jog from my driveway to the front door, but because of the adrenaline coursing through me.

"I had to get out of the house and didn't have anywhere else to go." She ran her perfectly manicured fingers through her stick-straight, black hair, pulling the silky strands away from her face. Then her ruby-red lips tipped into a smile and her onyx eyes glistened with mischief. "Whose car is that?"

It wasn't that I wanted to lie to her, but I had to be careful with how I explained it, while also being mindful that I didn't speak too loudly in the event Janelle stood on the other side of the door, listening. I took my guest by the arm and walked her to the driveway where we stood in front of the garage. "Matt's little sister."

Her smile grew wider and the glint in her eyes brightened. "Does Matt know?"

I nodded without offering more.

She'd get the information she was looking for without me having to offer it all up at once. And she didn't disappoint when she asked, "Visiting?"

"No. She's living with me for six months."

Her eyes widened in surprise, and her mouth rounded into a bright red *O*. "This is going to be fun. And exactly what I need to take my mind off the shit going on at home. Tell me, Holden. Tell me everything. And don't even think about leaving out a single detail." She poked me in the chest with her pointy nail that sparkled like aluminum foil. "Are you two together?"

I rolled my eyes and heaved out a long and controlled exhale. "Nope. But she knows about the chapel in Vegas. She came here like a week ago and asked me to sign her divorce papers, and I told her the only way I'd do that is if she moved back here and into my house for a while."

The giddy surprise in her expression quickly turned to complete amazement. "And she fell for that? She didn't know she can still get the divorce without you agreeing?"

Worried that Janelle could overhear, I shushed her and lowered my voice. "I told her I'd drag it out, and she didn't question me. Shut up, okay? I'm doing what I have to do for her family. They need her, and if this is the only way to get her here, then so be it."

"I'm pretty sure if you just tell her what's going on, she'll stay. I can't imagine anyone from that family being so coldhearted they'd find all that out and still turn their backs on their loved ones. Are you sure there isn't some ulterior motive behind your actions?"

I knew where she was going with this, but I refused to give in. She may have known more about me than anyone else, including Matt, but that didn't give her the right to jump to conclusions. "No. I've told you a million times, but I'll say it again…I'm over her. I knew it that first Christmas when she came back and made no effort to see or talk to me. And then it was further substantiated that next summer when she refused to come home. I knew then that I meant nothing to her, and that's when I moved on."

"Sure thing, Holden. Keep telling yourself that," she practically sang in her sickly sweet, singsong voice. "So tell me…how's it going having her under the same roof? Made any babies yet?"

"It makes total sense why you were kicked out of your house. What'd you do this time?"

"Bought a pair of shoes." She thrust out her foot to show off some fancy-looking pair of heels that she for whatever reason paired with jeans. "Apparently, it wasn't in the budget, and this wasn't the first time I'd spent money on myself without discussing it first."

"How long do you have to be gone?"

I DO

She shrugged. "Longer than normal. Do you mind?"

With an exaggerated huff, I said, "Fine. Come on. But you aren't allowed to say anything to Janelle. Do you understand? *Nothing.*"

"Don't you think that'd be awkward if she tries to talk to me and I just ignore her? I may look like a bitch, Holden, but I'm not one."

"I beg to differ. I've heard you answer the office phone before. Anyway...*obviously* you can talk to her, but don't throw me under the bus. Got it? I sign your paychecks, and if you want to afford those heels and have a reason to sleep in your own bed anytime soon, I highly suggest you play nice."

Her feigned shock made me laugh, which died on my lips as soon as we stepped inside. Janelle stood in the middle of the living room, as though she'd just gotten off the couch, and it made me wonder if she had tried to peek out the window to watch me.

"Janelle, this is Veronica. Veronica, this is Matt's little sister, Janelle." I didn't miss the way Janelle flinched when I introduced her, probably a reaction to my calling her someone's little sister. However, before I could get any other words out to explain who Veronica was, Janelle's claws came out.

"UPS never came. I called them, thinking they might've delivered it to the wrong address, but they informed me there was no package to be delivered today. They didn't have your address on the route—or your name. Please, Holden...for the love of all things holy, tell me you didn't make me stay home alone today to teach me a lesson. Tell me there was some mix up with your order."

Hurt burned in her stare and lit the anger coiling in her posture. This was when I had planned to admit that there was never a delivery. But as I glanced around the room and noticed how clean it was, smelled the presence of cleaning products in the air, I knew I couldn't do that to her.

"Oh, yeah. I'm really sorry about that. Turns out I had the wrong dates. I totally got my days mixed up. It'll be here later this week. I'm really sor—" My apology died on my tongue when my sight swung around the room and landed on the flat screen mounted on the wall. "What happened to the TV stand I had?"

"I put it in the other room. I figured now that you have furniture in there, it'd be nice to sit and watch a movie when you're in here using this one."

"What TV did you put in there?" I asked while peering around the corner to the hall, as if I could see through walls and answer my own question.

"The one I brought with me. You don't have cable jacks back in those rooms so there was no use in having it in there with me. Plus, you made it very clear that this is your house and you don't want me making any permanent changes."

"I don't have a cable jack in the formal room, either."

"No, but I hooked up my DVD player so we can watch movies, and when it's connected to Wi-Fi, we can get Netflix."

Fiery anger bubbled up in my chest, and I had to steady my breathing before I lost my control. "Then why couldn't you just keep it in your room and use it the same way?"

"Because then you wouldn't be able to use it, silly." She smacked my arm and shook her head in humor. But she didn't fool me. I knew this was an act. And it took everything in me to not call her out on it in front of Veronica.

Ignoring the issue regarding permanent changes and the holes in my wall where the flat screen now hung, I moved on to a more important question. "How did you mount that? Did you leave the house to get the brackets from the store?"

I DO

"No. I called Connor." Just the sound of his name made me want to crawl out of my skin. "I told him what kind it was and he picked up the recommended hardware."

"So he was here? While I was gone?"

"Well, yeah. I mean, I couldn't hang that thing on my own. It's like fifty inches."

I wanted to yell. I wanted to fight. I no longer cared about hurting her, because I couldn't remember a time I had felt more pain than I did right now. She'd invited *him* into my home while I was gone. I couldn't even say his name—not even to myself. The thought of them being together, alone, right here, made me sick. It made me seethe. It made me feel like I had lost my mind.

"You told me this morning that this is my house now, too. And I could invite people over without asking you first. I didn't think you'd mind. You don't mind…do you, Holden?"

Veronica must've sensed how close to the edge of sanity I was, because she didn't give me a chance to respond. She put her hand in mine and said, "Come on, baby. Let's get you showered. You still smell like sunscreen." Then, she turned her nausea-inducing, sweet voice to Janelle. "It was really nice to meet you. I've heard so much about you, and it's about time I finally get to put a face with the name."

It wasn't until we made it into my room with the door closed behind us that I managed to snap out of the rage-filled trance. It was like the last sixty seconds had been on pause until I walked away from Janelle, and now, standing in my room with Veronica, my brain hit play and I realized what she had done.

"I could fucking kiss you right now, Ronnie."

Her lips curled in disgust and she took a step back. "Please don't. That's repulsive."

"Whatever. We both know you used to dig dicks."

She waved me off over her shoulder and sashayed into my bathroom, where she started the shower for me. Her heels clicked on the tile on the way back out. But before she said anything else, she grabbed the remote off the nightstand and turned on the television, cranking the volume up loud enough to keep Janelle from overhearing.

"Just to be clear, I've never found any interest in a dick."

I stumbled on my words for a moment, trying to figure out the right way to ask my question without sounding like a complete moron. "Never? Like…not even when you were younger before you knew you liked vagina?"

She snickered while moving through my room, obviously comfortable in my space with as many times as she'd been here. "Holden…how do I put this? Let's see…I've always known I liked vagina. Well, wait. I always knew I liked girls. The sexual side of that came later with hormones."

"But you're so…feminine." I stepped back to appreciate her womanly figure dressed in tight jeans, her tank top hugging her curves, and her ample breasts practically spilling out of the deep V neckline. Her long, dark hair made her olive tone seem lighter, almost creamier. Without her admitting she liked women, or seeing her with her other half, no one would've ever been able to guess her sexuality.

"Thank you." She kicked off her heels and began to unbutton her jeans. "But that has no bearing on what gender I prefer in bed. Whether I wear a good pair of Jimmy Choo heels or Nike sneakers doesn't determine which genitalia I want in my face."

I sat on the edge of the bed and watched her step out of her jeans and then pull off her tank top. She stood before me in a bra and lace thong, and oddly enough, neither of us seemed to care. "So what's the plan. You just gonna hang out naked in my room to make her jealous?"

I DO

She grinned and pulled one of my T-shirts over her head. "I need a place to crash tonight. I originally hoped I could borrow your couch, but this seems like a way better idea. Trish needs time to cool off and realize I didn't bankrupt us, and you need to teach little miss thing in there a lesson. So...right now, go take a shower, and make sure to slap the wall a few times for good measure."

I raised a brow and contemplated her suggestion. "I like it. Make her think we're getting dirty in the shower."

She shoved me and rolled her eyes. "Hurry up. When you're done, I'm going to need you to bring me food." And with that, she reclined on my bed and settled into the pillows to watch whatever show was on the screen.

About an hour later, I left my room to get us something to eat. To my surprise, I found Janelle in the kitchen with a can of soda in her hand, as if she'd just pulled it from the fridge. I wasn't sure where I expected her to be, or why I found it so uncomfortable to be in the same room with her, but I couldn't shake the feeling that she was upset.

"Everything okay?" I asked while preparing to make a couple sandwiches.

"I thought we agreed to not bring anyone here."

I couldn't ignore the raw pain in her voice. It ran through me before settling in the center of my chest. When I turned to face her, I wished I hadn't, because I was sure I'd never forget the betrayal in her eyes. "We did, but that was before you brought your boytoy here."

"My what?" Her eyes narrowed and her top lip curled as if she just tasted something sour. "First of all, he's not anything to me. Just because some show deemed us made for each other doesn't mean I have any interest in dating him. The *only* reason I agreed to marry him was for the money. Nothing else."

I faltered, unsure of how to proceed. Part of me didn't want to believe her, because that would mean I'd perceivably broken our trust first, and the reason she appeared so broken was because of me. And those were two things I couldn't accept.

"I'm sorry," I whispered before turning my back on her.

Nothing else was said. The soft sounds of her feet padding down the hall were all I heard before the click of her bedroom door. Somberly, I finished making our sandwiches and went back to Veronica, where I confessed to feeling like a complete prick. Luckily, she knew most of the situation, and I filled her in on the rest, so she was able to give me solid advice. She did, however, pout about not being able to jump on the bed and practice her best fake orgasm noises. But I made it up to her by bringing her a glass of wine and talking to Trish on her behalf, getting her to agree to let Veronica back home in the morning.

SIX

(Janelle)

Warm light drifted through the slats in my blinds and woke me up. Like the last few mornings, it took me a second to figure out where I was, confused by the unfamiliar room. However, unlike the previous mornings, I didn't find myself consumed by determination. Instead, a deep sense of sadness filled me. A move originally meant to show Holden that I wasn't a pushover and couldn't be easily controlled ended up blowing up in my face. By telling him Connor had been there, I'd hoped it would've pushed his buttons, but not once did I think he'd get back at me by having a woman in his bed while I slept under the same roof.

I groaned and rolled off my mattress, realizing how pathetic I sounded—even to myself. I shouldn't care who he had in his room or what they did behind closed doors. It had nothing to do with me. But that didn't stop the pang of jealousy from forming within my chest. Veronica was gorgeous. Everything any sane woman wishes to be. I was sure I could've looked at her under a microscope and still not found a single flaw. Even her voice was the perfect pitch of sexy. Which made it so much worse. The least I could've hoped for was that she sounded nasally or whiny; that way, her sex noises would've offset everything else. But I was sure—even without hearing them—that her moans were symphonic.

While standing in front of the mirror hanging over my dresser, an idea smacked into me and left me winded, like the thought literally knocked the air out of my lungs. I remembered he had checked me out yesterday morning in the kitchen. I had no idea if Miss Perfection was still here or not, but I didn't really care. Legally speaking, she was in bed with *my* husband. So really, she had no right to say anything…and if she had a problem with it, maybe it would push Holden to give in and sign the papers.

Not wasting a second, I shimmied out of my cotton shorts and exchanged my everyday panties for the cheeky pair no guy could resist. No matter what brand, this style made every shape of ass look good. And instead of the loose T-shirt, I settled on a cami—the kind *without* the built-in shelf-bra. I made sure my hair was brushed, but I still piled it on top of my head, giving it that "I don't care" look. After one final glance in the mirror, I approved and set out to win this war.

I stepped out of my room and took the hallway like the New York Fashion Show runway. Ignoring the chill on the insides of my thighs normally covered by clothes, I put one foot in front of the other. And I didn't stop until I made it into the living room, where Holden sat on the loveseat, his cell phone in one hand and a mug of coffee in the other.

Taking a seat on the couch next to him, I propped one foot on the coffee table and arched my back into the oversized pillows, reclining as though I were under the hot sun on a beach in a bathing suit. He glanced over at me and then turned back to whatever he had on his phone, but in a split second, as if my presence just registered to him, his body turned rigid and he slowly brought his attention back to me. It started with my exposed leg, where I watched him trace it with his eyes. His focus then settled briefly at the apex of my

I DO

thighs before traveling north, taking a break to admire the obvious peaks on my chest due to the cool temperature he kept his thermostat set to. But rather than meet my gaze, he cleared his throat and took a sip of coffee, his attention back on his phone.

Taking matters into my own hands, I asked, "Veronica didn't stay for breakfast?"

"Nah," he answered without glancing up again. "She left about an hour ago."

Well, that wasn't the answer I'd hoped for. I wanted to hear him tell me how he'd kicked her out last night after our meeting in the kitchen. Then again, I wasn't sure *why* I wanted to hear him say that. Nor did I understand the sense of jealousy I couldn't shake. I told myself I wasn't green with envy over them being together.

I didn't want to be her because she had Holden.

No. I wanted to be her because she was perfect.

Holden got up from the couch and took his mug to the kitchen, and I inwardly cursed myself. He had Veronica in his bed last night. I was an idiot to think I could prance out here in panties and a tank top and make him turn his head. Yeah, right. His thirst was more than quenched last night. I had more of a chance to convince a vegetarian to try filet mignon than I did getting Holden's attention after a night with Miss Sex in Heels.

Even so, I watched him move around the kitchen, while taking note of his T-shirt, gym shorts, and sneakers. They looked so good on him. The way the silky material hung on his hips and hit him just below the knees made me pant with desperation. I'd seen my share of hot guys on campus, but nothing compared to Holden first thing in the morning. That's a lie. Nothing compared to him right after a shower.

Holy I've-seen-you-naked, Batman.

Every time I saw him with his hair wet, I couldn't help but call upon the single memory I had of when we were in the shower together, *before* I ruined everything. The one glimpse I'd had of his man meat. I was sure my imagination had embellished it over the years, because there was no way he truly was *that* big. But in my mind, he was. And it was glorious. And as I stared at him in basketball shorts, it was all I could think of.

"Need a napkin?" His voice brought me back to reality, and his smirk let me know he'd caught me checking him out. Thank God he didn't know exactly what I was thinking. "You got some drool there." He pointed to his chin, which brought my attention to the dark spatter of hair along his jaw.

"Very funny." I offered a fake laugh and pulled myself from the couch. I made a beeline for the fridge where my morning caffeine resided. "Where are you headed off to this morning? And are you planning on going to my parents' this afternoon for dinner?"

"I'm going for my jog. Wanna join me?"

I scowled in his direction. "No. Unless someone is chasing me, you won't see me run."

"Whatever. You don't know what you're missing."

"Bouncing boobs, sore thighs, cleavage sweat, swamp ass…I'm well aware of what I'm missing. Back to dinner. Are you going to my parents'?"

"I go every week. I'm not suddenly going to stop now that you're here. I didn't make this arrangement for you to take my place at the family table." For whatever reason, his answer got to me, and I didn't like it. He must've recognized it on my face, because his shoulders relaxed, and he tried again. "Yes, Janelle. I'll be there. Did you want to ride together?"

My heartbeats tripped over each other at his offer. "Sure." I added a shrug for good measure, hoping he hadn't noticed the palpitations he caused. "Save on gas and whatnot. Good for the environment. Eco-friendly and everything. It's a good idea. Ozone layer. Carbon dioxide." I poured cold, carbonated soda down my throat to keep me from spouting out more random words as if they somehow made sense and gave cause for us riding in the same vehicle together.

However, it hadn't stopped him from laughing at me. But at least he tried to be polite and keep it under his breath. Although it didn't matter to the burn in my cheeks over the absolute humiliation that covered me like a blanket. I had no idea what had happened to me over the last twenty-four hours, but I needed it to stop. Apparently, finding out Holden had sex with a goddess stole every last brain cell I had in my head and left me acting like a bumbling idiot.

"You sure you don't want to jog with me? The fresh air might do you some good."

I quirked a brow at him and finished swallowing my drink. "I'm positive."

"Suit yourself," he called out over his shoulder.

I didn't wait until I heard the door close before running back to my room to put clothes on. What seemed like a fantastic idea had turned out to be the worst thing I'd ever come up with. I was confident in my body, knew I didn't have anything to be ashamed of, but I was no Veronica. And had I shared a bed with her last night, I wouldn't have wanted to see me, either. I wanted to hang my head in shame and disappear, but I couldn't. I had to march on. Keep my head up. Eyes on the prize.

After collapsing on the couch, I learned the batteries in the remote had died. So I helped myself to every nook and cranny in his house looking for extras. I gave up when in what seemed to be a very organized junk drawer in the kitchen, I found an old photo of Holden and Matt. They couldn't have been older than twelve since that was the cutoff for trick or treating. Both of them were dressed head to toe in a costume—Matt was Superman, and Holden was Batman.

I had basically no memory of my life before Holden. He'd come into it at such an early age for me that it was easy to believe he'd been there since day one. Not to mention, he'd spent nearly every day at our house from the moment he'd met Matthew until…well, it seemed he still spent time at my parents' house. So there weren't many aspects of my life he wasn't there for. When I closed my eyes and thought about Holden, a lot came to mind. However, in everything I could conjure up about him and our past together, the bad times were never the ones that came to me easily. Those were the moments I had to consciously bring to the surface. They weren't the defining moments of him or how I felt about him—then or now.

The parts of him that had lingered over the years, even when I didn't want them to, was the way he'd hang his arm over my shoulders and tuck me protectively into his side. Or how calming it was to feel the pad of his thumb wipe away an errant tear. Every important male figure in my life had a role: Dad was the gatekeeper, the lawmaker, and overall police. Matthew was my bodyguard. But Holden…he was my Batman.

"In a fight between Batman and Superman, Superman would win every time." This seemed to be a constant debate between Matthew and Holden. And no matter how many times it was discussed, neither person changed their views. My brother defended the flying superhero as if he had a personal interest in him, and Holden argued his case for the dark knight with equal enthusiasm.

"Take away his superpowers and he wouldn't," Holden argued with a smug grin on his boyish face. He'd just started to shave and thought he looked like a man; we all had a good laugh at that one.

"You can't take away his powers, that defeats the whole 'superhero' aspect."

I DO

"Then it's not a fair fight. Superman is only a hero because he's from another planet and has powers. He doesn't bravely fight against crime. He just does what his body allows him to do, what his powers allow him to do. Whereas Batman protects people without a single superhuman strength." I'd heard these points so many times before I could've recited them, but I loved to hear Holden make them. The determination behind his arguments could've made anyone a believer in his opinion. *"He could get hurt, shot, he could die, but that doesn't stop him. He wasn't infected with some mutated venom or born on another planet. He wasn't created in a lab or pumped with chemicals. He's a normal person. And there's not a single superhero worth believing in more than Batman."*

"What about you, Jelly?" Matthew turned to me, probably hoping I would weigh in instead of just sit there, listening to their arguments. *"If you were in trouble and needed to be rescued, who would you want? Which hero would you call for help...Batman or Superman?"*

I looked right at Holden and said, "Batman."

———

The entire way to my parents' house, I couldn't stop thinking about Holden in his little costume with his cape hanging behind him. It made me curious if he still had the same opinions as he did back then. If he still cared as much, or if he looked back on it and thought it was ridiculous and childish.

I stared at his profile while he drove, mumbling about something I wasn't paying attention to, and mentally compared him to the memories I had of him. He was no longer the boy who used to apologize for teasing me. Nor was he the sweet teenager who hated to see me cry. But I knew that boy wasn't lost. He wasn't gone forever. I'd only lived with him for five days so far, but it was enough to see glimpses of him. I saw it yesterday when he came home, after I questioned him about the delivery. Regret narrowed his

97

eyes. And again last night, after his shower when I reminded him of our agreement. He seemed rather high and mighty until I explained my "relationship" with Connor to him. Then guilt weighted his tone and darkened his aura.

I started to think I was wearing him down. I grew closer to getting him where I wanted him. But then I stopped and wondered if things had changed. Rather than play him the way I was, I wondered if things could be different. I couldn't help but think about how the next six months would play out if I stopped fighting him and gave in. Mended our broken friendship and found our way back to one another. And again, it made me question if that was truly what I wanted. The money would still be there at the end of this. He'd given me a free place to stay. I didn't have any real rush, and I found myself more tolerant of the idea of waiting.

When we pulled into my parents' driveway, he shifted the car into park and turned to look at me. "Did you hear anything I said?"

"Nope." I dramatically popped the *P*. "Not a word. So, Cliff, give me your notes. What did I miss?"

He closed his eyes and huffed a chuckle. It was so sexy I nearly missed the condensed version of whatever he said on the ride over. "Just remember, you promised to not bring anything up. Don't pry. If anything comes up in conversation that you're confused about, then by all means, ask about it. But don't throw me under the bus by acting all weird and asking random questions."

"I still think you're making all this up. But don't worry, I won't ask anything unless it's warranted."

"I'm not fabricating anything, Janelle." His wit quickly evaporated, and his irritation became known when he jammed his finger into the ignition button, swiftly shutting off the car, and forcefully throwing his car door open.

I DO

In a panic, I grabbed his forearm and waited until his stormy eyes found mine. "If you're not making it up, then that means it's real. It means it's true. And without anything to go on, my mind resorts to the worst-case scenarios. Meaning...someone in that house is about to die, someone is on dialysis for kidney failure, and there's a good chance three more have some infectious disease they aren't aware of. But in reality, you could just mean someone has lice and someone else has a rash—a *non*-life threatening rash. So I'm not accusing you of making anything up. I'm telling myself you are because if I don't, I'll go crazy wondering what's wrong with who and why no one told me."

His eyes softened and his shoulders relaxed when he pulled in a deep breath. "Come on. Let's go inside," he whispered and climbed from the car.

It only took about thirty seconds to see how much my *entire* family loved Holden. Not that I had any doubts or couldn't remember it from before. But now, I almost felt like an outsider, like I was Holden's dinner guest or something. It was extremely awkward, and I wasn't sure how to handle myself. Since moving in with Holden, I'd seen my mom once, and my dad briefly at the same time. But that was it. I hadn't seen my sisters in a year and a half since I didn't make it home this past Christmas. That was the last time I'd seen Matthew too, but at least I talked to him on the phone from time to time. Now, walking inside behind Holden, watching my sisters greet him with smiles and excitement, made it hurt that much worse when they turned their attention to me and it lacked the same enthusiasm.

What hurt even more was when I headed toward the kitchen for a drink and stopped short of the entryway when I heard Stacey and Rachel talking in low tones, hushed, as if holding a surreptitious conversation. I paused, leaned against the wall, and waited a moment to figure out what they were talking about, hoping to get some kind of insight into these family secrets Holden kept hinting at.

"It's obvious she doesn't want to be here, so I don't know why she is."

"Just give her a chance, Stacey. We're a rather intimidating bunch, and walking back into this can't be easy. I'll admit, it would've been nice if Mom had told us she was coming. Or better yet, it would've been nice to know she was coming with Holden. Or *living* with him. We were a little blindsided, I'll give you that."

I held my breath and blinked, willing my tears to stay put.

"She wants something. That's the only thing that makes sense," Stacey continued.

"You don't know that."

"Why else is she here? I asked Mom if she got a job in town, thinking maybe that was her reason for coming back, and she said as far as she knew, Janelle was still looking for one. Which means she's *not* here for work. What other reason would she have to move back?"

There was a long pause before Rachel, my youngest sister—who was nine years older than me—spoke again. "Are her and Holden together? They used to be close before she left. Maybe they have a thing and she came back to see where it'd go."

Silence stretched out before the sound of a smack filled the room, followed by Stacey gasping, "Ouch." After a few hushed giggles, Stacey finally said, "I highly doubt that. For several reasons. One...if they had something before she left, that would've put her at seventeen or eighteen, and he would've been twenty-one or twenty-two. I doubt at that age, in or fresh out of college, he would've found anything in common with a girl in high school."

I DO

"You never know. I met Steve when I was a senior and he was in college."

"I guess it's not *im*possible, but I just don't see it. She's too immature. He runs a private accounting firm with Matt—who's married and very much an adult. He's got far too much going for him to waste his time with Janelle."

The burning behind my eyes grew more intense, and I wasn't sure I'd be able to stop it.

"Why are you hating on her so much?"

Stacey huffed, and even without seeing her, I knew exactly what she looked like—head thrown back, eyes rolling, and mouth agape. Her typical frustration tantrum. "I don't mean to hate on her. She's my sister, and I obviously love her. But it's irritating how she gets away with everything. It's like we're all held accountable to such impossibly high standards, and she gets to do whatever the hell she wants." The more she talked, the louder her voice became until Rachel quieted her down. "I know you see it, too. You feel it, too. I'm not the only one. We're all here—physically, mentally, *and* emotionally. But where is she?"

"Being young, Stacey. She's in her early twenties. She just finished college."

"That's not an excuse. When we were her age, we had jobs—full-blown *careers*. When Nikki was twenty-three, she was a mom. She had a baby, and a husband, who was still in school. She had a family to take care of. Look at Matty. He was already married to Christine when he was fresh out of college, getting ready to get his CPA license. Making preparations to open his own accounting firm…with *Holden*. So no, her being in her early twenties, just out of college isn't an excuse to be so flighty."

I couldn't take any more. For all I knew, they continued their conversation. Maybe Rachel agreed with her. Maybe she didn't and actually stuck up for me. I would never know, because I refused to stick around and hear the rest. I ran away from the kitchen, down the hall, and didn't stop until I twisted the doorknob to the bathroom and pushed it open.

Only to run face-first into a very hard wall of muscle.

I glanced up, tears streaming down my cheeks and blurring my sight, but they didn't stop me from recognizing Holden as I held onto him, steadying myself after the harsh impact. Without hesitation, he pulled me into the newly remodeled bathroom and set me up on the fancy vanity. Once the door was closed, the latch clicking in place, he situated himself between my legs and held my face in his hands.

Tears came for many different reasons, and people reacted to them in many different ways. For me, if I cried, there was a good chance it was because I'd found myself in that tight space between rage and frustration. The point when the anger implodes and you don't know if you want to punch a brick wall with your bare knuckles or drink your weight in tequila, because you know once you get the anger out, you'll feel better. For me, that's the moment I break down in tears. That's how I got the anger out. When I got sad, I became quiet and withdrawn, so my friends always said if I had tears in my eyes, it was time to run.

Unfortunately for Holden, he never got that memo.

He shushed me softly, his entire demeanor full of immense sympathy. However, that only made things worse. Not only did I despise being hushed, I also couldn't stand pity. It only served to make me angrier, which made me cry harder, all of which Holden had no idea how to handle.

Aside from the typical tears of a child, the only time he'd ever seen me lose it like this was after my breakup with Justin. Even then, there was enough separation between the physical breakup and finding myself crying on his couch. He never witnessed the blinding rage that poured out of me in the form of saltwater coating my cheeks.

"What's wrong? What happened?" The level of concern in his tone was noted, but it wasn't enough to calm the storm. It wasn't until the pads of his thumbs traced over my cheek bones, wiping away my liquefied frustration, that I finally stilled. With my hands fisted in his shirt, our gazes locked together, I was reminded of him being my hero. And rather than fight him like I had been since coming back, I gave in and let him rescue me. "Babe...what happened? Talk to me."

Ignoring the term of endearment, because I didn't have anywhere near the right amount of headspace to analyze that blunder, I sniffled and tucked my chin, prepared to explain to him what I'd heard before running into him. "I overheard Stacey and Rachel in the kitchen. Stacey doesn't want me here."

"That's not true. I'm sure she wants you here very much. I know she's missed you a lot over the years."

"You're a horrible liar." I tried to laugh, but it just sounded pathetic and made me cringe. "She said I get away with everything, and I'm too immature. Oh, and you'd never be interested in me because you're far too good for someone flighty like me."

"I'm sure she didn't say that. And if she did, she's probably taking her stress out on you. It's not right, and she shouldn't have said any of that, but if they were talking in the kitchen, behind your back, you were never really meant to hear it."

I peered up at him and blinked slowly, as if I'd misunderstood him, like the more I stared and the slower I blinked, I could rewind time and hear the words he really said. Unfortunately, that didn't happen.

"I'm sorry, *what*?"

SEVEN

(Janelle)

I shoved at his chest in a vain attempt to push him away. I should've known it would be futile—you can't budge a brick wall. But that didn't stop me. My anger fueled my need to add distance between us, which outweighed my hormone's desire to have him wedged between my legs. Had we not been wearing pants, the outcome might've been rather different.

"I don't mean to sound like a dick, but sometimes, people need to state their frustrations out loud. They have to purge them so they aren't obsessing about it or letting it fester until it ruins their day. It's not right to talk about people behind their backs. I will fully admit that. But if she's upset about something, isn't it better that she gets it out to her sister, someone who can defend you in your absence, rather than hold it in and take it out on you to your face?"

"How about she not be mad at me, period? She doesn't have any reason to be pissed off. I haven't done anything to her. To accuse me of always getting what I want, like I'm some spoiled brat…?"

He lifted his left shoulder and tilted his head toward it, giving me the scrunched-up face that said, *"well…they're right and you're wrong, but I'm not going to say that so I'm just going to shrug, cock my head to the side, and curl my lip like I just ate old cheese."*

I DO

"I am not a spoiled brat." I shoved at him again and fought to slide off the vanity.

But he refused to let me. Instead, he remained between my legs, his hands on my shoulders with his thumbs beneath my jaw, forcing me to look at him. "I wouldn't say 'spoiled brat,' and I'm sure your sister didn't use those words, either. But you do get away with a lot. And you pretty much get everything you want."

I was pretty sure my eyes were about to bug out of my head with as wide as I opened them to stare at him. "Did I get what I wanted on my first day of kindergarten? When I was so excited to finally be in school like everyone else, with a backpack on and my hair neatly braided, only to hear my mom do nothing but brag about Nikki going to college? Her first baby, away at school. Out of the nest. And it wasn't just once, either. I understand that my memory isn't so great from that long ago, and there's a chance things have been exaggerated over the years, but from what I recall, she brought it up a thousand times."

"Really? A thousand? You sure it wasn't like a hundred million?"

"Don't be an ass," I whined and slapped his chest. "You know what I mean. And as if that wasn't bad enough, when she picked me up that day, she spent the entire drive home on the phone, talking about Nikki. So I don't recall getting what I wanted then. Or how about when my parents told me they'd let me take piano lessons when I was ten, providing I made good grades? But when I did what was asked of me, earned straight As, I was told piano lessons were out of the question because Nikki got knocked up so they had a wedding to pay for and not much time to save. Which means my piano money funded her shotgun wedding. And after that, they had to help financially support them because Shane was still in college."

Even though he didn't move and continued to force me to look at him, at least he stopped talking. Instead, he stood there, perched between my parted legs, hands on my face, with his thumbs ever so gently removing the streaks of exasperation from my cheeks.

"And Stacey has no room to talk. She moved away for college and only moved back when her husband lost his job and she couldn't afford to solely keep her family afloat. So who the hell does she think she is, saying anything about me being gone? At least I didn't come crawling back to Mommy and Daddy, begging for their help because my man couldn't hold onto his paycheck."

"Don't…Janelle." He shook his head, sorrow filling his eyes. "You don't know anything about that situation. So until you do, maybe you shouldn't throw stones."

"Then tell me. He didn't lose his job?"

"No…he did. He was let go."

"Okay then." I refused to listen to him argue in her favor. "I didn't say anything wrong. He was let go. Laid off. Fired. Forced retirement. I don't care what term it's given or what they're calling it. Bottom line is, he lost his paychecks so they came back with their tails tucked between their legs and let everyone else take care of them."

Finally, with a hearty intake of air, he stepped away from me. "You're angry over hearing her say hurtful things about you behind your back. I get it. You have every right to feel upset, but how is what you're doing any better? How is it any different?"

I refused to answer him, because I didn't like admitting that he was right.

"Surely, you can understand the need to get it out to someone you care about, knowing it's a safe place, rather than let it fester and ruin your day."

I DO

"So it's okay for her to talk shit about me, but I can't say anything about her? What's going on, Holden? Do you have a thing for her? Are you two fucking behind Tony's back?" As soon as he leaned toward me, his hand in a fist with one finger pointed angrily in my direction, I knew I'd overstepped my bounds.

I just didn't know how far until he started to talk.

"This is your family. There will be highs. There will be lows. But no matter what, at the end of the day, they are yours. They share your blood, your sweat, your tears. If you ever find yourself needing them, they will rally together and come for you, no questions asked. The least you can do is show them the same courtesy."

"Why are you on their side?" I asked in such a desperate whisper I had to close my eyes, not wanting him to see me as exposed as I felt in that moment.

"I really wish you could see this for what it is. I'm not on their side, Janelle. I'm on *yours*." And with that, he yanked the door open with enough strength, I worried he'd torn it off its hinges. Then he stalked away and left me alone on the vanity, tears tracking down my face.

I'd never felt so alone in my life. Rather than lock myself in the bathroom, I followed Holden out. But where he turned left to meet everyone outside on the back patio, I turned right, heading to the front door. I made it outside but stopped on the top step, realizing by the sight of Holden's burnt-orange Challenger, that I didn't have a car. Which meant I had no way of leaving. I was stuck here, whether I liked it or not.

"What's cookin', good lookin'?" Matthew asked from behind me, probably seeing me run out and knowing something was wrong.

I quickly wiped my face and took a seat on the front stoop, not speaking until he joined me. "No one wants me here, but they don't have the balls to tell me to my face. Instead, I have to hear it being whispered behind my back."

"I'm not sure what you heard or who you heard say it, but I'm willing to bet you misunderstood something. We're all very excited to have you back. I know Christine and I were thrilled when Holden called to tell us you were going to stay with him for a bit while you looked for a job."

Knowing Holden had lied to his best friend to protect me—and him, too—made my chest constrict. Sure, he wouldn't risk telling Matthew the real reason I was living with him, but he didn't have to elaborate and offer extended fabricated pieces of information to make me look better.

"In fact, I was just talking to Nikki, and she's so happy that we're all local again. Mom won't stop talking about having all her babies under one roof." He made sure to say that with a mocking tone, making Mom sound like some old, frail lady with no teeth. We laughed for a second before he placed his hand on my back and grew serious. "Really, Jelly, I'm not lying. I don't know what you heard—or what you *think* you heard—but I'm willing to bet you misunderstood."

"As much as I want to believe you, Matt, I can't. I heard what she said. Stacey doesn't want me here. She's *mad* that I'm here. I'm not sure if she means 'here' as in Mom and Dad's house, or in general, like mad that I moved back. Oh, but she *loves* Holden. It's very clear that he fits in with everyone better than I do...all because I went off to school and was busy getting a degree."

He sat next to me with his back hunched, his arms resting on his knees, and stared at the empty lot across the street through squinted eyes. He had something he wanted to say, but needed a moment to organize his thoughts, so I waited patiently for him to get it all together. However, I didn't expect to hear him say what he did.

I DO

"Don't listen to her. She's bitter—but she has a right to be." He turned his blue eyes—true blue, not some odd mixture of whatever leftover color I got—to me and silenced me with his stare. It was eerie, but at the same time, trusting. "Stacey and Tony waited way too long before they came home. I guess they kept hoping they'd be able to dig themselves out of their hole. She hung on until the last possible second, because the thought of asking for help made her sick."

"That's not my fault, though."

"No. It's not. And she shouldn't take her anger out on you. I'm not justifying her actions—never have and never will. Hell, I disagree with the majority of what Stacey does. But it's not my life, so my opinions don't matter. Who am I to judge what they do? In my opinion, I think they should've come to us, as a family, long before they did. They wouldn't have needed half as much help had they come to us sooner. But I can't dwell on that. I have to be thankful they're okay, and they've made it through."

"How bad was it? He lost his job…what am I missing?"

"He lost his job months and months before anyone knew."

My mouth fell open, and I stared in shock at my brother. "He didn't tell her that he was fired?"

"He wasn't fired. He was let go. But that's beside the point. She knew, but no one else did. Meaning, *we* didn't know. Stacey didn't tell Mom and Dad until close to a year later. They had bills they couldn't pay, more than normal, and even though she took on extra nursing shifts, they couldn't cut it. So Dad offered him a job selling insurance, and Stacey got hired as an at-home care nurse, but that still didn't cover it. Finally, about a year ago, Holden pulled together enough money to pay off their bills to get that monster off their backs."

There was so much to say, but I couldn't form any words. I couldn't lie—it made my heart happy to hear how Holden had helped my family, knowing he'd never see that money again. It wasn't a loan, but a gift, and I had trouble wrapping my head around that kind of generosity. Not that it was foreign to me, because heartless people did not raise me. I guess more than anything, it proved how much Holden was an intricate part of this family.

"So if all that happened a while ago—the bills being paid off a year ago—why is she still so bitter?"

Matthew took a deep breath and slowly let it out while staring off into the distance, almost avoiding eye contact. "I don't think she's a bitter person, if that makes sense. But I do think she holds some sort of resentment for you. I don't know if it's jealousy-based, because while she was going through one the most difficult points in her life, you were off living it up and having fun. Or if she feels like you didn't care because you weren't here when she needed you the most."

"I didn't even know—"

He held up his hand to stop my screeching argument. "I know, Jelly. And deep down, she knows, too. I don't think that's where her bitterness comes from, because I want to believe she's capable of seeing the entire picture. I've had to point it out to her a few times, and I know Tony has, as well. She kept us all in the dark, and because of that, she can't blame anyone but herself. However, if I'm being honest here..." He caught my attention and waited a few blinks before continuing. "I think she found herself hanging by a thread, at the end of her rope, clinging onto life itself as if she were down to her last breath. And now, she has all the air she wants and her rope has been extended, but her nerves are still fried. Have you ever been so stressed that even after it's passed your heart still beats fast and your chest remains tight? I think that's how it is for her."

"But you just said the bills were paid a year ago. How much longer does she plan to hold onto the anxiety? Maybe she should seek help, talk to someone."

Complete and utter desolation covered his face like a veil, darkening his features. "She is talking to someone. Has been for a while now. And I don't think her anxiety is over what happened as much as it is simply caused by it. I think she's more worried about the other shoe dropping than she is about the past."

I nodded, finally understanding what he tried so carefully to explain. However, it left me feeling certain that whatever Holden thought I needed to be here for, it had something to do with Stacey. It was obvious she needed me, and even more evident that she wouldn't lean on me willingly. I'd promised Holden I wouldn't pry, so I resigned myself to sitting on the sidelines and waiting for the invitation to come, hoping at some point, it would.

"Thanks, Matthew. I appreciate the pep talk. It's been a bit stressful coming back, and nothing made me feel more estranged from my own flesh and blood than walking inside and being treated as if I were a stranger."

"Well, you haven't been here for a long time. A lot can happen, sis. And a lot did. But that doesn't mean you're not welcome or wanted. It just means we have to adjust to the final member of the Brewer clan returning and make room within the circle for you."

"That circle seems rather tight at the moment."

He knocked his shoulder into mine and said, "Eh…it is, but that's not a bad thing. Being part of a strong support system is far better than being part of a weak one. And it doesn't mean there's not enough room for more people to squeeze in. Just imagine how much tighter it'll be when you worm your way back in."

"You're very uplifting, has anyone ever told you that before?" My words practically dripped with sarcasm. "You should be a motivational speaker. In the event being a CPA fails you, and Brewer and York falls apart, at least you know you have something to fall back on."

Laughing, he leaned forward until he pulled himself to his feet. "You coming inside, or do you plan to isolate yourself even more and stay out here, staring off at an empty lot? I could tell Mom you're thinking about buying it so you can build a house on it and live across the street from her. I could really make her day if I told her you planned to live there with Holden and have all his babies."

"Ew." I scrunched my nose and curled my lip in faux disgust, when secretly, my ovaries were throwing a party and saying prayers. "He's your best friend, and I'm your *baby* sister; don't you find that repulsive?"

He shoved his hands into his pockets and grinned. "I don't like the idea, so don't go taking me seriously and try to make it happen, but I can't say it repulses me. Ultimately, I want someone for you who will take care of you. You deserve someone to love you unconditionally and stand by you every single day of your life. I know Holden is the kind of guy who could do that, which is why I don't hate the idea. Although, I feel certain there are others out there capable of treating you just as well, which means you should find one of them. My statement was in no way a blessing or a show of support."

"Whatever, Matty. You know you two have been planning our wedding since you were kids so you guys could finally be brothers." We both laughed in unison while he helped me off the porch and led me back inside.

Matt grabbed a beer from the fridge and then headed out back where it seemed everyone else gathered. I found a single can of my favorite soda hidden in the back on the bottom shelf, and as soon as I pulled it out and let the door fall closed, I shrieked in surprise at the sight of Holden standing there. I glanced around the room and then peered down the hall, pleased to see we were alone.

When my heart slowed down enough to talk without sounding like I'd suddenly picked up jogging, I moved closer to him and lowered my voice. "Matthew told me about you giving Stacey money. He said they had bills even after moving home and you helped pay them off. That was really nice of you."

It took him a beat, but he finally pulled away from me and turned to leave without speaking.

I grabbed his hand, unintentionally slipping my palm against his and lazily lacing our fingers together. "You don't have anything to say? You're just going to walk away as if I didn't just speak to you?"

"You didn't ask me a question, Janelle. Therefore, I'm not required to say anything. And honestly, I don't even know what to say to that. Are you asking me if that's true? Then yes. I did. They needed help, and I had the resources to help them, so I did. Should I thank you for the awkward compliment? In that case, thanks for telling me how nice my gesture was. I didn't do it to look nice."

I swallowed thickly and glanced around once more, needing to be sure no one could overhear my next words. "You got really defensive in the bathroom when I accused you of having an affair with her. I understand I was out of line and what I said was uncalled for. But I can't stop thinking about your reaction, which wouldn't be more than an errant thought had I not just found out about the other thing."

"What other thing?"

"You giving her money. I wasn't lying—that was really nice of you to do. And I understand that you did it because you're a good person with a good heart. I know I have no right to ask this, but I'm begging you to tell me the truth. No matter what your answer is, I won't tell anyone. You have my word on that, especially since you have so much against me. But I need the peace of mind one way or another." I licked my lips and paused to swallow past the knot in my throat.

But Holden didn't give me the chance to finish my question. He leaned into me, walking me backward a few steps until the counter met my back and stopped my retreat. Rather than hold himself up by the edge of the granite as he towered above me, he gripped my hips and held me against him. I had my head all the way back in order to see him as he peered down at me, my breath catching in my throat, my heart racing as each second passed.

"You wanna know if there's anything going on between me and your sister?" With most of our fronts pressed together, he lowered his mouth to my ear, completely forming his body along mine. "I've been inside you, Janelle. Just because you forgot doesn't mean I did. It doesn't mean it didn't happen…all four times. And I remember every single second of it. I know in detail what it was like to break through your virginity, to be the first one to ever slide all the way into you. To be buried balls-deep in your pussy. I'll never forget the way you sounded when I made you scream for me the first time. And every time after that. The way you gasped my name as you came on my cock."

Seconds before I gave in and humped his leg like a stray dog, he took a step back and leveled his heated stare with mine. "I have a strict policy against keeping things in the family. Once I'm with someone, all siblings are added to the no-touch list."

I DO

I nodded…and blinked…and fought desperately to catch my breath without looking like a panting whore in church. But I failed. Miserably. Luckily, all Holden did was laugh and leave me to recover alone in the kitchen, where I melted against the counter with the cold can of soda pressed against my feverish neck. If anyone walked in right now, they'd more than likely offer me one of Mom's estrogen pills and the ice pack she kept in the freezer to combat her hot flashes.

I was so screwed.

EIGHT

(Holden)

We managed to make it through the rest of dinner without another issue. However, I did see what Janelle was talking about regarding the awkwardness with Stacey. I made sure to keep an eye on them without being obvious, and even though Stacey wasn't rude to her, she wasn't exactly accommodating, either. I only hoped after another week or so it'd all be back to normal, and maybe she'd start to open up to Janelle.

By the time we got back home, it was still early enough to hang out, so I asked her to watch a movie with me. Ever since she came out of her room this morning nearly naked, I'd plotted my revenge. And this seemed like the perfect time to execute my plan. She headed back to her room to change, and I quickly stripped out of my clothes, leaving me in nothing but my boxer-briefs. Then I sat on the couch, much like she had this morning, and waited for her like a lion waits for its prey.

"What movie did you have in…?" At first, she didn't see me as she came down the hallway from her bedroom, but the second she made it to the living room, she dramatically slowed and her speech halted. It wasn't like she'd put on the brakes or acted like she'd hit a brick wall. It was far more slow-motion than that. First her body—her feet continued for a few more steps after she'd made eye contact. Then her

116

words rolled to a stop after a couple syllables, and finally her expression—eyes wide with shock, mouth agape. And then, as if someone merely decelerating to rubberneck at a traffic accident, she began to come back and gradually continue. "What are you doing?"

"Waiting for you. And I'm not picky; we can watch whatever you want. Free movie channels this weekend, ending tonight, so you have plenty of options."

"No." She waved her hand in front of her, gesturing to me. "What are *you* doing...like that?"

I glanced down at my state of undress with mock confusion and ran my hand down my torso before meeting her gaze, ensuring she saw me. And she did. Her chest rose and fell with each desperate breath she took while her eyes methodically traced every body part—*every* last one of them. When she turned her attention back to my face, I couldn't help but rejoice in the sight of her flushed cheeks.

"Oh, I just got comfortable for a movie. If this makes you uncomfortable, I'll gladly go put some more clothes on. I didn't think it would bother you." I might've laid it on too thick, because as soon as I finished, her eyes lit up and the faintest hint of a smile shadowed one corner of her mouth.

Had I not been looking, I would've missed it—the slight twitch in her left brow and the seamless transition from surprise to confidence in her body language. "No need to put clothes on for me," she said without a hitch in her voice as she sashayed toward me, stalking me. "What you have on is perfect."

She was calling my bluff.

This was the part where she expected me to get up, on my own accord, and either change or hide in my room. As uncomfortable as I knew playing this out would be, I couldn't back down just yet. Janelle had to learn I wouldn't concede to a fight. So instead of caving under the intense pressure of her gaze, I locked my hands behind my head and reclined into the overstuffed pillows behind me. "Then let's get to it. Feel free to peruse through what I have…*to watch*. Check it all out. Let me know what looks good—what you just *have* to see."

I'd known Janelle for a very long time. If I had to place a bet on who'd cave first, I'd pick her without a doubt. So when her brow arched and her lips curled into the most devious grin I'd ever seen on her glossy lips, I knew she not only called the ante, but she also raised it.

"I already know what I want to see." She'd lowered her voice to this sultry, phone-sex operator level that seemed to hum through her. She had me so wrapped up in the way she purred, along with her bright-blue eyes and deceitful smirk, that I nearly lost my composure when she straddled my thighs and pressed her blazing palms against my shoulders, as if holding on.

"W-what—" I had to clear my throat, close my eyes, and take a deep breath before continuing, pretty sure I'd just given her an idea of my poker hand. But I wasn't ready to fold yet. I knew well enough to predict we were both bluffing, and it basically was nothing more than a game of who could last the longest. "What movie did you decide on?"

"I'm torn. There are so many to choose from. Maybe you can help me choose."

At some point—and I honestly had no clue when, considering I'd lost most of my brain cells after she perched herself on my lap—my arms had fallen away from behind my head to settle against the cushions. It'd been many years since the last time I didn't know what to do with my hands in the company of a woman, but apparently, it could still happen. I dropped my gaze to her neck, thinking if I didn't look her in the eyes, I would be fine. That's when I noticed the rapid thrumming of her pulse just beneath her skin. It seemed she was just as affected as I was, and not at all cool, calm, and collected like she wanted me to believe.

I slid my hands up her outer thighs, running my palms over her smooth legs until I reached her shorts, and then took hold of her waist. But I didn't move her. Instead, I kept her where she was, only flexed my fingers so she couldn't forget where I touched her.

"What are my options?" I tried to make my voice husky and sultry like she did, but I doubted it worked. In my head, I sounded like a twelve-year-old boy getting ready to dive into the most exciting experience in this lifetime. There were some things women could do well that men had no business attempting, and phone-sex voice was one of them.

"Good Will Humping." She widened her legs to pull herself closer to me, and breathing became difficult. "Legally Boned." When she rolled her hips toward me, I had to close my eyes. Which did nothing to block her assault when she lowered her mouth to my ear and whispered, "Whorey Potter."

It was now or never. I tightened my hold on her hips and flipped her onto her back, and then pulled myself over her. I couldn't look at her, knowing the competition would end if I did, so I kept my cheek pressed against hers and used my other senses to assess the situation. Like the way her chest heaved with exertion, as if falling onto the couch from a sitting position wore her out. Her heart thrashed inside her chest, ricocheting against mine. But nothing affected her as much as when I rotated my hips to cause friction between our legs.

"I'd much rather prefer watching Missionary Impossible," I whispered against her neck.

"That's a good one." Her voice sounded strained, like the words were forced out.

Nearing the breaking point, I pushed up with my forearms to hover over her and met her heated stare. "It seems we're both incredibly stubborn, and there's a good chance I'll wind up balls-deep in you before either of us caves. We can either keep this up or both agree to give up at the same time."

"Keep it going."

I groaned and closed my eyes, knowing I'd have to be the one to put an end to it. I didn't like losing, but this went beyond my need for victory. Being between the legs of a woman—especially one named Janelle—and calling it quits would cost me a handful of points on the man-meter. If the reason had nothing to do with whiskey dick or lack of protection, I basically deserved to bury my head in the sand.

I opened my eyes and found hers, shining back at me, full of challenge. "As appealing as that sounds, it's not a good idea. At all. You're here for a divorce, right? Starting something up between us would only complicate that."

As if her need for me was nothing more than an act, she fluttered her eyes and pushed against my chest. "Fine. We both win—or lose, depending on how you look at it. But good game, York. I didn't expect you to take a play from my book, especially so soon after I played it."

I sat back and let her pull herself to a seated position at the end of the couch, where she grabbed the remote off the table and began flipping through the channels. With my hands cupped over my erection, I stood and headed toward my room.

"Where are you going? I thought we were going to watch a movie." She giggled to herself and shook her head, turning her attention back to the screen on the wall in front of her. "Oh, yeah. You should probably put on clothes to cover that."

"Actually, I'm headed to take a cold shower and ice my bruised ego."

I DO

"What happened to your ego? You're the one who stopped this."

Pausing at my door, I called out over my shoulder, "You could've at least acted distraught for a few minutes, maybe pretended to be a little upset."

Her laughter floated over me as I locked myself in my room and prepared to finish what we'd started—only this time, alone.

As if that wasn't bad enough, it seemed Janelle was on a roll. By the end of the week, I didn't think I stood a chance anymore and started to question if bringing her back for her family was worth it. I didn't even want to look at the scorecard, knowing I was not in the lead—not even close.

Monday after work, I came home and found her finishing up whatever dinner she'd made for herself. She stood at the sink and rinsed the bowl, while I rummaged through the fridge, searching for *anything* to fill my empty stomach.

"You know...it'd be nice to have supper ready to eat when I got home. I mean, it doesn't have to be coming out of the oven as soon as I pull into the driveway, but what good is it to have a stay-at-home wife when I still have to make my own food after busting my ass all day in the office?" I'd meant it partly as a joke, but in all honesty, I was serious about how nice it would've been to come home to something to eat.

"Are you seriously suggesting I cook dinner for you, and then serve it to you when you get home? You're sadly mistaken if you think having me here would be similar to ordering a wife through a catalog." She threw her head back and released a bellowing laugh.

"No. I think you're my wife who's living in my house for free, and considering we both need to eat something around this time every day—that bowl you're cleaning proves my point—I figured it wouldn't hurt if you made enough for two."

She huffed but didn't object, so I left behind a grocery list on the counter before I left for work the next day, along with cash to cover it, and came home to a fully—overly—stocked kitchen. She definitely got every item on the list, so I didn't have much room to complain. I'd asked for milk, but apparently, she needed me to specify which kind, and "there were so many options ranging from whole to reduced fat, and then the soy, cashew, and almond varieties, I just got them all to make sure you had what you wanted." I now had an entire shelf dedicated to every option of milk one could imagine. Although, rather than grumble, I simply smiled, thanked her, and said, "At least I won't have to worry about a calcium deficiency."

As for dinner, I did come home to something to eat every night.

Much like the milk debacle, I wasn't specific enough.

It seemed I was looking at six months' worth of ham sandwiches for supper.

But again, I didn't protest. I made sure to thank her every single night and tell her how amazing it was. She more than likely expected me to have some comment, but I didn't give her anything. Honestly, had we not been against each other, I would've given her a high-five and bragged to everyone I knew about how devious she was. But we weren't partners, and I was the one who ended up on the wrong end of that conspiracy.

With everything that had gone on last weekend—Ronnie showing up at my house, finding out that fucker had been there, the family drama Sunday evening, and then the underwear-on-the-couch scheme that blew up in my face that night—I'd totally forgotten about the package being delivered.

I DO

The original one, the one I'd made her stay home to sign, never existed. But after I got back from the lake and noticed she'd cleaned the house, I felt bad, and before going to sleep that night, I'd ordered something so I wouldn't look like I'd lied, and she wouldn't feel as though she'd stayed home for nothing. There was only one problem—I'd forgotten *all* about it.

After devouring my home-cooked peanut butter and jelly sandwich for dinner on Thursday, I sat on the couch and played a round of poker on my phone while she lounged on the loveseat with her face in a book. Suddenly, out of nowhere, she dropped her feet from the coffee table and jumped up. Returning about a minute later from her room, she held up a small brown box.

"Something was delivered for you today."

I exited the app and locked my phone, giving her my undivided attention. "Oh, good. I'm glad it finally got here. It's only a few days late, huh?"

"Funny thing…I didn't have to sign for it."

"Huh." I ran my hand along my jaw in mock intrigue, praying like hell I didn't lose yet another battle. "That's strange. But you know how those delivery guys can be. So many things going on they probably didn't even think about it. Oh well. At least it got here."

Even though I held my hand out for her to give it to me, she refused. With one fist perched on her hip and the other holding up the small box as if it were evidence in a murder trial, on display for the jury, she cocked her head and continued. "Yeah…except UPS didn't drop it off. It came with the regular mail."

"Damn. I guess I mixed that whole thing up, didn't I?"

"Well, you see, I opened the package—"

"Which is a federal offense."

"I'm your wife. Sue me." She flashed an arrogant grin and went on. "I just wanted to see if it was the watch you had ordered, the one you expected to come last Saturday, because if it was, I planned to raise hell over the delay of the delivery, as well as the lack of signature required. And you know what I found on the packing slip, Holden?"

At this juncture, there really was no point in doing anything other than sitting back and scrutinizing the show. So rather than keep up the pretense, I shrugged and let her finish.

"It seems the watch wasn't even ordered until Saturday. What I don't know is…did you order it before or after making me stay home all day instead of going out on the boat and having fun with my brother?"

It seemed I'd reached the proverbial fork in the road. I could've come up with some kind of lie, or at the very least, something to prolong it and give me more time. Or I could've told her the truth, that I made her stay behind to get back at her for something I claimed didn't bother me. It was a tough decision to make, but in the end, I did what was best.

I glanced at my phone, pressed the home button until it lit up, and said, "Oh, hold on. I have to take this." I then held it up to my ear and pulled myself from the couch. "Hey, so good to hear from you. Listen, give me a sec, I have to go to the other room."

I made it five steps away from my bedroom door before the universe proved how much it hated me. With my phone to my ear, in the middle of talking, the damn thing rang. Luckily, I had my back to Janelle, but that didn't end her maniacal laughter that followed me into my room, even long after I closed the door behind me.

However, none of that stopped me from spending the day on Saturday with her.

I DO

"Tennis shoes? You want me to wear tennis shoes? Where are you taking me?" Her shrill voice coupled with her wide eyes made me laugh.

"I already told you—it's a surprise. But I swear, there won't be any running. Or jogging. Or even fast-paced walking. I'm suggesting sneakers because we will be walking—leisurely," I added to keep her from freaking out. "And I don't want you to get blisters."

"Why do I have a feeling I'm going to regret this?" she muttered under her breath on her way back to her room to grab different shoes. By the time she rejoined me in the living room, she seemed less than impressed and even less excited about the surprise I had planned.

I'd always loved being outdoors, whether for a run, out on the lake, tossing around a ball…anything. It didn't matter the reason. If the sun was out, I wanted to be, as well. But Janelle was the opposite. She blamed it on being the youngest and never having kids her age in the neighborhood, which kept her inside most of her childhood, and therefore, groomed her to be the indoorsy woman she is today. However, that didn't prevent me from finding something to do with her that would appeal to both of our desires. It may have been hard, but not impossible.

"Come on, Jelly. Look, there's a bench right up there. Let's just go a little more and then we can take a break." She stood about ten feet behind me, hunched over with her hands on her knees, panting like she'd just climbed a mountain.

"You did this to get back at me, didn't you? I can't believe a word you say anymore."

I couldn't help but laugh, which turned out to be the wrong thing to do. It only irritated her more. "Janelle, babe, I'm not getting back at you for anything. I swear. I really did think this would be something fun we could do together."

"*Fun?*" Her anger only served to make it that much more entertaining. "We're outside, Holden...*babe,*" she spat and finally walked toward me. "It's hot and I'm sweaty and there are bugs. *Bugs,* Holden. What about a nature hike made you think I would enjoy it? Admit it, you did this to even the score after the air freshener incident."

My laughter turned to cackles when she reminded me of that. A few days ago, I'd made some comment about an odor in the house. I had no idea what caused it, but something had left a muted stench inside. I never asked her to deal with it or make it go away, nor did I ever accuse her of being the cause. Yet that didn't stop her from taking matters into her own hands. In every room, she plugged in air fresheners, which would've been great had they all been the same scent. Then she lit candles—again, all different fragrances. As soon as I'd walked in after work that evening, I was assaulted by a migraine-inducing aroma war. While I slept, I was convinced I was in Hawaii surrounded by lavender and brown sugar with clean sheets waving in the breeze. As if that wasn't a bad enough combination, there were also whiffs of cinnamon and baked goods.

I hadn't found it funny at the time, especially when I had to deal with a mammoth-sized headache, but Janelle made it better when she disposed of all but a couple air freshener plug-ins. She never admitted to why she got rid of it all, but I chose to believe she'd done it for me. What I'm sure started out as a way of being a royal smartass turned into something far worse, and it wouldn't surprise me if she felt bad about it. Regardless of *why* she aired out the house, I was just thankful she had. And now I could laugh at it.

"Janelle," I finally said after composing myself. "It's not a hike. In fact, there is no hiking involved. This is a nature trail, meant for leisurely walking and enjoyment."

I DO

"I swear to God, Holden, if you say *leisurely* one more time, I'm gonna leisurely punch you in the throat."

I held up both hands in surrender. "The trail is even covered with trees—from start to finish. I looked into it before planning to bring you here, because I know you hate the sun."

"I hate the heat. Which is derived from the sun, but not always the same thing."

"I'm sorry. I wanted to spend the day with you and do something we'd both like. I thought finding a place we could enjoy a...*laidback stroll* would be fun. There's this creek-slash-tiny river, trees, birds, pretty flowers."

Her expression softened, and so did her tone when she said, "I'm sorry. I really thought you dragged me out here to be a dick and pay me back for all the shit I've given you this week. I didn't know you truly wanted to hang out. I appreciate the time you spent thinking of this. Now...let's get to that bench." And with that, she walked ahead of me and took a seat at the observation area.

I joined her and stared off at the greenish-looking water in front of us. I suddenly saw this place through her eyes. Once I stepped out of the blissful bubble of us finally spending real time together, I was able to see this place with a renewed sense of sight, and I wouldn't have doubted if those bird sounds were filtered in through a speaker somewhere. The water was stale, and I was sure the only living thing in it was bacteria. What I imagined to be flowers turned out to be weeds, and I'd probably lost more blood to mosquitoes today than I did when I split my head open as a kid.

"I can see now how you convinced me to marry you," she teased without looking at me.

"Wait...*what*?" I angled my body to face her, utterly shocked over her statement. "First of all, I didn't convince you of anything. It was all your idea."

"Mine?" She turned to me with confusion lining her brow, probably mirroring my own surprise. "Why the hell would I suggest we get married? That makes no sense. You know I don't remember it, so you're probably making this whole thing up, knowing I can't disprove it."

"Not at all. I swear. We were in front of the Bellagio when you brought it up."

"How did I bring it up?"

For whatever reason, I never anticipated having to explain this to her. I knew she had no recollection of that night—no matter how much it pained me to admit that—but I guess I never thought we'd have this conversation. With a long sigh, I resigned myself to revisiting that night all over again, and giving her the details her brain had blocked out.

"Well, we were making out. I think I might've said something about not wanting to ever stop kissing you, and you suggested we get married. At first I thought you were joking, but as it turned out, you were very serious."

"What were my reasons?"

I couldn't keep eye contact with her while I told her this, and I didn't know why. It was nothing bad, and nothing she would hate me for, but it just felt awkward to look at her while explaining why we got married. "We both said we'd likely never make it down the aisle. Then you brought up some book you read about two friends who agreed to marry each other by whatever age if they were both single, and before I knew it, we had made the same pact. But somehow, it went from 'in ten years' to 'right now.' It made sense at the time."

"How the hell did that make sense? At *any* time?" Her high-pitched voice broke the romantic spell I'd been under while traveling down memory lane. It was as if thinking back on that night caused soft music to play in the background and a familiar warmth to settle over me. But as soon as she spoke up, reality came crashing back, and I realized that warmth was nothing but the summer heat and the soft music was really a group of people behind us murmuring to themselves while the birds chirped.

"Well, we got along, we were friends, and we trusted each other. Rather than wait a few years until you graduated from college, it made more sense to go ahead and do it so that when you got home, we wouldn't have to make a big deal about it. We both discussed how big weddings were a waste of money, and even though we thought Matt and Christine's was small and nicely done, it still seemed like too much of an effort neither of us were willing to make. Plus, taking care of it then would've eliminated the chances of your mom taking over. You even said if we waited, we'd end up eloping anyway because you wouldn't be able to take her meddling."

She tilted her head from side to side and lifted her shoulders a bit. "Yeah. That totally sounds like something I'd say. I guess I'm just confused as to why. Ya know? Like…why did you agree? Why did neither of us stop and think about the ramifications? Or at the very least have a conversation about our intentions and expectations."

"I can't answer most of that, but I can tell you why I agreed. I've always loved your family, Janelle. You know my mom wasn't around much, always chasing the next guy, but your mom was. Your dad filled the empty father role in my life, and for once, I finally stopped feeling alone. You complain about being the youngest, imagine being the only child—except getting *none* of the perks. It's not like I ever thought one way or another about marriage. It was more of a take-it-or-leave-it thing for me. But I found myself really enjoying your company over those months before Vegas. I liked spending time with you and taking care of you. I realized then that I actually *liked* having someone depend on me, and knowing that marrying you would solidify my place in the family made it all that much better. So it was a no-brainer for me."

"So you married me because you wanted to be a part of my family." It wasn't a question, although she did sound highly confused when she said it...doubtful maybe. "How romantic. That's exactly what every girl dreams of hearing."

"Whatever. You only married me to win the power struggle with your mom."

She waved me off and leaned against the back of the bench. "What else can you tell me about that night? How was the sex? Good? Great? Could've been better?"

My mouth opened and closed as I tried to come up with the right thing to say. Rather than anything intelligent coming out, it was a bunch of stammering and stuttering—basically, single-syllable garble.

"I totally rocked your world, didn't I?" She wagged her eyebrows, and effectively left me speechless.

Once we finally finished our walk—which Janelle adamantly referred to as the hike through Death Valley—we headed home. It wasn't that I had expected to eat dinner with her, but I would've liked it. Instead, as soon as we got back to the house, she left to go "shopping." However, when I climbed into bed at ten, she still wasn't home, and I couldn't help but assume the worst.

And by worst, I meant her being out with that fucker or another guy.

NINE

(Janelle)

"How much longer?" Holden called out from the living room.

I sat on the edge of my bed and slipped on the new pair of heels I'd purchased last night while I was out. I couldn't stop thinking about how good Veronica looked in them, and I wanted to see if I did, too. I knew I'd more than likely get teased for wearing them to my parents' house for Sunday dinner, but I didn't care.

I tucked my cell against my chest and yelled back, "Two minutes."

"I don't understand how going anywhere with him will make him divorce you faster," Connor droned on in my ear from the other end of the line. "I was for sure he would've kicked you out on your ass by now, so why hasn't he? Are you doing everything we talked about?"

I rolled my eyes, even though he couldn't see me. "Yes," I huffed into the receiver. "He's not going to cave easily—if at all. So you need to be prepared in the event he makes me wait out the entire six months. But we're getting ready to leave for dinner, so I have to go."

"Stop going out with him, and maybe he'll give up sooner."

"Oh my God. For the last time, it's my parents' house. I don't have a choice in the matter."

"Sure you do. He wants you there to reunite with them, so if you don't go, you'll piss him off, and eventually, he'll kick you out."

"It doesn't work that way, Connor. Just let me handle it, okay? It's been less than two weeks. Chill. I know what I'm doing. Not to mention, even if he doesn't give in earlier, it's not like we'll lose the money. We still have time." I stood and took a moment to steady myself in the heels. "Listen, as entertaining as this call was, I'm gonna have to let you go."

A minute later, I hobbled into the living room, where Holden waited for me by the front door. He drew his attention from whatever he had on his phone to my feet, and then slowly dragged his gaze up my legs. However, rather than say anything about my appearance—or the new shoes I struggled to walk in—he asked, "Ready?"

I wanted to stomp my foot and throw a tantrum, spin around in a circle, and scream, "do you not see how hot I look?" But I refrained. Instead, I nodded and followed him outside to his car. Which, to my dismay, wouldn't start due to what he assumed was a dead battery, so we ended up taking mine. And for reasons I wasn't willing to divulge, I hated taking my car.

Luckily, between the effort it took to steadily walk in heels, coupled with obsessing over Holden being in my car, I didn't have time to worry about how I'd be treated at dinner. And what helped even more was walking inside first—meaning, I didn't have to wait until everyone greeted Holden before they said hi to me. It also meant I didn't have to witness the sudden shift in reaction, either.

"I feel like I didn't get to talk to you much last week." Nikki took the empty seat next to me on the back deck, where I sat alone and watched the guys and kids run around with a

I DO

football in the yard. "There just seemed to be so much going on, and I didn't even realize it until we all left. So...how's it going? Are you enjoying being back?"

At first, I thought this was a trick. I halfway expected one of them to come ask me things to get on my good side, and then congregate in a corner, or the kitchen, and discuss it like some clicky high school group of girls. But when I turned to take in Nikki's stare, I realized how wrong I was. Her completely genuine interest shone back at me, and it nearly made me melt, because this was the first time since returning that I felt like one of my sisters actually wanted me here.

"It's an adjustment, but Holden's keeping me on my toes." I couldn't fight the burning grin tugging on my lips when I focused my sight on the men running around in the grass and found Holden, carrying Nikki's youngest daughter, Maggie—who was eight—over his shoulder.

"I bet he is." The way she said it made me face her once more, picking up on the teasing in her tone. "Oh, baby sis...I have so many years on you that you should know it's pointless to hide it. Not to mention, I've been through this with two other sisters before you, don't forget."

"Been through what?" It was easy to play dumb. Because I seriously had no idea what she was talking about. "I'm not trying to hide anything."

"You're not? So you don't care if we all know you and Holden are more than roomies?"

"*What*?" Shamelessly, my voice came out so high I was sure it rivaled one of Mariah Carey's soprano notes. I wanted to look away so she wouldn't catch my flaming cheeks, but I didn't—I knew doing so would give me away faster than a preacher at his daughter's shotgun wedding. "Why would you think that?"

"Aside from that?" With her finger pointed toward my face, she gestured to my expression using imaginary circles. "How about the way you came staggering in here like you just got off a bull? Or the glow you're exuding, which can only be derived from a good orgasm. And let me just say this, Jelly." She leaned forward, which I mimicked to prevent her from being overheard. "You're lit up like the Christmas tree in Times Square, so I know it must've been good."

Suddenly, it dawned on me. "You think…" I smiled for many reasons, but mainly out of relief that she didn't know about Vegas. She could think Holden spent every day buried between my legs for all I cared, just as long as she didn't find out the truth regarding my marital status.

"Oh, I don't think…I *know*."

"What if you're wrong? What if it's not Holden?"

"Really?" Her eyes widened, and her back went ramrod straight. "I want details. Who is it?"

"I'm not ready to talk about him quite yet. It's still so new." I waved her off, hoping that would've ended the conversation. I figured leading her to believe there was a mystery man in my life, one I wanted to keep a secret for now, would hold her off for a bit, at least until I could devise a breakup I'd want to keep on the down-low for obvious reasons.

Unfortunately, that didn't happen.

"Holden!" Nikki grabbed his attention as he tried to walk by to go inside.

When he glanced over and noticed us in the corner of the deck, he grinned and started to head over. Apparently, he completely missed me mouthing to him "*go away*" because he didn't, in fact, retreat. He came all the way over and perched himself on the railing, wearing the same shit-eating grin he used when he knew he had an advantage in a situation.

I DO

"Do you know who Janelle's mystery man is?" She was like a dog on a scent trail.

Before I could interrupt, Holden perked up and cocked his head in my direction. "Mystery man? I might have a clue. But it depends…what do you know?"

They were like co-conspirators the way they seemed to gravitate toward each other, practically rubbing their hands together in excitement. "She won't tell me anything, but whoever it is has given little Janelle over here the orgasm glow."

Humiliation weighted my eyelids, almost forcing them closed in a desperate attempt to save myself. However, before I lost sight of him, I noticed his shoulders sag and the lines between his brows deepen as he turned his attention to me. I thought to shake my head, to let him know it wasn't true, but then I reminded myself that I didn't owe him an explanation. I'd given him one last weekend regarding Connor, but he didn't need to know anything else. Plus, he'd never provided one to me when he invited Veronica into his bedroom right in front of me.

Holden pulled in a deep breath and straightened his posture, rolling his shoulders back. "Well, she went out last night and didn't come home until after ten."

"Interesting." She turned her attention to me and asked, "Where were you?"

"I went shopping." It was true. I even had a new pair of shoes to prove it.

"Alone?" When I nodded, my eyes glued to Holden, she continued. "What about after that? What did you do for dinner?"

"I ate at the food court in the mall." Again, not a lie.

"Well, you weren't there until after ten, so where did you go after shopping?"

That's when my gaze fell from his face. "I drove around, listened to music. Parked at the sports complex near the house. And then I went home. Nothing to know, no juicy details. You're looking far too hard into something that's not there."

Holden mumbled some excuse to get up and walked away, leaving me alone with Nikki, who I desperately wanted to strangle. I knew she didn't do or say any of that to be malicious; she had no idea. But it didn't stop me from being upset over the whole situation.

"I know you didn't think about it, but you just made things really awkward between us."

She stared at me with confusion brightening her eyes for a second, and then narrowed her gaze. "I'm sorry, Jelly. I had no idea. I guess I figured you two are friends, and you live together, so I didn't imagine—"

"It's okay. You didn't know. But from now on, please refrain from talking to Holden about me and relationships. We're just now getting to a good place where we can act normal around each other as roommates, and I don't want to jeopardize that."

"I guess I didn't know there was anything wrong between you two."

"I wouldn't say wrong, but as you know, a lot of my relationships here became strained when I moved away. That was one of them."

Remorse darkened her hazel eyes, and after a moment, she reached over to take my hand. "Don't let any of it get to you, okay? We're all happy you're home, and we want you to stay."

"I appreciate that, Nik. I really do. But let's be real—every single one of you got to go to school. You, Stacey, *and* Rachel all attended college away. I don't recall you guys being home much during those years. You got to live in a dorm, make friends, go to parties, and no one here gave you a guilt trip for not spending every holiday at the house. But when I do it, I'm crucified and treated like a runaway when I come back."

She squeezed my hand in a genuine show of support. "I fully understand where you're coming from, and you're right, it's not fair. You've been held to a different standard than the rest of us, simply because you're so much younger than we are. And I hate that for you. You had just as much right as we did to do all those things and be young, it's just hard for some of us to recognize that, because we've all moved into a different period in our lives."

"Exactly, and I'm the one being punished for being young. Just because I don't have a kid like you did at my age, or married like Matty and Christine, that somehow means I'm less. Maybe I don't want to get married or have kids. Maybe I want to own my own business and focus on that. That doesn't mean I'm somehow not as valuable as any of you."

"No one said you're not. And I'm not making an excuse, only offering you something to think about in the event you want to see things from our perspective. We were so used to you being here all the time — at least, I know I was. So when you went away, it was hard, but not as hard as it was when you stopped coming back. It's like…you were here, then in the blink of an eye, you were gone. Add to it, we were all older and moving into the land of parenthood and dealing with real life. The age gap between us was so monumental during that time. We kind of all banded together, and now that you're back, we're realizing we had left you out of major things in our lives. I can't speak for the others, but I'm willing to bet any resentment you're picking up on isn't meant for you. I know I, for one, feel like shit for not keeping you in the loop over the last few years. And I don't think I'm alone in that."

I hugged my sister, thankful for the insight she bestowed upon me. I felt it was the first time someone other than Matt had opened up to me honestly since I'd returned. Rather than try to convince me everyone was happy that I was back, she actually gave plausible reason to the hesitation I felt. I agreed that it wasn't my fault, and it shouldn't have been taken out on me, but at least now I could try to understand the issue and work toward finding a solution.

Holden, however, acted very strange for the rest of the evening. He behaved normal around my family, but in my presence, he refused to look at me, and any conversation was short and awkward. Most of his dialogue was mumbled and barely understood. It bothered me, but what I found more frustrating was that I had to wait until we left to make any effort to fix it, considering he avoided any possibility of time alone with me.

However, I tried to block that out and attempted to make the most of my time with my family. Rachel and I carried on an easy, surface-level conversation at the dinner table about the event-planning business I wanted to start. It drew in others, and eventually, I felt as though I belonged again.

I rode that high all the way up until it was time to leave. That's when anxiety hit me, knowing I'd be alone with Holden the entire ride home. After his silent treatment this afternoon, I expected him to be quiet, ignore me. Needless to say, I was rather surprised when he had so much to say once we backed out of the driveway.

"You went to the sports complex last night? The same one I took you to the night of your prom?"

"Yup." I avoided looking in his direction, even though I could feel his stare burning into the side of my head. I debated on telling him the truth, but I didn't have the nerve. I had no idea how he would've taken it, and I didn't care to hear his opinion.

I DO

"So if Nikki's right, and you're telling me the truth, that means you got off in the car."

I closed my eyes and groaned inwardly. "Maybe."

"I can't imagine there'd be that much room over there with the steering wheel in the way, unless he's a really small guy, and since this is your car, I'm assuming he was here. Which means..." He shifted in the seat and held his hands out as though he was afraid to touch anything. "Which means his bare ass was right here. I feel dirty."

In my peripheral vision, I saw him lean forward, but it wasn't until I realized he'd reached for the glove box that I jerked into action. My right arm swung into him—like a mother protecting her child in the front seat—and I screamed, "*No!*" Although, I elongated the two-letter word until it sounded more like an obnoxious cry of desperation comprised of eighty-seven of the worst sounding syllables ever put together. And yet even that wasn't enough to stop him before the latch came open.

The car swerved, and as soon as I saw something purple fall out and land at his feet, I gave up on righting the car and just pulled over to the side of the road, thanking the Lord we hadn't made it out of my parents' neighborhood yet. In fact, I not only pulled over, I threw the door open and got out. I had no idea what the plan was, but at that moment, I was more than willing to walk home—even in the most painful set of heels I'd ever worn.

"Wait, wait, wait," Holden called out when he, too, left the vehicle and ran around the front to stop my irrational retreat. "Don't take off like that. Let's get back in the car and head home. If you don't want to discuss it, then we don't have to...although I am kinda intrigued."

I rolled my eyes and tried to step out of his hold, but the way he gripped my shoulders made it hard to get away. "No.

This is really embarrassing, and I'd very much like to just disappear if that's all right with you."

He snickered and pulled me closer to his body, where I tucked my face into the space below his chin and pretended I was invisible. And while we stood there on the side of the road, he wrapped his arms around me and began to rub my back in soothing circles. "At this point in time, I could literally make half a dozen assumptions, and any one of them could be accurate. I understand you don't want to talk about it, and it's none of my business, but I'm *really* interested in the reason why a dildo just fell out of your glovebox."

I groaned again, this time out loud. His shirt absorbed most of it, the material holding in the heat of my breath and warming my face like I sat too close to a fire. "I bought it at the mall yesterday."

"And you couldn't wait to use it?"

"No." I pushed away from him and huffed. "I opened the package while I was at the baseball field last night because I wanted to see it. I've never had one before. I didn't use it," I added, feeling as though it needed to be said. "I saw movement in my side mirror, and I freaked out, so I tossed it on the floor. It must've rolled under the seat because when I got home, I couldn't find it, and I didn't want to stand out in the driveway all night looking for it. There was a dog barking and it freaked me out. I had all intention of getting it today, but then forgot all about it until you said we had to take my car. I didn't exactly have much time, so as soon as I found it, I shoved it in the glove box, assuming you wouldn't look in there. Why the hell would you look in there? Honestly, what are the odds you'd open the glove box?"

His laughter rippled through his chest. "So there's no mystery guy?"

"Really? A purple vibrator nearly fell into your lap just now, and all you're worried about is if I'm seeing someone?

I DO

No. I'm not. I'm hard up and desperate for an object that runs on batteries."

His hands floated down to my hips where he held me tight, digging his fingertips into my flesh hard enough to possibly leave bruises. When my gaze met his, the world quit spinning and I feared I'd float away. The lack of judgment in his calming green orbs ignited a fire within me.

And suddenly, it was as though the earth no longer had any oxygen.

He lowered his forehead to mine, not once breaking eye contact, and whispered, "There's no need to be embarrassed. We all do it, so pretending we don't is just silly."

"Is this supposed to make me feel better?"

"That's the goal, yeah. Is it working?"

"Not until the evidence of you doing it falls at my feet." If only I hadn't been staring into his eyes before I made that proclamation, I just might've been able to hear it in my head before ever allowing those words to tumble out of my mouth.

His huffed mirth burst across my face in a rush of air. "If you really want me to…"

"Forget I said that." I turned my head and pushed out of his hold, finally giving in and allowing myself to laugh at…myself. "Come on. Let's go home."

He made it around the front of the car, back to the passenger side, but as I turned to climb back in, my heel must've skimmed a rock and I went down. In order to protect my knees from landing on the street, I extended my arms in a thoughtless attempt to catch my fall, and immediately felt the burn in my palms. A split second after the sting tore through my hands, a bone-deep throb shot up my shin from my ankle. I twisted around to sit on my bottom and pressed my back against the front tire so I could pull my leg to my chest.

No matter how much pain radiated through my body, I held in the sobs. With my eyes squeezed closed and my teeth gritted together, I lowered my forehead to my knee and fought to maintain control of my breathing. Then, what seemed like hours later, I heard my name called out in panic. It was rough and cracked and desperate, and it sank into me.

Holden came around the car again and knelt in front of me. "What the hell happened?"

I rested the back of my head against the car and took several long, slow, deep breaths. "I think I twisted my ankle. I stepped on something and my foot went one way and my leg went the other. It hurts so bad, Holden."

Wordlessly, he slipped one arm behind my back and the other beneath my knees, encouraging me to wrap my arms around his neck so he could lift me bridal style. With every step around the hood to the passenger seat, where he carefully set me down and buckled me in, I fought against the tears. Yes, my ankle hurt, but I was also embarrassed—even more so than before—and just wanted this day to end. But thankfully, I didn't have to worry about anything. Holden took care of it all.

He drove me home, holding my hand the entire time, and then carried me inside, where he placed me on the couch while he pulled an ice pack from the freezer and a few pain relievers from the cabinet. Then he came to sit next to me, settled my legs in his lap, and proceeded to be my hero.

"What in the world made you wear high heels?" His fingertips lightly traced my foot while it rested on a pillow over his thighs. The TV was on, yet neither of us watched it. Instead, we kept our attention focused on each other.

"They were on sale and I thought they were cute—which they are, but it seems I'm not meant to wear them. I'm much happier in flats. You know…closer to the ground."

I DO

He pulled back the ice and winced. "It's ugly. It doesn't seem like you broke anything, but it's swollen and quickly turning colors. You need to keep it elevated tonight, and probably stay off it tomorrow."

"This is going to suck. You're going to be at work, and I'll be stuck here all alone, the cripple, unable to take care of myself."

"I'll see if Christine can come over and keep you company."

"Oh, joyous. Just what I've always wanted…a babysitter."

"Stop. I'm sure if you quit assuming everyone is against you, you'll probably start to see how much everyone enjoys being around you. Christine loves you. And the best part about that is she doesn't have to. She's not your sister and didn't grow up with you. She wants to be around you because she chooses to. Take a step back and you'll see the truth."

I waited a moment and watched him. He had his head reclined, eyes on the ceiling fan in the center of the room, and I found myself desperate to know what went through his mind. "Are we okay, Holden? You seemed upset today at dinner, but I don't know what I did wrong."

"You didn't do anything wrong," he responded, but he didn't look at me.

"Then what happened?"

"I don't know. I wish I had an answer for you but I don't. I guess the thought of you hanging out with me all day yesterday before meeting up with some guy for sex bothered me. I can't tell you why because it doesn't make sense."

My chest tightened with anticipation, praying he'd admit he was jealous, which only confused me more. "You know, I'm sure the next five and a half months would be a lot easier if we stopped fighting each other. If we called a truce and stopped trying to one up the other, maybe we might understand our feelings better."

His head fell to the side, and he locked eyes with me. "Like actually be friends again? For real and not pretend just to keep the other person from doing something crazy?"

"That'd be nice, right?"

"Yeah. I think so. Plus, that way, after our time is up and you get your divorce and gameshow prize money, we might want to hang out like normal people." He squeezed my good foot and offered a strained grin. "My biggest fear has always been that this would end and we'd have nothing to show for it. Because had I known when I knocked on your hotel door after the wedding that what we did that night would end our friendship, I would've gone straight to my own room."

My heart swelled at his honest, raw, and kind thoughts. However, it also fissured, knowing that no matter what, at the end of our arrangement, we would end. I wasn't sure why that bothered me, considering that had been my purpose in coming here. That had been my reason for agreeing to live with him, and it'd been the only thing I had thought about since hearing the news.

I wanted a divorce.

I wanted to end what we never had the chance to begin.

And knowing I'd get it broke my heart.

TEN

(Holden)

Ronnie sat on the edge of my desk after reading through an email she'd received and asked how I wanted her to proceed. Matt was off for the day, so everything seemed to land on my plate, and as if that wasn't enough, I'd somehow gotten stuck to her. Literally. As in the button on my shirt sleeve became attached to her skirt, and the more I pulled, the worse it got.

Apparently, things hadn't quite gotten bad enough, so the universe decided to choose that moment for Janelle to walk into my office. Of all the days, of all the times, she chose now to come visit me for the first time.

I glanced up, mouth hanging open in shock—and burning irritation. Ronnie peered over her shoulder, and Janelle froze, her gasp ringing out in the room. I didn't even get her name out of my mouth before she turned and fled out the doorway.

"Fuck it," I grumbled and tore my arm away from Ronnie's skirt, effectively ripping the button off my sleeve. "Janelle, wait."

We caught up with her in the hallway—her limp came to my advantage—and I grabbed her forearm to keep her from retreating.

"I didn't mean to interrupt anything." Aside from the apologetic tone in her voice, I could also pick up on the testiness. "The door was open so I didn't think to knock. I'll leave you two alone."

"Janelle, wait. Come back to my office. You came here for a reason, right?" That's when I noticed the bag in her other hand, and by the logo on the side, I knew it was food from my favorite deli down the street. "You brought me lunch? In that case, you're definitely not leaving."

"But what about...?" She turned her attention to Ronnie, whose smile gave away that she enjoyed this a little too much.

"Don't worry about me," Ronnie practically sang. "I'll be running off now. Enjoy your lunch."

Knowing Janelle would have a plethora of questions and more than a few vengeful statements on the tip of her tongue, I dragged her back to my office and closed the door behind us. "I had no idea you were coming up here." I sat in the seat next to her on the front side of my desk. "Why didn't you say anything?"

Even though we were the only ones in the room, her cheeks still turned pink and she refused to meet my gaze. "I was out running a few errands and noticed the time. I wasn't too far away from the office, and when I realized that I'd never seen where you and Matthew work, I thought I'd check it out. I knew he wasn't here today—therefore, I figured this would've been the best time to come so he wouldn't ask questions."

"What do you mean ask questions? About what?"

"You know...like why I'm here, what's going on between us. That sorta thing."

"Janelle, you live with me. I think it's safe for you to bring me lunch at work or come see my office. We don't have to be in a romantic relationship for you to do that. Friends visit each other at work all the time. And have lunch together." The more I talked, the darker her cheeks became. "Has anyone said anything to you already?"

I DO

"Not really. Last weekend at my parents' house, Nikki had assumed we were more than friends—that's where the whole mystery man came from. She said I had a glow and concluded it was you who put it there, and as soon as I told her we were just friends, everything spiraled."

I leaned back in my chair, slouching almost, and glanced down at the bag of food sitting next to her feet, which brought my attention to her ankle, reminding me of the slight limp she still had. Grabbing her leg by the calf, I directed it to my lap so I could take a closer look at it. There was still a little discoloration, but the swelling had almost all gone away.

"It's good to see you in sandals again," I teased after taking off her flip-flop.

She shook her head but huffed in laughter. "Yeah, I've accepted I'm just not meant to be sexy."

"What's that supposed to mean?"

Janelle gestured to the door and shook her head. "Like Veronica. She makes heels with jeans look like sex on a plate. Obviously, that's what guys go for. I can't pull that off. I'm a jeans with flip-flops kinda girl, and I guess I always will be."

I ran my hand over the top of her foot and up her shin, mesmerized by how smooth her skin was. Her feet seemed so tiny, even though I knew they were probably average, and her red toenails made them look dainty and unbelievably sexy. When I glanced up and met her stare, I realized I'd grown lost in her *feet*. I might've been embarrassed had it been anyone else, but this was the same girl I once caught stuffing her bra with water balloons.

"Jelly," I said with a grin, knowing she would assume I was teasing her, but I wasn't. "If you ask me, I prefer flip-flops on a woman. If I see someone dressed like you, I know they can hang. Whereas if I meet someone in jeans and heels, I would assume they're high maintenance. And for me, personally, I don't want someone who has to spend hours getting ready to go out. Or someone who can't leave if it's raining because of what it'll do to her hair. I like laidback." My words bounced around in my head, and I realized what I'd said, so I quickly tried to cover. "And I'm almost positive I'm not the only one."

She blinked at me as if I spoke in tongues. "You don't like people like Veronica?"

"I mean, I like them. I would just never choose to date them."

Her wide eyes swung from the door to me, back to the door, before finally settling on me. "So…is she only a booty call or something? I guess I got the impression she was more than that. Spending the night? I'd never sleep over at a guy's house if we were only hooking up. And I'd certainly never go to their office." She must've realized where she was, because she shook her head and waved me off. "Well, you know what I mean."

I couldn't help but laugh, and the more I did it, the quieter she became. When it turned into bellowing chuckles, she squinted her eyes and silently willed me to answer her unasked questions, her confusion coloring her entire face.

However, I decided to have a bit more fun before I gave in. "Oh, I'm not interested in Veronica."

"But she…" Her eyes moved to my desk, where Ronnie and I had been stuck together when Janelle had first walked in, then she glanced back at me. "And she spent the night a couple of weeks ago. Unless you lied to me."

I held my right hand up, as if taking a pledge. "I didn't lie to you. She did stay over that night."

"Oh." Her brows arched, her mouth rounding to mimic her gasped word. "I guess I just thought that meant you guys were…" She shook her head. "Never mind. What you do in your time—and on your desk—is your business." She tried to

I DO

pull her foot from my lap, but I held on and refused to let it go.

"What do you think happened on my desk, Jelly?" I cocked my head and raised an eyebrow.

"I honestly have no idea, nor do I care to hear."

"My button was stuck to her skirt."

"Like I said, Holden...I don't care. It's none of my business. And I think you know me well enough to know I won't tell Matthew about it, either. What you do here when he's gone is on you. You both own this place, and—"

"She works here, Janelle."

That seemed to stop her. After blinking a few times, she asked, "Veronica works here? What is she? Wait, no. You know, I said I'd stay out of it, but if we're really friends, I feel like I should give you some advice. Take it or leave it, that's up to you, but I strongly suggest you not get involved with people who work for you. Aside from it being messy, there's a whole legal thing I'm sure you don't want to deal with."

"She's the office assistant."

"Regardless of what she is—" As if just now realizing the words we'd both spoken, she abruptly stopped and shook her head. "The *office* assistant? What happened to Ron...or Ronald, or whatever his name was? And does Christine know about her?"

"Yes. And Christine loves her very much."

"Again...what happened to Ron?"

I smirked and leaned closer. "Janelle, do you mean Ronnie?" I waited for it to click in her head, but I apparently had to spell it out for her. "Ve*ron*ica?"

Finally, with the added emphasis on that one syllable, Janelle got it. "Really? This whole time I've imagined an older, balding, fat guy named Ron. And *that's* who it's been all along? I feel bad for any girl you end up dating...having to

149

worry about that sex kitten while you're at work. Knowing at any point she could be in here, perched on your desk with your hand up her skirt...pretending your button got stuck."

I held up my arm to show her the sleeve, which had thread hanging and an empty button hole. "It really was stuck. I had to rip it off in order to break away from her to come after you and my lunch."

"Sounds tragic." She seemed bored, but I told myself it was because she didn't believe me. And I pretended she didn't because she was jealous of Ronnie. And then I lied to myself and said I didn't care if she was envious or not.

"Any woman I date never has to worry about me cheating on them with Ronnie."

"Why? Are you that much of an asshole that you'd have her fired?"

"No. They just wouldn't have to worry about that. If anything, I'd have to worry about Ronnie hitting on them." When she turned her confused eyes at me, I couldn't hold back the widening grin stretching my lips. It was time to end the charade of Ronnie and my pseudo-sexual relationship. "She very much prefers your gender."

"Veronica? She likes women?" It was as if I could hear the wheels turning in her head. "But she slept in your room."

"Yeah, like I said...high maintenance. Trish, her wife—significant other, better half, whatever you want to call her—has an issue with Ronnie's spending habits and got mad over her purchasing a pair of shoes, so she came over to give Trish time to cool off. It's happened more times than either of us cares to admit."

"Then why didn't you tell me that? You let me believe you'd invited a woman over after we agreed we wouldn't do that. We talked about it in the kitchen that night...so why not tell me then?"

I DO

"I was pissed, Janelle. You invited your future hubby into *my* home while I was gone, and I assumed—just like you did—that more happened. I didn't go out of my way to get back at you, but I also didn't do anything to stop it. I'm sorry."

"I can't believe I almost broke my ankle to look like her," she muttered under her breath.

I wanted to say something about that remark, to question her motivation, but I knew to leave it alone. It was none of my business why she wanted to emulate Ronnie, and any reason I could've come up with on my own only opened the door for hope. And that was something I couldn't handle again. I'd lived with it on and off for a year or more after our night together in Vegas before I decided to get over it and move on. I couldn't afford to have my insides twisted up like that again.

I was a numbers guy...I needed certainty, and questioning Janelle's feelings toward me would never equal anything that concrete.

Knowing we needed to move on from the topic of Ronnie, I grabbed the bag of food and opened it to see what she'd picked up. We each took a container, and after I moved around the desk to sit in my office chair, we began to eat.

"The other night, you mentioned you wanted to be an event planner? I think I missed half that conversation, because I don't understand what you meant by not being able to get hired anywhere." I'd wanted to ask her additional questions when she'd brought the topic up, but it hadn't felt like the right time. Not to mention, I'd spent most of my time around her pouting and acting like a wounded puppy.

"If I worked at one of the hotels in the area that offers that service, then I wouldn't be able to open my own business in town due to the non-compete clause I'd have to sign. Not to mention, there are only two hotels around here that have space big enough to offer events."

"Why can't you just get hired by someone else?"

She swallowed her bite and then set down her fork, as if she needed all her energy to explain. "Event planning isn't usually this big industry—unless you're in New York City or a metropolitan capital like Los Angeles. In smaller areas, there isn't much of a need. Aside from weddings, why would you need to hire someone? Think about it...a birthday party or graduation is something you can put together yourself. And most people do. Weddings are different because no one wants to be responsible for something going wrong, but nowadays, most of those are housed at hotels."

"So what's your plan? You want to start your own business? Even though you just admitted there's no demand for it?" I thought about her explanation, and my stomach knotted up at the only plausible answer. "Or are you planning on moving to a big city?"

"Oh, no. I would never survive in a big city. I want to build a foundation here by simply offering what others don't. Be unique and stand out, and make it possible for ordinary people to afford an event planner. Organizing any event is stressful, and I want to take the burden off a mother's shoulders so she can enjoy her daughter's sweet sixteen."

"But I thought you just said those types of jobs aren't available here."

"I think the event opportunities are here. The people just don't know they need me, or more importantly, afford me...yet. You don't have to throw a big-budgeted occasion to hire an event planner."

"So what are you waiting for? It seems to me like you have everything planned out."

She licked her lips and turned her attention back to the container of pasta in front of her. "I don't have the money, remember? I won't get it until I marry Connor, and I can't do that because I'm playing house with you."

"Then let me help."

Her bright-blue gaze snapped to mine. "No. I won't take your money."

"Consider it a loan. You'd have to get a loan from a bank anyway, right?"

"Yeah, but I'd much rather get it from an actual institution than you."

I had no idea why, but hearing her say that wounded me. I didn't want her to know the pain she caused, so I played it off. "Well, let me know if you change your mind or want to start looking at office spaces. I'd be happy to help you get things prepared so when you do get the money, you don't have to wait."

She offered me a genuine smile. "Thank you."

We finished eating in silence, but once all the trash was thrown away, desperation ate at my core. I knew she'd be leaving soon and I didn't want her to go. "We should do this more often. Not lunch—that's not what I mean. But eating together. You know, at home, after I get off work. Why do we have to eat separately every night?"

Ever since our truce last weekend, she'd started to make me other things than just sandwiches. Monday night, she'd fixed hot dogs—although we didn't have buns so I had to eat mine on sandwich bread. Tuesday, I got buttered noodles. Still, I didn't complain. I was happy with what I got, and actually enjoyed every bite.

"You want us to eat dinner together?" The way she asked made it sound like I'd suggested we intimately eat off each other's naked bodies.

"Yeah. You know, like two ordinary people. Friends. Roomies. Kinda like we just did, but in the evening, at home, at a table not a desk." Finally, that got her to smile and relax. "We can try it tonight, and if it's just too uncomfortable for you, then we can go back to eating at two completely different times, and not even sit with each other."

To my utter surprise, when I walked inside after work, beat and exhausted from a rough day, I found Janelle in the kitchen with a fucking apron on. I bit my tongue to halt all the smartass remarks that were begging to surface. Instead, I stepped up behind her and watched as she proudly scooped macaroni and cheese onto two plates. I helped grab drinks and spoons and then met her at the table.

Conversation was stilted for a few minutes while we both adjusted to the company, but after a couple bites of the noodles coated in orange sauce that had originated from powder and meant to pass as cheese, I hummed and said, "This is amazing. Thank you."

She smiled, and it may have just been me, but she seemed to relax and eat easier.

I felt good about this—but I refused to analyze why.

ELEVEN

(Janelle)

Over the next few weeks, Holden and I had grown closer, and it definitely repaired the core of our friendship. However, we still hadn't brought up anything major. Other than our initial conversation about why we'd gotten married to begin with, that night hadn't come up again. There had been many times I'd wanted to question him, ask about what else occurred and the following day when he left. My mind refused to let go of the past, specifically what had taken place the rest of that summer, and basically, the last five years. But I never asked. Things seemed to be going well between us, and the last thing I wanted to do was drudge up the past, so rather than poke and prod, I went with the flow and tried to enjoy our time together as much as possible.

"Have you given any additional thought about the space we looked at yesterday?" he asked on the way to my parents' house for our weekly family dinner. "It's a really good location, so I worry it won't be available for long. The realtor said something about it just being listed in the last week—I think that's what he said."

For the last three Saturdays, Holden had taken me to look at storefront options. To entertain him, I went along and pretended to show interest. After all, it wasn't like I'd even be able to afford these places. But I kept my mouth closed and humored him with it because he'd told me it was nothing more than looking at options so I could have a plan for when I received my money. Needless to say, this was the first time he made any mention of doing more than "window shopping."

"We've discussed this already, Holden. I can't sign a lease yet."

"Yeah, but if we find something perfect, we should go ahead and grab it, because it more than likely won't be available later. These shops go quickly...trust me."

I ignored how he spoke of this as if it were a joint venture. "It doesn't matter how perfect it is, because I can't afford it right now. You keep finding these places smack dab in the heart of town. In order to find something within my budget, I'll have to get something on the outskirts, probably shoved back in the wooded area off Herron Street." I shuttered and added, "Who knows how many bodies are out there in those woods. Everyone knows they're haunted, and that won't be much of a selling point to welcome people in the front door."

"Exactly, which is why you should pick one of the ones we've looked at. Stop worrying about the money. I can help, and before you freak out, let me explain. You already know you're getting that money from the show, right? So you should let me help you get what you want and deserve now, and then you can just pay me back when you get the cash."

Moments like these, when he made comments about the money I'd get for marrying Connor, left me extremely confused. There were days where we got along so well, even I could've been convinced we were a real couple and had a strong chance of ending up together. I could've allowed myself to believe he was in love with me, always had been, and his motive from the very beginning was to make me feel the same. Yet it never failed, as soon as I began to believe we were both on the same page, he'd go and mention Connor—

without actually using his name—or nonchalantly bring up how much time we had left before he signed the papers. I couldn't understand why those words would leave me so dejected.

"I don't know for sure that I'll be awarded that money. What if Connor randomly decides he doesn't want to do it anymore, or there's some other twist in the rules? That's too much to risk. I'd rather just wait to make a move until I have the check in my hand. As of right now, this is just a pipe dream. It's just something I want to start without any clue at all that I can pull it off."

Surprising me, he reached over the console and took my hand, lacing our fingers together. "It's not a pipe dream, Jelly." He'd started taking on the nickname more often, except now he used it as an endearment and without the teasing implied. It puzzled me, but for whatever reason, I kind of liked it when he used it affectionately. "Look at what Matt and I did. We graduated from college, got our CPA licenses, and without ever working for another firm or even owning a business, we opened Brewer and York. Trust me, I know all about the pressures of starting your own dream—from the ground up—and the money you have to borrow and pay back." He squeezed my hand once. "I get it. And that's why I want to do what I can to help. We can start small. That place we looked at yesterday would be perfect. It's not too big, but at the same time, you won't outgrow it within a year, either."

"I know...but the *price*. And I have to sign a two-year contract. What if I manage to start it up and then I fail? Then I'm stuck with a lease I can't afford for two years."

"I really don't think you have anything to worry about."

"You don't know this, because you've never seen me work. How could you possibly have any faith in me to plan events, when you've never seen me put one together?"

"You're incredibly organized, and I think that illustrates quite a bit. Not to mention, when you go to the grocery store, you always find the best deals. Like when we went to get stuff for your bathroom, you made sure everything was practical — not just for now, but for after you leave, too. It's those little things that make me know you'll succeed and be amazing." The entire time he spoke, he kept his attention to the road ahead of him and refused to look my way. "Not to mention, I've heard you talk about your selling points and how you want to run the business. You've told me how you plan to offer services others don't. I believe in you, Janelle."

"Regardless, I would hate it if I couldn't repay you. It's not like I plan to stiff a bank on a loan, but I'd feel better doing that than taking your money and having to alter our agreement. You mean too much to me to do that."

When we pulled into the driveway and parked behind Matt's Jeep, I glanced around and noticed we were the only two cars here. I knew Nikki and Shane had taken their three girls on vacation to Disney before the start of school in a couple of weeks, but I had no idea where the others were.

"I wonder where Stacey and Rachel are." It was more of an outspoken thought to myself than anything; I didn't expect Holden to have the answers.

He met me around the front of the car on the way toward the front door and said, "Oh, they aren't coming. Tony isn't feeling well, so Stacey decided her and the kids would stay home with him, and Rachel's in-laws are in town. They're leaving tomorrow, so Rachel and Steve will be back next weekend for Labor Day."

My mouth hung open while I stared at him and blinked for added dramatic effect. "How do you know all this about my family? I was here last weekend, same as you, but I don't recall any discussion about in-laws, and how in the world do you know about Tony being sick?"

I DO

Holden grew quiet while he continued to the front porch. "Matt told me about Tony, and you must've missed the conversation last weekend about Steve's parents, because it was talked about exhaustively. Your mom even commented about taking suggestions from others for the weekly family meal since Rachel's usually the one who picks for her."

"Oh…I guess I must not have been in the room."

We made it to the door, but right before opening it, Holden turned to me with a straight face and intense gaze. "It was talked about at the table, during dinner."

I was speechless, confused as to how I could've missed an entire conversation happening around me.

Then his lips parted to show off his cheesy smile, the one that made it obvious how funny he thought he was. "You had taken the kids to the bathroom to wash up before supper. It didn't occur to me to say anything to you about it later because I didn't think it was that big of a deal."

"You're an asshole." I shoved at him and made him open the front door so we could walk inside. "You let me believe I'd blocked out an entire conversation."

Christine pulled herself from the couch and greeted us both with hugs before dragging me into the kitchen to help Mom with dinner. Apparently, with only half her daughters here, Mom couldn't be alone while cooking and needed our assistance. At least, that's what Christine mumbled under her breath on our way to the kitchen.

"Anything new going on with you and Holden?" she asked after we took our seats on the barstools in front of the sink.

I quickly glanced at my mom, hoping she hadn't heard, and then stared at Christine, offering her a death glare for bringing it up in front of my mother. Christine then waved me off just as Mom said, "You think I haven't been just as interested? There's a reason she brought it up in front of me. Poor girl is probably tired of hearing me ask if she knows anything."

"Really, Ma? You're talking about me when I'm not around?"

"No." She glanced up and gave me a very serious expression. "I've simply called Christine a few times to ask if she's heard anything about a possible budding relationship between you two. It's not like I'm talking behind your back. I'm purely seeking information about my youngest child." And just like that, she went back to layering the lasagna in the pan.

There were so many things I wanted to point out, if not question, but decided against fighting a battle I couldn't win. With my arms folded in front of me, I settled in to explain—apparently, to both of them. "We're not going to get together, so you both might as well stop waiting for the impossible to happen. And where did your sudden interest come from, Christine?"

"I don't know. I love you both and think you're so good together."

"Yeah, because we're friends. That's all we've ever been and that's the end of it. It'd be too weird if we were more than that. He's like a brother, for heaven's sake."

"No offense, but I don't see you look at Matty like that, Jelly." Christine smirked.

I shot her a thankless glare.

"Your father is my best friend," Mom added in her singsong voice. She closed the oven door and leaned against the counter with her hip, pointing her motherly stare my way.

"And Matty's mine." Christine propped her chin on her fist and offered me a smug grin. "I think that's the whole point. Right? You marry your best friend. So your argument isn't very valid."

160

I DO

"Well, at the very least, you should love the person you marry, and more than the way you love a friend. Unfortunately, we don't feel *that* way about each other. He's a great guy, and I love him the same way I love you," I said to Christine. "But that's about it. And I'm rather confident he'd agree with me."

"Agree with what?" Holden's deep voice filled the room from behind me.

My breathing stalled. Quit. Mid inhale, it just gave up and decided to go on strike. I craned my neck to peer over my shoulder and caught the sight of his devious smirk—the epitome of *the cat that ate the canary*. Of all his expressions, it had always been on the top of my favorites. But it was special, because he didn't hand that one out often, and only those close to him got to witness it.

His soft eyes shone, the mossy green turning more steel, while the bursts of brown took over and lit up like gold beneath the sun's rays. His high cheekbones heated with the tiniest dusting of blush, and that mouth...curved to one side, the top quirked higher to add the illusion of a sneer entwined with his grin. However, no matter how many times I'd seen it before, or how it made me feel, this one was different.

He directed it right at me.

And only me.

Normally, everyone in the room would've been rewarded with it, but not this time. While he approached the breakfast bar where I sat perched next to Christine, his fiery gaze and panty-melting grin practically hypnotized me. And as if I were in a movie, everything around me faded into nothingness as he drew closer, almost cautiously.

It made me wonder if he felt the same thing.

A magnetic pull. A need to be close.

He gripped the back of my stool—as well as the back of Christine's—and peered down at me, almost hovering over me. When he spoke, his husky words danced over my face and brought me back to the present. "What would I agree to?"

"That we're friends."

"Yes. I definitely agree with that."

Other than adjusting her elbow on the counter to lean into it more, Christine didn't move. She watched us, and out of the corner of my eye, I could see her Machiavellian grin. "I was convinced that after living together for over a month, one of you would be bald. Or on blood pressure medication." Then she lowered her voice and added, "Or suffering a severe, on-going case of blue balls."

"Christine!" I locked my stare on her and reprimanded her with a hiss.

Holden dropped his chin, shook his head, and laughed beneath his breath. And somehow, after all that had been said, nothing crippled me as much as his next words when he said, "You couldn't be more wrong."

I wanted to smack Christine or run away—or both—but I wasn't given a chance. Just then, Mom decided to rejoin the conversation. "I wouldn't have guessed hair loss or blood pressure issues. Maybe diabetes with as much crap as Jelly eats and drinks. Although, my money would be on Holden making her healthier, because he's such a well-balanced young man." Her rambling had me rolling my eyes and Holden puffing out his chest in exaggerated pride. Then, when we all thought she was done, she narrowed her questioning gaze at us and inquisitively asked, "But what are blue balls?"

Had I been drinking, liquid would've spurted out of my mouth like a sprinkler turning on for the first time all summer. Instead, all three of our mouths dropped open, and you could've heard a pin drop with as silent as we all went—

considering we probably all stopped breathing and our hearts ceased to beat.

Thankfully, Mom realized it on her own. Her eyes turned abnormally bright and her mouth fell agape. Then she clutched her chest with *both* hands—which was a sure sign that her response was genuine and not leaning to the side of dramatic. "Oh, never mind. I wasn't thinking."

My mom's reaction must've been too much for Holden, because he backed away and made some comment about joining Matthew and my dad outside. And the second he left the room, Christine pointed her know-it-all expression at me.

As if we hadn't just been taken by surprise by my mother's gaffe, Christine picked up where we left off prior to Holden's interruption. "Something has to be going on between you guys. The way he looked at you when he came in here…" She shook her head and fanned her face. "If you didn't see the way he looked at you like you were about to be his next meal, then you're utterly blind."

"Speaking of meals…" My mom leaned over the counter with her arms folded in front of her chest. "You're at least cooking for the boy, aren't you? When he comes home after a long day at work, the first thing he needs is a good meal. Please tell me you're giving that to him. None of that canned food garbage, right?"

"Don't worry, Mom. Every day when he comes home from work, he has dinner waiting for him at the table. Dinner I made myself. In fact, tonight will be the third time this week we've had lasagna—granted, the second time was leftovers." I only hoped she didn't keep prodding, because I wasn't sure how much more I would be able to spin her words around to keep her from knowing the truth.

"You need to give him variety, Jelly. Haven't I taught you anything? Men like options, and the less you give them on the dinner table, the more they'll give of themselves in the bedroom. The trick is to keep his mind occupied with food. Spice it up one night, keep it mellow the next. Dress it up with parsley or lay it on thick with gravy. As long as his stomach is full, his taste buds are satisfied, and dessert includes either chocolate or whipped cream, you'll be good to go."

"Mom!" Christine and I both shouted at the same time. Christine covered her ears, but I was too taken aback and shocked to move.

"Hold on." Mom waved us off and went around the bar to the pantry. "I have a couple cookbooks you can use. The trick is to never make the same meal twice, so once you make one, go on to the next."

Christine adjusted her stool so she faced me. She leaned closer and lowered her voice to say, "Had I known you already made lasagna this week, I would've asked for something else. Now I feel bad that Holden has to eat it again."

"Don't feel bad. This one might actually taste good, so I'm sure he won't mind at all."

She quirked a brow and tilted her chin down to eye me. "How do you mess up lasagna? I honestly don't think I've ever *not* liked it, no matter who made it. I mean, unless you forget an ingredient or something. Is that what happened?"

"Not quite." I'd been cooking for Holden for a few weeks now—and by that, I mean more than sandwiches and hot dogs—and not once had I felt ashamed about the dinners I'd offered him. At least, not until this very moment when I knew someone other than myself would find out my secret. "It was one of those family-sized frozen meals."

"Ran out of time to make dinner? Been there, done that. Although, those are typically the nights I play it off like I did it on purpose and make Matty take me out to eat. He never needs to know I simply forgot to take meat out of the freezer."

"Yeah...ran out of time. Forgot to thaw meat. We'll go with that."

With a puzzled expression, she asked, "What do you mean?"

"Christine, I can't cook. I lived on buttered noodles and pizza in college. How in God's name am I supposed to give Holden dinner every night without offering him the same thing over and over again if I can't prepare a decent meal?"

She fought against her smile, which tightened her lips yet still curled them in the corners.

I dropped my forehead to the bar top and groaned. "Mom's getting me a cookbook I won't be able to use. When I say I don't cook, it's not because I don't like it. It's because I literally don't know how." I sat up straight again and met her stare. "Well, I know the concept of cooking. It's just every time I try, I mess it up in one way or another."

"It's all in your head. You just have to start off small and work your way up. Like make chicken and rice and go from there. No one can mess that up." She studied my expression for a moment and then giggled to herself. "I'll call you in the morning so you can write it all down. It's really the easiest thing to make and barely takes any time at all to prep."

Just then, Mom returned from the pantry and set the book in front of me. "Your grandmother gave this to me when I first married your father. The other three used to help me in the kitchen when they were younger, so I didn't think about giving it to them when they got married. But I guess that was a good thing, because now you can have it."

"I don't need this, Ma. I'll be fine."

"No. You're my last daughter, so take it. If I wait to give it to you as a wedding gift, I might be long gone by then. So I might as well do it now."

All I could do was swallow my need to groan and roll my eyes. "Enough with the dramatics. You're sixty, not a hundred. Both Rachel and Stacey were older than I am when they got married, so you never know, I could surprise you all and be married in six months."

"Then good, take this and maybe it'll bring you wedding-bell luck."

I ran my fingertips over the front of the cookbook, taking note of the worn edges and grooves. If I believed in magic, I might've suspected this old book of having powers, because for some reason, I found the idea of cooking something new for Holden exhilarating. "Thank you, Mom."

And deep down, I had a strange yearning to discover what it would be like to be a real wife, one who could actually cook instead of just heat up premade meals. And with my mother's unknowing help, I felt confident I would be able to find out—I would be able to experience the role of a wife, without all that comes with it.

If only I could convince Holden to let me experience *all* the good marital parts without the baggage. Then I really wouldn't have an issue staying with him until the divorce papers are signed...not that I really had one anymore.

TWELVE

The timer on the oven beeped as soon as I closed the front door behind me. I heard Janelle in the kitchen moving around and the clang of pots and pans. My stomach rumbled, something smelling good. A smile immediately took over my face as I made my way through the living room. This was the first time I'd come home to actual food—not that country fried steak in the microwave isn't real food, but I could tell just by the aroma that this wasn't bought on a frozen food aisle. I made it to the edge of the kitchen when I heard her curse beneath her breath.

"Something smells good." It may have been the same line I recited every day when I walked through the front door, but I *really* meant it this time. I moved to stand behind her, and with a hand on her hip, I lifted the lid on the stockpot and peered inside from over her shoulder. "What's for dinner?"

"Christine called this morning and gave me detailed instructions on how to make this recipe. She swore up and down that it was foolproof, and there's no way I could mess it up." It was obvious she was extremely irritated by the melodramatic way she spoke, overly enunciating her words, and for some unknown reason, saying them in a lower octave as if mimicking a man. However, Christine wasn't a man, which only meant one thing—Janelle had long ago passed

167

frustration and had moved toward downright furious. "But apparently, it is possible to mess it up...*because I did*. No matter how long I cook the rice, it's still hard and there's still water on the bottom."

She proceeded to elbow me out of the way in order to pull the chicken out from the oven.

After setting it on an empty burner, she tossed the oven mitt aside and huffed. "And the chicken doesn't look right. I'm pretty sure it shouldn't still be clucking."

I tried not to laugh, I really did, but I couldn't hold it in. The way she pouted was not only adorable, but hysterical, as well. Once I got it all out, and she finished slapping me for the last time, I glanced over the food she lovingly attempted to cook me. And it dawned on me. Really hit me like a two-ton truck...

Janelle Brewer cooked for me.

And if salmonella wasn't a real threat, I would've eaten it just like that. However, I didn't care to spend the night in the bathroom due to food poisoning, so I held onto her shoulder, my fingers extending to the back of her neck to keep her attention, and said, "It's not a total loss. The chicken just needs to be cooked a bit longer."

"I set it to three fifty and put it in there for as long as she told me to. I even moved the rack to the middle like she said. I did *everything* she told me to do. Foolproof, my ass."

I was rather certain I knew what the problem was, but I worried I would insult her if I were wrong. However, I didn't care and asked her anyway. "Did you wait until the oven had preheated, or did you just stick it in there as soon as you set the temp?"

"I never preheat ovens and haven't had a problem yet."

"You mean...when you heat up frozen dinners that are technically pre-cooked?" I honestly hadn't meant it as an insult, but the way she stood in front of me, eyes blinking rapidly, no words coming out, I knew she was more than likely contemplating the quickest escape route. "You know what? Let's just stick this chicken back in the oven, and we'll make a new pot of rice."

"It's pointless. I'll throw this out, and we can order pizza or something."

"Why can't we just stick the chicken back in the oven and start a new pot of rice?"

"Because you're probably hungry. Not to mention, it's very obvious I don't know how to cook. Like, at all." She shoved the paper with the recipe on it in my face. "I'm pretty sure an illiterate chimpanzee could've followed these directions better."

I set the handwritten recipe down, choosing to ignore the obvious reason the rice didn't cook—she used a sixteen-quart stockpot for two cups of rice with a lid that didn't fit properly. Instead, I held her face in my hands and attempted to calm her down. However, I didn't actually think about the words before I said them. "Can you not cook? Is that why you've been feeding me Marie Callender's for the last month?"

She gave me the death glare and tried to shove me away.

"Don't be embarrassed. I'm not at all making fun of you— I swear. Hell, the only reason I know how to cook is because Matt moved out, and I had to learn. It was either that or starve. Well, I guess I did have the option of takeout, but I didn't see the point in throwing money away. What kind of accountant would that make me?"

At least she stopped pushing me away. Her lips split into a wide grin, and it seemed as though her giggles refused to relent. "Dude...I've been feeding you Stouffer's for weeks. Did you think I was just lazy and didn't want to fix dinner or something?"

Her lips were mere inches away. Her body so close I could easily touch her. Realizing just how dangerous that was, I stepped away to give us space. I grabbed the pot off the stove and dumped the rice down the drain before setting it aside. "Honestly? I thought you were trying to prove a point. Kind of like you've done with everything else."

"I will admit, at first, I fed you sandwiches to spite you. You made me feel like hired help, someone who's at your beck and call for all the *womanly* duties of the house. You'd leave behind a list of things you wanted me to pick up at the grocery store without so much as a 'could you please grab these things if you go out?' And then you said you wanted dinner every night when you came home, like I'm technically your wife so I am expected to provide you these things. Your chauvinism bothered me. Pissed me off to the point that I sought revenge. I didn't want to feel like that was all I was worth."

"I thought we—"

"We did, Holden. That's why I said *at first*. Then we called a truce, and after that, I can honestly say I gave dinner a genuine attempt. When you mentioned wanting to eat together, I figured you meant *real* food. Like…not macaroni and cheese from a box. I assumed that was your way of asking for *real* meals. Except I can't cook *real* food, so the only option I had was frozen crap from a box—which you were never supposed to know about."

Measuring water for the rice, I stood at the sink and asked, "Did you think I was under the impression you cooked all that? Yourself? From scratch? You do know I've eaten food before, right?"

She elbowed me before grabbing the stockpot from the counter. And rather than explain to her why we couldn't use it, I moved around her and pulled a smaller pot from the cabinet and continued with the rice, knowing she was watching me and *hopefully* taking notes while we finished our conversation.

"Well…maybe not from scratch, but yeah. I thought it was good enough to fool you. I mean, I used the oven. There were a few things I made on the stove, and I opened some cans. Not to mention, I stored them in the freezer in the garage and threw the boxes away *outside*. How could you have possibly known?"

"Even if I couldn't taste the difference between food someone prepared from scratch versus something that had been previously frozen and bought at a store? Janelle, I came home several times before you had a chance to move them from the cardboard they came in into a real dish."

"Whatever. I put a decent effort into those meals. I can't help it still sucked."

I placed the lid on top of the rice to simmer and set the timer before turning my attention back to Janelle. With my hands on her face, I silently took her in. I admired her exotic and intoxicating beauty, how effortless it seemed to be for her. Even without all the paint on her face, she was…perfect.

"And I appreciated every single one of them," I whispered, not having a clue as to where my voice had gone. Just then, we were interrupted by the obnoxious buzzing sound from her phone vibrating on the countertop next to us.

We both glanced over, probably reading his name at the same time. Never had two syllables bothered me the way those two did.

I stepped back, as if she had ignited into flames and burned me, while she lunged for her phone. It didn't matter how fast she grabbed it, because the damage had been done. In fact, I didn't even care if she ignored it or answered it.

My stomach had soured, and I couldn't stop my mind from racing. Aside from randomly mentioning the money she'd get for marrying this asshat, we hadn't spoken about him. She hadn't brought him up or even said his name aloud. I had no reason to believe she wasn't in contact with him, but for whatever reason, I had convinced myself she wasn't. Which proved to have been a horrible idea, considering the truth could be crippling.

I excused myself from the kitchen, went to my room, and closed the door behind me to change clothes. It didn't take me that entire time to put on something more comfortable to eat in, but I didn't come out until I heard the timer on the oven go off. I refused to risk hearing her converse with him. I didn't even want to acknowledge there had been a conversation I'd ignored.

When I made it back to Janelle, we both fell into place, moving silently around the kitchen as though this was our regular, nightly routine. I grabbed the pan of chicken from the oven just as Janelle reached around to turn off the burner on the stove. She got the dishes, I pulled out the silverware, and as if we were some well-oiled machine who'd done this for the last fifty years, we helped our plates and then made our way to the table.

I cut a piece of chicken, scooped up some rice on the fork, and much like every other night, hummed as soon as the food touched my tongue. "This is amazing, Janelle," I mumbled between bites, like I did with every meal, after every first mouthful I took.

Normally, she'd smile and take all the credit for whatever meal she'd transferred from the freezer to the table, but this time, she didn't. Rather than say anything, she sat there, fork in hand, food untouched on the plate in front of her, and stared across the table at me. Just stared. With a grin lazily tugging on her lips, and my heart beating with so much gusto I could hear it echo in my ears.

"Everything all right?" I asked with caution, worried about her reaction.

"Yeah. Everything's great."

"You're kinda making me worried with the way you're staring at me instead of eating. Like maybe your fork is going to haphazardly land in my chest instead of your chicken."

"You clearly know how to cook. Not just crap, either, but real food. Good food. You can do it without a cookbook or recipe, and you don't have to stand in the kitchen to make sure you don't mess it up. So how come every night when you eat the shit I've fed you, you tell me how good it is? You and I both know it's not *amazing* like you claim."

Slowly, I set my fork down on the side of the plate and used a napkin to wipe my mouth. "I've never had anyone cook me dinner...not like this. I mean, I used to eat at your house when I was younger, but your mom didn't cook specifically *for* me, she fixed food for everyone. And my mom...well, she worked a lot. So when she wasn't home, the delivery guy fed me, and when she was home, we ate reheated takeout."

The infectious grin fell from her expression, and her eyes turned soft with concern.

"Don't feel bad for me. Most kids used to beg their parents for pizza or fast food. Me? I got that shit shoved in my direction without even asking for it. I was in heaven. In case you've forgotten, I wasn't some sad, lonely child. I wasn't neglected. I had your family, and got to enjoy plenty of meals around a bunch of people sitting at the same table every week."

"Yeah...I don't think my mom ever had food delivered to the house. And if we had fast food, she was probably sick and couldn't cook—although..." She tapped her chin and stared above my head. "There was at least one child at home who was old enough to make dinner if she couldn't."

"You'll never hear me complain. That woman fed me some of the best meals of my life. I used to tell Matt I needed to find a woman who knew how to make the same stuff your mom did, because I'd marry her and never let her go." I laughed beneath my breath and shook my head. "He told me she made up every recipe, and they were secret, that she would never tell anyone how to make them. So I said I'd marry her and be his stepdaddy, and he'd have to call me Father Dearest."

We both shared a laugh, followed by brief silence while we took bites of our food. "Who cooked for you in college when you lived with Matt?"

I winked and said, "Take a wild guess."

She pondered it for a moment before her lips tightened with mirth. "My mom?"

"Yup. She used to bring us pre-prepped meals for the week. All we had to do was heat them up."

"Oh my God, you two were so spoiled."

"I wasn't complaining." I shrugged while chewing another bite. "But all that changed when Matt started to date Christine. Your mom said it was time to grow up—I'm pretty sure those were her exact words when we went over there to collect our weekly meals, and she handed us each brand-new frying pans. Somehow, Matt convinced Christine to come over and she took over duties as head chef for at least a few nights out of the week. Then they got married and moved out, and I had to finally learn to do something for myself."

"Well, it's amazing. The food, I mean. *This* food." She snickered before shoving a forkful of rice into her mouth, and then swallowed it down with some water. "But at least we know one thing...our marriage was doomed from the start. You want a wife who can cook like my mom, and it's evident

I DO

I can't make anything that doesn't come out of a box with microwave instructions."

"Janelle…" I waited until I had her full attention, and then said, "Regardless, if it was a peanut butter and jelly sandwich or Hamburger Helper, I appreciate the time you spent to make it for me. So believe me when I tell you it's amazing."

She fluttered her eyes and went back to her plate.

She didn't believe me, but she didn't have to.

We joked while we finished eating, but she seemed quieter than normal. Part of me wondered if it had to do with her phone call, but I wasn't about to ask. I didn't care to know anything pertaining to that prick. Granted, I didn't want her to stay quiet, but if it was between that or listening to her talk about the loser, I'd take her silence in a heartbeat. I figured if it got too bad, I'd give her a book and ask her to read it out loud—maybe a cookbook, but only if she didn't find that offensive.

However, while washing the dishes, I realized something was wrong. When I asked her about it, she just said she was tired, but I knew it had to have been more than that. Her eyes were distant and she appeared worn out, exhausted. So I sent her to bed and finished cleaning the kitchen.

That night, I realized how lonely the house was without her. Even though we didn't always spend the evenings together, at least we were both home bustling around. Sometimes we watched TV, while other times, I watched it and she played on her phone—or vice versa. There had even been a couple nights we weren't in the same room, but I could hear her from across the house, and I was sure she could hear me, both of us knowing the other was within reach.

But this night, it was silent.

Eerily so.

I couldn't help but wonder what it would be like with her gone.

Forever.

And I didn't like how that made me feel.

THIRTEEN

(Janelle)

My phone buzzed on the table next to me, but I couldn't answer it. My head pounded and any amount of light only made it worse. Even the slightest movement exasperated my pain. And to add to that, my throat felt like it was on fire and punished me every time I swallowed. So I not only *couldn't* answer the phone, I had no desire to. It could've been the Pope himself calling, and I wouldn't have cared—unless he called with a magic prayer to heal me. That I would've gotten out of bed for. But nothing less.

I had no sense of time, no idea as to how many days I'd stayed curled up on the mattress, burrowed deep beneath the covers. It could've been a month for all I knew. I'd briefly wake up, immediately remember how much pain I was in, and then surrender to sleep once more. That's where I wanted to stay—in the unconsciousness where I didn't hurt and things were good. It's where I was able to live in sheer bliss with Holden forever and ever.

"Janelle," a soft voice whispered, sounding very much like an angel coming to take me away. *This is it*, I thought to myself, *I must've died, and now I'm going to heaven.* The angel touched my forehead and said, "Come on, Janelle. You need to get up. We have to take you to the doctor's office."

I groaned and rolled over, and that's when I knew I wasn't dead, nor was I on my way to the pearly gates in the sky. I cracked my eyes open enough to see Christine perched on the side of my bed. I tried to speak, tried to ask her why she was here, but all that came out was a sob followed by a hiccup of pure agony caused by the sob.

"Holden called me because he got worried. You haven't answered any of his calls. Now I can see why he was concerned. You're burning up, Janelle. We need to get you to a doctor."

Even the thought of getting out of bed was painful. I'd reached the point of desperation where I began to imagine taking an ice cream scooper to my tonsils and digging them out. I also imagined setting my bed on fire, because it was the only thing I could come up with that would keep me warm. As far as curing the headache, my only option at that point was to crack my skull open to allow room for the swelling.

Christine was right—I needed a doctor. A real one.

It wasn't normal to contemplate self-induced brain surgery to relieve a headache.

With her help, I managed to get up, dressed, and in her car. Although, it wouldn't surprise me to find out I was unconscious most of that time. I certainly couldn't recall the drive to the clinic or somehow making it inside. I was shivering under my covers one minute, and sitting in the waiting room of a very noisy clinic the next—still shivering, except without a blanket, and even more miserable than I'd been at home.

Christine sat in a chair next to me, her foot bouncing and her fingers twisting in her lap. She seemed jittery and anxious, and I wasn't sure why. The only thing I knew was when I focused on her, I felt a little bit better. Just enough to hold a conversation without crying.

I DO

"What's wrong?" My voice cracked and the words scratched their way out.

She turned to me with a knitted brow and darkened eyes. "What do you mean?"

"You can't sit still, like this is the last place on Earth you want to be. Which I totally get, by the way. I don't particularly care to be here, either. It's like an open invitation to get sick with all the germs just hanging out, waiting for a host to grab onto." As if my head and throat weren't bad enough, I was about to tack on a weak stomach. "If you have other things to do, you're more than welcome to leave and take care of them. I can just wait when I'm done for you to pick me up, or I'll call my mom to come get me. Or I could just curl up in the morgue and take a nap there…and hope the Grim Reaper takes pity on me and claims my spirit."

The worry lining her face began to lessen and morph into more of a sympathetic concern. "Hush. It's a clinic, not a hospital. There's no morgue here for you to go die in. You'll live, I promise." She paused and inhaled deeply. "And I don't have anything else to do. It's not that at all. I just don't like doctors' offices. They make me nervous…remind me of horribly sad moments in my life. It's rather depressing."

I reached over the armrest and took her hand in mine. "You're right. This place is horrible. You can totally take me back home now and let me sleep this plague off. I feel very confident that it'll kill me shortly, so there won't be much suffering."

"We're not going anywhere. Hopefully, they'll call you back soon."

The more I sat there with my hand in hers, watching her fidget, I couldn't help but think about her reason for disliking clinics. And not believing it for one second. There was something she wasn't telling me, something she kept to herself, and I felt compelled to get her to open up to me.

"No one likes to see the doctor, Christine. But unless it's a child afraid to get a shot, no one freaks out—especially if they aren't the one waiting to be seen. So really, what's going on?" I couldn't talk too loudly, but I knew she heard me.

She squeezed my hand and turned to offer me the saddest smile I'd ever seen her give. "It's nothing you need to worry about. You're sick, which is why we're here, so let's focus on that."

"You wanna focus on me being sick?" Had I not felt like I was teetering on the edge of hell, I would've scoffed. "Okay, let's do that. I have a fever, and I'm freezing cold. It's probably hot outside, it's summer, and I'm wearing sweatpants and a hoodie, yet I'm shivering and can't get warm. My throat is on fire, and at some point in my sleep last night, I snacked on broken glass because even swallowing my spit hurts. And I'm pretty sure my brain is turning into mush because it's swollen and has nowhere to go."

She pressed the back of her hand to my forehead and apologized with a sympathetic glance.

"There...we've focused on me. Now it's time for you to talk."

"It's nothing, Janelle. Really. I'll be okay. This isn't the first time I've been here and it won't be the last, so there's no point in obsessing over it. Let's just worry about getting you well so we can get you home and in bed."

I curled into the uncomfortable seat and closed my eyes, but not before uttering, "That's okay. I'll just ask Matthew. I'm sure he'll tell me what's going on."

My eyes may have been closed, but I could still hear her strangled breathing, as if I'd pushed her to the verge of breaking, and as much as I hated it, I knew she needed to talk. Christine and I had always been close ever since she first started dating my brother. We may not have been best friends or even spoken all the time, but we always seemed to have the kind of relationship that time couldn't affect. No matter how long we went without talking, as soon as we picked up the phone, it was like it'd been no time at all. So to know she suffered from something and I didn't know about it, even though I'd been in town for over a month and had seen her on many occasions, I couldn't help but feel crushed that she didn't feel like she could confide in me.

Unless…it had to do with Matthew.

My eyes snapped open in fear. I couldn't help but think about Holden saying my family needed me. I thought it had to do with Stacey, but as I sat here with Christine, my gut twisted, and I couldn't ignore the panic settling into my chest. "Is…is my brother okay?"

She turned to face me, sorrow deep in her eyes. "Yeah, he's okay."

"But whatever your issue is has to do with him, doesn't it?"

With a deep breath, she shifted in her seat like I had and curled into it while facing me, making our conversation as private as possible while being in the middle of a waiting room. "Do you really want to know? You want me to tell you here, at the doctor's office instead of at home?"

Home—or hell, even in the car when we leave here—would've probably made more sense. The most sense. But I couldn't wait, not now that I knew there was an issue, and whatever it was, I realized it had to have been serious with the way she looked at me.

"If you don't want to tell me, don't. If you want to, but not here, then wait. You have me really worried, I can't lie about that. But I understand if you don't want to tell me now. Just know that I'm always here for you. Always, Christine.

For you and Matt. Just because I'm younger, not in the same place in life that you two are, and haven't been around much over the years, doesn't mean I don't care or want to know what's going on with my family. At the end of the day, you're my sister-in-law. He's my brother. And whatever you're going through affects me, too."

Her eyes glistened with unshed tears, but they didn't fall. Instead, she took a moment to gather herself before taking my hand again in hers. "We got pregnant a couple of years ago. After a few months of trying, the test had a plus sign, and we were beyond excited. So we told my parents, your parents, and our close friends, because even though they say to not tell anyone, we couldn't keep it a secret."

My stomach flipped and knotted, knowing her next words even though I'd never heard them.

"We made it to nine weeks."

"Oh my God, Christine. I'm so sorry." I couldn't fight back the tears filling my eyes, which in turn made my head pound harder. But I pushed it away because Christine was more important.

"This is why I didn't want to say it here. There's no need to cry, honey. We're okay. We've made it through each and every time."

The world stopped spinning. "What do you mean…each and every time? How many times?"

"Enough to know there's something wrong."

"Which is…?"

She wiped away the errant tear from my face. "Doctors have no idea. All the tests have come back inconclusive. No one knows why my body rejects pregnancies. But don't say anything to anyone, please. We've never told your sisters about any of it, even though I wouldn't be surprised if they knew something. Your parents know about the first two, and I'm pretty sure Holden knows about the third. But since then,

I DO

Matt and I haven't said anything to anyone—not when we've found out about being pregnant, and not after we've lost it. We've dealt with this together. We've made it this far, and I know we'll make it all the way."

Had I not been sick and practically knocking on death's door, I would've probably come up with something better to say. But unfortunately for me, I didn't have that luxury. So I squeezed her hand and gave her all I had. "I'm so sorry I wasn't here for you guys. And I hate that there's nothing I can do. I just hope you and my brother know I'm here for you any way you need me, anytime you need me, no matter where I am."

"We know." A single tear tracked down her cheek before falling from her chin. "We'll be okay, though. There's no reason to worry. But right now, we need to focus on getting you well. And I'd like to point out something huge—Holden called *me* to go check on you. You may not see the importance of that, but I do. And I'm going to tell you."

I loved how she effortlessly switched gears, as if she hadn't just dropped a bomb the size of the Atlantic into my lap.

"You may or may not know, but he couldn't leave the office today because of meetings. I guess he tried to call you several times to see how you were feeling because you went to bed early last night, and he didn't hear a peep from you. Then when you weren't answering the phone today, he got concerned." She lifted one eyebrow and tilted her head, giving me feigned attitude. "I doubt basic friends would do that, but I'm sure you already know that by now. And who does he call to check on you? Me...knowing full well if it was as bad as he thought, I'd have to take you to the doctor. And he *knows* I avoid this place like the plague. And *that* means something. Something you can't deny."

"Yeah, it means he needs me to get better so I can continue making his dinners and doing his grocery shopping." Even as those words came out of my mouth, I knew they weren't true. They didn't even taste right on my tongue. But I wasn't about to tell her that. Even if Holden fell at my feet right now and confessed his undying love, I still wouldn't tell her.

Probably because if that *did* happen, it would be a sure sign of my untimely death. And if I were no longer walking the earth, I *couldn't* tell her, even if I wanted to…for obvious reasons. Just knowing I even entertained these thoughts troubled me and made me even more concerned over whatever horrible disease I'd contracted. Thinking of Holden falling in love with me and all the reasons I couldn't tell Christine had me worried this wasn't some normal illness, and there was a real chance I wouldn't make it to see the next day.

"It makes no sense, though. I never even told him I didn't feel well. We had dinner, started to clean the kitchen, and when I complained about being tired, he told me to go to bed. I don't recall at all saying I felt sick or that I was coming down with something. I don't even think I was running a fever. I only had a headache when I went to lie down."

"You can deny it all you want, Jelly, but you two will end up together. I can feel it." For the first time all morning, I noticed a genuine smile spread across Christine's perfectly painted pink lips. "I knew your brother was the one for me when he stopped by my apartment early one morning before a test. His class started at eight and mine didn't start until almost nine, so he came knocking on my door at seven fifteen with flowers and a cup of coffee fixed just the way I like it."

"Why did he do that?" I was intrigued, having never heard this story before.

"No one else noticed, but I was terrified of the test I had that day. I didn't feel prepared enough because I hadn't had much time to study. But I'd never told anyone because it was my fault. I chose to do other things than study, so I wasn't about to complain. Needless to say, Matty knew. He recognized how stressed I was and somehow knew it was about the test. So he came over early in the morning to tell me how confident he was that I'd pass it."

"Well? Did you?"

"With flying colors. But that's not the moral of the story. What I was trying to say is he knew me well enough to pick up on things others overlooked. So if you didn't mention to Holden last night that you weren't feeling good, that means he saw it. He picked up on it."

I wrapped my arms around my shins, pulling my legs tighter to my body while curling into the awful waiting room chair, and closed my eyes. I was convinced they put these seats in clinics to will people to get better. The longer you had to sit in these, the higher the probability was that you'd take the chance with your cough, hoping it didn't turn out to be life threatening, because you just couldn't take it anymore. There'd probably be less deaths if they spent a few extra dollars on real chairs that weren't made of hard plastic to place in waiting rooms.

"Yeah," I mumbled. "That means we know each other well. It doesn't mean we'll end up together. Considering we've been in each other's lives for eighteen years, I would hope that he could pick up on a few things others didn't."

"Say what you want, but you won't change my mind."

Luckily, she dropped the conversation, and we waited in silence until someone called my name—which felt like a hundred years later. Christine walked back with me, and maybe it was my fever causing me to hallucinate, but she seemed lighter, less anxious about where we were. Either that or realizing she wasn't the patient and wouldn't be the one getting horrible news settled her nerves some. Whatever it was, she sat in the room and entertained me while we waited for the doctor to come in. Which, by the way, only lasted approximately ninety seconds. A hundred years in the waiting room to see an old man in a white coat for less than a hundred seconds. It took the nurse longer than that to scrape my throat.

However, at least I no longer had to sit in the waiting room.

I now had a pint-sized bed lined with crinkly paper.

I wasn't sure which was better.

"She's been asleep since we got back," Christine whispered, obviously having no clue that I had woken up. I blinked my eyes until I could focus on something and noticed her in the kitchen with Holden. He hadn't changed out of his work clothes, so I assumed he'd just gotten home.

He had his back to me, but that didn't stop his husky voice from traveling into the living room where I lay curled up on the couch. "At least the antibiotics should start to kick in by tomorrow. Don't those usually take twenty-four hours to kill the fever and dramatically lessen the symptoms? She'll start to feel better tomorrow, right?"

"I hate to say this, Holden, but I doubt she'll feel better for days. The antibiotics will help with the strep, but it won't touch the flu. I would love to stay and help out with her, but I can't. She'll probably sleep a ton for the next several days, but she needs to make sure she's staying hydrated. That fever is no joke."

There was a long beat of silence before he spoke again. "I can't thank you enough for all you've done. I want you to know I never would've asked you for help today if I had another option. I hope you know that and how much I appreciate it. Thank you so much for this."

Holden turned around to walk Christine to the door and noticed I was awake. I managed to offer her a wave, although she might not have recognized it as that, and then smiled weakly in response when she wished me well. She asked Holden to call her and let them know how I was doing and if we needed anything else, and then left.

After closing the door behind her, he came to kneel next to the couch, close to me. "How are you feeling?" he asked with his palm on my forehead. I wanted to slap it away and make fun of him for his intense show of concern, but I didn't have the energy. Not to mention, his reaction warmed my heart in ways I refused to acknowledge.

Instead, I groaned and closed my eyes.

"I stopped by the store on my way home and picked up some drinks. They're in the fridge. I'm sure they'll feel better on your throat once they cool down, but I can pour some over ice in the meantime."

I hummed at the thought of something icy on my throat. I'd had water, but no matter how cold it was, it was horrible and tasted awful. I was convinced it was poison and refused to drink much. Of course, I didn't tell Christine that. She had taken my prescription to the pharmacy and dropped it off so Holden could pick it up on the way home, and I knew if I complained about the taste of the water, she'd find a way to get me something else to drink. And she'd already done enough.

A crushing weight settled over me when I reminded myself once again about her anxiety while we waited to be seen. I knew she wasn't obligated to tell me, neither was my brother, and she even admitted that it had happened more times than anyone knew of. But that didn't stop my heart from breaking at the thought of their silent pain and secret battle.

The quiet in the room became almost unbearable, forcing me to open my eyes just to make sure he was still there. I wasn't sure if I'd fallen asleep or just gotten lost in my dark thoughts, but when I found him on the floor in front of me, tapping away on his phone, I knew he hadn't left me. "You didn't have to do all this, Holden. But thank you. It means a lot to me."

"Do what?" he asked, genuinely confused.

"Everything. Calling to check on me, having Christine come over and then take me to the one place she hates more than anything. Getting me something to drink and picking up my medicine. Being here. Everything, Holden. Thank you for everything."

Rather than respond, he ran his fingertips along my forehead, down my cheek, and paused on my chin. It was so close to my bottom lip I wanted to kiss it, but then he pulled it away and stood. And after regarding me without a sound for a long moment, he walked off. I had to close my eyes and curl into myself even more beneath the heavy blanket just to ward off the chill caused by his absence.

———

I didn't remember closing my eyes or falling back to sleep. But apparently, I did, because the next thing I knew, I opened my eyes and found Holden kneeling next to the couch. However, this time, he no longer had on work clothes, and a piping-hot bowl of chicken noodle soup sat on the coffee table in front of me. At first, I assumed he'd ordered it or had someone bring it over, because there was no way I could've slept through someone cooking a few feet away. But when I watched him through the walkway into the kitchen, I noticed the big pot on the stove and realized he'd cooked for me.

I DO

Which meant he had to buy the ingredients at the store while he was there.

If I'd had enough energy, I would've swooned.

Holden brought his bowl to the living room and sat next to me on the couch. He grabbed the remote, turned on the TV, and started flipping through the channels, as if this were any other night. I expected him to settle on one of the shows he liked to watch, but when he stopped on a reality show about wedding planners, I knew it was for me. He had no interest in a show like this, but he knew my dream was to plan events, and a wedding was considered an event.

"If you keep spoiling me like this, I may never leave," I croaked out.

He held his bowl close to his face and blew on it while cutting his gaze toward me. "You're sick, Janelle. Everyone deserves to be spoiled when they don't feel well."

This fever needed to go away, and fast. I wasn't sure what I expected him to say, but when he didn't make any comment about me staying, I felt like an idiot. I grabbed my bowl off the table and held it in my lap on a pillow, unable to look in his direction. It wasn't his fault I felt let down. It wasn't even like I had meant to fish for anything. But in the throes of my illness and the seeds Christine had planted in my head, I guess I'd hoped this meant more than him worrying about the health of a friend.

"You don't have to sit in here with me if you don't want to."

He whipped his head to the side so fast it was nothing but a blur in my peripheral vision and it made me glance up at him. His narrowed gaze silenced my argument long enough for him to respond. "Why would I want to eat at the table all by myself? And leave you in here alone?"

Without moving my head, only my eyes, I studied the kitchen table. It sat right behind the recliner—maybe ten feet away at best. Either way, not far. "It's right there," I muttered, my words comprised of confusion. "It's not like we wouldn't be able to talk or see each other. There's not even a wall separating it, so I wouldn't be alone."

With his eyes on the show ahead of him, he brought his spoon to his lips, blew on the broth, and then swallowed it. "It's too far away. Plus, you'd have to raise your voice to talk to me, and that'd make me feel like crap." He turned to look at me and hesitated for a few blinks before saying, "If you don't want me in here, just tell me. I can sit at the table. It won't hurt my feelings. I know some people prefer to be alone when they're sick."

"That's not it at all. I just don't want you to get sick."

"I'll be fine. Don't worry about me." And just like that, he dismissed my concerns.

I blew on my soup—at least, that's what I thought it was…until I tasted it. Then I realized it was heaven in a bowl. It soothed my throat and warmed me up all at once, and I never wanted to stop eating it. Being upright didn't help my headache, and my joints protested with every move I made, but that didn't stop me from sitting there, hunched over my bowl in my lap, bringing spoonful after spoonful to my mouth. I slurped as much of it down as I could, and thought about how wonderful it would've been to have a long, bendable, wide straw so I could eat-slash-drink the broth while lying down.

That was something that definitely needed to be invented.

I managed to finish half the bowl of soup and drink almost half a bottle of Gatorade before lying back down and falling asleep. At some point, not sure when because I didn't

I DO

bother to check the time, he picked me up and carried me to bed.

It was the most comfortable bed I'd ever been in, and I thought to myself how much better a mattress felt when you're sick. The sheets were softer and the comforter thicker, warmer. In fact, it was so warm, I finally stopped shivering. The pillow molded to my head and absorbed the weight evenly, which left me feeling as thought I were in a cocoon.

And it made me sleep so peacefully, I didn't wake up once.

FOURTEEN

(Holden)

"Take messages, and if they need to be addressed today, please email them to me. I'll check in periodically and do what I can from home." When my alarm went off this morning, I checked Janelle's forehead—not that I needed to, considering her body radiated enough heat to suffice a small town in Maine for the winter. There was no way I could've left her alone in that condition. It didn't matter if she ended up sleeping all day, she didn't need to be by herself. So I sent Matt a text and called Ronnie with instructions. "Yes, just tell them my wife has the flu, so I'm at home taking care of her. She needs me. You know how to get ahold of me if you need to."

I made sure to keep my voice as low as possible to keep from waking her while I concluded my phone call outside my bedroom door. I had no idea why I brought her to my bed last night, and then crawled beneath the covers with her, but I told myself it was to be close in case she needed me.

Apparently, I must've also convinced myself that she was dying. Because I wasn't sure what all I could do for someone with the flu, or what she could've possibly needed other than a drink. But that didn't matter, because in the event she needed something, I was there. Right next to her.

All. Night. Long.

I DO

God, I seriously needed help if I anticipated making it to the end of our agreement.

When I walked back into my room, the early morning sunlight drifted in through the window across from the bed and painted the walls in a warm glow. It also made Janelle appear to be an angel in my bed...who was no longer peacefully asleep, but lying there, staring at me with intense eyes.

"Sorry, I was trying to be quiet. I thought leaving the room and closing the door would've helped. I didn't mean to wake you up." I crawled beneath the blankets and crossed my arms behind my head. I more than likely wouldn't be able to fall back asleep, but that didn't keep me out of bed.

She stared at me, and I stared back, neither one of us making a move—physical or verbal. Finally, she cleared her throat and said, "You didn't wake me up. At least, I don't think you did."

"Do you need anything? Something to eat...drink? Anything?"

"No." Her voice was groggy, but it didn't seem to stop her from talking. "I'm just freezing. I think that's what woke me up. I was nice and warm all night, and now I can't stop shaking."

I pulled the covers to her neck and then tucked them around her body. Without delay, she curled into my side and rested her head on my shoulder, so I wrapped my arm around her and held her tighter. And as if that still wasn't close enough for her, she slipped her hand beneath my white T-shirt and settled her palm against the middle of my chest.

"You know, you're like a furnace when you sleep," I mumbled into her hair.

"I'm also running a fever."

When I laughed under my breath, it jostled her body, so I pulled her even closer into my side, as if it would protect her more. "Well, there's that, too. I would've taken my shirt off but I worried about how you'd react if you woke up and noticed me next to you half-naked."

"You're warm, so I doubt I would've reacted any other way than grateful for your body heat."

Without saying anything else, I eased her off me and sat up to pull my shirt over my head. After tossing it to the floor, I reclined against my pillow again and then lifted my arm, inviting her to reclaim her position by my side. Once she got comfortable with her head on my shoulder, cheek against my pec, and arm draped along my chest, I wrapped my arm around her again.

"You called me your wife," she whispered while her fingers absentmindedly fiddled with the small patch of hair in the middle of my chest. "A minute ago, when you were on the phone, you called me your wife."

"Oh, yeah. I had called the office to let them know I wouldn't be in today. It's just easier than explaining who you are, and if I called you my roommate, it wouldn't have the same effect."

"But what about Matt? What if he hears you say that?"

I grinned to myself and stared at the ceiling. "He's the one who started it. A couple weeks ago, Ronnie had suggested we all go out for a drink after work, and I said I couldn't. Matt's the one who said I had to get home to my wife, and it's been an ongoing joke since then."

Her body seemed to stiffen with my explanation. I only hoped I hadn't made her uncomfortable—either by calling her my wife to someone else, or for telling her how her brother had been the one to start it. But for some reason, talking to someone else and calling her my wife did something to me, something I couldn't explain. My chest felt bigger and my heartbeats felt stronger.

However, admitting that felt like jumping out of an airplane without a parachute—absolutely frightening. Which boggled my mind considering I wasn't much of a fearful person. Once I made up my mind I wanted something, I went after it. For all things except Janelle. And the only reason to explain that was our history and connection to one another. We had been close friends once, and I believed we had made it back to that place in each other's lives.

The last time our friendship had been taken to another level, we spent five years not talking. I wasn't willing to chance that again. Not to mention, if things between us didn't work out, it would only make everything harder. Losing someone you care about because of a breakup is always difficult, no matter what the reason. But losing an entire family and possibly a business partner and best friend is far worse. It's unfathomable. And a risk I adamantly refused to take.

Breaking me from my thoughts, she sighed and stilled her hand. "I can't believe I've slept in the same bed with you twice, yet can't remember either time. Not to mention, you're starting to give me a complex. I've woken up both times alone."

"If it makes you feel any better, there was nothing about last night worth remembering."

Her fingers began to move across my skin again, but this time, it wasn't mindlessly. I could sense her hesitation by the way she circled them in the same spot, as if mentally preparing herself to say something. Finally, I gave in, unable to handle her inner torture any longer.

"Whatever you have on your mind, Janelle…just say it."

"Did you wear a condom?" She must've sensed my body turn rigid, because she pressed her palm against the center of my chest, right over my racing heart, and rephrased her question. "In Vegas, did you wear a condom?"

I tightened my arm around her, not hard, but enough to hide how much her question made me react. At least I hoped it was enough to hide it. I took a moment and attempted to control my breathing in order to slow my heart rate. I had no idea how to answer, and had I known *this* would've been her question, I never would've prodded her to speak up. But I did prod and she did ask, so the only thing left to do was answer. And I had to be truthful. "Um…the first time, yes."

"But not the other times?"

It was such a simple question, one that required a one-word answer. Yes or no. However, the problem was how she'd react to that one word. And in all honesty, the complete answer was far more than yes or no, because it required an explanation—one I wasn't sure she'd be okay with.

"I think I have the right to know if we had unprotected sex."

I tightened my arm around her briefly before loosening my hold and dropping my hand to rest against her lower back. "No…not the other times. Right before the second time, you told me you were okay. So I didn't mention it again. I never asked you what you meant by being okay…I just assumed you were on the Pill or something."

She shook her head against my chest and my heart quit beating. "I wasn't. I mean, I'd gotten a prescription for it when I had planned on having sex with Justin, but after that fell through, I didn't see the point in starting it. I didn't actually start taking it until after Vegas."

I was almost afraid to speak when I asked, "So you weren't…*okay*?"

I DO

"Well, I mean, yeah. I didn't get pregnant or anything. So I guess that means I was fine." She craned her head back and leaned away slightly to peer at me. "My God, Holden. It could've been so bad. Babies aside, what about diseases? I understand we were both drunk, and there really isn't any reason to be upset knowing the outcome was fine, but that shouldn't be an excuse."

I brought my other hand up to capture her face, force her to keep her head back and eyes on me. I needed her full attention when I told her this. "That was the *only* time I've ever had sex without a condom. Even to this day, you're the only person I've ever had unprotected sex with. Pill or not, I've never gone bareback with anyone but you."

When her body relaxed, muscles loosening, I released her face and let her curl into my side once more. As soon as I had her settled against me, I rested my cheek against the top of her head and whispered, "And trust me, you were a virgin. You certainly didn't lie about that."

"If you had been sober that night, would you have still slept with me?"

I tried my best to mentally go back there, but in an alternate universe in order to give her the most honest answer. But no matter what, hypotheticals were always impossible, because what you *think* you might do, isn't always what you *would* do in that situation.

"I don't know, Janelle," I said with a slight shrug. "I can't answer that. I would like to believe I wouldn't. Obviously, sleeping with my best friend's little sister would be wrong. It would also be wrong to take your virginity after you cried on my shoulder when your boyfriend left you for not sleeping with him. I want to say I'd have more respect for you than that."

"But…?"

"But if I'm being honest...I'm a guy. You're a girl. You practically threw yourself at me, begged me to take you, so I doubt I would've had much self-control whether I was stone-cold sober or not. You absolutely refused to hear the word no. I was fearful—you totally took advantage of me."

She giggled and then groaned, immediately filling me with guilt for making her laugh when she was still so sick. "So you're basically saying you slept with me because I was your best friend's pathetic little sister who begged you to do what no other guy had done and deflower me. And you were too much of a horndog to say no. Is that it? That's why we slept together?"

I stroked her back and contemplated how I should answer. Her questions evoked a winless battle. It was no secret how much I enjoyed going back and forth with her, teasing and laughing and egging each other on, but I also knew she was sick. Most importantly, she deserved the truth. So that's what I decided to give her. "Not at all," I whispered against the top of her head while my fingers trailed down her back, dancing along the curve of her hip.

"So then why did you sleep with me?"

"I can't answer that."

"Why not?" she pressed, unwilling to let it go.

"Because I don't have an answer for you, Janelle. I've tried to understand my feelings for you that summer, but I can't. I couldn't then when it was going on, and I can't now. No matter how much I pick it apart. For whatever reason, I was into you back then. But it's obvious it wasn't meant to be. Is that what you want to hear?"

Rather than respond or follow up with more questions, she tucked her chin close to her chest and clung to me even more, as if I were a life preserver and she couldn't swim. It was the same way she had held onto me that night, right before we both finally fell asleep. It was the last time I'd felt

I DO

her arms around me like this, and I never wanted this moment to end.

But I knew it had to.

I secured her to me as if on instinct. "I know you don't feel well and you should be sleeping, but if you want to talk—about that night or anything else—I'll answer everything I can. You deserve to have all your questions answered."

"I'm not sure what to say, Holden. I don't know how I'm supposed to feel." The heat from her shaky words wafted across my bare chest. "My stomach is in knots, like I could throw up at any second, but I don't understand why. I'm angry, yet I have no right to be. I'm upset...for no reason. I have no idea what you want me to say."

I curled my fingers beneath her chin and lifted it, forcing her to look at me. "You have every right to be angry and upset. That's how I've felt about myself since it happened—well, since the next morning. I hate that we slept together after you had so much to drink. I swear, Janelle...had I known, I never would've touched you. I never would've taken you to that chapel."

Her eyes closed and a sigh escaped through her parted lips. She seemed so sad, and I wanted nothing more than to make her smile again. It was as though I needed her happiness to keep going.

"Well, that's not entirely true. Had I known how drunk you were, I would've made you drink a shit-ton of water and coffee and force-fed you until you were sober enough to truly make up your mind. Then I would've hauled you off, over my shoulder, to the chapel, and then taken you back to the room to have my way with you. And you better believe it would've continued the next morning, too."

Even though the corner of her mouth didn't move, I could tell by the way she relaxed into me that she already felt better.

"Was it good? I mean…" She didn't finish her question, but I didn't exactly need her to in order to know what she meant.

"You didn't hold onto your virginity for nothing, if that's what you're asking."

"Did it hurt? Me, I mean. God, I hope it didn't hurt you. If it did, I'm glad I can't remember."

I was happy to see some of her humor return, especially in the middle of such a serious conversation. "You cried, not much, but there were tears. At one point, I stopped because I thought you were in pain. I thought you were crying because I had hurt you. But you kissed me and told me you had never felt better." I closed my eyes and recalled exactly what she had said that night. I had replayed her words so many times I knew them by heart. *This is everything I've ever dreamed of. I wasn't sure anyone would ever live up to it. But you, Holden, you have; you're everything.*

"Did…did you like it?" The fever had to be the cause of her insecurity, because I'd never known her to be this way. However, I didn't let it stop me from telling her the absolute truth, needing her to never doubt herself again—whether it be with me or someone else.

"Hell yeah, I did. Best sex of my life."

Her shoulders shook with her muted laughter. I could tell she thought I meant it as a joke, but I decided against arguing with her or going out of my way to convince her of it right now. I would at a later time, when she was no longer delirious with a fever.

"Tell me a story," she begged in a sleepy whisper.

"What kind?"

"A fairy tale. But no Prince Charming. I want one about a knight."

"In shining armor?" I teased.

"No. No castles, no royalty, no white horses or shining armor."

I DO

"Then what kind of knight are you talking about?"

"The dark one."

I thought to myself for a moment before asking, "Batman? You want me to tell you a fairy tale about Batman?" Instead of speaking, she simply nodded against my chest. "To give you that, it'll take more than one day."

"Then break it up and tell me more each day until I get better."

The thought of being by her side until she got better made me almost want her to never get better. Except, I hated to see her sick. Just knowing she wanted me here made me want to never leave. Taking a deep breath, I closed my eyes, rested my cheek against her hair, and stroked her back as I began to tell her the best and worst fairy tale ever told.

"Once upon a time, there was an eighteen-year-old with a broken heart who'd locked herself in a room in a really high building. With her, she had twenty tiny bottles of…magic potion. She believed they would take her problems away, so she twisted the top off one and poured the entire thing down her throat. But after a few minutes, she didn't feel any different, so she opened another…and another…and another, until they were all gone. Little did she know, her very handsome—no, *sexy*—hero was on his way upstairs."

"This sounds familiar," she mumbled against my chest.

I shushed her and held her tighter. "Just listen. No interrupting…"

The elevator seemed to take forever, so the strong and handsome and amazing hero raced up the stairs, two at a time, on his way to the girl with the broken heart. As soon as he got there, he realized she needed him, more than she'd ever needed anyone.

She gripped the front of his shirt to keep from falling over. Her knees had gone weak, and she kept repeating, "Thank God you're here."

It didn't take long, but he finally calmed her down enough to be able to escort her from the room. They frantically ran outside, hand in hand, and everywhere she looked, there were lights. Bright lights of all different colors and shapes, blinking and flashing, as if beckoning them to follow. It was the most remarkable sight either of them had ever witnessed. But they'd been warned that it wouldn't last forever. They had limited time to uncover the secret world they sought, for as soon as the sun's first light peeked over the horizon, it would all vanish.

They had heard tales of dancing ribbons of water and an entire city locked within stone. Of men with sticks for legs and beautiful women scantily clad in breathtaking costumes. They wanted to leave no pebble unturned, so they quickly began their race against the clock, their sprint against time.

It was an adventure that started off at Treasure Island, just in time to see the Sirens of TI pirate show, complete with lights, music, and fire that burst clear up to the sky. The two young tourists watched with wide eyes as excitement filled them. It was certainly something at least one of them would never forget.

They traveled from the pirates' cove to Venice, Italy—or more realistically, the Venetian Hotel. She squeezed his hand as they rode up the escalator to Venice—or more accurately, the hotel's interpretation of the city. An indoor river ran between the shops with bridges and walkways paved like an authentic Italian street. Seeing the excitement in her eyes when she noticed the traditional Venetian rowboats—or more precisely, the ones designed to travel through a narrow, shallow lagoon inside a hotel—the hero with a body of steel and heart of pure gold raced to the ticket counter and purchased two seats for the next gondola ride.

As they floated along the water, Italian music playing around them, she couldn't take her eyes off the sky above her—more specifically, the high ceiling painted blue, complete with white fluffy clouds, and lit up to give a rather realistic illusion of the sky. He couldn't take his eyes off her, feeling as though this was the first time he had truly seen her for her worth…

(Bedridden fairytale day two)

Bliss practically carried them across the street. They arrived just in time to witness the volcano in front of the Mirage. A crowd had gathered, but neither one had an issue seeing the show. She stood with her back against his front, his arms around her shoulders, protectively crossed over her chest, with his cheek resting against the side of her head. Music played in time with the fiery explosions, and with each unexpected burst, she jumped and gasped, causing him to grin. He wouldn't remember much of the show, but he would be able to recall her reactions and excitement for years to come.

They walked on tiring feet down the crowded strip, taking in the hustle and bustle only Vegas at night could offer. As if following a tour guide, they made their way to Caesars Palace and trailed the people to the shops, finally stopping to wait near the Cheesecake Factory.

"I'm going to get something to drink. Do you want anything?" the hero asked the girl, whose heart seemed as if it were on the mend. He refused her request for an adult beverage, reminding her she wasn't of age, but she argued with him, batted her lashes, and in the end, got her way. The hero didn't think he'd ever in his lifetime be capable of telling the beautiful woman no.

Luckily, the crowd surrounding the indoor fountain concealed the drink, preventing questions. Not that anyone cared, considering everyone's attention became glued to the talking animatronics in front of them. Over the people talking, the sound effects, and water from the fountain, it became hard to hear the show, but they knew enough about it to adlib. The Fall of Atlantis was a show about sibling rivalry, which the young woman knew very much about, and the hero had somewhat experienced while staying with her family on numerous occasions. The couple began to create their own script, getting sideways glances when their giggles became too loud to be covered by the music.

Eventually, the two made their way outside. As though someone had lit a fire beneath their asses, they made a beeline to the Bellagio Hotel in time to watch the thrilling fountains. They stood amongst the crowd for nearly five minutes, as giddy as children on Christmas morning. And as soon as the first notes began to play to "Billie Jean" by Michael Jackson, they were enamored with the show.

Regardless of the lack of slow, romantic beats, they found themselves huddled tightly, arms around the other, needing to hold the other person as close as possible. There was something magical in the warm air that night, and it descended upon them while the water and lights danced in time with the music.

When it ended, they both turned to each other, arms still wound around the other, and stared longingly into one another's eyes. "I wanna kiss you so bad right now, Janelle." He worried his confession would scare her off. They'd been friends for so long and had just recently grown close, closer than ever before.

Rather than push him away or freak out, she whispered, "Then do it…"

(Bedridden fairy tale day three)

He didn't waste a second. She told him to kiss her, so he did. And then they stood there in the middle of the sidewalk, in the center of the crowd, experiencing the taste of each other for the very first time. Holding on tight, their lips shifted from soft and tentative caresses to frantic and needy, punishing kisses.

Eventually, they had to come up for air, and when they broke apart, he said—

I DO

"What did he say?" Janelle asked, fully invested in this story that somehow led to a piece of information I couldn't give her. I'd already lied about it, and if I changed it now, it could lead her to question everything. Plus, holding her in my bed as she recovered from the flu wasn't the right time to tell her that I had given her the one word I'd never spoken to another before.

"He said, 'I wish I could kiss you forever...'"

Then she said, "Let's do it. Let's get married and kiss each other forever and ever."

"That's a silly idea. And completely irrational."

"No it's not. It's perfect. Think about it..." She listed all the reasons they should tie the knot. When she told him how they would end up together anyway, since that was where the friendship was headed, it didn't make sense to the hero to wait a few years only to waste money on a celebration when none of that mattered to her — and he was a guy, so it shouldn't have mattered to him. His points were no longer valid and he couldn't think of one reason to argue that this union shouldn't be.

They planned to head off to a chapel and make it official. And then the next day, they would fly home, where they'd keep it secret from the family. In the unlikely event something went awry, neither wanted to chance upsetting her parents or siblings. The only details worked out in the back of a taxi were what would take place after she finished college. There was no mention of how they would interact or what to expect in the years between the vows and her college graduation.

But neither of them cared.

In front of Elvis, they promised their lives to one another.

She vowed to always be his sidekick.

And he swore to always be her hero.

FIFTEEN

(Janelle)

For four days, Holden stayed home with me. On the last day, seeing that I was feeling much better and not nearly as close to death as I had been at the beginning of the week, he went into the office for a few hours in the morning, but he was home by lunch and didn't leave my side again. Every night, he slept with me wrapped in his arms, because he claimed he wanted to make sure he was there in case I needed him for anything.

When questioned what I could've possibly needed in the middle of the night, he could only come up with "something to drink." As if my legs were broken and I couldn't get out of bed by myself. But I didn't complain, mostly because I loved his bed. Well, if I were completely honest, I had a list of other things I loved about sleeping next to Holden, but I ignored those, knowing if I gave them much credence, I would only end up with a bigger broken heart when he signed the divorce papers.

By Saturday, I finally deemed myself human again, but Holden still refused to let me resume my regularly scheduled activities. "The reason most people relapse after being sick is because they feel better, so they jump back in, not recognizing their bodies haven't fully recovered. There's a big difference between feeling better and returning to normal."

I DO

"Not in my book, there's not," I argued while he slipped on his shoes. I'd woken up and found his side empty — something I needed to stop saying before I actually believed *I* had a side. When I went out to the living room to look for him, I found him on the couch, dressed in workout clothes. "I was actually feeling better yesterday and decided to take one more day to rest. Which means today, I'm back to *normal*."

"Okay…wanna go for a jog with me?"

I scrunched my nose and curled my lip in disgust. "No. I think I'll pass."

"Good then. You stay here, watch TV or do whatever, and when I get back, we'll spend the day on the couch watching all the comic movies — in any order you want. Sound good? A lazy day without being stuck in bed?"

Holden left for his run, and when he returned, we did exactly as he suggested. We took a break to make dinner — both of us. Together. He grabbed things from the fridge and pantry and basically made up something with the ingredients we had. I chopped, he sautéed — or whatever he did on the stove to cook our dinner. We moved around each other fluently and stood within breathing distance of one another while sharing tasks. We ate together, like we did every night, but for some reason, this time just felt easier. Natural. Like we had been doing this together all our lives. And when we were done, we headed back to the couch to finish our movie marathon.

However, it was anything but a lazy day for me. I couldn't stop thinking about the way it felt to have his arms wrapped around me, my spine pressed along his chest. I missed his smell, his firm touch and large hands exploring my flesh, his words reverberating through his body. I wanted it again. More of it. All of it.

But I couldn't.

I needed to sleep in my own bed. Alone. I needed to wake up the next morning without the urge to touch him, or for him to touch me. So after one of the *Iron Man* movies ended, we turned off the TV and made our way off the couch. It was a bit awkward while we silently had an entire conversation about sleeping arrangements. And I didn't miss the slight droop in his posture when I slowly shuffled my feet toward the hallway that led to my bedroom, away from his. But he didn't question or fight it, so I resigned myself to believing the slouch in his shoulders meant nothing more than he was tired, or maybe he had a kink in his neck from sitting around all day.

We said goodnight and went in opposite directions.

Although, as I lay all alone in bed, sleep refused to come. I stared at the dark ceiling, ignoring how late it was and trying to forget how long I'd been in bed. But I couldn't close my eyes and relax. I'd had enough of that over this past week to last me a few years, but even if I hadn't, my subconscious refused to shut down. I couldn't stop replaying Holden's "fairy tale" in my mind, the one that had taken him days to tell me. Every night, he would narrate a little bit more until I fell asleep, listening to his voice rumble through his chest. Even though I couldn't remember that fateful Vegas night, there were so many things that sounded familiar as he recalled them.

And then I laughed at myself.

It wasn't like I had amnesia and there was a slim chance my memory would return. I had been black-out drunk. Far too intoxicated to trust anything resembling a memory. However, that didn't stop the overwhelming feeling of déjà vu when I imagined the scenes in my head as he revealed the story.

Refusing to obsess over it anymore, I rolled onto my side and closed my eyes. I fell into a light sleep and dreamed of water. Rather than vivid visuals dancing behind my closed eyelids, I heard sounds. Laughter, car horns, traffic, people passing. Then came the peacefulness of splashing, even though I couldn't see it. Nothing made sense, especially the bright lights flickering. Some were blurry, others more like streaks of color. Then there was warmth. At first it was at my back, over my shoulder, and then it moved to my front. My face heated with it. My pulse accelerated and my chest tightened, yet my knees weakened. Amongst all the other noises, one became clear. Closer almost.

Deep and penetrating.

So close to my ear.

"I want to kiss you so bad right now."

My heart beat faster, harder, more intense, while my knees buckled and my breathing hitched. I didn't move my mouth, but that didn't stop the words from coming out, in my voice, off my tongue. "Then do it." So breathless and filled with desperation.

My lips tingled, and I felt so light I was convinced I floated away. But then his voice shook, and the heat lingered closer to my mouth. He said something, but I couldn't hear it. A burst of air brushed against my lips as the words escaped him, but for the life of me, I had no idea what it was. Then he spoke again, saying, "Tell me you feel this, too. Tell me I'm not the only one who's felt what's between us the last few months."

"I feel it."

And then I *did* feel it. His mouth on mine, his lips leading the way. His tongue finding mine. Then our hands, roaming and touching and sensing. Our breaths combining, mingling into heated pants of air between us. A need, so large, so deep, so overwhelming came over me—and more than likely him, too.

Whoever he was.

But I knew who he was.

Even without seeing his face, I recognized him. As if his name had forever been carved deep into my soul, never to be erased. He was in me. All around me. In each heartbeat, every breath. Every waking moment. He had always been there. Always would be. Part of me.

I knew who he was.

And as I blinked my eyes open, breathing frantically into the dark, empty, quiet room, I knew who he was. Even though I couldn't recall that night, and the memory was fuzzy and unclear and disjointed, I knew it was real. It wasn't simply a dream. It was my subconscious telling me something.

Something I couldn't ignore.

So I didn't. I tossed the covers off my overheated body—only this time, it wasn't from fever—and sat on the edge of my bed, desperately trying to catch my breath before pulling myself to my feet. I needed strength if I wanted to make it to the other side of the house. And with one last full intake of air to completely expand my lungs, I left my room.

I headed down the hall, past the living room to his.

I turned the knob on his door.

Opened it.

And brazenly walked in.

I only meant to crawl in bed with him and sleep, like we had done all week. I did everything in my power to not disturb him, to not wake him, staying as still as possible. But as soon as I rested my head on the empty pillow, he rolled toward me until we faced each other. Half asleep, he put his arm around me and pulled me flush against him, the heat of his bare chest surrounding me.

"What are you doing, Janelle?" His slumber-filled voice rumbled in my ear.

"I couldn't sleep. Your bed is nicer."

I DO

"Does this mean you want to swap beds?"

I smiled against him, my head tucked beneath his chin. "Your room is nicer, too. The sun doesn't beat through the windows first thing in the morning. And I'm pretty sure the air hits here first before the back of the house."

"So…are you suggesting we swap rooms?"

"It might just be easier if we share. Ya know? Less hassle."

His body shook with silent mirth. "Roomies sharing a room. Sounds messy."

"Ah, Holden. What are you so scared about? We'll be fine."

"Yeah, we will," was the last thing he said before we both succumbed to sleep, as if our bodies refused to surrender until we were back in each other's arms.

I'd slept so well it felt like I only blinked.

Careful movement woke me up, and when my sight adjusted to the soft morning light filtering in through the blinds, I was able to focus on the set of dark-green eyes in front of me. I reached up, ran my fingertips over the spatter of facial hair that decorated his face, and smiled. "Morning."

"Morning, beautiful. Sleep good?"

"Yeah, did you?"

"You were in my bed…of course I did."

I melted at his compliment, and the sight of his first smile of the day nearly did me in. "I really want you to kiss me right now."

"Yeah?" he asked and slowly dropped his mouth to mine.

It started out sweet, probably meant to test the waters, but I had no patience for that. Between my caressing and groping, moans, and twisting my legs around his, I made it obvious what I wanted, and when he finally dropped his hand to my thigh, I almost shouted in praise.

There was just one minor problem. We still had clothes on, and he wasn't taking the initiative to remove them. I realized if I wanted it, I would have to go after it. So, without taking my mouth off his, I hooked my thumb inside the waistband of my panties and slid them over my hips. I didn't get far before Holden must've realized what I was in the middle of; that's when he took over and eagerly yanked them the rest of the way down my legs.

With a burst of confidence, I pushed myself up to lean over him, forcing him flat on his back. I didn't waste a single second—or give him a chance to intervene—while I straddled his waist. I pressed my hands against his firm pecs, sat up straight, and kept my eyes on his. The only time I broke the hungry stare was when I drew my shirt over my head to toss it on the floor, leaving myself completely bare on his lap.

His face heated, and his breathing became labored while he clearly fought himself for control.

Feeling his dick grow impossibly harder and bigger beneath me, I ran my finger down the center of his chest, and in the sexiest voice I could muster without making a fool of myself, I said, "I want to ride your cock and use it as my own personal dildo until I've come so many times I can't think straight."

Without hesitation, he lifted his hips and shimmied his boxers down, and then I reached behind me to finish taking them off without removing myself from his lap. I wanted to maintain control, to take matters into my own hands before I lost my nerve. Steadying myself, I took hold of his hardened shaft, lined him up with my entrance, and then slowly lowered my knees as I sank down onto him.

We both hummed at the same time, more than likely experiencing the same euphoria. My head fell back, the loose strands from my ponytail draping along my spine. I worked myself up and down his cock while balancing myself with my palms splayed on his bare abdomen.

"Baby...I need you to move faster." His hoarse voice did something to me I didn't expect, reached inside and touched places I never knew existed. "This is torture."

I dropped my chin and met his impassioned gaze. Ignoring his pleas of desperation, I seductively moaned while grinding my pubic bone against his, creating friction along my clit. I licked my lips and took a few breaths, trying to curb my appetite, to draw it out. "It's like your dick is made for me, made to reach that perfect spot inside, and I'm not ready to stop. I don't know when I'll ever feel this again, so I'm not stopping."

His fingers dug into the tender area over my hips as he attempted to gain dominance over me and entice me to move quicker. "If you stop torturing me, I'll make you feel it every night. I'll hit that spot anytime you want me to. But, Janelle...baby, you *have* to move. I can't handle it."

"This feels so good," I practically moaned, my eyes on the verge of rolling into the back of my head.

With his hold on me, he started to speed up my movements, and then lifted his hips to meet me thrust for thrust. "You're driving me crazy, Janelle. For God's sake, do something. Or I'll take over and fuck you into tomorrow."

I stuck my fingers into my mouth and wrapped my tongue around the middle two, making eye contact with him to ensure he watched me. Once I had them wet enough, I pulled them past my lips with a *pop* and skirted them over my breasts, toying with one nipple, and then I skimmed them down my belly and circled my clit while he continued to try to top me from the bottom.

In an instant, he sat up and held me to him, his face breaths apart from mine, our bodies completely still other than our chests heaving between us. "I know you're enjoying this, but I need you." He toyed with my bottom lip, gently biting it and then slowly dragging it out. "I need you so bad."

"If I only get this once, I want to make sure I get the most out of it. I have no desire to rush this."

I was in his lap one second, and then on my back the next. In some quick, magician-like maneuver, he switched positions until he hovered over me with my shoulders, neck, and head extending past the end of the mattress. His large hand held me in place by the crook of my neck where he gripped me so hard his fingertips dug into the muscle above my shoulder blade. "I don't know where you got the idea that this will only happen once, but you couldn't be more wrong." He punctuated each promised word with a deep thrust.

My back arched naturally, which gave him the perfect angle to hit the right spot. And it didn't take me long to realize that this position gave me an even bigger advantage. I'd never thought the pleasure could increase, but it did. Every push, every pull, hit it, driving me closer and closer to the edge. Needing to secure myself and ensure I wouldn't fall off the bed, I wrapped my fingers around his wrist with one hand and reached out to grab ahold of his other arm next to me. Between the angle of my overextended throat and the force in which he drove into me, I was unable to make a sound.

"You feel so good, Janelle. I don't think I'll ever be able to quit you."

The burning ache low in my abdomen grew until it left me holding my breath as I chased the high. The harder I gripped him, the more intense his thrusts became, which made me more desperate to catch the ever-eluding orgasm.

"Baby, I can't..." His voice came out strained, like his words choked him. "I can't hold on much longer. Please." More thrusts, more grunts. More intensity. "I need you to come. Please, Janelle."

I DO

As if on cue, I lost control as the orgasm took over my body. Every muscle coiled tight, and my mouth opened wide, yet no sound other than strained air came out. I'd never experienced anything this powerful before. It was almost paralyzing. I couldn't move, couldn't breathe, couldn't utter a single sound. My eyes remained clenched as I rode the wave, convincing myself it would never end.

The only thing capable of breaking through the cocoon of ecstasy was Holden's growly grunt. It grew louder and deeper until I found myself pulled into him, my arms latched around his neck as we sat upright. Either he tugged me up by his hold on my shoulder, or I somehow found the strength to lift myself off the side of the bed and into his arms. I straddled his hips with him on his knees and his arms wrapped around me, guaranteeing his ability to remain in control. With each thrust, he held me tighter and pushed me farther onto him until he couldn't possibly go any deeper. His girth stretched me in the most delicious way each time he became fully seated within me, and with every stroke, his length deepened his reach inside until the lingering effects of the last orgasm caught me off guard and dragged me back under like a riptide of ecstasy.

This time, I wasn't silenced. An aching scream tore past my lips while my nails sliced into his flesh. His grunts flooded my ears like music, along with his garbled promises of filling me completely. And then, without warning, he turned to the side and practically tossed me onto the mattress, my back meeting with the soft sheets. He hovered over me, holding himself up with one hand pressed into the comforter next to my head, his other arm still wrapped around my hips. Our cheeks grazed constantly with each move of our frantic bodies, the stubble on his face nearly chafing my skin.

"I need you..." he stammered, voice strained. "Fuck, I need you, baby."

"You have me." My reassurance was nothing more than panted words, but it was all I could offer. He'd exhausted every ounce of energy I had, and all I could do now was hold on tight and take what he gave me.

His movements turned rigid and jerky. And with one final thrust, he held himself deep inside me for an elongated beat. He collapsed on my chest before rolling us onto our sides. We were both so spent, neither of us cared how messy the bed was or that we were completely sideways on top of it.

"Oh my God..." I huffed out, in desperate need of air and oxygen and water. I felt depleted of everything a body needed in order to survive, and I wasn't sure when or how I'd get it back. I barely had enough energy to scratch his cheek, feeling the short, coarse hairs beneath my nails.

"You love being upside down, don't you?" His question held a note of nostalgia, and it made me wonder what thought or memory played in his head.

"What do you mean?"

When he lifted his lids, his eyes found mine immediately, and even without confirming it with his mouth, I could see a smile dancing in his gaze. "Doesn't matter. I wasn't thinking. Just something from that night, but you don't remember, so it's a moot question."

"Maybe you should share it with me."

He trailed his fingertips along the curve of my waist, over my hip, and along the outer side of my thigh, producing goose bumps on nearly every surface of my skin. "Well, that night...we were kinda all over the place. At one point, you started to slip off the side of the bed while we were right in the middle of it. I tried to pull you up, but you were determined to keep going, mumbling something about feeling weightless."

I DO

I couldn't help but laugh at myself along with him. It definitely sounded like something I'd say after having a few drinks. But at least I could state with certainty that I hadn't ever been in that position—or anything remotely similar—with anyone else. Yet with Holden, I'd managed to dangle off a bed twice.

"If it was anything like just now, I'm sure I enjoyed it immensely."

"You seemed to enjoy it then, too. I was worried I'd drop you, so I just grabbed you as hard as I could and held on, while continuing to fuck you like you'd begged for. The only parts of your body I could really hold onto were your hips." His voice rumbled in his chest and vibrated in his throat, intensifying every single sound as I curled closer to him with my leg pulled over his. "You got off twice and were too worn out to pull yourself back up so I had to lift you onto the bed."

"So that's where the bruises came from…"

"Yeah…" He let his sentence linger in the air for a moment while I did nothing but wait for him to finish. I could tell he had more to say. "I noticed them the next morning in the bathroom, but with everything going on, I didn't mention it. It wasn't until like a week later when I stopped and realized what that must've been like for you. To wake up covered in bruises, aware that you'd had sex, but not remember any of it. I honestly thought you probably assumed I was into some kinky shit and so you avoided me."

I giggled and pushed against his shoulder in jest. "I didn't think about it too much. I had more important things to ponder. Every single one of my friends had told me how painful losing their virginity was, so I was completely flabbergasted how I had so many bruises and no actual discomfort. Just soreness. And if we're being honest here, I kind of came to the conclusion that you had a small dick, and that's why it didn't hurt."

He stifled my laughter with a pointed stare. Then he rolled on top of me, pressing my back into the twisted sheets beneath me, and ran his dick along my inner thigh. "Small?"

I swallowed, fighting between being turned on and wanting to finish this conversation. "I've got to say, Holden...I'm far more confused now that I know you're *not* small." My breath hitched, and I had to close my eyes the closer to my sex he got. All I could think about was the orgasms he gave me, and how desperate I was to experience it all over again. "How did you not rip me in two? And how in the hell did we have wild monkey sex my first time and I didn't need a wheelchair the next day?"

His airy laughter fanned across my face seconds before the heat from his lips spread out across my shoulder. His taunting movements stilled in favor of his entire body quaking with humor. "I don't know if you're trying to insult me or give me a compliment. But the good news is...we don't have to worry about you giving me a big head."

Unable to bite back my retort, I turned my head to whisper in his ear, "But I like making your head big." Hooking my legs around his waist to keep him in place, I said again, "Really, Holden. I would love to finally hear the story of how I lost my virginity. I know all the details leading up to it, and I have a general consensus of what happened after. But my first time...I wanna know how that was."

Pulling his face away from my neck, he met my stare. "You really wanna know? You want me to tell you..." He swiveled his hips, stroking himself between my legs "Or would you rather I *show* you?"

SIXTEEN

(Holden)

Her cheeks were flushed and a thin layer of perspiration glistened on her skin, reminding me of dew first thing in the morning. She was absolutely beautiful, always had been, but *nothing* compared to the post-orgasmic glow she wore right now. And there was no higher high than knowing I'd done that to her.

She'd wanted to learn about her first time, so I'd shown her exactly how it went, in explicit detail. I'd taken my time to enter her, the same way I had our first night together. I made sure our gazes were connected, our mouths close together but not touching, and I had her hand clasped in mine above her head. And as if her memory had returned, she locked her ankles behind me at the same time she had before—the moment I fully settled deep inside her.

Janelle was right—my cock was made for her. And her cunt was made for me. I had to fight off the need to go caveman on her and remind her that I'd been here first. I'd staked my claim, raised my flag, dominated the fuck out of that territory. That didn't mean I wouldn't...I just had to find a way to do it without her knowing.

"How the hell am I supposed to keep my hands to myself around your family today?" With it being Labor Day weekend, everyone decided to meet up for a barbecue at

Lakes Park instead of gathering for our normal Sunday dinner. When the idea was first mentioned, I thought it was great—an excuse to see Janelle in a bathing suit. But now, after spending all morning tangled up in her, I wasn't sure I'd be able to see so much of her and not touch her. It would be pure agony. Absolute torture.

She groaned and curled into me, tucking her head beneath my chin. "I don't know, but you have to. They have to keep thinking we're just roommates." When I didn't respond, she pulled back enough to look me in the eyes. "Holden, I'm serious. We can't tell anyone about this. It'll only complicate everything."

Hiding the sting her rejection caused, I blew out a huffed chuckle. "Whatever, you just don't want them to find out because you know they love me more, and when you leave me, they'll take my side."

She slapped my shoulder and shook her head. "You're so full of yourself."

"That makes two of us…because you're so full of me, too." I quickly rolled away; she'd definitely hit me for that one. When I made it off the bed unscathed, I ignored her snicker and held out my hand to help her up.

As if the bed were some safety zone, once we both had our feet on the floor, it seemed like reality slapped us in the face. Janelle's shoulders curled in slightly; her modesty had reemerged. This was a woman who—moments ago—had brazenly taken her own panties off when I apparently didn't move fast enough for her. She was the one who climbed on my lap and told me she wanted to use my appendage as her own personal sex toy. This was the same woman who shamelessly stripped herself bare and then rode me like I was one of those plastic horses outside Kmart—the ones you feed a quarter and it goes up and down at the speed of negative slow.

220

I DO

Without saying a word, she picked up her T-shirt and walked out. I watched her leave with bewilderment, unable to do anything other than stand in the middle of my room and stare at her bare ass. I shook my head at myself, feeling like an utter fool all over again. The only thing that kept me sane this time was knowing she had no escape route. Five years ago, she had college. She had a reason to leave and never look back.

But not this time.

This time, she was stuck with me for another four-plus months. Even if it was vital that she run and hide, she couldn't. I had her exactly where I wanted her. She had her sights set on the money, and in order to get it, she had to stay put. So I wasn't concerned. My ego might've been slightly bruised, my hopes and dreams thrown in my face to taunt me and serve as remembrance of the pain I'd lived with after she'd left me the last time. But I could get over that.

Because I had a plan.

Her phone rang in her purse on the floorboard of the car, but she ignored it. She didn't even glance at it to check the number. Either she didn't care, or she had a good idea who it was. I knew her well enough to know she couldn't ignore a call. Rather than answer a blocked or unknown number, she'd stare at the screen and wait for the voicemail alert, and then get pissed off if they didn't leave a message. That never made sense to me. If she needed to find out who it was that badly, she should've answered it in the first place.

"Are you going to get that?" I pointed to the muffled ringing by her feet.

"Nope. I'm sure whoever it is will leave a message so I can call back later."

As if her snubbing a call wasn't weird enough, her nonchalance definitely raised a red flag. That told me everything—she didn't want me to see who it was. And there was only one person she'd hide from me. Not that I'd ever said anything to her about him calling. I knew what the deal was with him from the beginning, and I wasn't an idiot. I was aware they spoke to each other. I didn't like it, and I chose to not be in the same room when anything transpired between them if I could help it.

I only hoped this meant something good. Like she ignored him because she didn't have any desire to talk to him, and not because she didn't want to talk to him *in front of me.* Because the latter would've meant something very different, and not in my favor.

"So everyone's gonna be here today." I hated awkward silence, and I never experienced it too much around her, which only made it worse that I did now. "I won't lie…as much as I love being around your entire family, it was nice last weekend with the smaller group."

"Yeah, it was nice. I'm just not sure how to act around Christine."

"What do you mean?" I hadn't heard her mention anything about Christine since coming home from the doctor's office. "Why wouldn't you know how to act? What's wrong with how you normally are around her?"

She grew quiet and turned away from me to stare through her window. If she didn't start talking now, we wouldn't be able to finish the conversation because we'd be at the park already. But before I could prod her, she finally answered me. "When she took me to the clinic on Tuesday, she told me about her miscarriages."

"Well, I can't speak for her, but I don't imagine she told you in private that day because she wants to have a conversation about it today. So I'm pretty sure she's not expecting you to sit down and bring it up. Just act normal. Talk about whatever else you two typically talk about. Have you heard from her since Tuesday?"

"Yeah. She's sent me texts asking how I was feeling, but that's about it."

"Then you're fine. She's clearly not avoiding you, and she seems concerned about your health. You have absolutely nothing to worry about." After turning into the main entrance, I reached over the center console and took her hand in mine, holding it in her lap. Pride filled my chest. She'd taken the reins and had started to slowly form deeper relationships with her family. "Whatever you do, don't act weird."

"Why would I act weird? Uncomfortable, maybe. Or a little standoffish. But I don't think I'll be *weird*."

I pulled into an empty space close to the entrance, only releasing her hand to shift the car into park. Just after we both took off our seatbelts, I twisted my body to face her, staring intently at her with as much seriousness as I could muster. "I know how badly you want me. It's in the way you look at me, how your pupils get all big. How you lick your lips, imagining they were mine. But you can't act on your desires for the next few hours. Okay? That means you can't follow me into the bathroom or touch me in inappropriate places while we're in the pool. You shouldn't corner me behind a tree when no one's around, and if you can, you should definitely avoid trying to eye-fuck me."

"Oh, please." She lost the fight against the smile curling her lips. Just before climbing out of the car, she mumbled beneath her breath, "You wish."

When I met her around the front of the car, I took the beach bag from her and carried it on my arm with my towel tucked against my side. "I'll try to keep my shirt on as long as possible, but I will have to take it off at some point. So we should probably come up with an excuse now."

After a long pause, she finally asked, "Excuse for what?"

"The drool. We could tell them you have a toothache, or maybe the strep did something to your tonsils and now you're having issues swallowing your saliva. You just let me know what story we're gonna run with, and I'll back you up."

She shoved me while laughing beneath her breath. "You're the one who won't be able to deal. You might want to stay in the pool most of the day to conceal your...you know, your erection. Because once you lay eyes on me in my bikini, it'll just be one constant salute."

"Considering what I'm packing...it's virtually impossible to hide it, even under water." I couldn't help myself. Ever since she made the comment about assuming I was small after Vegas, I made it my goal in life to remind her just how wrong she was—every chance I got.

Out of nowhere, someone sidled up next to me. "Impossible to hide what?"

My neck almost kinked at the way I jerked my head to the side, recognizing Christine with a coy grin on her face. "The hard, hot sausage in the fridge. Janelle can't get enough of it. Isn't that right, Jelly? I swear, if I'm not watching her, she'll take the whole thing."

Janelle's cheeks turned fiery red, but after a second of astonishment, she managed to pull herself back together. "Then I guess it's a good thing you only brought the Slim Jim with you, because I could do without that."

I couldn't even form a response, because anything I longed to say would give us away in front of Christine, and Janelle made it very clear she didn't want anyone to know about us. I shook my head and kept walking toward the pavilion her parents reserved while Christine and Janelle made small talk. I couldn't shake that word. *Us...* I wasn't even sure if there was an "us," or if this morning was just an itch she needed scratched.

The three of us made it to the pavilion near the pool and restrooms where the entire family had already gathered. The one reason I hated to be the last one to show up was the number of people all crowding around to greet you. I loved them all, but try having sixteen people come at you all at once, and by the time you've made it through, you'll be looking for a fifth of vodka and a smoke.

Luckily, everyone seemed rather dispersed into small groups rather than one large mob—probably because we were at a park versus the family home. Janelle joined the women, who appeared busy around the picnic tables getting everything organized. The five older kids ran around in the field while Rachel's three-year-old daughter sat unfazed on a picnic table with an ice-pop in her hands.

"He lives!" Matt shouted as he clapped me on the back with his large, burly hand. "I almost forgot what you look like. It's been forever since I last saw you." Then he elbowed me in the side, and with a disapproving shake of his head, he said, "And from the looks of it, you've put on weight."

I slapped his arm away, laughing along with him. "I've been lazy this week, only got in two runs. Well, one was more of a pitiful jog, but I powered through. Give me a week and I should be back to where I was. Then I'll be able to kick your ass again."

"Oh, and before I forget, you have papers on your desk at the office. I found them sitting on the fax machine when I went to use it, and I had no idea what it was. Looks like terms of a lease. You're not leaving the firm, are you?" His concern would've been believable had we been anyone else, but it was understood neither one of us would ever screw the other over.

"Nah. Before Janelle got sick I had taken her to look at a few places. Must be from that." I wanted the conversation to end before anyone could ask questions. Until I had a chance to talk to Janelle about it, no one else could know about the lease I'd signed without her being aware of it.

Just then, she slid up next to us with a cold can of soda in her hand. She didn't act out of the ordinary, so I took that as a sign she hadn't heard the conversation she practically walked into. "Did you want anything to drink? I'm still taking the antibiotics, so I won't have anything, but if you'd like a beer, I can drive us home."

"And what makes you think I'd let you drive my car?"

"That's your call, buddy. I just thought I'd offer." She shrugged it off like it didn't faze her. Then she lowered her voice, and with a devious smirk, added, "But if you have an issue with me driving your car, then maybe I shouldn't let you in mine anymore."

"We hardly ever go anywhere in your car." I didn't want to insult her, but it really was a clunker.

"You were in it a couple of times this morning."

I was mid-swallow when she said that, making me realize what she'd meant by her "car," and I started to cough. Not only because she made a sexual reference in front of her family—granted, none of them would've gotten it—but I'd mentally called her car a clunker, and I couldn't stop thinking what would've happened had I actually said that out loud when I thought it.

She didn't even give me a chance to regain my composure before throwing a wink at me and walking away. Matt seemed a little confused, but he didn't question anything. I wasn't sure how I'd respond if he did. However, that didn't stop anyone else from taunting me.

Steve was the first to mention my dating life—or lack thereof. He thought it was hilarious how Janelle managed to

I DO

kill my game. I laughed along with him, but not at his joke. I laughed because he thought I had a game to begin with. Janelle didn't "cock-block" me like Shane had insinuated, but I wasn't about to admit anything. If they wanted to believe I was a player who entertained women all the time, then who was I to tell them differently? Matt knew I wasn't, though. Thankfully, he didn't speak up. Instead, he sat there and laughed with us, everyone having fun at my expense.

Finally having enough of their mocking, I got up and walked away. They hadn't pissed me off, and honestly, I found much of their statements comical, but I was tired of hearing them essentially put Janelle down. It wasn't on purpose or done with malice, considering they all loved her, but it irritated me all the same. However, the breaking point was when Tony referenced us playing house. As soon as he said I had it made because I had a woman in the kitchen who had her own room and her own bank account, I couldn't take any more. I told them I needed a beer and excused myself.

They had a large cooler by the pool, where the women were. Christine and Janelle sat on the edge with their feet in the water, talking to Nikki, who floated in the shallow end. Stacey and her mom were off to the side, applying lotion to Stacey's two kids, Alex and Kinsley, while Rachel fed her daughter on a lounge chair.

"Holden, come here." Nikki waved me over. "We need a man's opinion on something."

I decided this was my golden opportunity to really get under Janelle's skin, so rather than just go over there, I took off my T-shirt and stepped into the water. Janelle groaned beneath her breath, but I ignored it. "Hello, ladies. What would you like my opinion on?"

"A woman's appearance." Nikki smiled and wagged her brows while Janelle groaned and covered her face. "Imagine

227

there are two women standing side by side, one has on jeans and a T-shirt, and the other has on a skirt and blouse, think executive style. The one with jeans has her hair in a ponytail and the other has hers styled. Which one would you look at? As in...which one would you be interested in?"

"I'm going to need far more information than that. Such as...the woman in jeans, are they tight and fitted, or loose and baggy? And this T-shirt you speak of...is it one of those that cuts low and shows off cleavage, fitted so it hugs the waist and hips? Or is it something she grabbed from the men's rack in Wal-Mart?"

Nikki snickered and shook her head in disbelief. "Should've known not to expect a simple answer from you, but fine. Tight and fitted to all the above. And before you ask, the other girl's clothes are just as tight. So now...which one would you choose?"

I pretended to think some more before asking, "Are they nice or bitchy? I mean, which one seems more approachable? And more importantly, what are they doing? Are they talking to each other, like would I be interrupting a conversation, or are they strangers?"

"You're impossible," Janelle said with a laugh. "I told you he wouldn't give you a real answer."

"Oh, I will. I just need all the facts first. You can't give me two vague options and expect me to pick one. For instance, what if the girl in jeans has a disgusted look on her face? That would be enough to make me not approach her. Is the woman in the skirt standing flirtatiously, just waiting to pull the next victim into her web? If so, I probably wouldn't come within ten feet of her."

Nikki paused for a moment, appearing to process my words. "Explain."

It took everything in me to not look at Janelle when I spoke, because if I did, I'd give myself away. "If I approach someone, it wouldn't be for a random hookup. I have no interest in that anymore. So if I stopped what I was doing to go speak to a woman, it would have to be someone I would want to become acquainted with. If she doesn't look like she could have fun lounging around on the couch with me on a lazy Saturday afternoon, then I wouldn't give two shits what she wore. It'd be a waste of my time. My ideal woman is someone who can joke and even laugh at herself when the occasion calls for it. If someone isn't comfortable in their own skin, then I have no interest in her."

"But how would you know all that by simply looking at her?"

"Easy." I chanced a glance at Janelle and almost became sidetracked by the shadow of a grin dancing at the corners of her mouth. "It's in the expressions. It's easy to tell if a smile is genuine or not. And you can't fake an effortless laugh. Even without hearing the sound, you can tell by the way her head tilts back and how much she closes her eyes if it's the kind that's capable of breathing life back into you. Because that's the kind of laughter everyone needs around them. We all have crappy days, but the one thing that can make them better is when you come home to that sound."

"You are thinking far too much into this," Nikki said with a giggle, bringing me back to the present. "And you're clearly the wrong person to ask. I told Janelle she needs to update her wardrobe if she ever expects to grab a man's attention, and she said if a guy isn't okay with her clothes then she doesn't want him."

"I'm sorry, Nik…but I have to agree with your sister on this one." I stared at Janelle, waiting for her to say something else, but she didn't. Instead, she narrowed her gaze at me, twisted her lips to the side like I'd seen her do dozens of times, and then nodded to herself, as if having an entire one-sided conversation in her head.

However, nothing shocked me more than the perceptive grin on Christine's lips.

"What did I just walk into?" Stacey asked while stepping into the pool. "Everyone got so quiet."

We all chimed in with "oh, nothing" at the same time, which only served to make us seem like we were hiding something. I was about to get out and leave them, unable to handle the stares and silent suspicions, when Janelle turned to Stacey and said, "I'm glad to see you're not hovering on death's doorstep."

"What do you mean?" Stacey showed genuine confusion, as well as the rest of us.

"Tony got me sick, and I swear I thought I was about to die. I'm not sure how you didn't catch it from him. You must have an amazing immune system."

I knew where this conversation could go, and I didn't want to walk away in case Janelle needed my support.

"How did Tony get you sick?" Stacey regarded her with sincere curiosity.

"Holden said he was sick, and that's why you guys weren't at Mom and Dad's last weekend."

"Oh, yeah…he wasn't feeling well so we thought it'd be best to just stay home. But he couldn't have gotten you sick."

My chest tightened when I noticed the confusion in Janelle's eyes. "I guess I just assumed it was him because I haven't been around anyone else who hasn't been feeling well. I ended up having the flu and strep at the same time. Talk about knocking on death's door. What did Tony have?"

Janelle had no idea the can of worms she'd innocently unleashed. Her question was akin to watching a tsunami on the horizon without being aware of the damage it would cause. Everything went eerily silent. We were outside in a

230

I DO

public area on a holiday weekend. Aside from going deaf, it was virtually impossible for things to be this quiet. My chest tightened, and I couldn't decide what to do. My sight bounced back and forth between them and it felt like decades passed during the wordless encounter.

Stacey turned to the rest of us to seek help, but we all kept our mouths closed and waited for her to make the decision. "He was just tired and weak. Nothing a little rest couldn't cure."

Janelle's hesitation spoke volumes, and as soon as I turned my attention to her, I found her eyes set on me. "What's going on?" She was smart enough to pick up on the body language that left thick tension behind. "Can someone start talking before I get pissed off?"

"Don't get mad, Jelly." Christine tried to calm her by placing a supportive hand on her shoulder.

But Janelle shrugged it off. "I've tried really hard since I arrived for you guys to stop alienating me. If you think I haven't noticed the unspoken innuendos, you're wrong. The only thing I've been told over and over again is that you all want me here. I've been assured countless times that everyone is happy I'm home and so thankful to have me back within the fold. I've truly tried to believe that. But I have to tell you…actions speak louder than words and I can feel what you aren't saying."

"You know why we moved here a couple of years ago, right? Because Tony lost his job?" Stacey waited until she received Janelle's nod before continuing. "Well, he lost his job because he'd gotten sick. He ended up missing too much work, and they couldn't hold his position for him any longer. No one could tell us what was wrong. We went to countless doctors and specialists searching for answers. Instead of answers, the information we received only created more questions. Medical bills started stacking up, and we couldn't survive on my paycheck alone, so we packed up and moved here."

"You finally got answers, though…right?" Janelle's eyes brimmed with tears.

"Well, it took over a year, but yes, we finally received a diagnosis—Lupus." It was obvious to us all that Janelle had no idea what that meant. Finally, Stacey picked up on her sister's silence and offered more information. "It's an autoimmune disease. Basically, his immune system attacks itself and causes him to get really sick."

"Stacey, I'm so sorry that you've gone through all this. Is he better?" Janelle's voice shook as she spoke the words, and I could tell what she'd heard had upset her. The amount of pain her sister had suffered while supporting her husband through this disease was unfathomable.

"We were fortunate to finally receive a diagnosis, but unfortunate because Lupus isn't curable. He'll have it for the rest of his life. Sometimes the symptoms can worsen until they become debilitating, which is what happened a couple of weeks ago. He has flare ups, but the more we learn about it the more we're able to manage his symptoms with medications and treatments. So we're hopeful."

As Janelle absorbed this news, she looked at each of us, and then turned her head to take everyone in, including the family members around the grill by the pavilion. "So everyone knew? Everyone, but me? I'm the only one in the family who didn't know about this?"

"They were all here when it happened, Janelle." Stacey's words were meant to calm the storm brewing inside her sister, but I could tell it didn't work.

"But no one has ever uttered one word about it. When I'd call Mom from college to check in, none of this was mentioned."

I DO

"It's not like we were intentionally keeping it a secret. No one said to not tell you. It's just you weren't here, and there was no point in calling you up to share this with you. They were here—"

"Yeah. I got that part." Janelle's voice remained even, calm on the surface. But I knew her well enough to see the act before me. The hurt clear in her gaze. "It doesn't matter, though." She took in an audible breath before continuing. "The most important thing is that Tony is okay. That's all I care about. And I'm sorry I wasn't here for you, Stacey. I'm grateful you didn't have to deal with it alone. And from now on, if you need me, I'll be here, too."

Janelle's act seemed to have worked on everyone else. They ate it up like chocolate cake at a birthday party. But I didn't. The blue in her eyes brightened—like they do just before tears make an appearance. If anyone else took notice of the same things, they'd assume it was sadness.

But I knew the difference.

I realized Janelle wasn't ready to be rescued just yet, so I excused myself from the pool, dried off, and went back to meet up with the rest of the guys. However, I refused to take my eyes off her so I'd be cued in to when to go to her. She was an adult, fully capable of taking care of herself, but if I were there, she had someone else she could depend on.

She remained with the rest of the women, but it took less than twenty minutes before Janelle vacated her spot by the pool. Once the kids joined them, she used that opportunity to leave the group and head over to the restrooms.

Acting as nonchalant as possible, I waited for her to exit the women's side. She yelped when I grabbed her wrist and tugged her around the corner, but as soon as I had her back pressed against the building with my arms caging her in, she seemed to calm down.

"What are you doing, Holden?" she reprimanded me in a harsh whisper.

"Just checking to make sure you're okay."

"I'm fine. Why wouldn't I be?"

I shrugged, wondering if I had made a bigger deal out of it than there was. "You seemed upset after Stacey told you about Tony. You don't have to pretend with me, Janelle. If you're upset, tell me. We can talk about it, we can leave, we can do whatever you want."

"I told you, I'm fine."

"You were on the verge of crying…just like you are now."

"That doesn't mean—"

"It means you're mad. You keep forgetting how well I know you, Janelle. Just like it's obvious you're upset about Tony having Lupus, but you're too angry over being kept out of the loop to fully absorb what your sister and brother-in-law have gone through."

Her jaw dropped, and her gasp spread between us. And as if finally giving in to her emotions, her bright eyes glistened with forming tears. "I have no right to be mad. But I am. And I have no clue how to change it. I get how selfish it is to be pissed off over them not reaching out to me when a family crisis occurred, but I still can't help how wounded I feel."

"Just get it out. Let me take the weight off your chest." I wiped away a tear.

She closed her eyes and resigned herself to the situation. "They've made me feel like I'm solely responsible for alienating myself from the family. Yet when I came back, they treated me like a stranger. They're the ones who locked me out and refused to budge even an inch to let me in. They created this entire support system and didn't need me. They've made me into an outsider. Even Christine and Matt. I didn't even know they were pregnant the first time." Her tiny fists slammed into my chest. "And you…they even told

234

you about all this. You were not only informed about Tony but you came to their rescue by paying off their bills. I'm literally the only one here that wasn't let in on *any* of these important situations of my 'loved' ones."

I had nothing to say, but she didn't need to hear my words. She only needed someone to listen.

"It's so stupid, because I have no right to be angry about any of this. I could've come home or called more often. I could've made a better effort to be included, and I didn't. I have no one to blame but myself. I'm fully aware of this…so why am I so mad at them?"

"Because it's always easier to blame others than it is to look in a mirror and accept the parts we played in it. No matter who you are or what situation you're talking about, we're all guilty of doing it. But at least you recognize your role and the blame you carry. Once you move through the anger, release it all, you'll be able to look within yourself and figure out how to turn it around."

"Why did you come looking for me?"

I wiped away one last tear, certain she wouldn't have any more. "Because I know you, Janelle," I whispered as I lowered my face to hers.

Seconds before I pressed my lips to hers, she turned her head and offered me her cheek. Her breath hitched, and she shoved against my chest, fear brightening her wide eyes. "Holden!" she scorned in a harsh whisper. "My family is here. They could see us."

With my fingers wrapped securely around her upper arm, I pushed her against the wall, ending her attempt at escape. I carefully held her face in my hand and covered her mouth with mine, cutting off the argument on the tip of her tongue.

The kiss didn't last long, though it didn't need to be to give her the message. As I backed away, lust draped my voice when I growled, "Let them see us. I don't care."

SEVENTEEN

(Janelle)

I was seconds away from exiting my car when the phone rang, making me pause and check the caller ID. It was an out-of-area number, the screen reading "New York," but I had no idea who it was. I didn't know anyone from New York, so I sat there and waited for the ringing to end. Then I waited even longer for the familiar alert, notifying me of a new voicemail.

"This message is for Janelle Brewer. My name is Samantha Verdurmen, and I'm with the Reality Bites production team on the show you participated in, *Soul Mates*. We have been trying to follow up with you and Connor Murphy to get an update on your progress. Please give me a call back so we can catch up. Thank you." Then she spouted off the same number that had been displayed on my caller ID before disconnecting the call.

I certainly wouldn't be able to outrun the situation, and at some point, I'd have to answer a phone call and provide answers—either to the show or Connor. But I wasn't ready just yet. It'd only been a little over a week since Holden and I had started…whatever this was between us, and I had no idea where things stood. I figured I'd give it a little bit longer before deciding my next step. I'd gotten the feeling from Holden that he wanted more with me, which I wanted as well, but I also had to think about the money and what part that played in my future.

I deleted the message and climbed from the car outside Holden's office. My heart pounded harsher with each step I took, and as soon as I opened the door to head inside, I thought I might vomit all over myself. My nerves had absolutely nothing to do with seeing Holden and everything to do with the chances of running into my brother. No matter how many times I tried to tell myself it was fine, I still didn't believe it. Maybe because I wasn't simply there to drop lunch off for my roommate and friend who'd left it at home on his way out. I was convinced Matt would take one look at me and know I'd slept with Holden.

A lot.

Like I somehow had it written all over my face in black permanent marker: **Your best friend has given me countless orgasms**.

And then beneath that in smaller letters: *with his hands, his mouth, and his very large and impressive cock.*

All I wanted to do was slip in and slip back out, unseen, absolutely no attention brought to me, whatsoever. Yet I should've known that was an impossibility. Ever since Holden had called me this morning, asking me to bring him the lunch he'd forgotten in the fridge, my stomach had been in knots and my heart refused to beat a normal rhythm. I'd told him this was a bad idea, but he swore nothing would go wrong. He promised there wouldn't be any issues.

It seemed he'd forgotten about the hot lesbian who sat at the desk by the front door.

"Good morning, Janelle. What are you doing here? Come to see your brother or...*Holden*?" The way she quirked her eyebrow and taunted me with his name rubbed me the wrong way. She hadn't meant it maliciously, but like she'd been

I DO

privy to more than she was supposed to. And if that were the case, I'd kick Holden's ass.

I held up the brown bag and smiled. "Holden left his lunch, so he asked me to bring it up to him."

"I'm surprised he's even thinking of food so soon after breakfast."

I knew if I waited around too long, I'd run the risk of seeing Matthew, and I couldn't chance that. Instead of continuing a conversation with Veronica, I scurried down the hall toward Holden's office. Not wasting a single moment, I grabbed the handle and turned it.

Like a ninja, I opened the door just enough to squeeze through, and once I made it inside, I closed it behind me. Leaning against the solid wood, I closed my eyes to take a moment, needing to calm my racing heart before greeting Holden. And it was a good thing I gave my heart that time to settle, because as soon as I opened my eyes, I noticed my brother standing in front of me. In Holden's office.

"Is everything all right?" he asked, appearing concerned.

"Yeah...everything's great. Just came to bring my friend here his lunch." Just like with Veronica a minute ago, I held up the bag, as if I needed the evidence to prove it wasn't a lie. "He left it at home and called to see if I could drop it off."

Matt turned to Holden and laughed. "How the hell are you still thinking about food after the breakfast you had? No wonder you're gaining weight."

This was the second time I'd heard someone comment about his hunger, referencing breakfast. The only thing I could think of was he'd gone out to eat before work, but he'd made no mention of that when he left the house this morning, or when he called to ask me to come up here. "Breakfast?"

Matt shook his head and moved toward me, heading for the door. "You didn't eat with him?"

"No. She didn't get out of bed." Holden's voice held an air of humor, but I didn't understand.

"What'd you eat?"

His eyes lit up and the corners of his mouth fought against a smile when he said, "Breakfast of champions. Really kick-started my day."

Matt opened the door and laughed. "Yeah, some vegetarian omelet. Doesn't sound like anything I'd like. I prefer meat with my eggs." And with that, he left the office and let the door swing closed behind him.

As soon as we were alone, I crossed the room and chucked his lunch at his head. My face flamed with untamable heat, and I wasn't sure if I wanted to hide under his desk and never be seen in this office again, or beat the shit out of him.

"It's not funny, Holden," I scolded him when he couldn't stop laughing. "You told my brother and Veronica that you had a *vegetarian omelet*? While I was in bed? What if one of them would've guessed what you meant?"

"I didn't tell that to Ronnie. She probably would've known."

"You told Matt!" I collapsed into one of the chairs across from his desk. "See if I ever let you go down on me again. This is so embarrassing."

He got out of his chair and came around the desk to lean against the edge in front of me. "He didn't figure it out."

"Are you sure?"

He snickered again, and it made me stand up, thinking my small frame would do anything to intimidate him. Somehow, two seconds later, he had us turned around so that I sat on the edge of his desk and he stood between my legs.

"Baby...your brother just said he likes meat in his omelets. I think that's enough proof that he has no clue what I'm talking about." He'd taken to terms of endearment more often now, but so far, it seemed restricted to the bedroom or during times like this when being condescending toward me. "Trust me when I say, he has no idea I was talking about eating your pussy."

I swallowed hard and fought to close my legs, needing to clench my thighs together to ease the ache in my throbbing clit, but he wouldn't move out of the way. Instead, he leaned into me, pushing me farther onto his desk, and bringing his mouth close to my ear.

"It was so good, I think I may want it again for lunch."

"It's not noon yet," I argued breathlessly.

"Brunch then. I need to taste you on my tongue. I need to have your legs over my shoulders and your fingers in my hair." His hot breath brushed my neck just below my ear, heating me up until I was about to explode. "I can't get enough of you, Janelle."

Just then, he slipped his hand between us and pressed his thumb against my clit through my jeans. Out of sheer desperation to ease the need he'd created, I allowed him to touch me, completely forgetting about where we were. Until the intercom on his phone came to life with Veronica telling him about some fax that waited on her desk.

I tried to shove at his shoulders, but it was no use. He wouldn't budge. "Holden, you have to stop."

"Why?"

"We're in your office, where my brother or anyone can walk in."

"Then you should probably make it fast."

"Why in the hell do you like to get me off so much?" And he did. There were times he'd touch me just to bring me to orgasm and then he'd leave. "How does this do anything for you?"

With his lips hovering over mine, grazing them as he spoke, he said, "It does everything for me. Your cheeks turn pink and your eyelids grow heavy. Your mouth parts just enough to show me you're breathing too hard for your nose to keep up. Then there's the sounds you make. The soft purrs and low hums. The way you whimper at the height of your orgasm...it does everything for me."

I didn't know how to respond to that. It once again had me all turned around. Conversations like this convinced me he wanted things to be more serious between us, but then he'd go and make a random comment about Connor and the money. He shared his bed with me every night while we slept naked, tangled in each other until morning. I wanted to ask him, but I also needed to make sure that when we did talk about it, I knew for certain what my decision would be. My biggest concern was choosing him, only for it to all blow up in my face. I couldn't handle the kind of devastation that would bring—not only for my family, but for my heart, as well.

He closed his lips over mine, effectively silencing the thoughts from my head.

"Let me see you come," he whispered, and a second later, he had me incapable of choosing an intellectual response. The heat ran through me, and he swallowed every whimper I gave him. But he didn't let up, and I rode the wave, completely coming undone on top of his desk.

After the last tremor subsided, I reached for his belt buckle. "Now it's your turn." But before I could get it undone, he side-stepped out of the way. "That's unfair. Why do you get to do that to me but I can't do it to you?"

His smile lit up his face and I almost became lost in it. "Because I'm at work."

I snarled at him, sliding off the edge of the desk. "Fine. Have it your way."

I DO

"See you at home, honey." His laughter followed me all the way out the door. I tossed a wave over my shoulder when I passed by Veronica's desk, not wanting to chance a conversation with her. Not because I didn't want to talk to her, but because I didn't want to risk running into my brother—especially after what Holden had just done to me on his desk.

I hurried to my car, not taking a full breath of air until I was behind the wheel with the ignition on. However, seconds before I shifted the car into reverse, my phone buzzed, alerting me to a new text message. I quickly checked the screen, seeing Connor's name, and my heart sank to the pit of my stomach. There was nothing in the world worse than being intimate in any way with Holden, and then receiving a text or call from the man I was supposed to leave him for.

It worried me how easily I could get lost in Holden, and how quickly he could vanish from my life like he had before. But I figured if I started to fall for Holden, I would know the right thing to do to prevent a broken heart. However, I didn't take into consideration how you aren't even aware you're falling until you're on your way down, and by that point, you can't *do* anything about it.

Connor: It's been 2 months. Whens he gonna sign???

Me: In no more than four months. No matter how many times you ask me, it will be the same answer. You really need to calm down. They gave us a year to get married. We have plenty of time. I can't do much more than what I already am.

Connor: Is he in love with you?

Me: I have no idea.

Connor: Are you in love with him?

My thumb hovered over the screen. I was unsure of which letters to touch, which words to create, or what answer was

243

the most truthful. Unwilling to think about it much more, I tapped out my message and hit send.

Me: No.

And then I stared through the windshield at the front of his office building, taking in the name on the door: *Brewer & York.* I'd always been aware of the name of the partnership between him and Matthew. But for some reason, this was the first time I paid attention to the names and *didn't* see Matt, didn't see an accountant's office.

I saw my name...next to Holden's.

Guilt flooded me, and I wasn't sure where it came from. I hadn't done anything wrong. The original agreement was still in effect. Holden had known from the beginning what my plans were, and that they involved marrying Connor, so talking to Connor shouldn't have left me wracked with guilt.

But it did.

And not only that, I'd just told him I wasn't in love with Holden.

Confusion ate up the guilt and made me want to flee. Whether my message to Connor was true or not, it was none of Connor's business. I wasn't interested in analyzing the reasons why I'd responded with those two simple letters instead of three.

Connor: Then what are you waiting on?

Feeling beaten down and helpless, I unlocked my phone and sent him a reply.

Me: Give me a week. I think I have an idea.

Connor: I don't have much choice do I?

It'd taken me long enough, but I finally began my apology tour. After licking my wounds, feeling sorry for myself after finding out how my entire family—including Holden—had excluded me from valuable information, I set out to make things right.

My first stop was Rachel. I figured I'd get the easy ones out of the way first. She used to be a teacher, but now she substituted when she was needed. With Kennedy at home, it made more sense for her to cut back the amount she worked without giving up on her dream of molding the youth of our future. I'd never admit it out loud, but she was definitely my favorite sister.

"You're so cute, Jelly. You didn't have to come over here to say you're sorry for living your life. I always knew if I needed you, all I had to do was call. But I appreciate the gesture." We hung out on her couch for about an hour while Kennedy napped, and then I left shortly after she woke up so Rachel could feed her lunch.

The next stop was to Nikki, because she was my second favorite sister—not that I'd ever admit that. As luck would have it, she was at Mom's house for lunch, and I knew Mom would feed me. They both thought my apology was silly but entertained the conversation. Then they decided to discuss breast implants. When Mom started to talk about getting them, I figured it was time to make my exit.

Stacey worked as an at-home health nurse, taking care of an elderly man in his home a few evenings a week, so I went to her house before she had to leave. I made sure I pushed my visit as late as possible in case things went bad. Stacey and I had never really gotten along. We were eleven years apart, but our differences had nothing to do with age, and more to do with our personalities. She was a lot like our dad, whom I loved very much. I was definitely a daddy's girl, but my age was probably *why* my dad and I were so close. I got what I wanted because I was the baby, not because we had much in common or spent a lot of quality time together. If that ever happened, I would be willing to bet I'd lose the title of being Dad's favorite.

"I was jealous of you," she admitted, nearly shocking the shit out of me. "You had a free ride to college where you basically partied it up. Even after you graduated, you did what you wanted. But at the same time, I was angry that you *wanted* to live that life instead of being an active participant in our family. I was hours away, too. Except I didn't have that choice. I was married to a man with a job who didn't have any desire to move closer. And there you were, no reason to stay away, but you did. So I guess it was an equal mix of envy and irritation."

Not many words came to me after hearing her confession, but it sure did help make things clearer from her point of view. "I guess I still have some growing up to do. It kinda sucks when everyone is so much older—I could be the most mature person in a group my own age, but being around my family makes me look like an overindulged child. It's hard to be mature when I feel like I'll never be old enough for you guys to treat me as an equal."

I must've finally gotten through to her, because her eyes softened and she huffed in resignation. "I'm so sorry, Janelle. I guess I never really saw it that way before." She gave me a hug, which seemed to last forever. Once it was over, it was like we had nothing left to say, so before things could turn overly awkward, I said goodbye and left.

Christine was last, even though I spoke to her and Matt regularly. There wasn't much to say other than the apology for being absent when they'd needed me the most. That took all of ten seconds, considering I'd already said it countless times before. And once we got that out of the way, I hung out on her couch with her and helped fold laundry.

With my day complete, I headed home to make Holden dinner.

I DO

Then I realized I'd referred to his house as my home. And I had actually looked forward to cooking him supper. Once again, guilt ate at me over the reply I'd sent Connor, when asked if I was in love with Holden. And once again, I pushed it to the back of my mind, refusing to give it credence until I grew more certain about what the future had in store for us.

I stared at the halos on the ceiling, created by the lampshade on top of his nightstand, while his fingertips danced delicately along my bare skin. "Are you not worried at all about this? About what could happen between us in four months when our time is up?"

"What do you mean?"

I turned my head and met his dark eyes. "There's no question anymore about where we're sleeping. We eat dinner, clean the kitchen, watch a little TV, and then we both stroll in here, strip naked, and then climb into bed. We've gotten really comfortable with each other, and as much as I enjoy it, I'd be lying if I said it didn't concern me."

"Then talk to me. What about our situation concerns you?"

I pushed down the urge to sweep everything under the rug again. I didn't want to be the one who had to say this out loud, but it didn't seem like I had much of a choice. However, I couldn't look him in the eye, so I averted my gaze back to the glow on the ceiling cast by the lamp next to him. "How is this supposed to end? Like...do we just shake hands? Hug? See each other on weekends and act like we didn't spend months in some fake relationship?"

He shifted onto his elbow and hovered over me. The tips of his free hand grazed my side on its way to hold my face. "It doesn't have to end, Janelle. This...what we agreed to at the beginning, doesn't have to be the way it all plays out."

"Then how does this play out? Because I'll be honest with you, Holden...the thought of forfeiting that money and choosing you, only for us to not work out, scares the shit out of me. Because then I'll have nothing. And I can't accept that."

"You won't end up with nothing. I can promise you that. But if it'll make you feel better, we can figure out an alternative plan. You said the show gave you a year to marry the toolbag? Let's go with that then. Forget the six-month agreement we made and base it all off the deal you made for the money. I wanted you to stay here so you could patch things up with your family, and from what I can see, you've done that."

"But that still doesn't answer my question about us. If we break up, it'll make things difficult with my family, with my brother, with *us*."

"Then we don't tell them. We can keep this between us for as long as you want or until they figure it out. That way, it'll buy you time to see how you feel about this. About me and *us*. And no matter what happens, I'll never erase you from my life."

"Why not?"

He lowered his lips to mine and breathed, "Because I need you," against them.

If I had a switch that took me from zero to sixty in a millisecond, he flipped it with those three words—*I need you*. I bent my legs on either side of him and dug my heels into the mattress just enough to feel him where I needed him most. And that must've been his switch, because without wasting a single second, he covered my mouth with his and dug his fingers into my hip.

"Baby, I need you...now."

I splayed my fingers across his bare back and said, "Then take me."

I DO

For a moment, I thought this had to be a dream. I was convinced it wasn't real. Not because the situation dripped with idealistic fairytale qualities, enough to ask for a pinch to tell if it was a figment of my imagination, but because it was so...raw. So...desperate.

His breathing became ragged when he found my entrance. Considering the sensual way my body responded when he'd kissed me, I knew he felt how wet I was for him. Holden seemed to be teetering on the edge of control. His face etched with desire and his eyes half closed in bliss. He thrust inside me feverishly, as if his life depended on it, but I didn't bother trying to slow it down. Truth be told, I craved him just as badly, and a part of me was happy I didn't have to wait.

He slid inside me again, but he stayed fully seated this time, exhaling into the crook of my neck. The heat seeped into my pores and set my insides aflame. But nothing could've come close to what his next words did to me. He gently nipped my earlobe, and in a husky, needy voice, he whispered, "You'll always be a part of me. Always. I'll never be able to quit you."

I dug my nails into his back and flexed my hips, urging him to move once again. At first, he rolled his hips in slow rotations, but then his momentum increased and became more intense. Not much faster than before, but harder. Deeper. He dragged his long, thick shaft almost the entire way out, leaving just the tip inside, before driving himself back in with enough force to knock the air from my lungs. All while never breaking the contact of his hungry stare.

He buried himself over and over, teasing the spot inside me that no one had ever found before. Not that I'd had many partners, but of the ones I did have, it'd remained undiscovered. Until Holden. He'd found it and continued to stroke it with each and every thrust.

"Don't stop," I begged, wrapping my arms and legs around him in an effort to drive him deeper, urging him to move faster, pushing me toward the explosion he'd sparked. "I need you…right there."

He had one arm behind my back and one holding my hip. In a swift move I didn't expect, he maneuvered his arm up just enough to wrap his fingers around my shoulder to keep me from sliding up the bed every time he propelled himself inside me. He snaked his other arm under my leg, locking my bent knee in the crook of his elbow, and then he leaned slightly onto his side. It had to have been the combination of the angle and having developed more control over my body, but within a few seconds, I was ready to shatter and could no longer hold on.

A long, pleading whimper ripped through my throat as I lingered on the peak, and the second I fell over the precipice, gripping him with every muscle within my body, the whimper turned into a full-blown cry of ecstasy. Before I finished riding out the wave, his gruff words filled my ear. "I'm coming." And they took me higher, prolonging my orgasm, and strengthening the hold I had on him.

The part I dreaded when being with Holden was when he rolled off me. Even though he remained inside me and we lay wrapped in a twisted knot of arms and legs, I hated not feeling his weight on top of me. Without him over me, the air cooled and I felt less protected.

Holden was more than my hero.

He was my cape—he could send me flying while cloaking me in refuge all at once.

And it made me even more worried about what would happen to me if it were suddenly taken away.

EIGHTEEN

(Holden)

I tapped my fingers on the manila envelope on the table while staring at Janelle in the seat across from me. I had no idea how she'd react to this, but it was too late to take it back now. "I was going to give you this weeks ago, but then you got sick. So I waited until you were better, but then obviously, I got a little sidetracked. And after our talk last night and our decision to see where this goes between us without time limits—"

"Except the limit set by the show," she corrected.

I rolled my eyes. *Like I'd be able to forget about the show.* "Yes, except that one…I thought this would be the perfect time to give you this." I slid the folder across the table, practically holding my breath, and waited for her reaction.

It was not what I had wanted, but everything I had expected. "I told you I can't afford this place. And now that I'm not sure if I'll get that money, I *really* can't afford it. Why would you do this?" She waved the signed lease papers in the air.

"And like I told you, don't worry about it. You told your family you were staying with me while you got on your feet. You've been here two months, and now you could end up being here for another eight or nine—or more." I reached across the table and grabbed her hand. "You don't have to work if you don't want to, but it's obvious how excited you are about doing something you love. I just wanted to give you every opportunity."

"I know, and I love that you did this for me, Holden. I really do. But that doesn't mean I can snap my fingers and suddenly pay for it. When we talked about this before, back when we looked at storefronts, you were aware I planned to use what I got from the show to cover it."

I got up and moved to the chair next to her. Then I pulled her into my lap where I secured her in place with my arms wrapped tightly around her waist. "I wish you'd stop looking at things in terms of dollar signs. Marriage shouldn't be about money. And you opening your own business should only be about you accomplishing what you've set out to do. So let me worry about the lease and rent for now. *We* are married, Janelle. Let me take care of this for you like any husband would."

She stiffened in my lap and her rigid posture concerned me.

"Baby, talk to me. What's wrong?"

After a harsh swallow and long exhale, she finally shifted to look me in the eyes. "I get that we are technically married, and we are intimate, and behind closed doors, we behave like any regular couple. But I can't stop worrying about what will happen if this doesn't work out. Because now, it's more than just signing the papers and me packing my bags. Now it's a binding two-year lease on a place to house my business. That goes beyond just breaking up and into the territory of an actual divorce."

I traced invisible lines on her back to provide comfort, knowing she needed it. "Don't worry about all that right now. I would never screw you over. Even in the event you decide tomorrow that I'm not what you want and you'd rather be with One-Pump, there's not a chance in hell I would do anything to hurt you."

She wrapped her arms around my shoulder and hovered her lips over mine. "I'm not worried about *me* being screwed over. I'm more concerned with you getting the raw end of the deal."

Growing up, I had always been told by my mom and teachers that I was such a smart, bright kid, but I never applied myself enough. At the time, I didn't think about the true meaning behind those comments. And even though they were right about some of my abilities, they were completely wrong about my thought process. It wasn't until some much-needed self-discovery that I realized I overanalyzed everything. I picked everything apart until I was left with the tiniest pieces. Rather than break away the outer shell to discover the answer, my method was to dismantle the entire thing. It didn't matter what it was, a math equation, work issue, or life problem, I picked it apart to the point where even the truth was destroyed.

Which is exactly how I'd dealt with Janelle.

When she had come to me—actually, she'd gone to Matt, but he wasn't home so she'd settled for me—I'd thought that meant something. So, four months later when she came up with the amazing idea to get hitched by Elvis in Vegas since we were already there, I saw it as a romantic moment. One we would retell while living the rest of our lives together, completely in love. Looking back on it, I had given our love for one another too much credibility. That night, I analyzed the pieces I wanted to see, while ignoring the blatant red flags that waved frantically in front of my face. The events that led up to our marriage and those that quickly followed should've told me everything I needed to know. And when she'd come back to me, showing up on my doorstep and asking for a divorce, I should've seen those fucking red flags billowing in the wind. But once again, I saw only what I wanted to see. Had I stopped at any point during our time together to evaluate the starting image, the one from before Vegas, I might've seen it all.

But I never did.

Instead, I took a blind leap of faith and dove in headfirst, without a doubt in sight.

I didn't actually take a step back until the following week at the office.

Matt barged in without knocking and took a seat across from me. He relaxed into it with his elbows on the armrests and his ankle propped on his knee. There was something in the easy way he sat there that told me this was the news I'd been waiting a lifetime to hear.

"Spill it." I turned away from my computer and crossed my arms on my desk.

"Spill what? I have no idea what you're talking about. I just came in here to see my best friend, find out how he's doing, maybe see if he wanted to go grab lunch with me while Ronnie takes messages for us. You know…nothing out of the ordinary."

I couldn't help but laugh at him. We rarely went out for lunch together because it seemed we had too much to do in the office. If anything, we'd order in and sit together in the conference room while going over a mountain of paperwork. Not only that, but I couldn't contain my enjoyment at seeing his smile. It reminded me so much of Janelle's when she seemed so full of excitement I thought she'd burst.

"I have no problem doing that. I'd be happy to grab a bite to eat, but maybe you should go ahead and tell me the good news now. I don't think I can hide my surprise until noon."

Matt feigned confusion with a tilted head, gaping mouth, and dramatically knitted brow.

I DO

"We've been friends since before we hit puberty, Matt. And if that doesn't mean anything, maybe I should remind you that we lived together for four years, then opened this place together, and I was best man at your wedding. If you seriously think I've been blind to your repetitive tardies, long lunches, stressed attitude, and the repressed hope you've had bottled up over the last few months, then you're a moron."

His fake confusion turned to genuine shock. "You knew?"

"Well, not at first. I had an idea, but there was one other time late last year I thought so, as well, and that didn't pan out. So I figured I'd keep waiting and see if anything changed. I mean, if all went well, you'd eventually say something to me. Right?"

"Maybe we're talking about the wrong thing…" He eyed me suspiciously.

"It's possible, but I doubt it. Every four weeks on the dot you either come in late or take a long lunch, and every time, you expect beforehand that it'll happen and you let me know—the same thing you did the two times Christine was pregnant, and you went with her to the appointments. That in itself isn't overly telling considering I'm aware you two have gone to see multiple doctors for other reasons, but it was enough to take an educated guess. And then there's the way you snap at Ronnie leading up to those secret appointments, and afterward when you finally make it back to the office, you're so pleasant to be around. It doesn't take a genius to guess what's going on."

"You seriously figured all that out by watching me?"

"Don't make it sound like that. Don't cheapen what we have or dirty it with insinuations of obsession and stalking." I pretended to flip the hair I didn't have and then crossed my arms over my chest, giving him the best impression of an offended woman as I could. "Most people would kill to have a man like me in their life, watching them, making sure they were all right. But you don't even seem to be grateful."

Laughing beneath his breath, Matt threw a pencil at me.

"That could've poked my eye out. I'm not sure what kind of Worker's Comp claims are typical at an accounting firm, but a pencil to the eye probably isn't one that's seen often."

"I don't think it can be fairly assessed as to how often it gets *seen*...I mean, they'd be missing an eye right? I'm sure visibility is lowered at that point." We both shared a good laugh, one I hadn't had with him in a while. After the hilarity lessened, he asked, "So now that you know, you still want to have lunch with me?"

I leaned back in my chair and shook my head. "I don't know anything, because you have yet to tell me anything."

"Good. Then I'll tell you at lunch." He got up and headed for the door.

"Pick me up around eleven thirty?" I teased with my voice high and flirty.

Matt stood with the doorknob in his grip, his upper body turned to face me, and a smile stretched across his mouth. "Yeah, but I'm not bringing you flowers."

"That's fine. But don't expect me to put out."

He laughed again, and just when I thought he'd open the door and leave, he relaxed his stance and said, "Christine's pregnant." His voice quivered, his words sounding on the edge of tears. I'd only seen the man cry twice—when he'd seen Christine walk down the aisle, and when they lost their first baby. "I'm going to be a dad."

"Congrats, Matt. You'll be the best. No doubt about it."

I really wanted to run over to him, hug the life out of him, show him exactly how ecstatic I was for him, but my feet wouldn't move. That didn't at all mean I wasn't happy or didn't care to celebrate with him. It signified the enormity of the situation, the delicacy, and it expressed how grateful I was to the universe for this. If anyone deserved this kind of happiness, it was Matt—and obviously, Christine.

Once the door closed behind him, and I was left alone in the silence of my office, I couldn't help but think about the future and what I wanted out of it. It was obvious Matt was getting everything he could possibly want and deserve, and I couldn't be happier for him. But that happiness made me reexamine my own life. It made me think about what I wanted for myself. What would make me happy and would it even be possible to achieve that level of contentment.

For years, my focus had been the accounting firm. Any goal I'd set had to do with my business, and in the grand scheme of things, they were rather short term. Aside from the brief moment in time when I thought I had a future with Janelle, I'd never thought about the long term.

The realization suddenly hit me—I wanted that, too.

Maybe Matt becoming a dad put things into perspective for me, since we were the same age. Maybe it was having Janelle at the house and getting a taste of what life would be like with her as my wife. Whatever the reason, I couldn't stop myself from imagining my life years from now, and what I ultimately wanted.

Without a doubt, I was certain I wanted Janelle by my side. I wanted her to take my last name, for real this time. And I knew I wanted her to carry my children. As many as she'd give me. I wanted it all, and I wanted it with her. The Sunday dinners with our kids and grandkids coming to our house while she heated up frozen lasagna in the oven—although, the more we had cooked together, the better she'd gotten at it.

My sudden awareness overwhelmed me.

And now I needed to figure out what to do about it.

"There's no time for that, Holden." Janelle smirked at me through the mirror while she got ready for dinner. Matt and Christine had invited us all over to their house to share and celebrate their good news.

I moved to stand behind her, my hands on the bathroom vanity on either side of her waist, trapping her in. With my chin on her shoulder, I locked gazes with her in the mirror. "I can be fast. You don't even have to stop putting on your makeup."

She snickered and shoved me away with her shoulder. I took a step back and observed my sink area—the one that used to have next to nothing on it. Now, her soaps and lotions filled the corner, and her toothbrush joined mine in the cup to the side.

"Do you know why they've asked everyone to come over tonight?" She finished swiping on her gloss and smacked her lips in the mirror. When she found my eyes again, she turned around and perched herself on the edge of the vanity. "You do know, don't you? Spill it. Is it what I think it is?"

"Depends...what do you think it is?"

She waved me off with an infectious giggle. "Doesn't matter. I have a pretty good idea. I mean, why else would they ask the entire family over to their house at the same time?"

Grabbing her by the hips, I moved her farther onto the granite and then fit myself between her parted thighs. I glanced down and took in her outfit, loving the long skirt. This wasn't her typical attire, but realizing how easily accessible it made her, I wanted to stock her closet full of skirts just like this one. Then a thought crossed my mind and made me still my movements—I didn't want her clothes in any other closet than mine. Ever.

I DO

As my fingertips skimmed the outside of her soft legs, I caressed her cheek with mine and closed my eyes, taking it all in. I wanted nothing more than to tell her everything, confess my love for her and beg her to stay forever. I wanted to confess how I felt and the things I wished for our future. But I knew I had to wait. We'd been through so much over the years, going all the way back to before Vegas, and I needed to warm her up to the idea of a *real* forever with me. So I bit my tongue and hummed while slowly dragging her skirt up, baring her to me.

"Really, Holden." My name was barely a whisper on her tongue. Her words said one thing, but her tone conveyed another—her mounting desires. "We don't have time. We'll be late if you keep this up."

"Do you really want me to stop?"

"No," she breathed out. And rather than say anything else, she unbuttoned my pants and slid down the zipper. "But I need more than you just getting me off by touching me. I need you inside me. Fuck me, Holden."

Her boldness fueled me. I yanked her off the vanity, causing her to yelp in surprise. But I didn't pause. I spun her around and held her by her shoulder, pressing into her until she caught herself with her hands on the granite, facing the mirror. I didn't even bother to drop my pants and remove her skirt. I simply bunched the fabric over her ass, pulled her thong to the side, and lined myself up with her entrance. One thrust and I was deep inside, her warm heat embracing me. It took everything in me to not come right then.

Her face flushed, and her mouth dropped open, but that didn't stop her from watching it all in the mirror. The one thing I hated was not being able to see her fingers work over her clit due to the skirt hiding it from view. But other than that, it was perfection. And when she squeezed me with her orgasm, I gave her everything I had, filling her with every drop, and in the back of my mind, I couldn't stop the thought of one day impregnating her.

We both stood there, weak and breathless, trying to regain our strength to finish getting ready. After a few minutes, I kissed her shoulder and left her in the bathroom to clean up while I went into the kitchen for a glass of water.

And I would take back that decision in a second if it was possible.

As I stood leaning against the countertop, gulping down the cool liquid, her phone chimed in front of me. Normally, I wouldn't have thought twice about it. I wouldn't have looked at it or even wondered who it was or what they wanted. But with the way it was angled, I couldn't miss *his* name as it lit up the screen. And as if that wasn't bad enough, I couldn't miss what *he* said: *Did he fall for it?*

It took full minutes, which felt like hours, to pick up her phone and unlock the screen. I didn't want to, for numerous reasons. I wanted to trust her, to believe she hadn't lied. I also wanted to live in the fantasy I'd created in my mind, if only for a little longer. I'd fallen in love with the picture I'd easily painted, the one of us years and years from now with an entire family built off love and trust and devotion.

But that all vanished once my eyes latched onto the words on her screen. The many, many words that created conversations between her and this other man. Syllables containing betrayal and lies, proving I'd been wrong about everything this entire time. Even if I wanted to fantasize and say she'd chosen me—or at the very least, chosen to see where things would go between the two of us—I couldn't. Not with their conversation in front of me.

Connor: Are you in love with him?
Janelle: No.
Connor: Then what are you waiting on?

I DO

Janelle: *Give me a week. I think I have an idea.*

Connor: *I don't have much choice do I?*

The time stamp showed a week had passed between that message and the next one. However, when I thought back to the dates around the last conversation, the one when he asked if she loved me and she told him no, it had been less than two weeks. And if my memory served me correctly, that had been around the time when she'd had a change of heart. When we'd decided to see where things would go between us before making any decisions regarding the divorce. When affection had turned from friendship to complete commitment. At least on my part. Now I knew it was only playacting on hers.

Connor: *It's been a week. I need an update.*

Janelle: *Be patient.*

Connor: *I've been patient. I want my money.*

Janelle: *So do I. Trust me, I have things I need it for.*

Connor: *Then what's taking you so long???*

Janelle: *I can't just walk out the door or force him to sign the papers. If I don't play by his rules, he won't sign, and then we'll have nothing. So you need to chill the fuck out. OK? We still have time.*

By that timestamp, I was sure we had already had *the* discussion. The one where she'd accepted the storefront I'd offered her for her business. Reading her words about wanting the money ate at me. They crawled into my chest and festered until I couldn't breathe. But I forced myself to continue reading. I needed the truth.

Connor: *The show wants an update.*

Janelle: *I know. They've been blowing up my phone. Figured they'd eventually reach out to you.*

Connor: *What am I supposed to tell them?*

Janelle: *IDC. We have until the beginning of July. Tell them we decided to get married in June.*

Connor: *Why the hell are we waiting that long?!*
Janelle: *I didn't say we were...just tell THEM that.*

The next text messages were random and all from the last few days. It didn't appear she'd responded to any of them, but I wasn't stupid. I was very aware you could delete texts. I wasn't certain if she had, and I hoped these being left behind meant she hadn't, because I couldn't fathom deleting only her texts and not the others.

Connor: *So what's the progress with him?*
Connor: *Hello??*
Connor: *What is this plan of yours?*
Connor: *Did he fall for it?*

But it didn't truly matter if she'd deleted them. There was enough damning evidence left behind that couldn't be ignored. I couldn't excuse anything she'd told him, and even more so, the questions her words created in my mind forced me to reexamine everything I'd thought to be true.

She wanted the money—that had never been a secret—but the one thing I'd always refused to think about was her taking any of mine. From the beginning, we had always discussed a clean divorce. I'd sign the papers, and she'd carry on with her life. Done deal. Clean break. No arguing, no fighting over possessions. Nothing. But now, I couldn't help but wonder if she'd had a different plan all along. One I didn't know about.

She was aware I had money. Maybe not how much, considering I hadn't gotten rid of my first house, the one I bought when Matt and I had first started out, before we began to actually make real money. I'd kept the house for a couple reasons; aside from it being my first home and that it held sentimental value, I'd also bought it thinking I'd one day share it with my wife—who at the time was Janelle. And aside from renting her that storefront, telling her she didn't need to worry about it for now, I'd never flaunted what I had.

I DO

Then again, I'd practically begged her to let me be her husband and take care of her financially until she was able to get on her feet with her own business. I'd even declared she didn't have to work. And then there were her words from a little over a week ago when she told me she wasn't worried about being hurt—her concern was *me* getting shafted in the end. When I'd given her the envelope containing the lease, she'd made such a big deal about what would happen if we were divorced, that this lease would make things complicated. Now it became all too apparent why it caused concern. She'd never stopped planning for divorce.

It had basically been spelled out in front of me, if only I'd opened my eyes to see it sooner. Instead, I'd chosen to live with my eyes wide shut, fooled by her naked body in my bed every night. She'd blinded me from the start with who she was—my best friend's sister, the girl I'd known over half my life and been in love with for years. Who would've ever thought someone that close to me would've been capable of stabbing me in the back? *I* never did. And even standing here now, staring at her own words—practically a signed confession—I still didn't want to believe it.

But it was true.

And I was the only one to blame.

This entire time, I thought I had the upper hand. I thought I was safe from harm, that she'd never do anything like that to me. For some stupid reason, I had it in my head that what happened between us was more than this, more than lies and stealing and heartbreak. I'd let my guard done, but I was wrong. Then again, all I had to do was take a good look at her actions and I should've been able to predict all this.

This was the same girl who'd turned her back on her family. She'd taken her parents' hard-earned money and used it to party for five years, going after a degree she didn't need.

Her dream job was to throw parties for a living. That should've been enough to slap me in the face, but it wasn't.

It all fit together perfectly, no matter how badly I didn't want to believe it. If she waited a little bit longer, she could take more from me than just my heart. I'd made all my money in the course of our marriage, which meant she was entitled to half of it. And then once she finished taking me to the cleaners, providing the given year hadn't expired, she could marry the asshole and make even more money.

I was such a fool.

I'd asked for this, all because I wanted to bring her family back together. Well, it seemed I had succeeded in doing so, only I'd managed to ensure that my position in the family expired.

"Hey, Janelle?" I locked her phone and set it back where I'd found it. She was still in my bathroom, but rather than walk all the way into my room, I stood by the doorway and called out for her. "This is a family thing, so I think I'm gonna stay out of it."

She peeked her head around the corner and scrunched her brow in question. "What? That's silly, Holden. You *are* part of the family. He's your best friend, and you've kind of been a big part in this since the beginning, right? You deserve to be there to celebrate with everyone else."

"Nah. This is a Brewer thing. Plus, Matt and I already celebrated the other day at lunch. Tonight is for the family. I don't think anyone has been told, and I suck at acting surprised, so it'd be best if I didn't go."

"That's not what's going on." She stepped into the room, and I feared if she came much closer, I would lose my composure and tell her everything—which I couldn't do until I had time to dissect it all. "What's wrong? What happened after you walked out of here a few minutes ago?"

"Nothing. I was just thinking about this whole thing and realized I really shouldn't be there."

"Are you just going to stay here? If that's the case, I'll stay with you."

"No. I actually think I'm going to meet up with some guys I haven't seen in a while and hang out. I don't want them thinking that just because I have a woman living with me it means I can't make time for them."

"Oh…okay." She nodded slowly, and I knew she didn't believe me, but I didn't have anything else to offer. "What time will you be home? I don't think the dinner will last too long, but I can come home whenever you do."

I licked my bottom lip, hoping the pain in my chest would lessen. "Eh, you take your time. This is a big deal for you guys, and it's an even bigger deal that you get to be included this time. The entire family will be together while your brother shares probably the biggest news of his life."

Rather than wait for her to say anything else, knowing I wouldn't be able to handle much more, I retreated and grabbed my keys off the table. She never came out of the room, and behind my closed eyes, I pictured her standing in the same spot just outside the bathroom, next to *her* side of the bed, confusion settling in every shallow crease on her perfect face. I didn't want to be responsible for putting the pain in her eyes, but I didn't have much of a choice.

And as I drove away from my house, from my wife, I reminded myself that I hadn't been the one to make the decision. She had. I didn't make her lie to me. She did that on her own. I didn't make her lead me on for money. That had been her choice. The only thing I had done was give her my heart.

Foolish me…I never thought to ask her to take care of it.

NINETEEN

(Janelle)

Dinner at Matthew's house was good — better than good. The entire family was excited to hear the news, and even more thrilled to find out how far along they were. At sixteen weeks, they were able to find out the sex of the baby, but they'd decided to keep that to themselves for a little bit longer. I didn't blame them. With the stress and worry over the last three months, praying every day that they'd make it to the next, fearful that saying anything or having the slightest bit of hope would somehow jinx it, they deserved to keep a little something for themselves.

So many things started to make sense. Such as why Christine never got in the pool over Labor Day weekend when we were all at the park. I noticed she had put on some weight, but I would've never guessed it was baby weight. She didn't even have a stomach yet. It also made sense why she was so anxious when she had to take me to the clinic. It wasn't just bad memories, but because she knew she had a life inside her, and when I realized that, it made my heart hurt for her. Even though it all worked out, I couldn't help but be upset with myself and Holden for having her around me when I was so sick. Had she caught it, things could've been made worse.

I DO

But I refused to allow myself to think negatively. It didn't matter what *could've* happened, the important thing was that it didn't—which Matthew and Christine made sure of. Apparently, their previous miscarriages all happened between weeks eight and eleven. This time, when they made it to week twelve, they didn't tell anyone because they wanted to wait until after the doctor's appointment. Once they saw their doctor and even got to see the baby, they still weren't ready, worrying that announcing the news too soon would cause bad things to happen. And each week they made it to the next, there was one more reason to wait. Finally, after their last appointment, in which they were able to find out the gender, they decided it was time.

I only wished Holden had been here to experience this.

Matt had asked where he was, and when I told him what Holden had said to me before leaving the house, he gave me an odd look, but I ignored it.

Something was going on with Holden, and I was afraid to say too much for fear my brother would figure things out. Then again, I began to wonder how bad that would be. I'd started to think a lot more about this at night while curled up in Holden's arms. While he slept, his soft, even breaths dancing along my chilled, bare skin, I'd lay there with my fingers playing in the short, curly hairs on the side of his head, imagining how everyone would react if they knew the truth.

Just thinking about the curly hairs on the sides of Holden's head made me want to rush home and climb beneath the covers with him, just so he could lay his head on my chest and I could run my fingertips through them. When he let his hair grow too long, the curls went away, and they're only noticeable just above his ears. The top of his hair had some body to it, but rather than give it a curly look, it made it seem more like he'd just crawled out of bed. Or ran his fingers through it a couple million times. Or really, it looked like I'd taken ahold of it while he buried his face between my thighs—which was a more plausible reason than anything else, considering how much he enjoyed spending time down there.

"I'm so excited for you two. I really am. As soon as you guys decide to reveal the gender, make sure I'm included. And if it's a party, let me plan it. I have so many ideas, and I can totally do it without knowing what you're having. I don't have the office set up yet, but this would be a really good reason to get my butt moving." I hugged Christine and patted my brother on his chest. "I'm really so happy for you guys."

After saying goodbye for the hundredth time, I finally got in my car and headed home. I'd spent hours at their house, all of us staying late, and had assumed Holden would be back by the time I pulled in the driveway, but I didn't see his car. I wondered if he'd parked in the garage, which he used to do all the time when I'd first moved in, but now he seemed to prefer to keep his car next to mine in the driveway. I never asked, and he never explained. It just was what it was.

However, when I opened the front door, I realized he still wasn't home. I tried his cell a few times, but he didn't answer. I figured it was noisy where he was so I switched to my text messages, thinking I had more of a chance of him answering that. But when I pulled up the app, I noticed the last message from Connor, and suddenly, Holden's absence made sense. Connor had asked if Holden had fallen for it—whatever "it" was. If that was all Holden had seen, I wouldn't be surprised why he took off. But it didn't show me I had an unread message, so I assumed he'd read it all. And if he did, he'd see I hadn't responded in a while.

Figuring he only needed a few hours out with his friends, maybe a few drinks to deal with Connor's ignorant text, I sent him a simple message: *I'm home...will be waiting for you naked in bed.* I added a winky face and prayed that would be enough.

I DO

As I lay in bed all alone, I realized far more than I ever did with him next to me, and I immediately hated how that happened. The line, *absence makes the heart grow fonder*, is rather accurate, but I loathed that it was. We shouldn't have to lie in bed next to a cold, empty spot to realize just how much we need the person who occupies it. We should know that every night *while* that person is there. But for reasons I'd never comprehend, it'd taken this long for me to see everything clearly. Either that or it was the news of Matt and Christine's baby. Whatever it was, I had a lot to think about, but at least I had plenty of time to do it in, considering it didn't seem like Holden would be coming home anytime soon.

I'd loved Holden almost my whole life. When I was younger, it could've been described as puppy love. Infatuation. It was hearts on a notebook and our names sketched in script on lined paper. As I got older, it developed into a deep friendship. He was someone I could trust, someone who would never hurt me and would protect me. He truly was my hero, and staring at the ceiling now, I knew when I had given him my heart.

Yes, I had been upset and heartbroken over the whole Justin situation, but if I stopped and truly looked back at that time in my life, I'd see how quickly I had actually gotten over that breakup. Most of my excuses for coming to see him, spending time with him on his couch, wasn't because I was upset over some kid who probably wouldn't have lasted longer than ten seconds in bed. I'd gone to see Holden so much because I'd *wanted* to. I'd *wanted* to see Holden and be with him, share the same air as him and *feel* him next to me.

The five years that followed that time had been a mistake on my part. Had I known then what I knew now, I more than likely never would've moved away to college. And if I did move away, I would've made sure to stay more in contact with my family—all of them. But more than that, I would've made sure to keep Holden in my life. Because I needed him. I needed him then, and I needed him now.

It wasn't like I'd spent all this time uncertain of what I wanted, whether it be Holden and a future with him, or the money from the show. I comprehended exactly what I wanted, even before Holden had discussed waiting it out to see how things would go. I was simply too scared to make a decision, because my entire future rode on whatever I chose. And no matter what Holden said about what happened after Vegas, how I'd disappeared and turned my back on him—*he* was the one who'd vanished. I had no recollection of that night, and he knew it, and rather than comfort me, fill me in on what I couldn't remember, he ignored me. I understood his reasons for staying away, how he must've felt during that time and the guilt he carried around with him. But that was no excuse. The last five years could've been so different had he acted on it, and no matter what he said now, nothing would make that fear go away. The fear of him doing it again. Of me giving up fifty thousand dollars for him, only for him to vanish once more.

Much like he did tonight.

When I opened my eyes, realizing I had fallen asleep at some point, the morning sun bathed the room in its soft glow. I stretched, and then immediately sat up, realizing his side of the bed was still empty. It hadn't been slept in. Fear choked me, worst-case scenarios flickering through my mind. I jumped out of bed, threw on the first T-shirt I came across, and flung the door open. I didn't find him in the living room, but when I peered through the front window, I noticed his car parked in the driveway next to mine. That's when I heard noises coming from down the hall.

I raced back there and found him in my old room, taking apart the furniture. He already had the dresser broken down, the mirror leaning against the wall, and the bed mostly dismantled by the time I walked in. He sat on the floor with a screwdriver in his hand, his tongue peeking out, and his hair in even more disarray than usual.

"Does this mean I'm officially staying in your room now?" I started to squat, to join him on the floor, but his eyes stopped me. The anger darkening the green and lining his brow kept me from sitting down. In fact, it kept me from breathing, as well. "What's going on?"

"Your clothes are in bags. I've already put them in your car for you. I'm not sure how you plan on getting all this out of here, but I figured I'd save time and go ahead and break it all down for you. It should make moving it out easier. The patio table will have to come out of the gazebo, and the chairs are still in the garage. I can't really do much with the couch in the other room, so it can stay there until you arrange for a U-Haul or whatever you plan on using to take this all with you. Just don't take too long, because I want it out."

"I-I don't understand. W-what happened, Holden?" I had to fight back the tears, but that didn't stop them from filling my voice and breaking my words. "Last time I saw you, you were fucking me in your bathroom, then you left the house and now you're...now you're kicking me out? Is this because of Connor's text message?"

His eyes snapped to mine, and the heated anger I saw reflecting in them shattered my heart. "I was a fool to think you'd actually choose me. To assume you'd give this an honest shot. Silly me...here I was believing you were putting forth the effort in seeking a long-term relationship with me. But I was wrong. Because the whole time, you were talking to that asshole, 'planning' things behind my back. And you know what? I had an idea you were still talking to him. I guess I just trusted that you wouldn't stab me in the back."

271

"I didn't—"

"No...you're absolutely right, Janelle. You didn't stab me in the back. You faced me, looked me right in the eye, and stuck your knife straight through my chest while I watched. I just want to know why. Was it the money?"

I had no clue what he was talking about, but I refused to give up without a fight. "I didn't stab you anywhere. Not in the back or the chest. And I did give it a fair shot—I'm *still* giving it one. I want *you*, Holden. Don't let one stupid text change anything. Clearly, you saw that I haven't been responding to him."

"Yeah. And I also noticed that you hadn't told him the change of plans."

"What is there to tell him?" I raised my voice, partly out of fear, but also from frustration. I couldn't fathom losing him, especially over something silly like this, but I'd be lying if I didn't say his refusal to calm down and talk about this rationally pissed me off. "You wanted to remove the six-month deadline and just let things happen and see where they'd go. So what was I supposed to tell him?"

"Exactly that."

"Why when I could just wait until either January, when he was already expecting this to be over with, or until I had a definitive answer? That made more sense to me, and I'm sorry for not explaining that to you, but I knew how much you hated talking about him."

"Just tell me, Janelle...was it about the money?"

I fought against rolling my eyes and decided to pause for a full inhalation instead. "Yes, Holden. It's always been about the money. You knew that from the beginning. If you chose to ignore it and not see it for what it was, then I'm not sure what else to tell you."

I had never kept it from him. He understood there was nothing between me and Connor, and that marrying him wouldn't ever be a real thing, only a way to get the money. Hell, he'd been informed of that from day one, yet he still offered to move me in with him as part of *his* deal. Not to mention, when we talked about exploring what we had between us, and again when he surprised me with the lease on the storefront, I was very open and honest with him regarding my fear over giving up the money and still losing him. I hadn't kept any of that a secret, yet now, he acted as if I'd never told him any of it.

"That's what I thought," he practically said to himself, as if his words weren't meant for me. But I heard them all the same, and they hurt more than I'm sure he intended. "Listen, Janelle...this isn't gonna work out. I should've never believed it would. I guess I got wrapped up in having someone with me. I didn't stop and look at the bigger picture. In the end, I got what I wanted, and you got what you wanted, so I guess we're even."

"I got what I wanted? What did I want, Holden? Huh? And what did I get?"

He stood from the floor and grabbed an envelope off the top of the empty dresser. I hadn't seen it in two months, but I knew exactly what it held. "Signed. Sealed. And delivered. Here's your divorce. Just like you asked for, except four months early. Our part of the deal is done. Completed. Feel free to move on and go after what you want."

I wanted to scream at him, slap him until he stopped listening to his own thoughts and heard the words I told him—the words proclaiming that *he* was what I wanted. But there was something in his eyes that prevented me from continuing. The severe coldness displayed left me unable to speak. The hope I'd held onto from the beginning started to float away and it became painfully obvious that nothing I said would change his stance.

"As far as the storefront goes…you haven't technically started your business yet. I was thinking I could sublease it out, but if you'd like, I could sublease it to you. But don't feel pressured to take it; I know how expensive it is and how much you never wanted it in the first place. I figured since you haven't done anything with the space yet, I'm not causing you any irreparable damage."

I clenched my teeth and balled my hands into fists, holding myself back from either wrapping my arms around him and pleading with him to listen and give me a chance, or physically attacking him. I couldn't decide if I wanted to love him or hate him, and that war only made things worse.

I nodded, acknowledging him without words, because I didn't trust myself to speak.

"There are still some clothes of yours in my room and in the laundry room. Feel free to finish getting ready—take a shower if you need to, use the bathroom, eat breakfast. I'll be in here finishing this. And I guess just keep me in the loop of what you plan to do with all this."

"I don't want any of this. Throw it all away for all I care." I swallowed down my need to cry. Although this time, my tears were made of more than anger. They were mixed with pain. Pure agony. An absolute broken heart, unlike I'd ever experienced before. If I thought flying home after Vegas alone was bad, *nothing* compared to walking back to his room alone.

After almost twenty minutes of sitting on the edge of his bed with my head in my hands, crying unlike I'd ever cried before, I finally managed to pull myself together enough to get ready and leave. As pathetic as it was to cry in his room by myself, it proved to be therapeutic, because it reminded me how I was the only one I could depend on to wipe away my tears.

And as I drove away with my clothes in bags in the back seat, I was reminded that superheroes don't exist. Not even the ones who didn't have powers from other planets. In fact, it was the first time I believed that I had a better chance of running into a man who could fly than I did finding a man who wore a mask at night to fight the bad guys. I learned I needed to start believing in the ones who'd been bitten by an insect and suddenly had superhuman powers, or the ones created in a lab.

Because real heroes didn't exist.

No one would come rescue me.

As I drove away from Holden York, I learned just how alone I was.

———

"I must say, Janelle, your call surprised us all." Samantha Verdurmen, one of the producers on the show, sat across from me at a large mahogany desk in New York City. "Last time we spoke to Connor, he said you two were planning a wedding for next summer."

"Well, things happened unexpectedly." Even though I sat here with a smile on my face, it didn't mean my heart had stopped hurting. It remained shattered in my chest, but I chose to ignore it, doing what I did best—moving on and turning my back to the past. "As you're aware, I had to get divorced, so that took some time."

"And I see you've gotten the papers signed?" She picked up the envelope and pulled out the papers with Holden's signature scratched along the bottom. I hadn't even looked at it, unable to see his name in ink, dried, dissolving the marriage I had just barely gotten to enjoy.

After leaving Holden's house, I didn't know where else to go, so I stayed at a hotel for a couple of days while Connor helped me sort it all out. He'd called the show and found out the next steps we needed to take. We'd planned this meeting so they could guide us in how to proceed. They'd even set us up in a fancy two-bedroom suite.

"I won't lie, Miss Brewer, I didn't expect you'd get these signed. We were thinking you had changed your mind."

I glanced at the other people in the room—none of whom I recognized. They were all suits, leaning back in their leather chairs, executives in every sense of the word, regarding me silently. Samantha was the only one who spoke, and even she remained vague most of the time.

"Well, if I'm being honest, I almost did change my mind. By the time those papers were signed, I wasn't the one who asked for it." I couldn't keep the pain from my voice any longer. It may have been a week since I walked out of his house with the envelope in my hand, but that didn't make it hurt any less. In fact, if anything, it only made it worse. Because I hadn't heard one word from him.

I'd spoken to my family—each of them—at least once since I left, telling them I had gone to New York with friends for a girls' trip I completely made up, and not one of them even mentioned his name. It hurt. A lot. But I had to forge on. I couldn't dwell on his decision, because in the end, he'd made it based on my actions. On my inability to communicate to Connor regarding my feelings and desires for Holden. I was the only one to blame.

But the thing that hurt most, even though I hadn't truly expected it, is that he hadn't come after me. He'd dropped me just like he had after Vegas.

"So what happened? Why the change of heart on his part?" she asked, sounding more like a reporter than the producer of a lame reality show.

"It doesn't matter." I sat up straighter, hoping my body language conveyed that this topic was off limits. "What's important is that I did my part, got the papers signed, and

I DO

now all that's left is to marry Connor and then collect our money."

"Well, you still have to file for the divorce. This is only step one." She held up the folder. "If you'd like, we have an attorney on staff who could represent you and have this taken care of on your behalf."

I hesitated, really thought about her offer. It sounded like a dream, not having to deal with the reality of the dissolution of a marriage I'd only recently started to accept. It would mean I could move on and lick my wounds, while working toward collecting the check—the whole reason I was even in this position to begin with.

We spoke a bit more. I asked her questions about the attorney and how filing the papers worked, about how long it would all take and when I would be able to legally marry Connor. She asked me some questions about my views on marriage and if I thought Connor and I would be able to make a real go of things. I almost laughed at her when she asked me that. Our prize money wasn't contingent on our relationship, so I didn't have to be in love with him or even pretend we were getting married for the right reasons. Certain I had nothing to lose—and no one else to talk to—I chose to be honest with her and everyone in the room. I opened up about Holden and where things stood before I woke up that fateful morning. I explained how I'd felt before and after he chose to kick me out of his bed, his house, and his life, all within fifteen minutes.

It seemed that was enough to get Samantha to finally cut the act. Her hard exterior began to soften as we spoke, and she offered me insight and even a few unsought words of advice. I replayed them in my head over and over on the way back to the hotel. On the way back to Connor. In all honesty, I felt lost. Her words helped more than they hurt, but that still didn't mean I had all the answers. At least I knew the game plan and what I wanted to do. I'd decided where I wanted to go after here and how I planned to get there. If only I could find out what I'd had to drink that night in Vegas that made me black out, because I'd get an IV of it this minute if it would erase all memory of this heartache.

When I opened the door to the suite, I found Connor in the living room, bending some blonde over the back of the couch. I groaned—he wasn't supposed to hear me, but this wasn't the first time I'd walked in on Connor fucking some random woman in our communal space, and we'd only been here two days.

"This is the reason I prefer to stay in my own room."

"If you spent more time with me, I wouldn't need to find company."

I opened the door to my bedroom and slammed it behind me, unable to deal with him any longer. I was just happy this process was almost over, and then I wouldn't have to worry about putting up with him ever again. I tossed my purse to the side and threw myself onto the bed, succumbing to the exhaustion I'd been living with since being kicked in the chest a week ago.

Even though I dreaded sleep—because I couldn't close my eyes without seeing his face, without hearing his voice or feeling his touch—I couldn't fight it. My body was spent, probably because I'd expended so much energy due to my broken heart.

As I gave in to the blackness, I released one final sob.

TWENTY

(Holden)

"You have got to be the biggest idiot in the world." Ronnie stood in my office with her arms crossed over her chest, staring at me like I was a moron who'd just tried to tell her two plus two equaled seventeen. "It's obvious you miss her, so why the hell are you here and she's there?"

"Have you not heard a word I've said?"

"Yes, Captain Asshat, I've heard them all. You went through her phone—without permission, might I point out—read text messages that weren't meant for you, and then spent almost the entire night sulking in your own rendition of what had happened. Because let's be real, you didn't ask her what he meant when he sent her those texts. You didn't ask her why she said those things to him. You looked at the dates, assumed you knew when everything took place—regardless of the fact you're a guy and guys are *the* most horrible timekeepers—and then you jumped to conclusions. Then you spent hours and hours drowning yourself in those assumptions, and not once did you bother to ask her about any of it."

"That's not true. I did ask her."

"Yeah. The next morning as you ripped apart her furniture. After you packed all her clothes and belongings. You kicked her out of your house, Holden. Not just your room, not just your life...the house you arranged for her to live in until at least January. Where did you think she would go?"

"She has family here." My words tasted like soured milk.

"Way to be a heartless asshole." She rolled her head and groaned before looking at me once more. "Stop being mad. Stop living in this bubble where she's the bad guy who did something wrong. You don't know what she's done because you never bothered to ask. Pack your sack and move to the land of benefit of the doubt, and we'll talk more then."

"There's nothing to talk about, Ronnie. It's over. She didn't even fight me on the way out. She took her stuff and left, and then went straight to New York. Why? Gee, maybe to follow through with the original deal and marry the loser for a check."

She stalked toward me, grabbed the back of one of the chairs in front of my desk, and leaned forward. "What did you expect her to do?" Ronnie asked with sincerity. "Really, Holden…you kicked her out, months before she expected to be on her own, after taking back the office space you had *just* gifted to her. Aside from a new relationship with her family and your signature on the divorce papers, what more does she have now than she did two months ago when she first arrived?"

"Why are you making me out to be the bad guy?" She was right, she always was, and she wouldn't stop until I recognized it, but that didn't keep me from arguing. I'd deny her for as long as I could, because I wasn't ready to accept that maybe I had jumped the gun.

"She's been gone for a week, and you haven't gone after her. You haven't called, you haven't chased her down. You just let her walk out, taking your future with her, and you haven't done a damn thing to stop it. That makes you the bad guy. Not only for yourself, but for her, as well."

I DO

"Again, Veronica..." I only ever used her full name when either introducing her to someone, or when I was angry with her. She knew that, too. "I'm not the only player in this game. She had a part in it, too, so why am I the only one who's in the wrong?"

"You're not. She should've been upfront with that guy about where it all stood. But not because of you. Because this guy has a right to the facts—if there's a chance he won't get any of that money. She was in the wrong for that, and I'd tell her the same thing if she were here. Except she's not, because you pushed her away. So I can't divvy up the blame between the two of you because you're the only one here."

I dropped my head into my hands and suppressed a growl, frustrated at her inability to take *my* side. She was supposed to be *my* friend, but whenever Janelle was brought up, she often chose to defend her. "You won't get it. You weren't there. I appreciate your help, but it's useless because you don't and won't see my side of things." I slid my hands down my jaw and raised my eyes to meet hers. "You're ignoring the fact that I was hurt. That she hurt me, and instead, all you're worried about is her."

Ronnie moved around the chair she had used to hold her up and sat in it. "That's not true. I am fully aware of how badly you're hurting right now, which is why I'm saying all this to you. Your pain comes from an assumption you made when you read text messages on her phone and didn't ask her about them. You didn't give her a chance to explain or provide accurate information. Had you done that, and she still told you everything you assumed, then I would be right there with you helping you pack her shit. You know that. But when you put words in her mouth and then refuse to give her the chance to correct you, I can't stand by that. And you wouldn't either if this were happening to someone else. Ask yourself this, Holden. Are you going to give up every time you don't see eye to eye?"

I took a deep breath and absorbed her words, as if I'd breathed them into my lungs and let them begin to pump life back into my veins. "So now what am I supposed to do? Call her up and ask for the answers? Isn't it a little pointless now? She's run off to claim the money with that douchecanoe. What good will her answers do now?"

"You really are a twit." She picked up a pen and threw it at me.

"Seriously, I think we need an office meeting to inform everyone about the dangers of throwing writing utensils at people."

She narrowed her gaze and bit back her smile when she said, "There are only three people who work in this office. What kind of meeting are you expecting to have, and how many people here throw pens?"

"You'd be surprised."

Ronnie picked up another and held it in the air as if threatening to throw that one at me, too. "Stop deflecting. We're talking about Janelle here. Let's get back on track. If she's moving on with this whole wedding for cha-ching thing, then that's your fault. You can't push her in that direction and then use that as an excuse to not right your wrongs."

"I get it, but I can't do anything about it. She made up her mind when she left. She didn't argue or fight with me like...like..."

"Like you expected her to? Like what, Holden? Like you think she should have? Did you do all that—take down her bed and pack her clothes—just to see what reaction you'd provoke? Did you honestly think you could load her belongings up in a car, accuse her of being shady behind your back, and she somehow *wouldn't* leave when you told her to?"

I DO

"No!" I slammed both fists on the desk, releasing my anger for the first time since Janelle walked away and never looked back. "But I expected more. Five years ago, she packed her bags and left. No phone call, no knock on my door. Nothing. She moved away and left me behind."

Ronnie scooted forward to the very edge of the chair and leaned as far across my desk as she could reach. With the calmest voice I'd ever heard her use, she held my hand and asked, "And what did you do for her?"

"Not sure what you mean."

"Janelle was eighteen, correct? She woke up in a hotel room, no longer holding her V card, learning she gave it to you but couldn't remember."

"And then kicked me out of the shower, making me feel like the biggest piece of shit that ever walked the earth," I added, filling in the rest for her in case she didn't remember that part of the story. "So again, what was it I was supposed to do for her?"

"Let me just go back a second or two...to the part where I pointed out that she'd had *sex* for the very first time, losing her *virginity*, something she had held onto all that time, and couldn't remember *any* of it. I've never had a real dick up in me, but I can tell you if I couldn't remember my first time— no matter how freaking awful it was—I'd be miserable. But if I woke up like she did, knowing the guy was basically part of my family and I'd never be able to hide from him again, I'd probably want to crawl into a hole and die. I most certainly wouldn't want to share a shower with him."

I couldn't do anything other than sit and listen, because I had never thought about this perspective before. And I hated that I never once understood what it had been like for Janelle. I'd thought about it, about how she must've felt, but not once had I ever been able to fully comprehend everything Ronnie was explaining now.

"Then she gets on a plane and realizes the seat next to her is empty. *Your* seat. You slept with her and then couldn't even stomach flying home with her. Imagine what she must've gone through on that plane. It takes effort to switch a flight—and money. Which basically means your empty seat told her you'd rather waste time and money than be forced to sit next to her. That's not the message I'm sure you meant to send, but I'm willing to bet that's what she received loud and clear."

"Didn't you say my entire problem is because I came to my own conclusions? Isn't that what you're doing now?"

"Nope. Not at all. I'm a woman, I have a vagina, I know how we think. Straight or not, we have the same thought process—well, most of us do. But anyway, I am willing to bet that's how she felt that morning. And to sum up the rest of her summer, you avoided her. Did you not? So now, after hearing all that, can you please explain to me why she should've reached out to you after she moved away?"

"What was I supposed to do?"

"You were supposed to do exactly what you should do now—go after her!"

"You mean go to New York?"

"Is she in New York, Holden?" she asked, full of sass and attitude. When I nodded, she clucked her tongue and fluttered her eyes. "Then yes, go to her. Beg her for forgiveness, tell her what a loser you are and that you'll spend the rest of your life making it up to her. I don't care if you promise her the freaking moon. Go get her!"

I sat at my desk, surrounded by Ronnie's words long after she fled the room. I knew she was right, I just wasn't sure how to go about the situation. It wasn't until I found myself standing in Matt's office, words falling off my tongue before I figured out how to handle it.

I DO

"You're taking *more* time off? Seriously, Holden, I feel like I've been here all by myself ever since Janelle got sick."

"That's not true. I took a few days off when she was ill, yes, but I worked from home and even came in for a few hours on that Friday. That's not fair. I've never held your time off against you."

He held up his hands and his eyes grew wide. "I'm messing with you. It was just a joke. Calm down and tell me what's gotten you so worked up. What do you need the time off for anyway? Is this what's got you wound tight?"

"I'm going to New York."

"Is there something going on there that I'm not privy to? First Janelle, now you."

"Well, I'm going there because of her. I want to go there to get her, because I was an asshole and pushed her away. So now I need to go grovel and beg her to forgive me."

"Are you trying to tell me you've got the hots for my sister?" His tone gave nothing away, so I had nothing to go on. Then again, it didn't really matter. I knew ahead of time that I would do anything, regardless of reactions or objections. Matt was my best friend, like a brother to me, but if he had a problem with me and Janelle, he'd just have to deal with it. Because I refused to let anything ever get in the way of us again.

"I'm trying to tell you I'm in love with her."

His eyes grew large, and he began to choke.

"I've been in love with her for a really long time."

"How long?"

"Funny story…so you see, when we were all in Vegas for your wedding—"

"I swear to God, Holden…" He rose from his chair, red faced and hands fisted. "If you fucked my baby sister—"

"I married her!"

285

We stood facing each other, a desk separating us, both breathing heavily and unsure of the other's response. Then he relaxed, the anger vanishing before my eyes. "You did what?"

"The night of your wedding, after the reception, we hung out. We walked the strip and watched some shows, and when we were done, we decided to go to a chapel and get married. We had the whole thing planned out. But you see, when we got back home, reality started to settle in and then she left for college...it didn't exactly turn out the way we thought it would."

"So...you guys aren't married?"

"Yeah, we are. Or, at least I think we still are. In a nutshell, I got pissed off over something I more than likely misunderstood, and I sent her away with signed papers that would dissolve the legality of our marriage. And I'm praying I can get to her before they can be filed, or before any other damage can be made."

Matt stared at me, blinking, for what seemed like forever. Then the corners of his mouth tilted, and I was certain it'd all be okay. "To be honest, I thought you had a thing for her. I noticed it at the barbecue at Lakes Park. But I didn't think you two had actually done anything about it, and when she left, I assumed that was the end of it. I had no idea about any of the other stuff."

"No one did. She didn't want anyone in the family to be told."

He nodded but kept on. "I get it, but I really wish I would've been informed. Ya know? You're my best friend, and she's my little sister. Of course there's no one who could take care of her like you, and I'm more than excited about you actually being my brother. What upsets me is the not being made aware of it. Since Christine and I got married?"

I nodded and shrugged, hoping this was something we could get past rather soon.

I DO

"So this means you guys have the same anniversary as we do?"

"Technically, it's the next day, because by the time it was all said and done, it was after midnight. But yeah, one day later. You can see why we never said anything to anyone, right?"

Matt came around the desk and clapped me on the back. "You should probably go get your wife. A week in New York City is a horrible idea for anyone, let alone Janelle. And you better make it grand. No fucking knocking on her door and giving her some lame excuse for your dickless decisions. Man the fuck up."

I couldn't help but laugh and shake my head. "I will. I promise you, I won't leave until she's mine again."

As I ran out of the office, Ronnie called out after me, "Where are you going?"

"To rescue my bride."

TWENTY-ONE

(Holden)

In the movies, when someone makes such a profound statement about chasing after the woman of their dreams, even flying across the country to do so, it looks like it takes maybe an hour, two at the most. They don't show all the hoops you jump through and red tape you have to tear down just to get there. Flights into New York at the last minute were outrageously expensive—*if* there were any seats available. Finally, after getting everything in order, I landed in New York almost nine hours later.

Then again, if the movies showed the reality of the trip, it wouldn't be as romantic.

Even though, in my opinion, any woman who didn't find a man spending half a day and a good chunk of his credit card limit just to get to her as being romantic had no heart.

However, the hours and hours of either waiting or waiting to wait gave me plenty of time to track her down. I wasn't sure how I managed it, but after many phone calls and more than my fair share of favors, I had gotten the information I needed regarding her whereabouts. The last thing I wanted to do when I landed was wait for a bag, so I hadn't packed one. I had everything I needed with me, and in the event she turned me away, I wouldn't have anything to drag back home.

I DO

I ran outside the airport and fought to find a cab to take me to her hotel. And as soon as we got close enough, I paid the man and hopped out, unable to handle waiting in traffic any longer. Even the ride up in the elevator was torture, and by the time I made it to her door, I pounded on it frantically with my fist because I couldn't waste another second before telling her how much I loved her.

How much I needed her.

And how fucking sorry I was.

But she didn't answer the door—*he* did. I shoved past him and invited myself in, ignoring the smug grin I was about to wipe off his ugly face. The sight of the room had me frozen in place after only a few steps inside. A bra hung off the back of the couch, clothes strewn all over the room. My gut twisted and knotted, and I feared I'd vomit all over myself.

"She's a feisty one, isn't she?" he asked with wagging brows.

My arm, as if having a mind of its own, extended out, delivering my fist straight into the center of his face. It happened so fast it even surprised me, but I didn't care. I wasn't the one with the bloody nose. Nor was I the one who screamed like a girl.

"Where is she?" I demanded, a sudden fierceness coming over me. The thought of him touching her bothered me more than I could comprehend, but I had to remind myself I had no right to complain. I'd pushed her away and straight into his arms, so I deserved to suffer the consequences.

"Probably cleaning my come out of her pussy."

It seemed as though my leg and arm ran on the same circuit, because while he remained hunched over, his hands covering his nose and mouth, my knee jerked up, right into his bloody face. This time, he fell to the floor, and I was pretty sure he started to cry.

"Oh my God!" Someone came running out of the room to the right. She had blond hair, but not like my Janelle. It wasn't the color of honey. It was almost white like she'd washed it with bleach repeatedly. Naked as the day she was born—which by the looks of it, wasn't that long ago—she ran to Pencil-Dick's side and began to fawn all over him.

I stared in confusion for a moment before I bent over and picked up the lacy black bra. It reminded me of some of Janelle's I'd seen around my room at home. Except when I did a double-take, this one had a lot of extra fabric in the cups, and I knew there was no way this would've fit her. She didn't have large breasts, they were the perfect size for me, and this bra was made for someone who more than likely had—

I peered over my shoulder and assessed the blonde who offered first aid to Connor and tried to frantically stop his bleeding. The first thing I noticed were her obviously fake tits. From a quick guesstimation, it seemed as though this bra belonged to her. After tossing it back onto the couch where I'd found it, I heard a gasp that drew my attention to my left, and that's when I finally found her.

"Janelle," I whispered, followed by a confident, "baby." My heart began to beat in a steady rhythm and my mind seemed to settle. It felt as if years had passed since my last interaction with her, instead of only one week. But one week had even been too long. I never wanted to be without her again. I was done wasting time on what ifs, could've beens and should'ves. No doubts remained that she was my forever.

However, she tried to slam the door in my face once I reached her.

"Come on, baby...please open the door. Let me in." I hoped smooth-talking her would do the trick. When it didn't seem to be working, I decided to go with force and apologize for it later. I shoved my shoulder into the door and pushed against it with caution to prevent hurting her in the process.

I DO

"Go away, Holden. I don't want to see you."

"Too bad, Jelly. Because I want to see you."

And just like that, the door flew open, almost causing me to fall on my face. Once I righted myself, I flung the door closed behind me, trapping the two of us in the bedroom together and blocking out the bleeder and the naked one tending to him.

"Hear me out, Janelle. Please."

She stood in the middle of the room with her arms crossed protectively over her chest. Her eyes mirrored my tiredness and her hair dangled all over as if she'd just woken up. "I heard you say enough during our last conversation. I don't need to hear any more."

"I know, but I'm asking you to hear me out, because I messed up. Please, baby, just let me say what I want to say, and if you want me to leave, I will." I moved to her and grabbed her hands, pulling her arms away from her chest. Then I settled her on the edge of the bed, where I knelt between her legs and wrapped my arms around her waist. Her willingness to move and her silence gave me the confidence I needed to continue. With her eyes locked on mine, I began the most important dialogue of my life. I had everything to lose.

"I'm so sorry, Janelle. I saw his messages, and the ones you sent back to him and I—"

"But I didn't send any back to him. I ignored him. Didn't you see that?"

"I did…but I'm talking about the ones prior to those. The ones where you told him you didn't love me, and that you had a plan but needed him to give you a week. I read the one where you talked about how you wanted the money, and I jumped to conclusions without speaking to you first. I can't even begin to tell you how sorry I am."

She ran her fingers through my hair, concentrating on her favorite spot right over my ears. The spot she always went to when we'd lie in bed together. "I just don't understand why you reacted that way. Why didn't you just talk to me about it? I would've explained it all to you. This could've been just a speedbump in our relationship instead of the end."

"I know, but I guess I thought anything you said would be a lie."

"You thought I'd lie to you? You don't trust me?"

"I do. Instead of giving you the benefit of the doubt, I thought the worst." I needed her to understand that I was telling the truth. "I trust you, but in that moment, I was scared shitless. Maybe what scared me the most was that you'd confess the one thing I feared the most."

"What?" She studied my face with confusion as she waited for me to explain.

"I feared you'd admit that you didn't have any feelings for me and were playing me all along. Finding out it had always been about the money devastated me."

"What? No." Her gaze narrowed and held me captive. "You thought that?"

"Kinda. No. Maybe." I shook my head and closed my eyes, needing a moment to gather myself. "Honestly? I wasn't sure how I felt after reading your texts. You'd told me that you worried I'd get the raw end of the deal. Then you told that dipshit you really wanted the money. I guess the final confirmation was when I asked you about it and you said it had always been about the money."

Her shoulders drooped and her expression softened. "When I told you I didn't want you to end up hurt, it had nothing to do with that. I just meant I didn't want you to go through all that trouble and then I end up failing at starting my own business. I didn't want you to be stuck with a lease on a storefront without anything to use it for. And yes, I told

I DO

Connor I wanted the money, because I do. Fifty thousand dollars is a lot to me. In fact, I don't know anyone who wouldn't *want* that kind of money. But that's it.

"The plan I was talking about was to talk to you, but I couldn't tell Connor that. That all happened the day I brought your lunch to you at work. We talked that night, that's when we decided to see where things would go. That was the entirety of my plan, believe it or not. I decided I'd bring it up and test the water to see where your head was at. I told him to give me a week in case I didn't have the confidence to bring it up to you right away. But I still didn't have an answer for him because you and I hadn't come to any conclusions. We only decided to wait…so that's what I was doing."

She had my head spinning in circles, unsure of which way was up or down.

"I couldn't tell him that we wouldn't be getting the money because I had chosen you, because I wasn't certain where we stood. So the last thing I wanted to do was give up the money and then end up losing you in the end. I wanted you, if I had my choice, it would've been you. Forever. But I didn't know where your heart was."

"You've always had it, baby. Always." I reached into my pocket and pulled out the gold band. Holding it between my fingers, I took her hand in mine and watched her eyes widen and turn brighter.

"W-what's that?"

"This is your wedding band. I found it on the nightstand the next morning when I was straightening up your hotel room. You didn't remember anything, so I took it with me, and I've saved it all these years. Many things have gone wrong with us on our quest to make it right. It started that morning—after one of the best nights of my life—when I didn't tell you the truth. I should've come clean then, once I realized your memory loss. Then I allowed the charade to continue for five years when I refused to reach out to you. Call it stubbornness or being pigheaded. I deserve every name you can think of to call me. Over the past couple months, we went about it all wrong. We tiptoed around each other instead of verbalizing what should've been said five long years ago. I want you to have this, to wear it again. I want to put it on your finger like I did years ago, but this time, I want it to stay there."

Her lack of words, the worry in her stare, and the harsh swallow she took while regarding me with a pained expression, made my stomach turn. Nothing about her actions set me at ease. They only served to heighten my fear that maybe I had been too late. That I had pushed her too far away.

I should've known it would take more than a plain gold band to make things right again. I would do anything to correct the situation. I would've strung up lights all the way to the moon and back if that's what was required.

"Please tell me you haven't filed for divorce yet. Fuck...please, Jelly. Did you meet with the producers? What did you decide?" The frantic words flew from my lips faster than I could stop them. But I didn't care, even though I had everything to lose. She needed to be made aware of how I felt, because I was done hiding. I was done playing it safe or trying to keep her from running off.

She licked her lips and closed her eyes for a brief moment before she finally spoke. "Did they ever call you, earlier this year to ask if we were married? Or did anyone for that matter?"

Her question confused me, but right before I answered her, I remembered something. At the time, I hadn't given it much thought, and I would've forgotten about it completely if she hadn't asked me with that curious glint in her eye.

294

"Uh…yeah. Last year, though. It was around Thanksgiving, maybe earlier. Someone from the Clark County Clerk of Courts had called, said something about records and verifying marriage licenses. I didn't think anything of it; it was all so formal. She just asked if I had married you on July fifteenth, twenty twelve in Las Vegas, Nevada. I said yes. She asked if it had been annulled or dissolved, and I said no. She didn't ask anything else, and I didn't think to question it." By the look on her face, she had more to say. "Why?"

"I was told before leaving the show — when they informed me I was legally married — that they had called you. To be honest, with everything going on, I totally forgot until now. This last week apart, I've replayed everything over and over again, and that was when I remembered. You were surprised to see me when I showed up on your front step. You seemed genuinely shocked when I admitted to knowing about the marriage. You didn't have a clue how I'd found out. At the time, with so much going on, so many things to say, I didn't think twice about it. But the producers told me something interesting when I met with them earlier."

I waited with bated breath for her to say more, but she didn't. I figured I had to pry it out of her before I died of heart failure. "So you did meet with them already…what happened? What did you tell them?" I frantically searched around the room, hoping to lay eyes on the folder containing our divorce documents without ever pulling myself from the floor at her feet. "Baby, tell me we still have a chance."

Her expression was difficult to read. First appearing soft, her lips almost seemed on the verge of smiling, but her breathing came off slightly labored, as if she were having a hard time confessing something. And that paralyzed me.

"You've called me 'baby' a lot since you got here."

I pinched my brows in thought, wondering why that somehow had any significance to her. But I didn't question it and only answered her, even though she had yet to give me a single answer to anything I'd asked. Although, I didn't exactly have room to complain. She didn't owe me anything—I was the one who owed her the world. "Yeah, I guess I have."

"Why? You have before, at completely random times, but never this much unless we're having sex. It just makes me curious."

I could tell she was doing this to test my patience. It was in her smiling eyes. "I'm not certain. Maybe because I'm not holding back like I have been. Because I don't care if you think I'm coming on too strong. Hell, Jelly, it could be a million different reasons. I love you. I'm *in love* with you. I want you to come home with me and be my wife—not like we have been, but for real. Like...for *real*, for real. Your last name matching mine and a house belonging to both of us with a deed that says Holden *and* Janelle York. I'm talking babies and mini vans and my firm and your event planning. I want it all. And I want it with you. I'm not hiding anymore...*baby*. This is me, being who I am for the woman of my dreams, the woman I love, the woman I will do anything for if she were to give me the honor of spending the rest of her life with me."

Her eyes brightened and became glassy, which meant she was on the verge of tears. Which wasn't a good sign for me, considering that usually meant she was pissed off...at me. So I sat there, on my knees, at her feet, with my arms wrapped around her and my eyes pleading, *begging* her to not give up on me, on us, quite yet. I cherished this moment between us, fully aware that it may be the last time I get to hold her.

"I like it," she whispered, almost to herself. I wasn't even sure I'd heard her correctly until she gave a demure grin and traced the taut lines on my brow with the tip of her finger.

I DO

When she went back to the sides of my head, running her fingers through my short hairs, I decided it couldn't be as bad as I feared. "The producers told me they had attorneys who could handle our paperwork for us, possibly speed up the process so we can get the ball rolling with the rest of it."

My heart sank to the pit of my stomach, and then my stomach twisted and knotted.

"I told them no." That one sentence breathed life back into me. "I came all the way here to follow through with the original plan. You kicked me to the curb, so I didn't feel like I had any other choice. I don't think I've ever thought very far ahead. It was always pick the stone up and throw it, and then focus on where it landed, make it there, and then repeat it all over again. I don't think I've ever picked my head up and looked beyond the stone to see where I was even headed. For all I know, I could've ended up in a lake or walking right off a bridge. Today, I looked past the stone."

My throat was so tight I wasn't sure I would be able to speak when I asked, "And what did you see?"

"You. It's always been you." And that sentence pumped life back into me. "So I told them I wasn't interested in their help with the divorce, because this time, I would be the one to fight it. I told them I have no desire to marry Connor for money or any other reason. That's when they explained the show to me."

I bit my lip and pulled her closer, hanging on her every word.

"They found me because they'd confirmed I was married. They were the ones who called you and asked for verification, and from when you said you got the call, it sounds like it was all part of the grand plan. There were ten guys and ten girls, all meant to pair off into ten couples. Half of us had been married in Vegas four to seven years ago. The other half were staged. It was part of some experiment, I guess to see if we'd end up figuring out our shit or follow the money."

Surprise made me speechless and I couldn't do anything other than stare at her.

"There were seven couples who actually did what they were supposed to—which as it turns out was basically pair up with one of the dummies. Out of those seven, so far they haven't written any checks. And aside from me, there's one other couple who forfeited the money. The others they're still waiting to hear back from."

"So was there ever any money?"

She shrugged and took a deep breath. "I assume so. I mean, they said they would give it, so I guess they would have to. But that doesn't matter to me, because I don't want it. I already turned it down and that's when they explained it all to me."

"You chose me before I showed up in New York?"

Her smile stretched across her face and it drew me up off my knees. It dragged me up her body until I hovered over her, laying her across the mattress.

"Then why did you try to close the door in my face?"

"I don't know…I guess I was caught off guard to see you here. That and Connor was bleeding and the sight kind of grossed me out. Oh, and I had just woken up so I'm sure I look like shit. There are a hundred reasons, Holden. But none of them make any sense."

I straddled her waist and held her hand in mine, making sure she watched as I slid the ring down her finger and over her knuckle until it fit perfectly in place, not giving her the chance to argue with me about it. "Oh, and by the way, I told Matt."

"About what?" Panic filled her wide eyes.

"Everything. I told him I was leaving work to chase after you, and then told him why."

I DO

"He knows about Vegas?"

"About the chapel, yes. But, babe, you never have to worry about me telling anyone about that night in its entirety. No one needs to know the details."

She smirked and pinned me with her comical stare. "Trying to keep it a secret how fast you blew your load?"

With my hands pressed into the mattress on either side of her head, I lowered my forehead to hers and whispered, "Nah. I was trying to save you from the embarrassment of people finding out how when you were on top, riding my cock like a motherfucking pro, you whipped your hand in the air and called out, 'ride 'em cowboy.'"

Her eyes widened and she released a gasp. "No, I didn't."

"Oh, yes you did," I mumbled against her lips. Leaving her in her state of shock, I lowered my mouth to her neck, then her chest, before slowly cupping her breast and massaging it with my fingers. The perfect handful. The urge to be inside her superseded anything else. But as soon as I squeezed her tit, she flinched and cried out in pain.

"Sorry, they're sore. I should be getting my period soon. I've been feeling it come on but it hasn't yet." When I started to back away from her, unwilling to cause her more pain, she gripped my shirt in her fists and yanked me back down. "I haven't gotten it yet...which means we're good. We can have sex. No need to freak out over the dreaded *P* word."

I wagged my brows at her but crawled off her body anyway. Her knitted brows said it all, until she realized I only meant to back away enough to remove my clothing. And just before I found myself over her once more, she lifted herself onto her elbows and asked me where my ring was.

"It's at home."

"I want to put it on you."

It took me a second, but then it made sense. "You have a thing for men wearing wedding bands?"

"I have a thing for my husband wearing absolutely nothing *but* his wedding band."

And if I hadn't been seconds away from filling her completely, I would've hauled her over my shoulder and dragged her home just so she could slide my band over my knuckle, where I'd keep it forever and ever.

"I love you so much, Jelly." It was meant to be this sweet, monumental moment, but when she smiled and stared into my eyes, I couldn't see past the sheen of tears lining her baby blues. "Why are you mad? What did I do wrong?"

"I'm not mad. Quite the opposite, actually. I'm happy. I didn't think I'd ever feel this content, but I do. You, Holden, make me feel so complete, it's like my heart will burst. And I'm pretty sure you've made me feel this way before, because it's familiar. Being with you like this, my heart pounding against my ribs, not from fear or angst, but from so much love it's almost unbearable."

"Are you trying to tell me you're in love with me?" I teased, hoping to make things easier for her.

"No." Her one-word reply stilled my heart. But then her explanation revived it. "Every action has an opposite reaction. So if I'm *in* love with you, that means there's an option to be *out* of love with you. And that's not possible. If anything, I'd say I *in*definitely love you."

I lowered my lips to hers and slowly slid into her tight heat, waiting for that sigh to pass her lips once I fit all the way in. When she gave me that, I swallowed it and said, "I indefinitely love you, too."

EPILOGUE

(Janelle)

I gripped Holden's hand and tried to suppress the need to hurl. I was so nervous and just wanted to hurry up and get this over with.

"I don't get it…you've said you were the life of the party when you were away at college. So what's the difference now? Why do you all of a sudden not want the attention set on you?" He held my gaze in an attempt to calm me down.

"That's different. This is my family. Around my peers is one thing…but these are people I can't escape. They have the ability to hurt me more than anyone else."

"You have nothing to worry about, babe. Yes, they are your family, which means they aren't going anywhere." He kissed me on my cheek and then opened his car door, leaving me to follow him.

The nausea only worsened when I glanced through the window along the front of the office, and I saw that my entire family had already arrived. Holden met me around the front of the car and laced my fingers with his, shoving his left hand into his front pocket. Ever since coming back from New York, we always wore our bands—except Sunday afternoons at my parents' house. Rather than take them off now, we hid it. Which only made my stomach flip and flop even more.

Everyone knew we had started to date, but that was as far as we let it go. Anytime Mom would start talking about weddings, I told her I would never walk down the aisle, so she needed to give up on the dream. I could easily tell her the one thing that would get her to shut up, but I just wasn't ready to offer that up yet. And honestly, walking into the office, facing the entire lot of my family members, I didn't want to tell them now, either. I wasn't ready to let the cat out of the bag just yet.

"Are you ready for the grand opening?" Christine met us by the door, just outside The Newest York Events office. Balloons clung to the handle, along with streamers, all colored blue and pink.

"This is your gender reveal—*not* my grand opening."

We had been back for four weeks, and almost every second of that time had been spent working on getting my business up and running. Luckily, I had Holden to help, considering he'd basically done this same thing—he hated it when I said that and had to point out how a certified public accountant firm wasn't at all the same as my event planning. I simply rolled my eyes and waved him off, telling him he could believe what he wanted.

Matt and Christine obviously knew about us, but we had sworn them to secrecy. We explained how we wanted to tell everyone at once, but I personally didn't want to do that until we had the business far enough along to share it all with them at once. They agreed, and somehow, I'd convinced them to use their gender reveal "party" to kick-start the opening. Apparently, neither Christine nor Matt thought there needed to be some big to-do when revealing the sex of their baby. I convinced them otherwise, under the stipulation that we share the event—half baby surprise and half grand opening for the family. They also made me swear to tell everyone about Holden and me being married. I begrudgingly agreed—not because I didn't want to share my news, but because I would've been happy keeping it our happy little secret for just a little bit longer.

"I already told you, Janelle…" Christine lowered her chin to pin me with her serious stare. "This isn't about us. It's not about the baby. This is about you and your store and your big news with Holden. I understand that you didn't want it to be *all* about you, but honestly, I don't want this to be a big deal."

"I figured you were just trying to be nice. Christine, this *is* a big deal. You and Matt have suffered for so long, been through so many heartbreaks…you guys deserve to celebrate. This is your rainbow baby—"

"Don't, Janelle." Her eyes turned glassy. "My baby isn't in my arms yet. I will celebrate then. When I hold my child and know everything's okay."

I could only nod, fully understanding her fear, and pray to God it was unwarranted. After a quick hug in an attempt to clear her tears, we all walked inside—Christine and Matt, and Holden and me.

We got the standard greetings, the hugs and handshakes, the well wishes and congratulations. I smiled and clung to Holden, ready to run and hold our secret safe. We hadn't been there for five full minutes before Mom started in on me.

"Why's it called The Newest York? Are you and Holden getting married?" Her eyes lit up.

And I'm sure mine did too when I said, "No. I already told you, Ma…I'm not walking down the aisle with Holden. I will never change my last name, and I will never file for a marriage license. I need you to accept that and be okay with it."

Christine stood next to me and snickered. I glared at her, hoping she'd stop before she gave everything away. Rather than stop, she muttered to me, "I don't think I can ever trust another word that comes out of your mouth."

I made sure to keep my voice low when I argued, "Technically, I didn't lie."

"I know. That's the scary part. Now I have to pick apart every single one of your sentences just to know what you mean."

I huffed a giggle beneath my breath and shook my head, turning my attention back to my mom just in time to hear more of her grumbling complaints. "You just have to be the only one, don't you? Living in sin, shacking up with your beau, never planning to get married. You wanna see your mother in an early grave? Is that it?"

"Christine and Matt would like to share with everyone what they're having—aside from a baby." I winked at Christine, hoping to move the party along and away from me.

She nodded to Matt, who crossed the room and quickly stuck a pin into the giant black balloon, letting the pink confetti fall to cover the floor. "We're having a girl!"

The entire family started to crowd in around her, making the small group feel like an arena full of excited partygoers. In an instant, her face paled and her hands began to shake by her sides. But before I could say anything to derail the frenzy, Matt stuck his pinkies in his mouth and whistled, causing everyone to immediately stop.

"Jelly is having a baby!"

Gasps rang out all around, soft murmurs and quiet questions. My head became light, and I started to feel dizzy. Not in a bad way, but in an out-of-body kind of way. It was like I had floated above myself and watched everything happen. I was completely cognizant of what was happening, but it was as though I had no control over any of it.

"You're what?" My mother's eyes couldn't have gotten any bigger, shining with utter excitement.

I DO

"I'm, uh...I'm having a baby," I repeated, turning my inquisitive stare to my brother.

He shrugged, and with giddy laughter, he said, "Holden isn't allowed to keep secrets from me anymore."

I whipped my head to stare at Holden, who stood next to me, shaking in uncontrollable laughter. As soon as his eyes fell on me, his mirth settled long enough to beam at me with pride and unadulterated love.

We'd found out shortly after coming home from New York. Turns out, antibiotics affect birth control, and Christine hadn't felt the need to inform me of that when I'd gotten sick because she didn't think there was a reason to. Holden was ecstatic, but I wasn't sure how much of that was because of the baby and how much was because he now had a reason to say I had a Jelly Bean in my Jelly Belly.

"And you're still refusing to get married?" Of course, that'd be my mother's one and only concern.

I held up my left hand, proudly showing off the plain gold band Holden had purchased to match his in a small, cheap chapel in Las Vegas. But I treasured it as if it were priceless. "I can't walk down an aisle because I already did. I refuse to change my last name because it's York, and I will forever be a York. I will never apply for a marriage license because I'll never have another reason to. Holden and I are married."

Mom gasped and covered her gaping mouth. Everyone else just stood in place with wide eyes, observing the comedy show before them. "When did you do that? Did you run off and get married when you found out about the baby? You know we would've been involved."

I glanced over at Holden and grinned. When he nodded, I knew that was his way of supporting me as I ran with it. "Actually, we got married over five years ago." As expected, the entire room broke out in a flurry, everyone talking over each other, questions being tossed around, not caring who answered.

The noise level grew even louder, but abruptly stopped when mom shouted, "I'm getting breast implants!"

"What?" I'm pretty sure we all asked at the exact same time.

"Everyone else was sharing their news. Thought I'd share mine, too."

All I could do was stare at her. And blink. And stare some more. Then, Holden came over and stole me away, saving me from dealing with that.

"Look at you, my Prince Charming, my knight in shining armor, coming to rescue me from the evil queen talking about filling her flabby boobies with silicone."

His laughter shook his body when he covered my lips with his. "No, babe. I'm not your Prince Charming, and I'm not in shining armor."

"But you're not a dark knight, either."

"Then what am I?"

"Just a regular man who chose to come sweep me off my feet and save the day."

"So I'm not a superhero?" He cocked his head to the side and pinched his brows in question.

"You're *my* hero. Isn't that enough?"

"That's all I've ever wanted to be." And then he sealed our words with his lips.

LEDDY'S NOTES

When I first started writing this book, it was going to be just like all my others, a highly emotional romance. But then, when I was ALMOST finished, I realized how wrong it was. The entire time, Janelle and Holden's relationship felt light, but the story was anything but. And so I finally decided to go back to the beginning and tell the story the characters wanted, not what I wanted.

There were nights I'd write and laugh my ass off at some of the things they were saying and doing, and then would wake up in the morning and freak out because I've never attempted light and humorous before, and feared my humor would be overlooked. But luckily, my friends and beta readers laughed at those same scenes.

So either I can be funny…or they're my friends for a reason. It could also be a mixture of both. We're just going to go with I'm hilarious!

Also, if you loved Ronnie as much as I did, you should totally check out "Girl Crush" by Stephie Walls, because there's a lot of her in there!

HEY (you!!!)

Let's see if I can make it through this without forgetting anyone. Probably not, considering I forget at least one person in every book. But hey…at least I'm consistent.

My family…I love you all more than you'll ever know.

Stephie…I thank my lucky stars every single day that you came into my life. We all know how much better of a person you are after having me as a friend, but you've made me a better person too. Either that, or we're delusional, in which case, I'd rather live in a delusional world with you, my woobie, than real life.

Marlo…my lobster. You are always there when I need it, and I can't imagine not having you in my corner. I love you more than you know. Your friendship and unwavering support means everything to me.

Kristie…Once upon a time, a whore named Kristie met an angel named Leddy. After a little while, Kristie convinced Leddy to be her friend, because Kristie really wanted to be as cool as Leddy. The end.

My TWOTs…you all fill my days with so much entertainment, support, and amazing friendship. I appreciate each and every one of you!

My betas…Shannon, Heidi, and Stefanie: I may have lost my shit a few (hundred) times, but thank you SO much for sticking with it! This book wouldn't have been half as good as it is now without you guys!!

Emily…you are my sunshine, my only sunshine. Thank you from the absolute bottom of my very large heart! You have been there from the very beginning, and you better be there until the bitter end. If not…I'll hunt you down. The end.

Josie…thank you for everything you do, and for making my words come to life!

Robin…your covers are like art! I'm so thankful to have you on my team, giving me amazing masterpieces every single time! You're a freaking rock star!

My girls…Sarah, Julie, and Joy: I couldn't do this without you guys! I love you all, and am so blessed to have you three in my little corner!!!

Robyn…you talked me off a ledge a few times, and pushed me when I needed it when it came to this book. I'm so unbelievably grateful to have you in my life! Thank you for being you. Soup, salad, and breadsticks means a lifelong friendship!

Bloggers…I am indebted to you for the time you've given me. Even for just a share, a like, a post, you'll never know how much I appreciate it all. So thank you, every single one of you!

My readers…I honestly can't thank each and every one of you enough for all the support you've given me! I wouldn't even be here if it weren't for you. I'd just be a small-town girl, living in a lonely world, who took the midnight train going anywhere…but here. I love you all! Thank you!!